Dorbyan

(A Lithuanian Jewish Stetl)

D.H. JACOB

With special thanks to

Mrs Leibe Katz of New York City
and to
The Chevra Kadisha of Sydney, Australia

whose timely generosity allowed the restoration of the Dorbyan
Jewish cemetery to proceed at a time when the outlook was bleak

Order this book online at www.trafford.com
or email orders@trafford.com

Most Trafford titles are also available at major online book retailers.

Print information available on the last page.

ISBN: 978-1-4251-1800-6 (sc)

Trafford rev. 06/18/2019

 www.trafford.com
North America & international
toll-free: 1 888 232 4444 (USA & Canada)
fax: 812 355 4082

CONTENTS

ACKNOWLEDGEMENTS

It goes without saying that a work of this nature cannot be the product of a single person, and that without the input of many others it would not have seen the light of day.

From my early childhood days when *Dorbyan* was simply the strange sounding name of the place my grandparents came from, until the point was reached where I felt I knew enough to attempt a novel on the subject, the quest for knowledge has led me to distant lands, and put me in contact with some of the most fascinating people on earth. Starting logically from a family base in eastern Canada I soon found that the story took me over the rest of Canada and most of the USA. From there the trail led to Israel, South Africa, and finally to Lithuania itself. Among the many people I have encountered along the way and to whom I am indebted are those whose names are to follow.

That this work represents a lifetime's work cannot be denied, but the lifetime spent was not that of the author. Raymond Whitzman of Montreal, Canada became fascinated with his family background some twenty years ago, and since that time has dedicated himself to this pastime almost to the exclusion of every other activity. His family tree is an immense work, and a valuable starting point for anyone interested in eastern European Jewish history. In the course of his work he has become expert on the subject of Dorbyan, and if there is anyone qualified to take issue with the material in this book, then Raymond Whitzman is that person.

Sol (Sliomas) Gilis was born and raised in Krettingen, some eight miles away from Dorbyan, and visited the town on numerous occasions. He lived in this area until the German annexation of Memel, upon which he fled first to Scotland where he met his wife Hilda, and finally to Yarmouth, Nova Scotia. Although in frail health and getting on in years, his amazing powers of recollection were matched only by his willingness to share his memories and knowledge. It is through my correspondence with Mr Gilis that I have been able to build up a picture of what life was like in Lithuanian Jewish society before it was snuffed out forever. The information gained from him has been priceless, and without it, this book would be lacking an integral part of its character.

Sara Yablon is a Dorbyan descendant and the historian of the Jewish community of Halifax, Nova Scotia. Her position has given her access to information which she has readily passed on to me and which I could never have acquired on my own. In addition she has provided me with anecdotal material from her own Dorbyan forbears, much of which appears in the pages which follow.

Antanas Kramilius is a journalist by profession and a prominent member of the Lithuanian community of Sydney, Australia. When first referred to Mr Kramilius I was told that he was "A man who knows where to look for things". This was understatement, for not only did his correspondence and translating on my behalf achieve in a short time what I would never have achieved, but his other efforts on my behalf went far beyond any reasonable call of duty. On business trips to Lithuania he broke his journey to visit Dorbyan (Darbenai) on my behalf, even taking it upon himself to interview villagers and return with video tapes and photographs to present to me. It was through Mr Kramilius' organization and Lithuanian connections that arrangements were made to clean up and restore the Dorbyan Jewish cemetery.

Lipman Bloch of Holon, Israel was born and raised in Dorbyan. He was in the town during the horrible days in 1941 and somehow survived it. Corresponding on the subject is not comfortable for him, and on the occasions he has done so his agony is evident in every word of his replies. I know that my questions to him have caused him to recollect greater misery than any I am likely ever to experience, yet not to do so means that his knowledge will be lost for all time, for unlike most other living Dorbyaners, he did not leave the town at an age too young to form memories of the place and its life.

Several people have departed during the time I have been preparing this work. Betty Crone of Sun City Arizona was a daughter of Joseph Jacobson, and granddaughter of Hersh and Chana, so often mentioned in this book. When I learned of her death I remember the empty feeling of knowing that never again would I learn anything from her, for she was instrumental in passing on to me the experiences as told her by her father.

Bernie Bloom of Saint John, New Brunswick was the son of Chaia, eldest daughter of Hersh and Chana. Although terminally ill, he corresponded with me to the end, providing me with photographs which I had not dreamed could still exist. Another empty feeling when I learned that his contributions had stopped, forever.

Morris Attis was born in Dorbyan and lived there until the age of nine, making him one of the few who had vivid memories of the town before he left. It is to him I am indebted for the description of the synagogue, and for many of the glimpses of life as it once was.

Finally, sadly, word has reached the authour of the recent passing of Sol Gilis. His health was poor in recent years, and when his wife passed away shortly before him, it would seem that without his lifelong companion and carer, he lost the will to live. His contribution to this work can't be measured, and the information received from him would fill a full sized novel in itself.

There is an expression that when an elder dies, it is similar to a library burning down. This expression has never had greater meaning than when applied to the four people mentioned above.

There are others who deserve mention: Liebe (Libby) Katz of New York City; Eric Goldstein of Atlanta, Georgia; Professor Konrad Kwiet of Sydney, Australia; Vincas Augustivicius also of Sydney; Rina Ruizguiliene and Albinas Simkus, both of Darbenai, Lithuania. To these, and to all those whose contributions were smaller but nonetheless pertinent, I dedicate this book.

DARBENAI

In the fertile Kretinga district of northwestern Lithuania, lies the peaceful village of Darbenai. It is situated in what is considered to be lowland Lithuania, and known to its inhabitants as Samagothica. Here a dialect of Lithuanian is spoken which differs sufficiently from the mainstream language as to cause occasional problems in communication.

The main thoroughfare is wide, having once served as the village marketplce. As with so many other places in this part of the world, the major landmark is its stone Catholic church. The building is impressive, having been constructed over one hundred years ago with little regard for the cost. It towers high above the town and provides a prominent landmark far into surrounding countryside. At both both ends of the marketplace are bridges crossing branches of the river Darba.

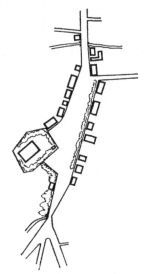

One side of the thoroughfare is for the most part occupied with the church and its assocated buildings. On the other side are several comfortable homes partially hidden by trees and shrubs.

Curiously, almost directly across from the church in what would be considered the very centre of the village, is an empty, overgrown space, which for some reason lies unused.

There is a strange unexplained sleepiness about Darbenai, a village whose existence can be traced back more than four hundred years. The houses that one would expect to be crowded about the village centre are found instead on the periphery and outskirts. There is little activity in and about the main square, and apart from church prayer days, it is largely empty.

It takes but a brief investigation to discover the reason for the sleepy atmosphere of Darbenai, which is the same in hundreds of east European villages.

Its heart is missing.

IN THE BEGINNING
CHAPTER 1

Almost 4000 years ago, in the ancient Mesopotamian city of Ur, a wealthy herdsman named Abram was preparing for a journey to the west which would change his life and alter the history of the world. His vision had told him that his flocks would lead him westward to a new and better land. For Abram had strange and radical ideas, and legend has it that his beliefs brought him into conflict with many around him, not to mention his own father.

It was Abram's belief that the idols then universally worshipped could not possibly contain any divine power, and he is said to have smashed the idols of his father to the ground, and then taunted him with the fact that he had suffered no divine retribution.

Somewhere after his departure from Ur, Abram received the inspiration that a single, almighty, supreme being created and regulated the entire known universe, both rewarding and punishing humans according to their individual deeds. It is said that the clear tranquility of the desert nights can provoke deep thought, and perhaps this is what happened to Abram. He became inspired by his new found beliefs, and as an act of faith towards the Almighty he changed his name and became known as Abraham. In return he believed that he was promised by his Creator that his descendants would prosper and multiply, becoming even more numerous than the stars in the heavens.

With his entourage he continued westward, passing through Haran in what is now eastern Turkey, and finally arriving at and settling in the Land of Canaan, which had been promised to him and his people by the Almighty.

By legend Abraham is considered to be the first believer in one God, and the first Jew. The exploits of his descendants in their Promised Land are well documented, and form the basis of the Old Testament, and the beliefs which he founded have become the bases of three great modern religions, Judaism, Christianity and Islam. His two sons, Ishmael and Isaac, are considered to be the patriarchs of the Arab and Hebrew nations.

Very few people who have walked the face of the earth have ever had greater influence on the subsequent history of the human race than Abraham.

About the time that Abraham was making his way towards the Promised Land, another migration was coming to an end. Some 1200 years earlier, primitive Indo-Europeans, their exact place of origin obscure, but most likely from Afghanistan or farther to the east in India, had begun to migrate westwards, passing through the steppes of Russia and the Ukraine. Like Abraham and his company, they too were probably herdsmen, and followed in the direction that their flocks took them.

By about 2000 BC they had travelled far enough to the west to infiltrate parts of the middle East, Turkey and Greece. The migration continued. Some 200 years later these first Probalts, or Baltic ancestors, reached their final destination, making their way into what is now modern day Lithuania, Latvia and Prussia.

Probalts differed from the Mongolian races to the north, the Slavic races to the east, and the Germanic races to the west, forming a small ethnic island and speaking a language totally unrelated to any spoken by their neighbours.

Interestingly enough, some scholars can see resemblances between the Baltic languages and the Basque tongue spoken in the far western extremity of Europe, itself an isolated linguistic island whose existence defies explanation.

Unlike the descendants of Abraham, for almost 3000 years the Probalts remained in obscurity, with no written record of their history. The result is that very little is known of them until shortly after 1000 AD, when the name Lithuania was mentioned for the first time. Yet events passed slowly, and it was not until the year 1240 AD that the first state of Lithuania was established. The nation of the Probalts had altered considerably, with its largest branch, the Prussian language now extinct, and its people no longer recognizable as an ethnic entity, having become assimilated through the constant pressures of invasion by the Teutonic knights and other Germanic movements. The tiny kingdoms of Lithuania and Latvia now remained the last bastions of the ancient Baltic language in eastern Europe.

In no way could Lithuania and Latvia have been considered nations in the modern sense of the word. Divided into regional kingdoms, these lands had became polarised into spheres of influence under the rule of powerful noble families, each holding the power of life and death over those under their control.

By this time the descendants of Abraham had endured a long and varied history, from the greatest of heights to the depths of despair. Unlike other races, such as the Probalts, their history is well documented in the familiar passages of the Old Testament. Abraham's sons, Isaac and Ishmael had become the patriarchs of the Jewish and Arab races. Jacob, the son of Isaac, was the father of twelve sons whom history tells us became the fathers of the twelve tribes of Israel, another name by which Jacob became known.

The twelve tribes of Israel had prospered and multiplied, just as the Almighty had promised Abraham they would, but with every rise to grandeur they had suffered a downfall of equal proportion.

The sons of Jacob had left the promised land and followed their brother Joseph into the land of Egypt, driven from their homes by famine. There they prospered, for a time, until their successes became the cause of envy amongst their neighbours, a pattern which was to repeat itself countless times throughout Jewish history. They were expelled from Egypt, and through their leaders Moses and Joshua they made their way back to their Promised Land.

Under their kings David and Solomon they had prevailed over the peoples of Palestine and created a mighty nation, with its capital in Jerusalem, only to see it destroyed by the Assyrian hordes. They rose from the ashes, only to be conquered again and carried off into captivity by the Babylonians. They rose once again, and rebuilt their destroyed temple, only to be conquered by the might of Rome. This time their fate was sealed, for their ideas constituted a threat to the pagan religion of the Romans. Rome would not tolerate dissent or differing religious views within her empire, and did not hesitate to deal mercilessly with dissidents. The Jewish capital and holy city of Jerusalem along with its temple were again destroyed, and the Jews were expelled from their homeland and dispersed far and wide throughout the Roman empire.

A new phenomenon occurred, and for the first time in history a nation was no longer indigenous to the confines of its homeland. Jews could now be found in Babylonia and farther eastwards, southwards throughout Egypt and into the Nile valley, and throughout Europe to the west as far as Spain.

From Babylonia Jews had migrated northwards into the Crimea, where their isolation caused their beliefs to diverge from mainstream Judaism. From there they entered Poland and Lithuania in small isolated groups, where they became known as Karaites or Khazaks. At the same time small numbers were coming from the opposite direction, making their way into Lithuania from Czechoslovakia and the Germanic lands. But their numbers remained few, for Lithuania had little to offer a nation of wanderers in search of a better life. Pagan and backward, the chief characteristic of twelfth century Lithuania was its resistance to change. Divided amongst the noble families who ran their serfdoms as their own private estates, by the middle of the thirteenth century Lithuania was the sole European country which had not converted to Christianity.

Even with the coming of Christianity, there were still areas which retained their paganism one hundred years later, notably the district adjoining the Prussian frontier known as *Samagothica* (lowland Lithuania).

The old ways in most of Lithuania came to an abrupt end when Grand Duke Mindaugas came to power in 1251 AD and accepted Christianity as his religion. From this point onward most of Lithuiania followed the path of progress, increasing its contact with the west at every opportunity.

Mindaugas' successor, Grand Duke Gediminas, continued along the course that Mindaugas had set, forming a union with Poland and setting the stage for the following two centuries, when Lithuania was to expand into empire and achieve the height of its greatness.

Lithuania ceased to be the unattractive and backward land it had previously been.

At this time the Jews of western Europe were experiencing mixed fortunes. Sometimes welcomed, more often shunned or persecuted, they had begun a steady movement toward the east and hopefully a better future.

In western Europe, only in Spain did the Jews prosper. Allowed freedom of religion and expression by the Moorish rulers, they helped bring prosperity to that land, and at the same time they created a culture rarely matched during any other period in their 3000 year old history.

But the golden age of the Jews in Spain was not to last. With the Christian conquest of the land came the Inquisition, and the Jews became one of the main targets of persecution. Like so many of their ancestors before them, they chose to suffer rather than renounce their faith. Finally, in 1492, in that same year that a Spanish-led expedition was discovering the New World, they were banished from their homes, often leaving families as well as their entire possessions behind.

CHAPTER 2

"Cyganas! Cyganas!"

The three young children ran excitedly across the field to the adults at work with their farm implements.

"Cyganas! Look! Just over there! By the bridge!"

Several adults dropped their implements and followed the children, who pointed at the ragged group which had stopped just before the rickety wooden bridge over the river Darba.

At the head a wagon had creaked to a halt, driven by an old man with a long white beard. The wagon was precariously overloaded with baggage and furniture, on top of which sat two elderly women nursing small children. A second wagon had almost pulled alongside the first, and now it too came to a shuddering, squeaking halt. Slightly smaller than the first, it nonetheless carried the same amount of baggage, with a bearded man at the reins, and two elderly women nursing infants as passengers.

Then another group came into view, on foot, perhaps thirty persons in all. Burdened by as much baggage as they could possibly carry, they staggered up to the spot where the wagons had stopped, then relieved themselves of their burden before collapsing on the ground with exhaustion.

"Cyganas!, Cyganas!", repeated the children.

"No, Cyganas, no,.. Zydu," answered one of the adults knowingly, as the others turned back to their toil in the fields, leaving the children to gaze at the scene unfolding before them.

As Eliezzer gently pulled back on the reins, bringing the wagon to a halt, he was conscious of the group of people watching from the field on the other side of the river. The sight of onlookers as his band made its way through the countryside was nothing new to him.

"At least they don't look hostile, only curious," he thought to himself, echoing the thoughts of every other member of the band. They had become expert in reading the moods of the local people in every town, city, village and farmyard they had passed through. Since leaving the Germanic lands the attitude had been different, and hostility has diminished, with curiosity becoming the normal reaction. Yet they had long learned not to take any form of acceptance for granted. The collective mood of an entire populace could change instantly at the whim of a single vociferous individual, and without warning they could find themselves the target of flying sticks and stones, causing a sudden emergency, and forcing them to quicken their pace and beat an exit as quickly as their exhausted limbs would allow.

Eliezzer's assessment of the onlookers was correct, as within a few minutes the adults of the crowd dispersed back to their toil in the fields, leaving only the children to stare at his band from the safety of the other side of the river.

The children continued their curious gaze as the elderly long-bearded man stepped away from the wagons and began to address the group.

"We stop today at this point", he said, "At the second bridge over the River Darba. It is a beautiful spot, and we give thanks to the Lord that he has brought us to such a place. This will be our resting-place for the Sabbath, and we shall pass the rest of today and all of tomorrow giving praise to him. The day's rest will give us the strength to continue our journey."

"This is a very fertile spot," observed one of the other older men. "Might it not be worth considering as a spot for us to settle down and end our journey?"

Eliezzer had heard this question almost as a matter of course at the end of every day's journey during the past several years. His people were weary, and footsore, but more than that, they were fatigued in spirit, and dreamed of the day when they would remain in one place and begin to build a life for themselves and their children.

"Yes, there is no doubt that this place is fertile," he agreed, "But we all can see that it lacks the one thing that we need to survive. We Jews are not like other people, We are not in a country of our own, we are not allowed to occupy land and to farm it . We have only one means to support ourselves. We must trade to live, and without other people to trade with, we cannot exist."

He pointed beyond the watching children to the small agricultural estate on the other side of the river. There was a manor house surrounded by a few humble huts at the edge of a cultivated field. A few people worked the fields, a few animals grazed, nothing more.

"This farm has always belonged to the noble Titschcovitch family, but only of late has it grown to the point where it can be given a name. It is known as Dorbyany, or Darbenai to the Balts of this area, and it has been given its name because of the River Darba which we see before us.

"I have no doubt," he continued, "That one day this will become a very important place, as it is fertile and situated where the river crossing meets the road. But for the moment it is too small to support us. Where we are going is not far from here, and is known as Loigzim. From all that we have been told, the Loigzimer estate is much larger and will be everything that we need. But for the moment we shall stop and enjoy the pleasant surroundings."

How often, he thought, had he made this same statement to his people, and how often had their hopes risen, only to be dashed? These people were not like Gypsies. Their wandering was not a way of life, but a necessity, to be ended as soon as possible.

He motioned to the spot alongside him which would be their resting place, and at his signal the women and children descended upon the wagons and began unloading the baggage to the ground alongside.

The work was done quickly and efficiently, for these were people who had known many spells of wandering, and many of the younger children had experienced no other way of life. It was not long before canvasses were suspended from wagon to wagon and from the wagons to the ground. Although it was late spring, and the weather was becoming warmer with each day, the possibility of rainstorms was constant, and the skins and hides placed on the ground for sleeping had to be kept dry at all cost.

Eliezzer and the men unhitched the two horses from the wagons and carefully examined each one for any bruises, cuts or other injuries which might have occurred during the day. They then led them to a bank of the river where the slope was gradual, and eased them gently into the clear water where they bathed and drank. The people of the band were impatient to refresh themselves in the inviting river as well, but the rule was that the horses' needs came first.

After scrubbing the horses down, they then led them back up the bank and to a grassy area near some trees which marked the beginning of a forest. There they tethered the horses securely and left them to graze in peace.

The women lit the fires and began preparing the meals that would have to sustain them over the Sabbath. There could be no cooking on the Lord's day, and sufficient food would have to be prepared to last until the following evening.

Today there would be no schooling for the children, for the hours leading up to the Sabbath were to be used for rest. On other days of the week, the children as young as three years of age would be taught without exception, even if it meant breaking the journey, for the teaching of the children and the bringing them up into the way of their forefathers was a sacred duty.

The men and the male children now took their turn to bathe in the river. Modesty required that they choose a spot out of sight of the women, so they selected an area on the other side of the bridge around a slight bend in the river. The children laughed and frolicked, their happy screams contrasting with the more serious conversation of the adults. Their language was a contrast as well, for while they spoke to each other only in Yiddish, the adults spoke a language which still contained some vestiges of the old Ladino dialect brought with them from Spain more than two generations earlier.

Finally, when the men and boys had finished bathing, it was the turn of the women and girls. They too went to the out-of-sight spot beyond the bridge, and before long their happy screams too could be heard. They remained in the water for far longer than the men and finally had to be called to return to the camp.

The company was now cleansed and worthy of honouring God on His Sabbath, according to the ancient commandment handed down to Moses on Mount Sinai some three thousand years earlier. Bathing was not always possible for these wanderers, but special effort had always been made to find a source of water before the Sabbath. Sometimes this had proved impossible, and in such cases water intended for drinking had been used for ritual cleansing instead. Often during the winter months precious fuel had been used to heat the water in order that the ritual bathing be carried out.

Eliezzer and the men had found a level area away from the campsite and had begun their prayer services. The children on the opposite bank watched in fascination as a box was taken from a wagon and leaned against a tree facing the sunset. They stared at the men, their backs to the sunset and facing the box, as they broke into what sounded like a mournful, mysterious chant. When the box was opened, they could see a parchment scroll being taken out and unrolled, and the old man who led the congregation taking it into his arms as the others joined him in the chanting.

When the prayers had ended and the parchment scroll returned to its box,, Eliezzer and the men began watching the sun with serious discussion, and finally, following nods of agreement, he gave the word, and the Sabbath candles were lit by the women of each family. There was never a shortage of candles, for candlemaking was one of the skills possessed by the members of this band.

Thus it was, that even as homeless wanderers. they were able to maintain their devotion to the Lord on His day. As they faced the east in the direction of their holy city Jerusalem, they carried out their sacred traditions which first had their origins in the days of Abraham, over one-hundred generations before them.

As the dusk began to settle, the children on the other side of the river, still entranced, turned and made for home, in answer to the hoarse calls of their parents.

Later that evening, their devotion to God fulfilled, His Sabbath properly ushered in, the smaller children fed and put to bed, the adults were able to sit about a small fire and speak their minds. As was the custom, Eliezzer, the leader, was the first to speak.

"I know what is on all of our minds. I know how weary we all are of wandering. I know that it is not even an adventure for the children anymore. I know that we could have stopped at many other places and ended our journey much sooner than this. But I also remember what has happened to us in the past, and what would happen to us again if we place our future in any of the lands which belong to the Germanic peoples."

"But Eliezzer, what is the point of wandering further? The Germans have been cruel to our people, that is sure. Many of us are old enough to remember Ravensburg, and noone wishes to go through that experience again, but how can we know that the Balts or the Slavs will be any better?"

"No one can answer your question, Reuven," answered Eliezzer, "But there are some signs which seem clear to me, which is the reason that I have insisted that we make no more stops in the lands of the Germans, even though there were many opportunities for us to do so."

"There were many nobles in Germany who would have been happy to have us on their estates, and there were many who would have allowed us to remain in their towns and villages," interrupted one of the women."

"Yes, Dvorah, yes, that is true. But how many times did we accept offers to settle in some place, only to see years of toil stolen from us as we were forced to flee? It would have been very easy for us to stop and remain in one place if we had been willing to renounce our God and His teachings. It would have been easy, but we would no longer be Jews. Was it not to remain Jews that we fled the Inquisition in *Safarad*? We could have remained there, and converted into Christians, but that is the one thing we can never do. Our teachings show us that the way of the Lord is the only true path, whatever pain and suffering it may cause us."

"But how can you be so sure that we would perish as Jews amongst the Germans, and not amongst the Balts or the Poles?"

"The land we have just passed through, Shimon," answered Eliezzer, "Is known to all of us as Prussia. Most know it as a land peopled by Germans, but it has not always been this way. Once, perhaps a thousand years ago, Prussia was peopled by Balts, like the people of Lithuania where we now find ourselves. Then the Germans pushed eastward, killing many of the Prussians and forcing the rest to change their ways and language. This continued for hundreds of years, and the work was finished by the German crusaders, the same ones who slaughtered so many of our people everywhere they went. Today there is not a person living in Prussia who knows a word of the old Prussian language, which I am told was not greatly different from the Lithuanian spoken by the people here.

"If we had remained in a land peopled by Germans, this would have been our fate, perhaps not at once, but eventually in the future. As it is, I fear for those of our people who have chosen to remain in German lands."

"But what kind of a life is this for our children?"

"It is not the best life, I cannot deny this," said Eliezzer, "But although we suffer, we are at least able to bring our children up as Jews. We all know what would have happened to us if we had not chosen a life of wandering."

There was silence, and the group thought back to the days when their families had lived in Spain. Their knowledge was based entirely on what they had learned from the generations before them, for amongst their band, Eliezzer alone had been born before the flight from Spain, but his infancy at the time precluded him from having any personal memories of the event. They had been told of a prosperous existence, of Jews gaining positions of great influence and respect, of Jews gaining great wealth through commerce, of Jews owning great farm estates, of Jews who excelled in religion and philosophy, and even of ordinary Jews leading a prosperous existence.

This their parents had been willing to give up when forced to make the choice between their religion and traditions and a life of comfort and prosperity.

The changes in Spain had come gradually, but had not seemed serious enough at first to warrant panic. Very few Jews left even when the Inquisition had begun its quest to convert the Jews in earnest. Ways had been found to circumvent the edicts, Jews had resorted to bribery, hiding, and even pretence under torture to convince the authourities that they had abandoned their faith. But eventually the Inquisition had realized that its methods had not been effective, and the decision had been taken to expel all Jews who did not convert publicly. The notice given to the Jews to leave Spain was short, no more than three months, and the consequence was the greatest upheaval in Jewish society since the exile from the Holy Land in the days of the Romans. Separation of family members was unavoidable in many instances, with many families never to be reunited. Some fled to England, many to France and Holland, but by far the greatest number crossed the border into Portugal which had offered them asylum.

The refuge was short lived however, as political considerations caused the Portuguese in turn to expel the Jews some five years later. The flight from Portugal was one of the first clear memories of Eliezzer's life, and he could remember his parents' attempts to explain the ensuing wandering to him in simple terms. The one thing that had been emblazoned in his mind and soul was that the leaving of Spain and Portugal was the price that had to be paid for remaining Jewish, and that for this blessing it was a small price to pay indeed.

First it had been by sea to England, and a stay of four years in that country. Jews had not been officially welcome, although small numbers had always managed to survive there. The reception had been hostile and the band had been subjected to injustice after injustice. The pressures to convert to Christianity had been immense, and certain of their number had succumbed. For these, relief had been only illusory, for they had never been accepted fully into the Christian community despite their baptism. Full acceptance would have to wait for the birth of their grandchildren, if it ever came at all.

Eliezzer's father, Shmuel, had recognized the symptoms, and had determined that what had happened in Spain would not repeated. He himself had not been witness to the glory days of the Jewish community in Spain, for the persecutions had begun before his birth. But he could remember the stories of his own grandparents, a generation which could remember prosperity and respect, only to see it come to an end as the Islamic Moors in Spain had gradually succumbed to the might of the invading Christians. He resolved that it would not happen to the band under his leadership, and that as soon as the first telltale signs of anti-semitism appeared, he would take his flock and depart for a less hostile environment.

The problem lay, of course, in finding a less hostile environment. Shmuel and his followers had sojourned in Antwerp for eight years, and gained a measure of prosperity. But the hostility was still there, and was growing, and he decided that once again, his band was better off in another place. Somewhere they would come across a kingdom where their worth would be appreciated and they would be made welcome.

21

But it was not to be, and the trials and tribulations faced by the band as they wandered from fiefdom to fiefdom made them long for Antwerp on many occasions and envy the few who had not heeded Shmuel's call to leave. France had been particularly unfriendly, and apart from remaining in one place each winter, they had found no sanctuary where they did not fear for their lives, no king or noble prepared to offer them a haven in return for their talents and their services.

As they made their way into the Germanic lands the reception was mixed. Many Jews lived in these lands, and they constantly encountered other bands either on the move or safely settled in some town or city. They settled in town after town, usually receiving a warm welcome from the local nobleman at first. Their skills and talents, particularly at commerce and crafts had made them sought after, but the ending had always been the same. They had no sooner shown signs of prosperity when a hardpressed landowner or ruler would require their services to fund either a war with his neighbours or an extravagant lifestyle. When his indebtedness reached a certain level, he would find it expedient to solve his problems by driving the Jews away from his domain, thus avoiding his debts and seizing their property in the process.

Then came Martin Luther, at first benevolent towards the Jews, in the hope that his benevolence might be rewarded by their conversion to the true faith. When his reason fell upon deaf ears, his attitude changed, and in 1543 he published a treatise entitled "On the Jews and Their Lies", which basically advocated that Jews were not fit to live amongst Christian communities, and that enslavement was the only fit treatment for them, with their books and sacred objects to be destroyed by burning. Luther's treatise gained widespread approval throughout the German speaking world within a short space of time, and set the stage for an anti-semitic indoctrination of the Germanic peoples that would never entirely disappear.

The large pogroms followed, with Jews expelled from the cities of Frankfurt and Ravensburg, as well from dozens of smaller towns and villages, more often than not with loss of life. Again they were given sanctuary when it suited the overlords, but the hostility was greater, and the periods of settlement shorter.

It was during this period, the 1540's ,that Shmuel, by now a very old man, died, leaving to his son Eliezzer the unenviable task of leading his people to the ever-receding resting place where they would find a welcome, to an existence where they could follow the teachings of their God in peace.

The words of his father had remained with Eliezzer constantly. A large measure of the problems of Jews was their success in matters commercial, success which invoked envy and hostility amongst those around them. The solution, as Shmuel had told him, was to forego the trappings of success, to achieve no more than that needed to support themselves securely, and to devote the remainder of their energies to the following of the teachings of the Lord. By not allowing themselves to rise above the surrounding populations economically they would not arouse the emnity that had been their curse since the expulsion from Spain.

They had made their way eastwards, having heard that in Prussia, Poland and Lithuania the attitude towards Jews was more lenient. Prussia had been better, but the country was no longer recognizable as a Baltic nation, the population long since having become Germanicized. The attitude however, was more lenient towards Jews, and Memel possessed a neophyte Jewish community which appeared to enjoy prosperity and freedom. Many of the band had pleaded with Eliezzer to stop at Memel, but he had held firm against their pleas. Farther east into the Baltic and Slavic lands things would be better, he argued, as Poland and Lithuania had ceased their hostility against Jews some fifty years earlier, and come to realize that Jews were a valuable asset to any kingdom, through their commercial acumen which inevitably resulted in greater prosperity. Besides, Eliezzer didn't trust the people of Memel, even though Memel bordered on the Baltic lands. The people of Memel were Germans, and ever capable of change, needing only a single Martin Luther to bring it out. They were getting close to their destination, he argued, and it would be folly to stop short of the target. The place they were seeking would offer peace and freedom for themselves and their children for the next ten generations to come.

The questions continued well into the night.

"And what was wrong with the place we stopped at during the

winter?"

"I am surprised that you have to ask such a question. You know that the landlord allowed us to stop in his abandoned huts for the winter only because he knew he could get rent from us by doing so. There was no livlihood for us there, and in a very short time we would not have been able to exist. It should be plain to all that this was not the place we need."

"And where will we ever find such a place?"

"Such places exist," answered Eliezzer, "And there is one such place very close to where we are now. It is called *Loigzim*, and from what we have learned about it, this could be the place where our wanderings come to an end. The estate is similar to here in Dorbyan, but larger. We have been told that the master of the estate is a nobleman who is looking for Jews to settle there, and will be generous to the right people. There is a river, the Kulse, which is not too unlike the river Darba where we now camp, and there is land beside it which could be made available for our use.

"But I must add that, despite all the good things we have heard, we can only make a decision after we have seen the place. We must speak with the master, and form an opinion as to his feelings towards us. If all turns out well, and he in turn agrees to accept us, then our journey will be over."

"How far from here is this place Loigzim?"

"Near, very near," replied Eliezzer. "When we leave here on the day after the Sabbath, we shall arrive there on the same day. If we leave early enough, then we may well arrive there before noon.

"And now I bid everyone, let us sleep well this night, for it is the Sabbath, and we have His day to keep tomorrow. Let us sleep well, for I am certain that before long He will lead us to the better days that we have been seeking."

On the following morning, Saturday, the Sabbath services were held as they were held in every Jewish community throughout Europe and the known world, as they had been held since time immemorial. The menfolk conducted the service, with the women and children looking on only as observers. The service was solemn, and the children, regardless of age, were trained to utter no word of interruption

24

or distraction. The service lasted until shortly before noon, and when it finished, the solemnity came to an end, and the campsite became a place of laughter as the band partook of the best meal of the week.

The rest of the day was a time for happiness, and the children were allowed once again to frolic in the river, an ideal place for them as it was slow moving and shallow enough to wade completely across at the place that had been selected for bathing.

Then as the afternoon neared its end, and the thoughts of the next day's travel once again came to mind, it was the children's turn to ask the questions?

"Zeide, why is it that we must always travel, when others are able to make homes in one place?"

"It is not true that we must always travel, my child, it is only that we have chosen this life until we find the best place possible for our home."

"What is wrong with this place? We like it here."

"You ask this question every Sabbath at every place we stop. You are right, it is a lovely place, but we would only starve if we remained here. As Jews, we would not be allowed to own land and farm it, so we must trade to live. There are not enough people here to trade with, so we must find a place where there are."

"Will we ever find such a place, Zeide?"

"You were sleeping when we talked about this last night. There is a place very near to here, which we shall visit. It is called *Loigzim*, and there is a chance that it may be the place for us."

"Will we be there before the next winter?"

"Yes, my child, we will be there much, much sooner than that. If *Loigzim* is the right place, than we shall be there tomorrow. If it is not, then there are other places which we shall visit within the next week or two."

"Does Loigzim have a river, Zeide?"

"Yes it does, my children, I am told. It would have to have water for people to be able to live there, but I am afraid that I cannot promise you a river as beautiful as the one we have here."

Later that evening Eliezzer lay beside Rivke and listened as her shallow breathing told him she was asleep. How anyone could sleep that night was a mystery to him, for the thoughts in his own mind would certainly keep him awake.

He found himself thinking of the members of his band, and the skills and abilities that they would be able to offer the Baron von Loigzim.

He and Rivke had been unable to have children, and so the next leader of the band would have to come from another family. His mind immediately settled on Judah ben Shimon, a generation younger than himself.

Judah was foremost a linguistic genius, and stood head and shoulders above every other member of a group which was almost to a person multilingual. A band of traders had little choice but to learn the dialects in the areas in which they traded, but Judah achieved mastery rather than mere survival in every tongue he encountered. The time needed for him to do this was minimal, and he seemed to possess the ability to communicate even in languages in which he had no prior knowledge. Such was his ability that even inflections and changes of voice were sufficient for him to pick up the meaning of a conversation in an unfamiliar tongue. His memory was phenomenal, and before long the unfamiliar tongue became unfamiliar no longer, and was added to the long list of those he already knew. The value of Judah throughout the wanderings had been inestimable, and would continue to be so even after the wanderings stopped.

There was Rachman ben Arieh, married to Rachel, with four children, one Bar-Mitzvah. Like himself, Rachman came from a line of farmers and grape growers, even though neither of them had never known a farm of his own. The traditions of his forebears had been passed down to him, and he was expert in the producing of wine. Their two families would locate a supply of grapes, and carry on with their trade, which never lacked for custom.

Shalom ben Israel, and married to Dvorah, had three children, all girls. Possessing no specialist skills, he was adept to a certain degree in almost anything that required the use of the hands. Whenever an unforeseen problem or a situation not previously experienced arose, it was Shalom who was called upon to come to the rescue; and he invariably succeeded.

Leiba ben Jaakov, like Shalom, was skilled with his hands, and together the two fashioned untensils for the band from metal, and furniture for the markets from wood. It was Leiba who ensured that the horses were well shod and maintained.

Because of the likes of Shalom and Leiba, the band had reached its present level of prosperity, enjoying the luxury of two horse drawn wagons for the first time in its existence. When a resting place was found, the band would be well placed to continue its trading and peddling livlihood.

David, eldest son of Mordechai, married to Sarah, with two grown up sons and a daughter, was the most knowledgeable in matters financial, and was the final word on most of the decisions of the band that concerned money matters. With Judah by his side, the trading which ensured the band's survival became a most effective and efficient operation. In the past, when the group had settled in one place, he had served the nobility as a tax collector and financial advisor, and there was little doubt that he would one day find himself in this role again.

There were the brothers Joseph and Arieh, the sons of Absalom, both unmarried. Joseph, the elder, had been well taught by his father in the production of leather, from the choice of skins right through to the final tanning process. Arieh, still learning, had become more interested in cloth as a material, and could be said to be a proficient tailor. But Arieh had another talent as well, one which had been learned since the exile from Spain and Portugal. He had long held a fascination for the art of glassblowing, and through sheer perseverance had become proficient in the trade. Unfortunately as they had made their way eastwards, the demand for his skill had diminished, but in the process of his learning he had picked up another skill which promised greater reward, and had proved useful in every location where the band had stopped. He was now an accomplished glazier, and his skill at the cutting and fitting of glass had found a ready market amongst the nobility everywhere, and even occasionally amongst the peasantry, who would often trade produce in return for the luxury of having a small pane of glass in their homes.

CHAPTER 3

The following morning, the band was awake shortly before first dawn, that the men could begin their prayers at the rising of the sun. Women and children scurried about the site, working efficiently, each to his or her allotted task. The articles not needed during the day's journey were packed away first, with eating utensils and food supplies remaining at the top of the pile where they would be accessible for a midday meal. A certain number of canvasses were kept at the ready in the event that inclement weather forced a halt in their journey. In such cases shelter if not naturally available could be found under the wagons with the canvasses used to block the entry of wind and rain.

Their prayers finished, their morning meal eaten, their wagons packed, the band started on its way, waving a final goodbye to the children watching from across the river. This time the children waved back at them, shouting a few words of Lithuanian in the process. After an appropriate time had elapsed, and the band was out of sight, the children's curiosity overwhelmed them. and racing across the bridge, they minutely examined the abandoned campsite for any treasure which may have been left behind. They found very little, and nothing of use, which did not surprise them, for most wandering bands were equally frugal with their belongings, and not in the habit of leaving anything of value behind.

The band continued along its way, along a rutted track through heavily forested and hilly terrain. As midday approached, a rest was called and a meal was taken. Eliezzer spoke.

"We are now very near to the place known to the Lithuanians as *Laukzemis*, but which is also known as *Loigzim*. We shall stop there and stay for the rest of the day while we speak with the baron who owns the estate. God willing, this may be the place where our journey will end, but we must not place too much hope on this until we have discussed the matter with the baron. This may take several days, and we must be patient, but I have a good feeling that our fortunes are about to change."

One hour later the wagons pulled up at the edge of a cultivated estate, larger than that at Darbenai, greeted by the usual committee of children staring from a safe distance across the fields. The wagons were unloaded and camp set up in the normal fashion. Although there was excitement throughout the camp, everyone was careful not to show too much optimism. They had been disappointed too often in the past.

Eliezzer and Judah left the campsite and walked the quarter mile to the manor house on the opposite side of the field. It was constructed of logs and easily distinguishable from the mean spartan huts surrounding it, some twenty in all, each very much like the others. In the distance stood another cluster of similar huts, no doubt also part of the baron's fiefdom. All in all it indicated some hundred and fifty to two hundred people under the baron's control.

As they neared the baron's home several large dogs barked menacingly,but Eliezzer and Judah maintained their pace. Unfriendly dogs were a way of life to these people, and experience had taught them that the best means of dealing with them was to show no fear and to act as though oblivious of their existence.

The growling and barking brought a woman to the door, who went back inside and called to her master. The baron appeared, and he stepped forward to meet the two strangers. He was a large, heavy set man, middle aged and showing the first signs of baldness.

"If you are who I think you are, I have been expecting you," he said.

He continued, "You are Jews, are you not?"

"Yes, my lord, we are," answered Eliezzer.

"Then come in, and sit down," said the baron. "I have been awaiting your arrival. There is much to discuss."

The two men walked inside the large but dingy home, following the baron through a hallway to a reasonably comfortable room a short distance from the front door. Inside the room was a heavy wooden table surrounded by half a dozen wooden chairs. At one end of the room were two more comfortable chairs which were padded.

Eliezzer observed the darkness of the room and of the house in general, and thought to himself that an opportunity for Arieh the glazier existed someday in the future.

The baron took two of the wooden chairs and turned them towards the corner. He offered them to the two visitors and then collapsed into one of the padded chairs.

"You are here, I presume, because you wish to settle on my lands. Is that correct."

Judah spoke a few words into Eliezzer's ear, and Eliezzer nodded.

"And for my part, I am interested in having you on my estate, because of the benefits you can bring.

"That is," continued the baron, "Providing we can reach agreement on this matter."

"Eliezzer spoke a few words to Judah, who then spoke to the baron in his own tongue.

My lord, you will not find us hard to deal with, for we are very reasonable people."

"Good, I am happy to hear this," said the baron. "In that case I will be happy to have you on my estate, providing you are able to satisfy me that it will be to my benefit to have you."

Eliezzer believed he had understood the baron's words, but did not trust himself to reply in case of misunderstanding. He spoke a few words to Judah, who answered the baron.

"My lord, after we have discussed everything fully, I believe that we will be able to convince you that our presence will be to your benefit."

"Very well then," said the baron, "We shall start the discussion. From the beginning we are assuming that your presence on my estate will cause no expense to me or to my estate."

Eliezzer spoke a few words to Judah, who replied, "My Lord, this should present no problem. We Jews have always been self-sufficient and paid our own way in everything we do.

"Good," said the baron, "And now, another thing that has been concerning me. I do not know how true these stories are, but I have heard of instances where Jews have become very rich and powerful, and become a problem in the places where they live.

"My lord," answered Judah, turning to Eliezzer for advice. "Our wish is not to become wealthy and powerful, but simply to live in moderate comfort and practise our religion, for it is the love of our religion that is most important to us. If we are able to do this, you will never have cause to feel threatened by us. Rather you will find us to be faithful servants who will do our best to bring prosperity to your estate.

The baron excused himself for a moment, then returned with a cask of wine and three small glasses. When Eliezzer and Judah politely refused his offer, he poured himself a drink which he downed in one gulp before refilling the glass and letting it stand. He studied the two men, choosing his words carefully.

"I make no secret of it, it is my ambition someday to rule over an estate much larger and more important than what is now here in *Laukzemis*. I am told that to bring this to pass, Jews are the best helpers that one can have, and that is why I let it be known that I am interested in having Jews on my estate...."

He paused, "....That is, if they meet my conditions, for you must be aware that there will be conditions."

"Of course we expected that there would be conditions to fulfill," answered Judah.

"Very well," said the baron. "We will start with the first, and the most obvious. No matter how wealthy any of you may become, as long as you are on my estate, no one will build a home larger than mine. Should you have any wish to do this, then you will be required to build for me a new home that is larger again. Is this understood?"

Eliezzer spoke to Judah, who answered, "Yes, my lord, we understand this. It is a very reasonable condition, and we accept it."

"The second matter," continued the baron, "Is the matter of tax collecting. It is known that you Jews are excellent tax collectors. I want you to increase my tax collections by being far stricter on my serfs than I have been."

Eliezzer understood the baron's words, but did not trust himself to express himself adequately in this instance. He spoke a few words to Judah who passed on the message to the baron.

"My lord, Eliezzer understands what you are saying. We have amongst our band those who have had much experience in collecting taxes. If you will leave it to us to do it our way, we are certain that we can increase the revenue that comes to you."

"Good, I am glad to hear this. Then I can count on you to be strict with my serfs."

"Not necessarily stricter, my lord, but more efficient. Sometimes strictness is not the best way. If you will allow us to do as we have done in the past, then we are certain that we can improve things.. After all, our chief concern is in seeing that your revenue is increased."

"Very well," answered the baron reluctantly, "You shall be free to use whatever methods you choose, but if you are not successful, then I shall demand that you Jews make up the difference yourselves."

"We accept this condition without concern, for we know that it will not be necessary. Amongst us we have David, son of Mordechai, who is expert at this task. We shall allow him to perform it, as he sees best."

"Another service which you must agree to." added the baron, "Is the purchase of all the produce from this estate. I have been taking the goods and selling them myself in the past, but I have little time for this activity. We will agree on a price for the produce, which you will be required to take off my hands. It is then yours to sell as you see fit. Whether you make a gain or a loss will become your problem, not mine."

Eliezzer nodded to Judah, who answered. "This poses no problem, my lord, for it is something we expected. If the price is fair, then we can all gain from this."

"The price will be fair," said the baron.

"And now, I have a question," he added, "And one that is important to me. Is there anyone amongst you who is able to produce wine? We lack a good winemaker on this estate, and bringing it from Kretinga is both expensive and unreliable."

"You will be pleased to know," answered Judah, "That both Eliezzer and I have come from winemaking families and are well versed in the trade. If you can but arrange a regular supply of grapes, then we are able to produce wine for you as good as any you have tasted."

"This is good news," smiled the baron." If you are able to make wine as good as you say, than you will always remain very welcome on my estate. Have no worry, one of the first things we will do is to arrange a steady supply of grapes."

The baron drank another glass of wine, then graciously offered Eliezzer and Judah a glass, which they again refused.

"And now, for the final condition. If you are to stay on this estate, we shall find a spot for you separate from my serfs, perhaps not far from where your wagons rest at the moment. There you will be free to build homes for yourselves at your expense, but you must pay me rent for the right to remain on my estate, and if you leave for any reason, your homes and property become forfeit to me."

Eliezzer smiled when he heard this last condition, for the terms were identical to those in every place they had stopped, but with a difference. This baron, unlike those previous, has been honest enough to spell it out. Others had promised a life of security for perpetuity, but had seized Jewish property without recompense upon the slightest provocation.

He spoke a few words to Judah, who replied to the baron.

"My lord, nothing could be more just than for us to pay you rent for the right to remain on your property, But how can we know that you will not drive us away sometime in the future simply as a means of seizing our property?"

"You have no way of knowing this," answered the baron. "The only protection you have is to know the man whom you are dealing with. I consider myself an honourable man. When I say that you are welcome to stop here, I mean what I say."

Eliezzer stared directly into the baron's face. Through the reddened alcohol-induced complexion he could see a basic decency and honesty. He made up his mind immediately.

"My lord, I trust you, and I believe that in our dealings with you there will be honour. But we also pray that the rent you exact from us will be that which will not place too great a burden on us, and discourage us from remaining, for after all, you must remember that we will be serving you in many other ways."

Despite the slight slur which was creeping into his speech, the baron answered politely.

"My friends, if you prove your worth to me, you need have no fear that the rent I demand will become too burdensome, for it will not be my intent to drive you away if you are performing well. The rent will be something you can easily afford, and may even be payable in wine or clothing or other things that you produce. Do you not remember what you told me a few moments ago, about your tax collector friend with my serfs, that the best results are often obtained if one is not too strict?"

Eliezzer felt a touch of respect for the baron, although even from this early meeting it had become obvious that there would be problems on the occasions that he chose to overdrink. When sober, there was no question that the baron was a clear-thinking, intelligent and decent man who would be an efficient person to deal with.

"And now my friends," he said, offering his hand to the two Jews. "I believe that we have covered almost everything. Perhaps we have missed something which we will think of later. No doubt there will be further questions, but we can discuss these over the coming days before we make any decisions."

"My lord, there is one most important question which we have not discussed, and which cannot wait. To us, our religion is the most important thing of all, and our religion tells us that we are to spend the Sabbath day performing no other task than worshipping our God. On that day, and on certain of our festivals, we must obey our laws, and we are unable to do any work, either for ourselves or for anyone else."

The baron did not seem surprised at the remark.

"Yes, I understand this and I expected it, for I have heard this thing about Jews and their God. I find it hard to understand, but I accept it. You will not be asked to do anything that goes against your tradition and laws, but you must know that if a task is to be completed, it cannot go unfinished because of your Sabbath. You will be required to manage your affairs in such a way that everything that is due to me is finished before your Sabbath begins."

"We accept this," answered Judah, "And we do not consider this an unreasonable demand. We are grateful that you respect our religion, and in turn we shall respect your right to everything that you are entitled."

"That is good," said the baron. "I believe we understand each other. I shall be willing to have you on my estate, if you are willing to remain here. You may choose a site near where you are, at the edge of my estate, and beside the Kulse River further downstream from where my people live.

"You may discuss it with your people over the next few days, and let me know what you have decided. Then we can talk about any other questions which may arise."

Eliezzer offered his hand to the baron, and in his less than fluent Polish, he spoke.

"The important questions have been asked. We are dealing with a man of honour. There is no need to discuss further. We know what our people want. We thank you, and we stay."

CHAPTER 4

Thus it was that a Jewish community was formed at Laukzemis in Samagothica in the Kretinga district of Lithuania, which came to be known as *Loigzim* to its Jewish inhabitants. The community was to exist for the next three hundred years, during which it developed into a *Shtetl*, or self-contained Jewish village, largely cut off from the outside world, and bound by its own strict religious and traditional laws.

The Jewish community of Loigzim became semi-isolated, providing for all its needs with very little contact or influence from outside. Children were taught at home by their parents, and eventually a special room was able to be provided for the teaching of all the children, the number of which never came to exceed a score. The room became known as a *Bet-Hamidrash*, Hebrew for "House of Learning", and the classes came to be known as *Cheder*, taken from the Hebrew word meaning "Room".

The room contained little more than a long table with benches running along its length on both sides, a cabinet to hold the books, and a blackboard where the teacher or *Melamed* stood. Children would have their first exposure to classes as early as the age of three, and never later than five. By the time they were six they were able to read and write fluently in at least two languages. In a world where only the nobility received an education of any kind, this set the Jews off as different from all the other inhabitants of the district. Although there was little to differ the Jews economically from the Lithuanian peasantry, in cultural terms they belonged to a different world.

The reason for the emphasis on education is obscure, but could be traced back as far as biblical times. It had since become one of the strongest facets of Jewish culture, and the depriving of a child of a Jewish education came to be considered as a crime against that child. Indeed it came to be accepted that no Jew should stop in a place where he could not properly educate his children.

Although Loigzim remained cut off from all but the nearest local communities, the education provided to its children was identical to that received by Jews in every community in the world. For Jewish education, no mater where it existed, was based on the *Torah*, and it had been decreed thousands of years earlier that the *Torah* was the word of God, and as such was perfect. The *Torah* could never be altered, and would remain as it was for so long as there were Jews to follow its teachings No matter where in the world a Jew happened to reside, his teachings would stem from the same unalterable word of God.

In the meantime the community eked out a precarious economic existence, surviving off its members' skills in basic crafts such as tailoring, wine making, leather work, and the trading at the local markets of any product which would produce a profit.

The community of Loigzim never grew and never prospered, but remained static, unchanged through the years, and centuries later as strongly committed to its Judaic faith as in the days of its founding.

By the early eighteenth century other Jewish centres in the area were growing and prospering, as Jews from the west sought refuge from persecution. Loigzim remained unchanged, stifled by a sequence of despotic overlords who spurned any thought of progress. To the Jews of the *Shtetl*, this was simply a burden to be born philosophically, providing that their most cherished values, their religion and traditions, were not interfered with. Poverty could be dealt with, even the loss of their children to neighbouring centres, but suppression of their religion was another matter. For so long as their ways were not threatened, they were prepared to accept their lot in life.

DORBYAN
PART 1

It was late in autumn of 1941, and work was proceeding feverishly on the tiny Samagothican peasant farm. It was necessary to harvest the crops before the arrival of the colder weather and the first frosts. The peasants in the field were dedicated to their task, making their way forward between the rows at a steady pace.

One of the workers stood out from the others, not because of any difference in the clothing he wore, or because of any major difference in his size and physique, but because of the manner in which he carried out his task. Whereas the others worked purposefully and singlemindedly, this young man seemed preoccupied with other matters. He would work with a purpose for a short period of time and then stop, gazing absentmindedly towards the sky or at the space beyond the fields as if in a dream.

From time to time one of the others would walk over to the young man and place a comforting hand on his shoulder whispering a few words of encouragement. The young man would then continue his work for a few minutes longer before lapsing once again into his daydream.

No effort was made by the others to chastise the young worker for his lack of contribution to their efforts, for they knew what he had recently experienced, and understood.

The other workers were watchful as they worked, for these were dangerous times, made still more dangerous by the Jew in their midst. The recent conquest of their land by the Germans had seen the extermination of almost all the area's Jews, with the few survivors maintaining their existence only through the goodwill of those Lithuanian peasants who were prepared to offer them safety and shelter.

The consequences of being discovered were too unpleasant to contemplate, for the Germans had made known that any Lithuanian found harbouring or assisting a Jew would be treated as if he were a Jew himself. However, it was not the Germans who were the main problem, for their numbers were small, but rather those Lithuanians who sympathized with and actively assisted the Germans. The only consolation was that this danger had diminished of late, now that the Germans had made their true intentions known. Earlier they had been enthusiastically welcomed into the country as saviours who would liberate the land from the hated Russians. The honeymoon had not lasted, as it had soon become clear that the Germans had not entered Lithuania as liberators, but as conquerors, and that their methods were at least as brutal and repressive as those of the occupiers they replaced.

Still, although the general mood was of hostility to the Germans, there were those who continued to admire their methods and ambitions. As a result, the presence of Moshe Bloch had been mentioned to no person outside the farm. The farm itself was isolated, more than three miles from its nearest neighbour, and as such was as safe a sanctuary for Moshe Bloch as was likely to be found in the district.

As Moshe Bloch worked in the field he found it impossible to concentrate on the task before him. He dearly wanted to make himself useful, to repay these kind folk for the lifesaving assistance they had provided him, but the thoughts in his mind, the events of the past few months had made this impossible. Indeed, it was a struggle simply hold his mind together, to retain his sanity and to prevent himself from descending into a morass of apathy and self-pity.

His ordeal had begun in June of that year, when he had left Dorbyan to visit the subject of his affections, Esther Salminis, in the nearby port town of Polangen. It was while he was in Polangen that the Germans had invaded Russia and marched into Lithuania. As expected, the Russians were no match for the Germans, and within the day the first German units appeared in Polangen. This had been followed by immediate measures against the town's Jews, who numbered some four hundred in number.

For some reason Moshe had decided to return to Dorbyan where the Germans could likewise be expected very shortly. The move saved his life. It was on his way home that he was told the news that was to alter his plans.

On June 27 the Germans had herded all the Polangen Jews into the main square, separating the women and children from the adult males. The males had then been marched to a spot on the outskirts of town and shot to death, their bodies being buried in a mass grave previously prepared. There had been rumours that the same thing had taken place in the nearby district capital of Krettingen. There could be no doubt that the same fate awaited his fellow Jews in Dorbyan within a very short time.

Lithuanian peasants pleaded with him not to return to Dorbyan and certain execution, and it was at that point where he had been forced to make a heartrending decision, one which he was still not certain was the correct choice.

Should he hurry back to the doomed town and spend whatever time was left with his beloved father and mother, or should he survive at all costs, even if it meant abandoning his family? The choice was agonizing.

In the end he allowed himself to be persuaded by the Lithuanian peasants that he must survive, if for no other reason than to bear witness against the Germans at some future date. He would be of no assistance in Dorbyan apart from providing some form of comfort to his family, who in any case would be disappointed that he had not taken the opportunity to save himself.

The massacre of the male Jewish population of Dorbyan came on June 29, with his father, Mordechai becoming the first victim of the Germans. He had heard the gruesome tale of how the males, almost three hundred in number, had been marched from the town centre to a spot beside an old water mill just outside of town. They had been shot and their bodies thrown into a trench, and covered with earth. In many cases the bodies so buried had still shown signs of life.

The women and small children had been imprisoned in the synagogue, the fittest of them being removed in small groups to labour in the fields of Lithuanians until the point of exhaustion, upon which point they were bludgeoned to death with farm implements. Finally, toward the end, when the number remaining was no more than one hundred, the synagogue had been set alight, burning and asphyxiating those inside to death.

Moshe had crept into the synagogue on several occasions shortly before the end, trying to persuade some of those inside to leave with him. Apart from three young children whom he was able to carry to safety, none of the others had shown any desire to escape their entrapment.

This was something that would haunt him for the rest of his days. He genuinely believed that he could have led his mother and his younger sister Chia to safety, but they had refused to accompany him, even at the last moment. There were others whom he could have likewise helped, but who had refused all assistance.

He had been strong during the ordeal, but now that it was over, his defence mechanisms could no longer cope, and every thought that entered his head simply caused him further depression.

One thing that troubled him was how little he knew of the place of his birth. How old was Dorbyan? How had it been founded?

He had never taken the trouble to find out these things, and now, apart from his younger brother Lipman, he was the only adult survivor of the Jewish community. Old Hersh and Chana Jacob would probably have known, but they had been amongst the victims and now it was too late. Perhaps his parents could have told him, but they too were gone. The only hope was those Dorbyaners who had migrated before the destruction. His parents had corresponded with *mishpoche* in other lands, but he had not known these people and would have no idea how or where to locate them. The correspondence, the letters from overseas, had all been destroyed.

He realized now that he must survive at all costs, to bear witness to the events which had happened, but he would be at best an imperfect witness, able to testify to recent events but to little more. He must try to recollect as much information as possible, before his memory began to fail him. How many Jews were there in Dorbyan before the Germans came? How many houses were there? How many businesses? These questions he could answer, but his knowledge of things that had happened before his own personal recollection was abysmal, and he knew of no one who could help. By his reckoning, there were eight survivors of the Dorbyan massacre, six girls aged between five and six years, his younger brother Lipman, and himself. The children would grow up to have faint memories of earlier loving families, but no knowledge or remembrance of Dorbyan itself. His brother Lipman, nine years younger than himself, would know no more than he did.

Could the story of Dorbyan ever be told?

CHAPTER 1

Arieh Lieb, son of Chaim Sender, and known as Leiba, was one of the few Jewish merchants who had succeeded in Loigzim, and yet he wanted to leave.

A wine dealer, he and his wife Breina Shora and their children lived a far more secure existence than most of the Jews and peasants who eked out a living from the Baron von Loigzim's run-down estate. The Baron worshipped his wine, regarding it as an absolute necessity of life, and frequently consumed it to the point of overindulgence, making life difficult for anyone who had dealings with him. The Baron frequently deemed it unnecessary to settle his debts with others, but because of the nature of the product he sold, Leiba knew that he could always be assured of being paid on time.

The Jewish community was small, but ancient and closely knit. It lacked a synagogue, having never achieved the size or the means to acquire one. But between the community members, facilities had always existed to maintain the cherished religion and traditions. The Barons had always been difficult men to deal with, but to their credit it must be conceded that they had allowed their Jews freedom to follow their faith. The Barons had long realized the advantages of having Jews in their employ, and if they did not understand or approve of the Jewish religion, they at least tolerated it, and made little attempt to interfere. A small Jewish cemetery dating back to the days of the Spanish Inquisition gave testimony to the generations of Jews who had lived and died in the tiny village of Loigzim.

The estate of Dorbyan had become larger than that of Loigzim, and in the year 1701 had been granted commercial privileges, amongst which was the right to hold its own market. Small at first, it had grown gradually at first, and then at an accelerating pace as more and more traders came to realize its potential. Within twenty years it had become a well known feature in the district and Leiba now found himself making the five mile journey on almost every Wednesday that he was able. His produce had sold well, and he could foresee a growing demand which far exceeded what he had been able to sell in Loigzim. The town was well located, at the junction of a river and an overland trade route. The baron there was known to be efficient and progressive, and there could be no doubt that a rosy future existed in Dorbyan.

He continually found himself wondering if it would be possible for him to settle there, abandoning his dealings in Loigzim and servicing the new market full time. He was certain that this was the way to make his fortune, and yet the hurdles before him seemed insurmountable.

He knew that if he took his wife and children and went to settle in Dorbyan alone.they would before long cease to be Jews, for without a community it would be impossible for them to carry on their faith. Since time immemorial Jews had generally migrated in groups, and with good reason, for their motivation had been usually to avoid expulsion or persecution. For a single Jewish family to move to a place where they would be on their own was unthinkable, particularly when they were not forced to leave in the interests of self-preservation.

And yet he could not get Dorbyan out of his mind; the opportunities were simply too good to be ignored.

There was only one way. He would simply have to convince others to join him. Since the days of the Babylonian exile, Jews had been bound by Jewish law to remain together, and with good reason. The necessity of having at least ten adult Jewish males to hold a prayer service had ensured throughout the ages that Jews stayed together in communities. When they had designed their laws, the ancient Rabbis had been very conscious of what they were doing, for as almost every other ancient nation had vanished, the Jews alone had maintained their identity, separate from all other nations. Those who had not remained part of the community and had gone off on their own way had become assimilated into other peoples. They were no longer Jews, or at least could no longer be identified as such.

Leiba had not mentioned his thoughts to Breina, for he knew that his ideas would devastate her. Her lot was not easy despite their relative affluence, and her sole joy in life was in knowing that she had succeeded in bringing up her children to be devoted Jews, knowledgeable in all the traditions and customs. In time they in turn would pass on this same devotion to their children. In Dorbyan this would not be possible.

There was only one way. He would speak to his brother ,Joseph Beir, the barber, and to Breina's brother, Nochum Joseph, the hide merchant. Between these two families were six sons, all Bar-Mitzvah. With his own two Bar-Mitzvah sons there would be eleven adult males, enough to form a proper Jewish congregation, that is, if the others could be persuaded to join him.

Leiba believed that he would find Joseph Beir receptive. Joseph had had dealings with the Baron von Loigzim that were far from satisfactory, and had come to tolerate his lot for the simple reason that he knew of no other alternative. His children would be leaving him in the next few years in any case, as he had no means of employing them. He and his wife Basha would not be difficult to persuade.

Nochum Joseph and his wife Rachel would be another matter. Their hide processing business had been anything but prosperous and they would be reluctant to take risks. In addition their leaving would be tantamount to abandoning a considerable debt owed to them by the Baron, probably uncollectable, but owing just the same.

"But Nochum," said Leiba, "If business is as bad as you say now, how will you manage when your sons are ready to earn their own living? They are Bar-Mitzvah already, and the time cannot be far away. If you cannot employ them in your business, then they will go to Krettingen, or even Memel. Dorbyan is already much larger than Loigzim, and is growing very quickly. Surely in Dorbyan you have a better chance to provide employment for your sons."

The argument was not sufficient, so Leiba returned to his wife Breina. She, as expected, was not impressed by the idea either, but agreed to follow her husband's wishes if he could find sufficient others to accompany him. Joseph Beir and Basha were of the same mind. They were uncertain, but were prepared to go, but only on the condition that others could be found to join them. The deadlock was finally broken when Leiba earnestly confronted Nochum Joseph and Rachel together in their home.

"Can you not see?", he pleaded' "In Dorbyan there is an opportunity for each of us to expand, your family just as much as mine."

"It could mean starvation for us. The hide business is not good, but at least it puts food on our table", said Nochum Joseph.

"It will be a barren life away from our friends and the Jewish community", said Rachel.

"Nochum, I will take your argument first. I do not believe that you are taking any risk in moving your business to Dorbyan. It will in fact be easier for you. As yet there is no hide dealer there, and yet the farm is larger, the market is larger, and there are more people there to buy your hides.

"And so certain am I that you will succeed that I am prepared to make you an offer. I have no fears that my own trade will not improve in Dorbyan, and that before long I will live a very comfortable existence. I am prepared to guarantee your success, by meeting all your expenses of your moving there. I will also guarantee all your business expenses until you are established, although it is my own belief that there will be not much need for this.

"And Rachel, I realize what a barren life it would be away from the Jewish life we love, and that is why Breina and I could never do it by ourselves. But if our families go at the same time, we are taking our Jewish way of life with us. We will be enough in number to do everything there that we do here. Just remember, we are still in reach of Loigzim if need be, and we will be nearer than we have been to the synagogue at Krettingen.

"Let us remember that our forefathers survived and brought us to this day because they were always willing to move to another place where the opportunity was greater. They came to Loigzim because it was better than wherever they were at the time. Now the time has come that there are better places than Loigzim for us to live."

"They came to Loigzim because no other place was safe for them. At least we are safe here in Loigzim", retorted Rachel.

"And we would not be safe in Dorbyan?", asked Leiba. "Of course our safety comes first, but if we can be safe in a better place, then why not?

"By moving to Dorbyan we would be doing ourselves and our children a favour. At the moment how many of our children remain with us in Loigzim? Why is it that everyone of us has *mishpoche* in

Memel and Krettingen? Has the community here grown since the time of our grandfathers? I doubt it, but in Dorbyan we have the chance to keep our children with us, and to grow."

Finally Leiba was able to prevail with his arguments, his offer of financial assistance swaying Nochum Joseph, and his play on the fears of Rachel that her children would soon leave her, swaying her.

Leiba's next task was to speak with the Baron von Dorbyan. With his wagon well laden with his finest wines he set out early on his five mile journey. His wagon creaked along, leaving behind the run-down Loigzim estate, and made its way along the rutted track leading to Dorbyan. He passed through fields, forest, and then more fields, this time better maintained, as he approached his destination. Ahead of him he saw the rough wooden bridge over the River Darba, but turned his wagon to the right before crossing it, following an earthen track into the estate. Four hours after leaving Loigzim he brought his wagon to a creaking halt and hitched his horse to the post in front of the Baron von Dorbyan's home.

The difference between the estate at Dorbyan and the one he had left behind was striking. Here the estate reeked of prosperity, with lush, neatly cultivated fields. The Baron's house was immaculate, and even the modest huts of the peasants were tidy and well maintained. Obviously the Baron here enjoyed a rapport with his workers that was missing at Loigzim, and the results were plainly evident.

There was no question in Leiba's mind that in a place such as this he and the other members of his and his wife's families would prosper.

Although he had dealt with the Baron von Dorbyan before, a wave of nervous energy welled up inside him as he was taken to the entrance of his home.

"Sir, you will remember me as the wine merchant from Loigzim. This time I would like to speak to you on another matter, and to beg a favour from you."

The Baron was a cultured, softly spoken man, and unlike his counterpart in Loigzim, totally sober. He welcomed Leiba in a polite but firm manner which put him at ease.

"Yes, come in. Of course I remember you, you have always been a good person to deal with. Just what favour is it that you ask? If it is reasonable and within my means I shall do my best to grant it."

As Leiba entered the doorway, he turned and pointed to his loaded wagon.

"Thank you sir, but first as a token of gratitude for this audience, I would like you to accept these casks of wine that I have brought with me. They are very good wines, and I am certain that you will find them to your taste."

The Baron was easy to deal with, although Leiba suspected that he could be very firm when the occasion warranted it. In Krettingen the baron had had considerable exposure to dealings with Jews, and had always found their polite businesslike manner a welcome change from his dealings with the illiterate peasants who worked his estate. Yes, there was land available in Dorbyan which could be made available to Jews wishing to settle there.

The wine was unloaded from Leiba's wagon and taken into the Baron's house. Then the Baron climbed into the wagon and sat alongside Leiba, pointing in the direction they were to go.

"I shall come with you, that there be no misunderstanding as to the area in which you may settle."

Together they rode the half mile from the Baron's estate in the direction from which Leiba had arrived. This time they crossed the wooden bridge which rattled precariously under the weight of the horse and wagon. With the River Darba behind them the baron motioned Leiba to stop the wagon, and the two men climbed out.

"Here," said the Baron, "we have a good view of the whole area. You can see the church on the right hand side of the road, and farther along you can see the bridge over the other branch of the river. The land on the right belongs to the church, and as you know, the area in front of it is the marketplace, but the space on the other side between the two bridges is not being used, and will belong to you and your people."

Leiba surveyed the scene before him and nodded in approval at the area being offered to him. The distance between the two bridges was almost a half mile, more than enough space to easily house the entire Loigzim Jewish community if necessary. He thanked the Baron profusely.

"I am very grateful, sir, for it is as much as I had hoped for, and even more. I am certain that the others will approve as well, and be grateful to you for what you have done."

"There are conditions of course, Leiba," said the Baron. "As you can see, this space is largely wooded, and many trees will have to be cleared, even though there are some empty spaces. You must bear the responsibility of clearing it yourselves, for it is a condition that no expense accrue to the estate because of your settling here."

This was nothing more than Leiba had expected, and he thanked the Baron again, assuring him that the condition would be met.

The Baron then added, "Another thing that will become your responsibility is the maintenance of the bridges. As it is you who will be living here, and presumably gaining benefit from the market, it will be in your interest to see that the bridges are able to handle the extra traffic that will be placed upon them. Is this understood?"

"Yes sir," replied Leiba, "Just as soon as we are established, our first task will be to see that the two bridges are strengthened."

The Baron nodded approvingly. For his part, he was pleased at the transaction, and considered the event a piece of good fortune that had come his way. He knew that in Memel and Krettingen the Jewish presence was an asset, increasing trade and bringing prosperity to the towns. The Jews somehow seemed to possess an acumen for commerce than others could not match. He was certain that with Jews living and trading in Darbenai the importance of his estate would only increase. On a personal note, there would be the benefit of having a reputable wine merchant located conveniently near his home.

After delivering the Baron to his home, Leiba returned to the site, examining the area over and over by himself, making plans on how each section might be used, and dreaming of what it might someday become. It was perfect! He could have asked for nothing more! The trees would have to be cut down, but the expense of felling them would be offset by the lumber they would provide for the houses that would be built.

Between the bridges the land was low lying enough to be fertile and easily cultivated, yet sufficiently elevated not to become flooded if the river overflowed its banks. The fields on the other side behind the church were of the same soil, and their lushness could one day be matched on the Jewish side.

He looked at the small wooden church on the other side of the roadway, built some eighty years earlier, and he thought to himself, "How wonderful it would be if we could have someday what Loigzim has never had - our own place of worship!, - right on this spot, opposite the church, with the market place between us!"

It was getting late, and reluctantly he tore himself away from his dreams, and pointed his horse back onto the dusty road to Loigzim.

Thus it was that, in early spring, in order to give themselves the longest possible time before the next winter, the three families began the burdensome task of moving to Dorbyan. Leiba had already made several visits to the area, At his own expense Leiba had paid for the clearing of a portion of the land. He had also arranged for the fallen trees to be stripped and cut into logs ready for construction. that work could begin just as soon as the families arrived.

Unlike so many of their ancestors, these people did not travel lightly, for they were not fugitives leaving their entire belongings behind. With them they brought enough to sustain themselves under shelter until the first of their homes could be erected. When this was done they would then be able to return to Loigzim to collect the remainder of their possessions.

Their problems were those of all pioneers. They possessed sufficient manpower for the task but not always the skills. There was not a carpenter amongst them, nor in Loigzim who would have been able to help them, so money was paid to the Baron von Dorbyan to procure a carpenter for them. The house construction had to be paid for, and was, courtesy of Leiba, whose savings were rapidly dwindling. Their homes in Loigzim would have no sales value and would be better given away to other Jews to whom favours were owed. They were now impoverished, but at least they had roofs over their heads, albeit considerably inferior to the homes they had left behind.

After several wagon trips their possessions were now in Dorbyan. Then came the farm animals, which had to be driven at a snail's pace, but finally came the day when there was nothing left of their property in Loigzim. Both they and the people in Loigzim knew that this was their last visit to their birthplace apart from the odd exceptional occasion. Farewells were spoken, and there was apprehension on the part of both those leaving and those left behind, for the community was now precariously split in two, with both halves barely above the point of remaining viable.

Leiba suspected that eventually the Loigzim Jewish community would die out, as more and more of its members moved to Dorbyan. Others had already considered the idea, but abandoned it as too risky. Now, with a Jewish community already established in Dorbyan, it would be a far more attractive proposition.

As more land was cleared and outbuildings built, Leiba insisted that a vacant space be left amongst their homes directly across from the church. Already he could foresee the day when Dorbyan would possess what Loigzim had always lacked, its own place of worship.

Nochum Joseph's fears turned out to be unfounded. His hide business prospered, and the small amount of financial assistance required from Leiba was quickly repaid. Nochum's sons were already helping him in his expanded business, and one of them was making regular journeys to Loigzim to maintain his earlier trade.

Joseph the barber's trade likewise increased, and one of his sons was able to assist him although the other had leanings towards the glamour of the large town of Memel. For the time being he was at home and also making regular visits to Loigzim to continue the work his father had left behind.

The three wives gradually became happier as their homes acquired the comforts they had known in Loigzim, and more. Hardship had been their lot since birth, and they were accustomed to it, but somehow in Dorbyan it seemed less severe. With the books they had brought with them they were able to give the younger children the upbringing they needed, and when more was required, it was but a day's journey into Krettingen.

The years passed, and Leiba's older children grew up. His eldest son was Sender, who surprised his father with the news that he did not wish to enter the family wine trade. Ever since his childhood he had always wished to be a glazier, from the days in Loigzim when he had gazed in fascination at the work being done by the glazier on his occasional visits. Leiba had known of Sender's desire, but had always assumed it to be nothing more than childhood fancy, which would disappear with adulthood.

After a long discussion, Leiba agreed to accede to his son's wish, and to assist him in his chosen profession. His other sons would inherit the wine business. He paid a visit to Memel, found a Jewish glazier who was known to him, and made arrangements for Sender to work one year in Memel. Sender would receive no wage, but would be fed and housed for the year, and was guaranteed to be proficient in the trade when he returned. Leiba visited him twice during the year when he had the occasion to conduct wine business, but although Breina talked about accompanying him, she was never able to make the trip. Memel, some twenty miles away, was too much of a trip to be made by a mother who was still raising young children.

The day came for Leiba to collect Sender from Memel. He took his largest wagon, in anticipation of the load of glass and tools he would be bringing back for Sender's business. It was fortuitous that he did, for it turned out that the wagon was filled to the point of overflowing. With Sender came another surprise, by the name of Hinda Bluma. Sender had been introduced to her, the daughter of one of his fellow glass workers, and they had become friendly at first sight. She and her parents would be accompanying them to Dorbyan to meet the family, and if everything went as hoped, a marriage would be arranged in the not too distant future.

A place was made for Sender's business in a shed behind Leiba's house, but plans were made for a home for Sender and his new bride. Dorbyan now had its own glazier.

Leiba's wine trade went from strength to strength, and with his younger sons helping him, his burden became lighter. The Baron von Loigzim, fearful of losing his regular supply of wine, did everything possible to make Leiba welcome on his visits.

On one occasion Leiba had noticed the sad state of repair of the windows on the Baron's estate, and had suggested to Sender that a visit to the Baron might pay dividends. Sender took his father's advice, arranged an audience with the Baron, and was immediately engaged to do the repairs.

For the next three weeks Sender lived in Loigzim amongst relatives, performing the very tasks he had marvelled at when he was a boy. Broken glass was replaced, mirrors were repaired, window sashes were made weathertight, and doors were glazed. When he finished he returned to Dorbyan, overjoyed to be back with his new wife and amongst family members. Loigzim was the place of his birth, but Dorbyan was his home.

It was not long afterward however, that Sender complained to his father that he was having difficulty in extracting payment from the Baron von Loigzim. He had visited and mentioned the subject, receiving nothing more than a vague assurance of future payment. He had left the matter in the hands of other Jewish community members, but their efforts to collect his debt had fared no better.

The time for payment had elapsed beyond the point of reason. Another Loigzimer visiting Dorbyan had reported to Sender that the Baron now seemed to have no recollection of the debt. Finally Leiba decided that it was time for Sender and himself to pay a visit to the Baron personally.

The Baron welcomed Leiba with open arms.

"Aah, my good friend Leiba!," he said eagerly, "It is good to see you! What fine wines have you brought with you this time? It is some time since I have seen you!"

"I have brought no wine with me this time, sir. Instead I have brought with me my son, Sender."

"Yes, yes, your son and I, we know each other well."

"Sender tells me has has done considerable work for you repairing glass on your estate. I would like to see for myself what he has done, and if it has been done satisfactorily. For if it has not, I would like to know."

"There is no need for you to inspect. The work has been completed and is to my satisfaction."

"Then why is it that after all this time my son has not yet been paid for his work?"

"He will be paid in due course," answered the Baron. "All is not always as it seems. This estate has its difficulties, and sometimes we struggle here. Times will soon be better, and then your son will receive all that is owed to him."

Leiba looked the Baron directly in the eye.

"Sir, Sender is my son. His well-being is my own well-being. If he has any problem, then it becomes my problem. If he is unable to deal with you to his satisfaction, then I too am unable to deal with you."

The Baron blanched.

"Wait a moment, perhaps there is something I can do."

He dashed into his home, and from the distance Leiba and Sender could hear abuse hurled at someone inside, probably his wife. A few minutes later he emerged with a small sack of money, which he began counting into Leiba's hand.

Leiba motioned him to give the money to Sender. "The money is my son's, not mine," he said.

"There, I believe that you will find this to be the amount we agreed upon," said the Baron.

Both Leiba and Sender thanked the Baron.

"And now Leiba, just when will you arrive here with a load of wine? I do not see you very often anymore, and there is nowhere else for me to buy wine as good as yours for the same price. My wine cellar is almost empty, and I cannot wait much longer."

"I will come on any day you wish, as long as it is not on our Sabbath or a holiday, or on Dorbyan market day. Just tell me what day you wish, and you may be certain that I will arrive with a full load of the finest wines that can be had."

As Leiba and Sender rode off, the Baron knew that he had been bested, and yet he was not angry, but relieved, for he knew that his wine problem was now solved for the foreseeable future. Whatever his thoughts about Jews in general, he knew that a Jew could always be counted on to uphold a business transaction.

Leiba's other sons found wives from the old community at Loigzim, where the weddings were held. Dorbyan's Jewish community had now grown from the uncertain days when the loss of an adult male could have meant disaster. By contrast the Jewish community in Loigzim was in decline, and some of its members were now moving to Dorbyan. Leiba was certain that within a generation or two, perhaps even sooner, the ancient Jewish community at Loigzim would die out altogether.

Leiba and Nochum Joseph were fortunate that their businesses could support their sons. Others, such as Joseph Beir the barber, watched as most of their sons left for Kretinga or the larger centres of Memel and Libau. But the numbers were growing, and the cluster of Jewish homes around the market place had increased considerably.

One of Joseph Beir's daughters married a carter, who was easily persuaded to locate his business in Dorbyan. Another arrival made a living in the buying and selling of horses. Yet another found profit in taking farm produce to towns of the Baltic coast and exchanging it for fish which could be sold at the Dorbyan market.

More and more homes appeared, more and more weddings took place. The first grandchildren were born. The community was growing.

Leiba, now well past middle age, rejoiced with every change. Now his heart was filled with joy. Before long the empty space amongst the houses opposite the church would be empty no more. A dream was about to be realized, for the community could now afford to build its own synagogue.

In Dorbyan the tiny Jewish community had found fertile ground, and had taken root.

CHAPTER 2

The years passed peacefully for the Jews of Dorbyan. Allowed the freedom to follow their traditions, and allowed the freedom to trade without hindrance, their community flourished and grew.

The single room building which had been the original synagogue had become inadequate in a very short time, and had been added to in two directions. One of the additions had been made necessary by a fire which had miraculously spared the ark housing the holy Torah, but which had gutted the entire opposite wall. leaving it open to the elements.

This side, the western side, and the side facing the roadway, had been barely restored and extended outwards, when the community realized that further extension would be needed. Now an additional room had been built on to the same side through which one would pass before entering the door leading into the synagogue proper. The new room would be the classroom for the teaching of children. No longer would this function be the responsibility of the womenfolk in their own homes.

Outside the synagogue on the side facing the roadway and the church there still remained the considerable empty space which had come to be known as the *shul platz*. Used as a town meeting place, it was the favoured venue for the holding of weddings and festivals, or simply a meeting place for gossip.

Since the days when the first synagogue was built, Jewish communities had always kept to the tradition of living as closely as possible to it, and Dorbyan was no exception. The area between the two bridges on the synagogue side soon became filled up to the point of overcrowding. Houses began to be built farther back from the bridge, and then along the roadway on the other sides of the bridges. New streets were created. Apart from the old wooden church and its associated buildings, the entire inner area of Dorbyan surrounding the market area had become a Jewish domain.

As the eighteenth century passed its mid-point and approached the three-quarter mark, Leiba, son of Chaim Sender, had assumed the role of village elder. Now closer to ninety than eighty, but still alert and active, he was by far the community's oldest living member, and was looked upon as its founder. He had long since ceased to operate his wine busness, and the two sons he had passed it on to had in turn passed it on to their own sons. His life had become easy and comfortable, yet there had been moments of tragedy as well.

There had been the heartbreak at the low survival rate of newly born infants, and he had often pondered the problem, finding no solution. There had been the sense of loss when a son or daughter had left the community to make a life in Krettingen or Memel. Experience had taught that these had seldom returned, their visits becoming less and less frequent as their new lives were made in the larger centres. But the greatest tragedy had taken place within his own immediate family, and the scar it had left on him would never heal.

It was now almost thirty years since the fire which destroyed his home had taken Breina from him, and the pain it had caused him was the more unbearable because he would always blame himself for allowing it to happen. He knew that he should have been at home at the time, and that if he had, he would have been able to prevent Breina from entering the burning house to rescue her valuables.

The questions still crossed his mind. Why, on that day alone had he lingered so long at the Baron's estate when delivering his wagon load of wine? Normally he had done his business quickly, and left. Why not this time?... If only....., if only.....He would not still have been in the Baron's fields when the Lithuanian peasant first pointed to the smoke coming from the direction of the village.

"It looks like it could be the church," the Baron had noted. "We'd better take some men with us and see if we can be of help."

Leiba had looked in the direction of the smoke and felt his heart sink. He knew by the angle that the smoke was not quite in the direction where the church stood.It had to be coming from one of the homes somewhere on the Jewish side!

He would always remember his wild dash home and the scene which greeted him on his arrival, the ruined remains of his home, with the villagers still pouring buckets of water over the smouldering embers, the sight of his entire family running towards him, weeping and wailing loudly, tragedy written on their faces.

"It's Mama!... She's dead, Papa!"

Between sobs the story had come out, and he remembered their futile attempts to comfort him as the shock had worn off and the realization had taken its place.

"She ran into the house, Papa!...... to try to bring out the books!....... It was so sudden,...she gave no warning!......No one could stop her..... and then a minute later.......it was too late......she was gone!......There was nothing anyone could do.....!

And then he could remember Sender's arm around his shoulder, and his comforting words. Shall we go over and sit beside Mama, Papa?"

He and Sender had gone over and knelt beside the charred body. As his lips formed the ancient prayer he had been conscious of a circle forming around him. Through his tears he could remember seeing the Baron slightly behind the circle, the son of the man who had first allowed Jews to settle in Dorbyan. With his Lithuanian peasants beside him, he had stood there silently, his head reverently bowed.

For Leiba the tragic loss had been ironic, and had destroyed what should have been one of the happy events in his life. Less than week earlier the whole community had rejoiced, and he most of all, for the newly built synagogue had been used for its first ever Sabbath service. Now, the second use of the building was to be for the heartbreaking funeral service for Breina Shora. No matter what might be achieved by the community in the future, there would always be an emptiness in his life without Breina to share it with him.

The fire had alerted him to another need of the community. There had been other blazes, but these had always been extinguished by villagers passing buckets from a well. The fire in his house, which had been well established before it had been discovered, could not be dealt with in this fashion. There was a need for a better system, such as was in use in some of the larger centres. A handpump, combined with a pipe or hose, would have brought water into play more quickly, and had one been available at the time, Breina's life might possibly have been saved. He had sent one of his sons to Memel to investigate this, and the result was that Dorbyan now had a more effective means of fighting fire.

There had been other tragedies as well. The death of Sender's youngest son from an unexplained illness but a year before his Bar-Mitzvah had left another scar, and had left Sender and Hinda Bluma broken and disconsolate for months afterward. The other trials and tribulations of the fledgeling community had affected him as well, and with every misfortune that occurred he had felt his own body die a little, for as the founder he somehow felt himself responsible for the well-being of every person in the village.

But, on balance, life in Dorbyan was better than the life they had left behind in Loigzim, where similar tragedies had been equally common. How happy Breina would have been to have seen the latest classrooms in the synagogue. The long but gratifying hours she had spent in instructing the children and grandchildren had now become the responsibility of the *Melamed* in his new facilities, and now there was talk of taking the task from the Rabbi and hiring a new schoolteacher for that purpose alone. Many of the articles Breina had been deprived of could now be found in Dorbyan, and with each new year the number of merchants and the variety of goods on offer was increasing.

Still in good health, Leiba continued to visit the synagogue twice daily, making the short walk unassisted. His home, which had been rebuilt after the fire, had been passed on to his youngest son, the son with the largest family, and now he lived with Sender and Hinde Bluma. Sender, likewise retired, would accompany him to the synagogue to make his daily devotion, after which the two would wait in the *Shul platz* and find someone with whom to share a conversation. There was no topic that did not interest him, and he was probably more aware of the local gossip than he had been as a younger man. Business matters still interested him, as did the goings-on of the younger folk. From time to time he would engage the Rabbi in religious discussion, but it was always an unfair match, the Rabbi always being careful to withhold his superior knowledge in deference to Leiba's revered position in the community.

Sender's own children had in turn given birth, and now Leiba found himself becoming a great-grandfather with increasing frequency. He had become the patriarch of a large and rapidly growing family.

Saturday afternoon after the Sabbath service and meal were his favourite time of the week, for his many grandchildren and great-grandchildren would come to visit and pay their respects to him each week. The children would always welcome the stories he told, and their faces would light up when he indicated that he would tell them of the beginnings of Dorbyan and Loigzim, stories of which they never tired.

"Tell us again about Loigzim, Zeide!"

"Please!"

"Again!", Leiba would ask with feigned incredulity. "Have you not heard about Loigzim often enough?....Very well then, sit down. What is it that you wish to know?"

"You and Papa have told us many times about life in Loigzim, and you have told us how Dorbyan began, but you have never told us how Loigzim began."

Leiba thought for a long moment.

"Perhaps there is a reason that I have never told you, for I am not sure that I know the answer myself. I am an old man, and I can remember the beginning of Dorbyan, but not nearly old enough to remember the beginning of Loigzim.......

"...When I was young like you, I too wanted to know, so I went to my Bobe and Zeide, but they too were not old enough to know. They could only tell me stories they had heard from their own grandparents, who themselves had been told by older people. I can only tell you what they heard and told to me, and we can hope that the story has not changed too much from the truth......

"In the land of Sepharad, far to the west, the Jews lived peacefully and comfortably......."

"Where is Sepharad, Zeide?"

"Shoosh!" One of the older children scolded the inquisitive one. "Let Zeide speak, and don't be so curious!"

Leiba looked from his chair to the children seated around him on the floor, and smiled.

"Now, now, there is no shame in being curious. Did you know that it is the curious of today who will be the wise of tomorrow. Any of you may ask whatever questions you like, and I only hope that I will have the answers to satisfy you."

He continued, "....Safarad is a land far to the west of here, several months' journey away. In fact it is the farthest to the west that one can travel before he comes to the great ocean."

"Why did the Jews go so far away to live, Zeide?"

"As we all know, the original home of our people was the Land of Israel, as Palestine was once known. It was the home of our forefathers, Abraham, Isaac and Jacob. But the land was rich, and the Jews were not allowed to live there in peace, for other nations coveted it.

"Many nations conquered the Land of Israel, and overpowered the people living in it, each nation changing the people they conquered to their own ways....

"With every other nation they succeeded in changing their ways, and they tried to do the same to our people, to make us worship their gods instead of ours....

"Although they succeeded with all other peoples, with the Jews they all failed, and when each nation finally departed, the Jews always remained, never changing.

".....Finally came the mightiest empire of all, the Romans, who conquered the land and all the peoples within it. Of all the peoples living there, only the Jews refused to bow before them, and worship their Gods. In the end the Romans realized that they would never change the Jews, so they drove them from their homeland and forced them to flee to other lands."

Leiba looked into the faces of the children. "...But surely you have learned all of this in your cheder classes."

The children remained silent. Of course they had learned all of this, but how could they tell Leiba the reason for their attention, that his version was so much more interesting than the boring lectures of their teacher?

Leiba continued, "The Jews fled in all directions, looking for a safe place to be free of the Romans, where they could live like Jews, and like ourselves, study their religion. The Romans controlled most of the known world, but in some places they were not as strict. In many lands they were not welcome, in others they were welcome for a time. Those who moved eastwards from Palestine towards Babylon found a home where they thrived. Those who moved westwards faced hardship and suffering.

"Jews travelled westward along the bottom of Europe and along the top of Africa. Finally when they had travelled as far to the west as possible, they found a haven in Sepharad. There they were allowed to worship God in peace and to prosper. In turn they brought prosperity to Sepharad, making it an important centre of commerce and culture. At the same time they produced many of the greatest scholars in history, such as the Rambam."

"Who was the Rambam, Zeide, and what did he do?"

"Who was the Rambam?! How can it be that you haven't already learned this? One of these days I must have a word with your teacher. I am sure that he will be only too happy to make a lesson of this subject if you ask. The Rambam was a man named Moses ben Maimon, or Moses Maimonides...."

"And how did he get his name, Zeide?"

"When you ask me all the things he did and how he got his names you are asking me questions that would take a week to answer, and for this you will have to ask your teacher. After all, we are trying to find out about the beginnings of Loigzim.

".....But we were talking about the Jews in Sepharad. They were the greatest scholars of the time, and of these the Rambam was the greatest. But there were other fields where Jews excelled. They were the greatest scientists, the greatest explorers, and the greatest merchants and traders. Even the kings and queens of the time had to depend upon the Jews for their finance....

".....But as so often before in our history, the Jews of Sepharad fell upon evil times."

"How could it happen if they were so powerful, Zeide? Could it happen here?"

"I cannot answer all your questions at once. Perhaps as I continue, you will find the answers to your questions.

".....The Jews fell upon evil times. As in the days of Pharaoh in Egypt, there arose new rulers who did not recognize the good that the Jews had brought to the country. Also the church, the same Catholic church that we see across the market place, had changed. Instead of practising their compassionate religion and being tolerant of Jews, they decided that all Jews should become Christians like themselves, and they made their own laws to force the Jews to change. The king and queen of Sepharad were weak people, and did not try to interfere with the church.

"And now I will ask you a question or two. What do you think the Jews did? What do you think we would do here in Dorbyan if we were told that we were not allowed to remain Jews".

Leiba waited patiently, but no answers were forthcoming. Finally, one of the older children said weakly, "I think that perhaps I would run away."

"You are not too far wrong," said Leiba, "And now I will tell you what happened.

"At first the Jews pretended to change, but they practised their religion in secret, but soon the church became alert to this. They began to decree that the Jews worship in their churches, that they eat *unkosher* food, and that they allow their children to be taught the teachings of Christians.

"And what did the Jews do then, Zeide?"

"The Jews did what they have done everytime in history when this has happened. They refused, for they knew that the laws of God were more important than any laws that other people might make."

"And what did the Christians do when they saw that the Jews were refusing?"

"They became angrier. They began taking Jews prisoner, and torturing them to make them change their religion. The people doing this were known as the Inquisition, and they punished any people that they didn't like, but mainly the Jews. A few Jews changed, some pretended to change, and many more went into hiding to avoid torture, for they knew that if they didn't change under torture, they would be put to death, and their children taken away to be raised as Christians.

".....Eventually even this did not satisfy the Inquisition, for they knew that many Jews were avoiding them, and worshipping God in secret."

Leiba paused for a moment, expecting a question, but the children were staring upwards at him, spellbound.

"Finally it was decreed that all Jews were to be banished from Sepharad.

"They were given little time, some say no more than three

months. It was a difficult time, for many had businesses, large estates and comfortable homes which they had to leave behind. Others had lost their children to be raised as Christians. They had always had hope that their children might someday be returned to them, but now they were forced to leave them behind. They were not allowed to take their belongings with them, and so with nothing at all, they were forced to leave Sepharad.

".....It is a miracle that they were able to survive at all, but they did, and it was only their faith in God that kept them alive and allowed them to remain Jews."

"But Zeide, why did God allow this to happen to them? You have not told us that they were sinful people?"

Leiba smiled. "This is a question that I cannot answer, nor can any Rabbi. God has always treated us differently from other peoples and, if it seems that he has punished us more often, perhaps it is that he expects more of us. For as long as Jews have existed, no one has been able to answer this question.

"To this day I am told that there are no Jews in Sepharad, but that there are those whose ancestors were Jews and who can still remember some of the old traditions."

"And what did the Jews do when they left Sepharad? How did they live?"

"Just as they did when they were forced to leave the land of Egypt, and as they did when they had to leave Palestine at an earlier date. They fled in all directions, they became wanderers. Some found refuge for a short time in a country called Portugal, but soon they too had to leave. They could not travel farther west, to they turned once again eastwards. Most of them went to the south and followed the Mediteranean, perhaps hoping eventually to return to Palestine. It was a lonely and difficult time for them, without possessions and children, but they had skills and good minds, and they survived. They stopped in many lands along the way, where I am told that their descendants still speak Sephardic.

".....Others went to the north, which turned out to be the most difficult direction of all. They went to France, and England, and Holland, where they endured a dismal existence until they managed to become established as traders. Many stopped in these places, but never felt secure. Others kept moving eastwards over the north of Europe, and passed from Holland through the Germanic lands and Prussia, where they gradually lost their Sephardic language and learned the Prussian that became the Yiddish that we speak today.

"But no matter how much they wandered, and how often they split up, they always remained in bands which had enough men to form a *minyan*, for without this they could not pray and remain as Jews.

"........And at least one small group made it all the way through France and Holland, through the Germanic lands and through Prussia, stopping in many places over many years, but never settling down, until they came to Loigzim."

"But Zeide, why Loigzim? It is such a small place! Was there no other place for them to stop along the way?"

"I'm sure there were other places, my children, but I'm sure that they had reasons for moving on. Perhaps their lives were in danger, perhaps their religion and traditions were threatened."

"Was it like Sepharad again, Zeide?"

"I'm sure it seemed that way, my children, for those who were forced to move on, but often there were other reasons as well. At first many kings and nobles welcomed the Jews, knowing that they would bring trade and prosperity to their kingdoms."

"Then why drive them away, Zeide?"

"Many of the kings and nobles were not good managers, and very often through waste and greed they found themselves in difficulties. When they saw Jews prospering, they believed that they were to blame for their misfortunes. They coveted the property of the Jews, which could then be used to solve their own problems. If they could seize the property of the Jews, they could use it to pay off their debts. Often their debts were to the Jews themselves, and it was easier to drive them away and take their property than it was to pay off the debts.

"This happened so many times that it is impossible to count. When the need arose, the Jews would suddenly be called 'Killers of Christ' or 'Bloodthirsty Child Murderers', or worse. This would be reason enough to drive them away and to take their property....

"....Later on the Jews would be missed and allowed to return."

"But why return, Zeide? Why would anyone wish to return to a place where this has happened to them?

"I agree, my children, but often a generation would pass, and the new group, tired of wandering and desperate to find a place to settle down, would think that times had changed, and return to that place.

"......When the Jews first arrived in Loigzim, or so I am told, there were still those who could remember the terrible times of the Inquisition and the flight from Sepharad. They could also remember their ordeals along the way through Europe. Although Loigzim was not a prosperous place, it was a new place, and it seemed to offer peace and shelter. There they found a Baron who was happy to receive them and let them worship God in peace.This was more than they had found in any other place. Some of the Barons von Loigzim were idiots and drunkards, some were greedy, but they never interfered in the Jews' way of life. Yes, life in Loigzim was difficult, and tedious, and few prospered, but at least the Jews always felt that they were safe there.

"......And you must remember that Jews have now lived in Loigzim for many generations, and at no time were they ever driven away from their homes.

"......And now, you have asked me if what happened in Sepharad could someday happen to us here in Dorbyan. I think not, but we can never be certain. You see, we Jews are always living in other people's lands, and if they should someday decide that they don't want us, it is always in their power to drive us away, and we can do very little about it, except leave.

"In Dorbyan we are fortunate that we have always had intelligent, well educated barons, who realize the benefits that we bring. But all this could someday change, and as happened in Egypt, Palestine and Sepharad, some future baron may decide to be rid of us."

"But where would we go, Zeide? ..What would become of us?.... Would we always just continue to wander from place to place forever?"

"I hope it never happens, but we must always be prepared in case it does," answered Leiba. "At the moment it would not be so bad, as there are Jews in many places who are happy and prospering, and we too would be welcome at these places. Already many of our people are to be found far to the east of Loigzim, and deep inside Russia. We would find a new home somewhere, just as other Jews are finding a new home by coming to Dorbyan.

"......But anyone can see that this is not the answer. The only real way is for us to have our own land, like other nations, where we can be certain of our future. This is why at every Rosh Hashanah we always recite the words, "Leshanah Habo B'Yerushaloyim" (Next year in Jerusalem). Only when we are one day again in Jerusalem will we be in our true home.

".......And that is why, my children, it is important for you to spend so much time in cheder, learning. As Jews, is more important for us to be learned than other people who are living in their own lands and do not have to face the prospect of being driven out of their homes without warning. I know that you don't like the mathematics that you are taught. I didn't either. but now , later in my life, I know the reason. If we are good at mathematics we will be good at business, and if we are valuable at commerce it is unlikely that some future baron will wish to be rid of us.

"....And if some unhappy day arises that we must move on, it is our skill at commerce that will keep us alive.

"Also I know that it seems unnecessary to be learning other languages, when Yiddish and Hebrew are enough for us to speak and pray in, but there is a reason for this as well. I know that it is difficult to learn to read and write in languages that do not use our Hebrew script, but we must master all the languages in the lands in which we live. We must speak Polish to the barons, German to the Prussians, Lithuanian to the peasants, and Russian to the Russians. If we wish to be good businessmen we must be able to conduct ourselves in all these languages, for it is certain that they will not learn our language. After all it is not they who are in our country, but we who are in theirs."

Leiba smiled, then winked mischievously.

"...And so, my children, I am now going to tell you what you have been waiting to hear! Tomorrow, when you are in *cheder*, pay attention to every word that your teacher tells you, for it is for your own good."

A mock groan arose collectively from the children.

".....And that, my children, is enough for today. I am not as strong as I used to be, and even speaking can take away my strength."

Reluctantly the children realized that there would be no further questions on that day. They would have to try again on the following Sabbath. Why was it that their Zeide Leibe could make any subject so much more interesting than their *Cheder* teacher?

Perhaps it was he who should be the schoolteacher.

One by one they dutifully kissed the old man, then dashed out towards the *Shul Platz* to play.

CHAPTER 3

In the latter years of his life, Leiba made another contribution to the Dorbyan Jewish community, a contribution he believed would endure long after he himself had passed from the scene.

He donated a new Torah to the synagogue.

The Torah in use had been brought from Loigzim, one of the three owned by the community there. Its origin was obscure, for it was the oldest of the three, and the most worn. To the knowledge of any Loigzimer, no Torah had been acquired by the community itself, and it could only be assumed that this one, if not the others, had made the journey from Spain during the expulsion. It was now in poor condition, and had been repaired many times.

Now, after further steady use in Dorbyan, after countless times being rolled and unrolled, it had deteriorated to the point where a religious authority would probably pronounce it *Unkosher*. The stitching was now perishing in so many sections as to make repair impractical, and many of the three hundred thousand letters contained within its pages were wearing away almost to the point of illegibility. The fading of the text could lead to an error in the reading of it, an unspeakable insult to the Almighty.

On numerous occasions, mention had been made of the need for a new Torah, but the expense involved had always been beyond the community's means,

There was a scribe in Kovno, but Vilna was the centre where the most illustrious authorities were to be found. A scribe could be sent for from Vilna, but this would take time and incur further expense. Scribes, particularly those sanctioned and cabable of working on Torahs, did not exist in large numbers. It could be several months or longer before a qualified scribe became available to make the journey to Dorbyan.

Sending the Torah away for repair was no solution, as the community would be without it until its return. In addition, the old Torah might well be pronounced beyond repair. A visit was paid to Loigzim to see if one of their remaining Torahs could be borrowed for a time, but the Torahs of that struggling community were in a similar state of repair.

Thus it was that Leiba examined his assets and weighed them up against the heavy expense of a new Torah. As a general rule communities acquired new Torahs when their finances permited. Leiba knew of larger communities which had prospered and whose synagogues housed a dozen Torahs or more, acquired gradually over many generations. Other communities, such as Loigzim, had never achieved the affluence necessary to contemplate their purchase.

It was impossible for a community to possess too many Torahs, for such an event would require the possession of a Torah for every adult male member of the congregation as well for every potential outside visitor who might appear on short notice.

Leiba reckoned that he still possessed a large estate, even though his breadwinning days had ended more than a generation earlier. He had planned to divide it amongst his many descendants, but gradually came to the conclusion that this was unnecessary. Each of his families was already enjoying a comfortable life, thanks to the assistance he had already given them. By using his estate to purchase a Torah, he would be bequeathing it to the whole community, most of which was in some way related to him in any case. There would still be a small estate left over to pass on to his family when he died.

When Leiba announced his decision, the community was stunned, for it had been slowly budgeting for the day when it could manage the purchase on its own. Leiba's gift became the subject of most of the talk in the streets for months to come, as it had become evident that Leiba had become a far wealthier man than anyone had realized.

What the community did realize was the unbelievable amount of labour which went into the creation of a Torah, which when finished was one of the most painstakingly crafted items produced by any culture on earth.

A Torah, to be *Kosher*, could only be made from the skins of animals themselves considered *Kosher* by Jewish law. Of these materials goatskin was the most popular, but *Shtil*, the skin of unborn calves, was preferred. This produced softer, whiter and less hairy writing surfaces than any other known material.

The Torah scroll, a roll by ancient tradition, because of its length, required the joining of full sheets of parchment. Remnants were not permitted. In fact, every stage of the production of a Torah was taken with respect to the Almighty as the sole consideration. Nothing that humans could do would be worthy of Him, but they could only do the best humanly possible. Anything less would be considered an insult to His name.

The joining of the sheets of parchment was in itself a work of art, sewn lengthwise to make the continuous scroll. The threads were made of dried animal tendons, once again only from permitted animals. These tendons were pounded with stones, forming them into flat filaments, so that the seams would be barely noticeable.

This was merely the procedure for the production of the material which was to receive the Torah writing. It was possible to produce a suitable vellum in as little as one month. The actual writing of the Torah could take as much as one year, and had been known to take longer.

The Torah could be written only by a qualified scribe, known as a *Sopher*. The word comes from the Hebrew word which is translated literally, "One who counts", for it was necessary that the three hundred thousand letters be counted on the finished Torah at the end. Omission of a single letter would render the work imperfect, and as such unsuitable for prayer.

Thus it was that a scribe was not permitted to write a single word from memory, but had to copy it from an existing Torah. He was to pronounce each word aloud before it was allowed to be written.

The physical writing of the text was equally painstaking. The sheets of parchment were written on before joining, and each sheet was permitted to contain between three and eight columns of writing, each line of which contained thirty letters. The ink, like all other materials, was in accordance with Jewish law, and all writing was done only with turkey feathers.

Writing had to be evenly spaced and legible, so that "a child not too bright and not too stupid" could read it. No letter was allowed to touch another letter. Errors could be corrected under supervision, but generally three or more errors on the same page were sufficient to render that page unfit for use. A single error in the spelling of God's name would have the same effect. A Torah could be written in as little as three months, but could also take a full year prior to final checking.

The entire process of producing a Torah was intended with but a single purpose, perfection, for the teachings of God were deemed to be perfect, and nothing must be allowed to detract from that perfection.

When word from Vilna reached the community that a Torah meeting their requirements had been completed, Leiba wanted to make the journey there himself to collect it, but he came to realize that his health would no longer permit such a strenuous task. Even his son Sender had reached the age where he felt such a journey to be beyond him, and so it was that three of Sender's sons were chosen to go. The day of their departure was a major event for the villagers, for in addition to taking a large sum of money with them, they were carrying the hopes of the community on their shoulders.

The road out of Dorbyan was little more than a well worn track, but once past Plugyon, thirty miles to the southeast, the roads became safer and were generally in good repair. The three Dorbyaners were able to drive their wagon from Shaharis prayers in the morning until Mincha in the afternoon, finding shelter in synagogues along the way, many of which provided lodgings for travelling Jews. They reached Vilna late in the afternoon and were able to find similar lodgings for the night, but as their journey had taken them five days, they had arrived to find that the Sabbath was about to begin. Their business would have to wait until after the Sabbath.

On Sunday morning they prayed Shaharis in the Jewish quarter, then sought out the address they had been given to collect the Torah. They made their way through narrow streets and lanes lined with tiny Jewish houses crowded tightly one against the other. From many of the houses came prayer, the sign of a Yeshivah or Rabbinical school inside. Vilna had an ancient Jewish community and had become one of the greatest centres of Jewish learning and culture in Europe.

They entered the given address, and found themselves in a

Rabbinical institute. The ancient Rabbi who showed them around escorted them to a dreary room where several Torahs were being painstakingly examined by scholars and scribes. Their Torah, they were told, had been finished some two months earlier, written by a Sopher in a small room of his own home. It had been checked according to law, and had been pronounced Kosher. Both the name of the Sopher and the seal of the institute had been affixed to one of the handles at the end of the scroll.

When they opened the Torah to examine it, they were dumbfounded by its beauty, and the clarity of its writing, for their only experience had been with the old Torah from Loigzim, which obviously was in need of a great deal of repair. They mentioned the Loigzimer Torah to the Rabbi, who said that with proper treatment it could probably be rehabilitated. As they gazed at the new Torah, they could not conceal their excitement, for the villagers of Dorbyan would be overjoyed when their treasure was delivered to them. With great joy they paid the purchase price to the Rabbi.

They returned to Dorbyan along the same route they had earlier taken. Five days later their dusty wagon creaked into the market square to a tumultuous welcome. There was dancing in the *Shul Platz* as the new Torah was blessed, then taken to its resting place in the ark on the eastern wall of the synagogue, and placed alongside the old Loigzim Torah which had served the community so faithfully.

On the following day, Saturday, the first person called to read from the new Torah was the aged patriarch of the village, Leiba, son of Chaim Sender.

It had been Leiba's hope that his example would inspire the community to continue to acquire Torahs, and that someday a large number might be housed in the ark, as in larger congregations, for there was no doubt in his mind that someday Dorbyan would become a large and important Jewish community.

CHAPTER 4

It was late in the autumn of 1779 that Arieh Leib Jacob, or Leiba, son of Chaim Sender, was laid to rest.

He had been waning for several months, and the death of Sender, the last of his sons, had finally destroyed his motivation to continue living. The entire village of Dorbyan was in mourning, and many came from neighbouring districts to pay their respects. There was not a villager who could remember life without Leiba Jacob, for he was believed to have approached the age of one hundred years, and a lively topic of discussion had always been whether he had attained the milestone or not. The smallest child old enough to remember knew the old man, who until recently had spent his days sitting at the edge of the Shul Platz after prayers, watching the children at play, waving to them, and deriving great pleasure at their antics.

A small party from the ancient community of Loigzim came to the village. None of the Loigzimers would have remembered Leiba's days in their village, but all would have been told of his exploits. Loigzim, despite all predictions, had continued to cling tenuously to life as a Jewish community, although more and more frequently were the occasions that they turned to the newer community for assistance, for the connection between families still existed between the old and new congregations.

From the agricultural estate came the current Baron von Dorbyan, now more widely known by his family name Tytschcovitch, and a grandson of the Baron who had first given Leiba permission to settle in the district. With him a small number of Lithuanian peasants in his employ slowly followed the procession which made its sad way from the home on the market street, pausing for a moment of silence before the open door of the synagogue which Leiba had played such a major hand in founding. They continued along the market street for a short distance until the came to the road to the right which led to the Wainaiker Forest. Following closely the River Darba, the weeping and wailing congregation walked the one and half mile distance to the cemetery where a freshly dug pit awaited. There, amidst the trees of the Wainaiker Forest, they heard the service over the open pit and the eulogy of the Rabbi as the shrouded body of Leiba was lowered slowly into its final resting place. Most of the mourners who paid their respects that day were two and three generations removed from Leiba, but to a person they were aware that an era had ended.

Many were the changes that had occurred during Leiba's time, and the precarious early existence was now talked about only as a piece of folklore.The entire Jewish community, and along with it the Baron Titschcovitch and his Lithuanian peasantry, had prospered. The market had grown, and now attracted merchants and vendors from farther afield. More and more shops had appeared along the main market street, and for these blessings Leiba had been responsible more than any other person.

In many other directions there had been hardly any change. The lifestyle of a Jewish family differed little from that of their great-grandparents in Loigzim. The traditional methods of cooking and baking, the raising and slaughter of animals and the growing of garden produce were unchanged, and labour saving devices were few and far between. Of course the practise of the religion and the teaching of the traditions to the children had never changed, and never would.

One event had occurred which had made Leiba outwardly a different person than his father Chaim Sender. Some ten years earlier a census had been taken throughout the land, but a census with a difference. It had been decreed that all inhabitants must register on the lists, for a practice was to be introduced which had already been long in force on the other side of the Prussian border. It was now ordered that everyone, Jew and Gentile alike, and not just the nobility as previously, would henceforth be required to adopt a surname.

When the census takers arrived in the village, Leiba had been the first of the Jewish community to be listed. When asked by which surname he wished to be known, Leiba proudly announced "JACOB", and gave as his reason that he was in fact a son of Jacob, the father of the Children of Israel, who personified the whole Jewish nation.

It look very little time before the census takers realized that they had a problem on their hands. The addition of a surname, instead of simplifying the task of identifying individuals, had made their task more difficult. Before the day was finished, almost half of the Dorbyan families had chosen "JACOB" as well, partially out of deference to Leiba, but also because so many of them were in some way related to him.

Many of the families named Jacob had members with the same first name, rendering the surname useless. Similar first names were of little concern when the father's name was also used, and now it remained necessary to continue using these as well.

Other names besides Jacob were chosen, such as Kahn, Kagan and Levi, which related to descendancy from the ancient priestly castes. Some names suggested the bearers occupation, whilst others suggested the origin of families which had migrated to Dorbyan from other villages or districts

Amongst the Lithuanian community the same changes also occurred, but the variety of surnames chosen was greater, and duplication did not take place to the same degree. Previously the monopoly of the Tytschcovitches, the Chodkovitches and other noble families, no longer would the Lithuanian peasantry live and die in anonymity. The Lithuanian surnames too reflected occupation, parentage and place of origin. Amongst the local names which appeared in and around the village of Dorbyan were such names as Lekasius, Zalys, Zavueras, Skripkavicius, Galdikas, Simkas, Yashinskas and others.

In the year 1797 a boy was born to one of Leiba's great-great-grandchildren. The boy was born into a village which now had a population of more than one hundred and fifty Jews distributed amongst some twenty families, and was able to boast many of the amenities found in older and more established communities. A synagogue existed, as did a school. There was a tiny library with books in both Yiddish and Hebrew. A *Mikveh* had been built a short distance away from the town centre on the road to Krettingen, at a site where the proper conditions existed according to Jewish law, namely that a source of natural spring water be available. Jews could now bathe there for ceremonial purposes as well as cleansing themselves during the cold winter months when bathing in the river was out of the question. Amongst the tradesmen to be found in the town were shoemaker, barber, glazier, winemaker and tanner. Other business activities included carting, peddling, buying and selling of hides and a fledgeling textile industry.

Two years earlier had seen the collapse of the federation between Poland and Lithuania, and now both had been absorbed into the Russian empire. The changes occurred slowly, and at first the general populations were not affected. The burdensome taxes and conscription into the tsarist armies would come later.

The boy was named Chaim Nochum Jacob, after the fathers of Leiba and his wife Breina. Although the parents had never known the namesakes, they had followed a tradition of naming children after departed forebears, thereby keeping the names of ancestors alive in perpetuity. In fact the names Chaim and Nochum had been passed down through the town founder Leiba himself, who named his younger son by these names, thereby ensuring the names' survival. It was inevitable that a generation later a child would be named for an existing grandparent or other relative, thus ensuring that the memory of that person would endure.

In the case of Chaim Nochum it had been in fact intended to name him Arieh Leib, a derivative of the word 'lion' in the two languages, Hebrew and Yiddish, and the namesake of the still fondly remembered Leiba. However, the boy came into the world a few weeks too late, and an earlier born child received the same name. Common sense had begun to prevail, and no longer was every second child named after the founder.

As Chaim Nochum grew up, it was naturally assumed that he would take his place in the wine business that had supported his family for generations, and which was large enough to support any male children wishing to enter it. The boy did not disappoint his family, and he began to take an interest in it even during his pre Bar-Mitzvah days when he was still being schooled. As he became able, he took a more and more active interest until the day came when the occupation became full-time.

Before long he had taken over the major role from his ageing father, and was in effect running the business on his own acumen. He soon proved to have a golden touch in all matters commercial, and under his directorship the business expanded far beyond the dreams of those who had operated it before him. Branches opened in Krettingen and Memel, and business was conducted in directions as distant as Libau and Plugyon. His other brothers lacked his interest in the business, being content to receive their share of the profits as an inheritance.

In order to realize the plans he had for the future, Chaim Nochum needed a partner, someone who could manage the affairs which were conducted out of Dorbyan, for he himself had little taste for the travel involved, preferring to spend the precious moments of freedom with his family and practising his beloved religion.

The partner was Phillip Jacob, son of Leiba Jacob and Hannah Levy, some six years his junior, and a distant family member. The partnership was not equal, but Phillip would have complete autonomy in the matters that were his concern, while Chaim Nochum would remain the brains behind the overall operation.

Together the two increased their trade beyond their wildest expectations, and although the ownership was more Chaim Nochum's, he began to look upon Phillip more and more as an equal. Chaim Nochum could forsee the day when he would leave more of the affairs to Phillip, for he had married Anna Kersusky and was well on his way to towards the building of a large family.

On the other hand Phillip had remained single, which was convenient, for his business dealings were taking him away from Dorbyan for increasing periods of time. His untiring efforts had enabled agencies to be set up in almost every district centre where wine was consumed. To these agencies he would regularly travel, making deliveries, collecting accounts and maintaining close personal contact with the agents as only he was able to do.

One day in the late spring of 1830, Phillip approached his partner, knowing that what he had to say would cause him distress.

"Chaim, it is not easy for me to say this, for you are the last person I wish to cause *Tsores* to, as things have always been well between us. You have been the best partner and friend anyone could have, and together our business has been very successful."

"What is it, Phillip? You know me well. Bad news I can always suffer, as long as it is not too bad!"

"I do not consider what I have to say bad news, although you may not agree with me."

"Good, I am glad to hear this, for I was beginning to wonder if I had offended you in some way."

"No, Chaim, that is hardly the problem, for I have never known you to offend anyone. What I must tell you is a simple thing. I have been thinking about it for some time, and now I have finally decided to leave Dorbyan."

Chaim Nochum stared at Phillip numbly. A full minute passed before he was able to speak.

"What?.....Wh.....Why?........You can't be serious!"

"Yes, Chaim, I am serious", answered Phillip calmly.

"Yes, I can see you are," said Chaim Nochum, still shocked. "I know you well, and your face tells me you mean what you say.

"....But why?....If anything has been lacking in my behaviour to you, just let me know, just tell me. You know I will do anything, anything, to make you happy. Can you not see that your place is here, in Dorbyan, near your family, with me in the business."

"No, Chaim, you do not understand. This is not my place. I must leave, and perhaps I can make you understand my feelings. I would have mentioned this much earlier but I could not face up to it. I was afraid of the effect that it might have on you, and was worried that you might blame yourself that I am leaving. Whatever you are thinking, I assure you that it has nothing to do with this. If there is any fault anywhere, it lies not with you, but somewhere deep inside of me."

"But Phillip, why?.....Your life is here in Dorbyan. This town has a future, and you should be part of it. You have a comfortable business, a mother, a father, two brothers, four sisters......"

"...But no wife or children," interrupted Phillip. "You, Chaim, are blessed with the contentment that comes with having a lovely wife and a large and lovely family."

"...But Phillip!...", exclaimed Chaim Nochum incredulously, "....If this is all that troubles you, then it can easily be solved!....I can't see how this can possibly be a problem. You are young and prosperous, and able to offer much to any woman. I can think of several who would be grateful to have such as you for a husband, and who would repay you by bearing you as many children as God will allow. There is no reason whatever for you to remain unmarried if you do not wish to!....

"........I'll tell you what, Phillip. Just tell me whom it is that you would like to have as your wife, make a list of all the women you like if you wish, not only in Dorbyan, but in Krettingen and Memel. Just let me know, and I will find a way of speaking to them myself, or through people I know. I promise you one thing, and that is that before long you shall have the woman of your choice as your bride."

"You are missing the point, Chaim. I am not complaining about the fact that I am single and not fathering a family. What I am trying to tell you is that I am not doing these things because I choose to remain single. Because I do not have a family, I am free to travel where I wish, to visit other lands, meet other people, and earn my living in the way that I choose.

"I told you earlier that the fault is not with you. The fault, if it is a fault, lies deep inside of me. In working in the wine trade, and travelling to other districts, I have found myself. So do not blame yourself, for you are the best friend that I have ever had. It is very simple. I wish to travel, to see other lands, and to learn new languages and ways."

Chaim Nochum looked sadly at his friend. When he spoke his voice was subdued.

"Phillip, I suppose that what you are doing is breaking no law, and that neither I nor anyone else has the right to prevent you from doing what your heart tells you to do."

"I wish my brothers could be convinced to feel this way about it," interrupted Phillip. "From the little bit I have mentioned to them to date they seem to feel that I am breaking every law of the human race. I know that when I tell them and my parents that my decision has been made it will be a most difficult moment."

"You have obviously given this thing a great deal of thought," said Chaim Nochum. "I only hope that what you do brings you the peace of mind you hope for, and does not turn out to be a disappointment. Should there be no Jewish life where you go, then your upbringing will be lost. I pray that this does not happen, and that everything turns out well for you.

"Tell me Phillip, if you are not happy on your travels, will you be able to admit the mistake and return to Dorbyan where you will always be welcome, or will you be too ashamed to face us?"

"I cannot answer that, Chaim. All I know is that the desire to leave Dorbyan is too strong for me to resist. If a desire is as powerful as this, then I do not see how it can be a mistake.

"By working in Memel and beyond, I have had a taste of other places, and I must confess that on occasion I found it difficult to return to Dorbyan. It is only my connections here that have made me return each time, and now not even these are strong enough to hold me."

"Phillip, you know that you are going to be impossible to replace in this business."

"Not impossible, Chaim. There are others who, if given the chance, and with your guidance, will do just as good a job as I. In fact, if you like, I can give you the names of several others who are worth considering."

"Very well, Phillip. I can see that there is no chance of my changing your mind, not that I have any right to in any case. Everything you have said that you want to do is completely within your rights and breaking no law of our religion or the land. But you must please forgive my shock, for it does not seem normal for someone with a good livelihood to be leaving Dorbyan. I can understand that farther to the east where our people do not prosper and they are subject to mistreatment, there are those who are leaving to the west, but Dorbyan is different. We are growing rapidly and doing well. Most people seem more interested in moving here, for it is a good place to be doing business.

"I cannot find fault with Dorbyan, except for the fact that it has become a Russian province. Although there has been no trouble here, I do not like what has happened further to the east and what someday may happen here. But even this is not my reason for leaving, for we all know that when one is prosperous it is always possible to buy the Russians off, and avoid conscription in their wretched army. No, my reason for leaving is simply to see new places, places which are different, places I have only heard about, places where the life is changing, places where the future has already arrived."

"And where will you go?"

"In Memel I have had a taste of modern life. The Prussians are very advanced. I am told that westwards into Prussia the life is even more exciting, and that to the west of Prussia it is better still. This is the direction I will take."

"And what of your family?"

"As I said, I have mentioned it quietly to my brothers, but to noone else except yourself. Now I must find the courage to tell Mama and Papa. It will not be an easy thing, but talking with you has given me courage."

"We shall have time to discuss the business later," said Chaim Nochum, "How much of it belongs to you, and how you are to receive your fair share. In the meantime I must learn to get over the loss of a dear friend and business partner."

As Chaim Nochum watched his friend leave, he felt confused and puzzled. More people were moving into Dorbyan than ever before, and the few that were leaving it to improve their lot were going no farther than the nearby larger towns and cities, where they remained within easy reach of their families and friends. What Phillip Jacobs was doing was strangely different.

Was it a suppressed wandering urge that lived in the heart of every Jew born since the expulsion from Palestine, hidden from time to time when life became comfortable, but emerging when adversity or danger threatened? How could this be, for life for Jews had never become more secure than here in Dorbyan? What urge could possibly be so powerful as to cause Phillip to leave his whole way of life behind? Why had he himself never felt this urge? Was it only Phillip, or would there be others?

DORBYAN

PART 2

CHAPTER 1

The years passed, and Phillip Jacob did not return to Doryan, nor was he heard from except for occasional letters to his family. Chaim Nochum had expected to hear from him, but did not, and was frustrated at his inability to learn of his whereabouts. All he knew was the little he could glean from Phillip's brothers, that he had settled down near a large town named Eindhoven, in Holland, that he had taken a gentile as a wife, and that he was not following the Jewish faith. In the eyes of his family, no greater disgrace could have fallen upon them, and Chaim found it hard to get any of them to speak on the subject. Not only had Phillip abandoned his family, but far worse, he had forsaken the faith which had sustained his people for almost 4000 years. Henceforth he would be considered as lost, and no longer amongst the living.

Despite his own disappointment, Chaim Nochum could not bring himself to condemn his old friend and business partner, and he dearly wanted to see him again, or at least to hear from him. While Phillip's family considered him dead, Chaim Nochum continued to hope that through some miracle the day would someday come when they could meet and sit together over a glass of the very wine that they had sold together.

It was not to be, however, and Chaim Nochum realized that with each passing month his hopes were receding, and that eventually all contact with Phillip would be lost. His family could not be persuaded to pass his letters on to him. They were not read by his family, and usually discarded before being opened. It was inevitable that the slow trickle of correspondence would eventually cease altogether.

Chaim Nochum himself had his own affairs to occupy him. He remained the major partner in a large and prosperous business, and yet he could foresee problems in the future. Through Phillip Jacob the business had been able to expand far beyond the limits of Dorbyan, but he had been able to find no replacement equal to the task of maintaining the empire. There were agencies in Memel, Libau and Krettingen, but the others had been either abandoned or sold to competitors. In his mind this spelt the eventual doom of his business, for Dorbyan could not provide a sufficiently large base to withstand the forces of the larger competitors which were springing up elsewhere and would someday move into his territory. For the moment he was safe, but he knew that the day would come when he would have to either sell out to a stronger competitor, or perish.

In addition to his business concerns, he had social obligations as well. He was now a pillar of society. His family had grown to be the largest in Dorbyan, yet because of his station in life his twelve children were privileged to receive the best schooling the town could offer. Unlike the children of many Dorbyan families, his children would not be called upon to help support the family as early as the age of eight. They would be able to continue their study until adulthood if necessary, and if private tutoring was necessary from the Rabbi or the Melamed, then it would be available as a matter of course. His utmost priority was to ensure that each of his children grew up with a devotion and sense of duty to the religion and customs that was at least as strong as his own.

Still, the saga of his friend Phillip Jacob continued to haunt him, and scarcely a day passed when it would not occupy a place in his thoughts. Phillip's Jewish upbringing had been second to none, and every other member of his family was a well respected citizen. Yet what had happened? Why? He could not avoid a feeling of deepest sympathy towards the members of Phillip's family.

If a person such as Phillip Jacob could lose his way, could it be that the same fate could befall anyone, regardless of upbringing?

"None of our children will turn out to be like Phillip Jacob," he told his wife Anna with as much conviction as he could muster. "As fond as I am of Phillip I cannot agree with what he has done. I only wish I could discuss the matter with him. Then perhaps I could find out the what has caused him to change so. There must be a reason."

"Of course there is a reason, Chaim. He is a *meshuganeh*, I have always told you so! How can anyone know what goes on in the mind of a meshuganeh? It is almost like, unlike the rest of us, he was born with the heart and soul of a goy."

"The heart and soul of a goy," Chaim Nochum mused to himself. "Can it be, is such a thing possible", and yet, as he thought about it more and more, perhaps this in some way explained Phillips unusual success in the business, his extraordinary rapport with his gentile customers.

"Maybe," he said to Anna, "But still I cannot condemn him until I have had a chance to listen to his motives. I do not believe it will ever happen to any of our children, but what if I am wrong, and someday we too suffer the same disgrace? Such a thing was once impossible, but now I wonder. I only know that I have great pity for Leiba and Hannah, for I can think of nothing they have done to deserve such punishment."

Chaim Nochum and Anna's children were now beginning to approach adulthood. As expected, the eldest son would enter the wine business and eventually inherit it. The others would have to find employment for themselves, but in their case they had the good fortune to have a father who was both willing and financially able to assist. There was no lack of opportunity. Dorbyan was growing at a rapid rate, and any business, if properly managed, was assured of success. Unlike earlier generations, children growing up could now expect to find employment within the confines of Dorbyan itself. It was unlikely that any of Chaim Nochum's children would ever have to move to Memel or Libau to earn a living.

One of Chaim Nochum and Anna's younger children, born in the late 1820's, was Joseph. The town he was born into was considerably larger than the place of his father's birth, for the Jewish population had more than doubled since, and now outnumbered the gentile population which tended to live on the outskirts and in the surrounding farmland.

The synagogue had been extended and the library increased in size. The cheder was now in a separate building from the synagogue. Most of the homes and all of the shops in the town centre belonged to Jews, and almost all the trading throughout the surrounding countryside was carried out by Jews.

Joseph was an extraordinarily studious and religious child who had seriously considered the rabbinate as a life's profession before finally deciding that he had not attained the perfection required for the task. With his father's assistance, Joseph had gravitated into the carting trade, a business becoming ever more popular with the rapid increase in trade and commerce in the district. The business appeared promising, and should have been, but no sooner had Joseph become independent than he had married Riva, and now the race against time began, whether his business could become sufficiently established before the inevitable large family arrived.

The family arrived first, and Joseph and Riva's six children were all born within the space of ten years. Despite the considerable assistance from a wealthy father, Joseph's life was a continual battle against financial adversity. Somehow he had been instilled with an even greater sense of religious devotion than his father, and to this his business took second place. Amongst Jewish traders business considerations were frequently deferred to avoid conflict with religious duties, but Joseph carried out the practice to new extremes. Any promise his carting business may have shown was nipped in the bud, as the business was pushed aside upon the slightest religious pretext.

If Joseph's family was lacking in material wealth, in matters spiritual it was amongst the wealthiest in Dorbyan. Joseph and Riva devoted their entire lives to ensuring that each of their children grew up with a knowledge and love of the religion that was second to none. A learned man himself, Joseph took personal interest in everything that his children learned, often debating and discussing the daily school lessons with them upon their return from school. On occasion his views would conflict with those of the Rabbi or the Melamed, providing the setting for a lively family discussion around the evening meal table.

Of all his sons, the most receptive was Hersh, born in 1856. Dorbyan at that time was a Jewish community of some one hundred and twenty families, making approximately seven hundred Jews, the vast majority orthodox in their views and devout to the extreme. The synagogue was now an imposing structure of brick alongside the Beit Hamidrash, or the seat of learning for the community. These buildings towered over the tiny wooden Catholic church on the opposite side of the market place which dated back to the early days of the village when it alone had stood between the two bridges which crossed the river Darba. Now the church and its buildings occupied a portion of one side of the market place, while the synagogue side was crammed with Jewish homes which spilled over to the other sides of the bridges and well beyond. In addition new streets were formed leading from the main streets, all of them lined with Jewish homes. The town had undergone a complete change of character, with the centre now a Jewish domain, and the Lithuanian peasantry looking on from the periphery.

Hersh was a bright and studious child who eagerly devoured the teachings from all sources, and then pleaded for more. When at the age of thirteen, Hersh became Bar-mitzvah, the simple ceremony had moved all present to declare that his reading from the Torah and his leading of the congregation on that day had been the most perfect within living memory. Here was a marvellous student, and a perfect candidate for a future Rabbi.

Joseph was troubled that he could not afford to provide a Rabbinate education for Hersh, and was frequently depressed as a result, despite the sympathies of his wife Riva, who reasoned with him that the money could no doubt be obtained from his father Chaim Nochum if necessary. This was of litle comfort to Joseph, who felt the task to be his own duty. The cost of sending Hersh to one of the great Yeshivot would be prohibitive, for not only would the fees have to be paid, but there would be costs of maintaining his son away from home as well.

He toyed with the idea of selling his carting business to pay for the venture, but realized that in its run-down state it would fetch little, and would only serve to leave him destitute, a prospect which did not frighten him personally, but which he bring himself to im-pose upon Riva and the youngest of his children.

Even when his father Chaim Nochum died, he still could not manage it. Chaim Nochum had left a sizeable estate, but by the time it was divided between twelve children, Joseph's share was enough to rescue himself from the dire financial straits he had been in, but little more.

Although none outside could observe it, and he did not mention it to Rive, it deeply concerned him that he had been unable to make a success of his carting business, for there was no doubt that in the proper hands it could prosper. Perhaps when his oldest son Yankel, now approaching adulthood, entered the business, more could be made of it.

The growth of Dorbyan had attracted increased trade from the entire district, with the town now a major centre of commerce connecting with such major centres as Memel, Krettingen and Libau, and smaller regional towns such as Plugyon, Polangen and Shkud. Textiles and handicrafts were now manufactured in Dorbyan, and shipped elsewhere. The amber trade on the Baltic passed through Dorbyan on its way inland, farm produce was transported to the coast, fish was brought back in return, and so on. All of this activity spelt an ever growing custom for those fortunate enough to be well positioned in the carting trade.

The prosperity of Dorbyan had also attracted a number of residents of other, sometimes larger centres, to locate themselves there, bringing their businesses with them. One such newcomer was Arieh Leib Jacob, born in Plugyon, but later of Libau. Known simply as "Leiba Zup", he was married to Shora Hinda, and the couple had two unmarried daughters, Chana Eta and Mere Gita. Leiba Zup operated on a larger scale than Joseph, but did not compete directly with him, for his main interest was in the fish trade, which he would purchase in the port of Polangen and then peddle at the various centres on market days. Upon his return to Dorbyan he would purchase produce from the peasant farmers of the surrounding countryside which he would in turn take to the coast to be sold. Although Joseph initially had little reason to have anything to do with Leiba Zup, their lives were eventually to be bound together.

Joseph's thoughts of a Rabbinate education for Hersh continued to plague him, and he felt the helplessness of one who considered himself a failure. In fact there had been little he had been able to do for any of his children, and in lesser years he would have faced the heartbreaking sight of seeing them leave for Memel or Libau one after the other. In earlier days he had never considered that finances would weigh heavily in his life, but had been proven wrong.

One day the problem of a Rabbinate education for Hersh was solved, when his son approached him with a proposition.

"Father, you know that of late I have been working for Leiba Zup Jacob, helping him with his carting business."

"Yes, my son, I know this, and I am both happy and unhappy about it at the same time. Happy that you have found something to occupy yourself, but unhappy that you had to go to another carter to find employment."

"Father, you need not feel unhappy about this, many families with several sons are not able to employ all their sons in the business. What has happened to me is nothing unusual."

"Just the same, my son, I feel that I have betrayed you. It has always been a regret for me that I have not been able to do more for my children, for when I was your age your grandfather Chaim Nochum was able to give me much more."

"Father, do not speak like this! You have given each of us the best upbringing possible, and you and mother with your love have made our lives the happiest of any people we know. How can you think of this as a betrayal?"

"It is a betrayal in that I should have been able to give you more. You especially, Hersh, for you have what it takes to someday become a great scholar, and maybe a Rabbi. Once the same was said about me, but you have far more talent than I ever had. Now this will never be, because I have squandered the inheritance your father left to me."

"Do not punish yourself, father. If I had been destined to become a Rabbi, and had God had willed it, I would have known it in my heart, and somehow it would have come to pass. Other Rabbis have come from poorer families and I could have also if it were to be. The money would have been found for it if it had been the will of God. I only know that I am a very happy person, and that all the knowledge that I possess has come from you and Mama, and that it can never be taken away from me for the rest of my life. If I am able to do my job as well as you, then hopefully I shall be able to pass on my knowledge to children of my own."

"It still troubles me, my son, that you have had to take employment by Leiba Zup Jacob, while at the same time our own carting business is unable to employ you. I know very little of Leiba Zup Jacob. Tell me, what is he like? Is he a good man to have an an employer?"

"He is a fine man, father, and I could not think of any other I would rather work for. He pays me fairly and he is very honest. I know of noone who deals with him who does not have a good word for him. One day you will meet him, and I know that the two of you will become fond of each other."

"Also working for Leiba Zup provides advantages for both of us."

"And what might these advantages be, my son?"

"Apart from an income for me, it is good for Leiba Zups. As you know, he has no sons no sons of his own, and it troubles him what will become of his business one day. He treats me as if I were his own son. Although I cannot say that I wish to remain in the carting business for long it has another attraction for me."

"I can see that there is much going on that I do not know, Hersh. Perhaps you had better tell me what other thing attracts you to Leiba Zup and his carting business."

"Through working with Leiba Zup," answered Hersh, "It has helped me to become friendly with his younger daughter Chana Eta. We are getting to be very fond of each other."

"Aah, your mother has noticed this of late, and mentioned it to me, but I must confess that I am not as observant as your mother. We are both pleased, for Leiba Zup and Shora Hinde seem to be very fine people, and their daughters Mere Gite and Chana Eta are both lovely girls."

"But this is not what I came to speak to you about, father. What I really wanted to do was to request something of you and Mama."

"Of course we shall grant you any request that is within our means. How could any parent refuse a request from a son such as you?"

"Father, since working for Leiba Zup, I have managed to save some money. With the money I have saved,... I wish to buy a horse."

"A horse! I don't understand. Perhaps you had better tell me a bit more."

"Yes, father, I am serious. I wish to buy a horse, to keep it and strengthen it, and then to sell it. In tending to your horse, and the horses of Leiba Zup, I have come to realize what I have known all along, that I love the animals. It is not the work of carrying goods that keeps me working for Leiba Zup. The travelling to Krettingen and Polangen and the peddling is not what interests me, but the tending of the horses and the feeding and grooming them when the day's work is done is the most rewarding thing I have ever done in my life. I have a feeling for horses, and I believe that I understand them as well as I understand humans. I am certain that I can make a living out of raising and caring for them."

"I do not know much about horses as a business, so I am not able to say," answered Joseph. "In fact, I am not the one to ask on any business matter, as I have not had much success in business myself."

"Father, I too have no experience in business, but I am certain that I can make a living here. Ever since old Hessel died there has been noone carrying on this trade, and whenever anyone in Dorbyan needed a horse, he had to go to one of the goyishe farmers or to the market in Krettingen or Memel.

"It is only a short time ago that one of Leiba Zup's horses became lame, and Leiba had to sell it very cheaply and purchase another, because his business would not permit him to be without a horse for even a single day.

"I know that I could have taken that horse, and given it good care and nursed it back into health again, and then sold it for a profit."

"My son, as I said, I cannot point to success as a businessman, but it seems to me that there are worse things that you could do for a living. On the face of it, what you tell me seems like a good idea. There are those in our family who are very clever at business matters. We will speak to them, and if they like your idea, then you have my blessing."

"Thank you father, I am certain that after I have spoken to them I can convince them of my idea."

"Very well, my son, I hope it works for you. If it does, then I too have a small amount of money that your mother does not know about. It was meant to be a surprise for her, but the surprise can wait. You shall have it, and with this money you will be able to start off with two horses. It is the least that I can do for my son, and my only regret is that I am unable to do more." Hersh jumped to his feet and embraced his father.

"Wonderful! I know what our relatives will say. I know that this will be a success, and that before long I shall be able to repay you and give something to mother as well!

"....But I have not yet asked you the favour that I mentioned. I shall need space to keep my horse. Our yard behind the house is large, and only partly used for vegetables. If I am able to fence off the remainder, will you permit me to keep the horses there? Do you think that mother will mind?"

"Such a question you have no need to ask, my son. Of course you may. Your mother and I gain our greatest happiness from seeing our children make successes of themselves. In fact, if you will trust your father with such a task, I shall be only too happy to help you with the building of the fence."

Thus it was that Hersh, son of Joseph Jacob, grandson of Chaim Nochum Jacob, entered into the business of buying, selling, raising and trading horses, a livelihood which was to occupy him for the rest of his life.

CHAPTER 2

One of Hersh's closest friends was David Wolff. Of almost the same age, they had gone through *Cheder* together and had been *Bar-Mitzvah* during the same Jewish calendar year. As children they had been inseparable, and had spent almost as much time in each other's home and yard as they had in their own. David's family were merchants, engaged in the lumber trade, and although not wealthy, through other family members had connections in the industry in the major centres of Memel and Libau. When at the age of seventeen, Hersh decided that he wished to marry Chana Eta, younger daughter of Leiba Zup and Shora Hinde Jacob, David was the first person in whom he confided his plans.

"But why now, Hersh? You're so young. Can it not wait? There's still so much to see and do."

"Why wait, Dodke? I love Chana. What reason is there to wait any longer? Why not have the extra time with her now?"

"I suppose.....," answered David Wolff pensively. "Perhaps you feel this way. How am I to know someone else's feelings? I only know that in my own case I see no reason to get married for a long, long time."

"But that's only because you have yet to meet the right girl," said Hersh. "I am certain, Dodke, that if you ever come to feel towards a girl the way that I feel towards Chana, you would quickly change your mind."

David Wollf shook his head. "No, Hersh, I don't believe this. I don't expect to get married because I don't plan to allow it to happen. I want to do other things with my life. In fact, I don't plan to remain in Dorbyan much longer."

"What! You have never mentioned this before, Dodke! I don't understand!"

"Hersh, during the past several months I have been doing a great deal of thinking, about what I want to do with my life and how I can best fulfill it. Everytime I think about it, I come to realize that my plans can never be completed if I remain in Dorbyan."

"And what is wrong with Dorbyan, Dodke? Compared with many other places in Russia we have been fortunate. We should be grateful for what we have."

David Wolff replied earnestly.

"Yes, you are right Hersh, there are worse places than Dorbyan. I cannot argue against this. I know that, despite the Russians, we are a happier people than in many other places. We both have had a happy childhood here. We have been taught well, and there has been a lot of pleasure in our lives. We swim in the river in summer, skate on it in winter, play games in the *Shul Platz*. The adults grow old happily, They enjoy themselves meeting and talking in the market place. Everybody here knows everybody else, and I can think of no two persons who would call themselves enemies. Apart from the Russians and their wretched army, this place is a place that many would envy, but still there is something missing for someone with ambition."

"But Dodke, Dorbyan is growing. Someday it will have everything that Memel has. If you have ambition, would you not be better to stay and become a part of it?"

"Dorbyan does not have everything," replied David Wolff, "Nor has Memel, and they never will. There will always be something missing."

"Sometimes I don't understand you, Dodke. You seem to talk in riddles."

"As long as we are here, Hersh, we will never be in our own home, we will always be in a land that belongs to *goyim*......"

"You have told me this before, Dodke. We have been this way for thousands of years. I think we can put up with it."

"But why should we have to put up with it?," replied David Wolff emotionally.

"Can't you see? Even though we do well here, this is not our home! The fact that we can always be taken by the Russians into their army should remind you of that! What about the peasants revolt against the Tytschcovitch family in 1824? Even though it was not our battle, and we took no part in it, it was still a dangerous time for our people, for it was almost impossible to remain neutral. Who is to say that something like this cannot happen again? Why should we have to put up with this, generation after generation?"

"But Dodke, where would you go where the life is better?...To the east, where the Russians are constantly making *pogrom* against our people, or to the west, where Jews are rapidly losing their traditions and religion? Here in Dorbyan we have the best of everything. We manage to preserve our customs, and we are far enough from the centre of Russia that they pay little attention to us."

"You know as well as I that it is not only the Russians, even though they are a cursed lot. We all know that they can be outsmarted or bought off with money. It is not hard for a man of army age to cross over the border into Prussia each time they come, but why should this be necessary?"

"If you can show me a place where none of this is necessary, where the life is better, then I would like to know about it."

"There is a place, it is Palestine."

"Palestine! You cannot be serious! Yes, I know that some of our people are choosing to go there, and to begin new settlements, but they are the exceptions. Only a complete *meshuganeh* would leave Dorbyan to go to a place like Palestine! Places like *Rishon L'Zion* are mentioned, but the stories one hears do not sound attractive to me. The people there face a life of enormous hardship for very little return. How can you possibly say that the life there is better than here?"

"I did not say the life there was easier, Hersh, only better, and the people who go there are not *meshuganim*.! Things there are not as comfortable in the way you imagine, but the life there is definitely more rewarding, and that is why the movement to return to Palestine is growing.

"I do not say that I will go there at once, but it is my eventual destination. My first task is to become successful, that I may be of more use to the movement, but wherever I may live my life, there is one thing I am sure of, and that is that I wish to die in Palestine."

"Perhaps, Dodke, but that is a long time into the future. If you wish to be successful, then what better place to begin than Dorbyan? It is a good place to do business."

"No, not Dorbyan. For one thing, I shall always be looking over my shoulder for Russians. Besides, should I stay here, sooner or later

I shall be pressured into starting a family and abandoning all my ambitions."

"Well, if you go to Memel, or even Libau, at least you will not be far from home."

"Memel will be just the starting point, Hersh. At least there I will find others who feel as I do. If I can make my fortune there, then I can then go farther west, where there are other people who share my dreams, and who are are starting to do something about it."

"But Dodke, after all this you have only told me that you wish to go to Palestine, but you have not really given me a good reason why. The life there is harder and more dangerous than here. In all the wanderings of our people since the days of Abraham, the reason has always been the search for a better life, not a more difficult one. If you had told me that you are planning to go to America, then perhaps I could understand."

"It is not the sort of thing that is easy to explain, Hersh,. because it is something that one feels in his heart. The life there is not easy, and when a man dies he may possess little more than when he started out, but it is a beginning."

"A beginning of what?"

"A beginning of a home for our people, a home that belongs to us and nobody else; a home where we do not have to worry about the Russians, or imbecilic noblemen, or anti-semitic *goyim* ; a home where we can speak Hebrew and Yiddish, and not have to learn another dozen tongues just to appease the *goyim* ; a home where our ancestors first came to know God and worship Him, and where we can do the same thing without the need to hide it; a home that is a nation of Jews, peopled by Jews, and run by Jews, according to Jewish laws and traditions."

"Do you honestly believe all this, Dodke? Which will come first, your dream, or the *Meshiach?*"

"Don't you understand, Hersh, it simply has to come! If it doesn't, then who can say what will happen to us someday? It only takes a change in the people's minds, perhaps only one person can do it, and we face the same fate our ancestors faced in Sepharad, and some of our people are facing right now to the east. I hope that it never happens, but something inside me tells me that it is bound to happen sooner or later."

"I do not forsee any calamity happening to us, Dodke," replied Hersh. "After all, times have changed, and we do not live in the same age as the people of Sepharad."

"I hope you are right," said David Wolff," But it still doesn't change the fact that we need our own homeland. I personally believe that it is not so far away as many think. If enough people believe in it and are prepared to act, then we can make it happen even sooner. I am certain that I shall live to see a homeland for us in Palestine in my lifetime...

".......And so, Hersh, our paths will differ,..... as we both follow the paths that our hearts dictate. You will remain in Dorbyan, marry Chana Eta, and raise a happy and hopefully prosperous family which I know will be well taught and faithful to our customs. I shall end my days in Palestine, which by then will belong to our people. Although our ambitions may differ, I know that we will always remain the best of friends."

"Well Dodke," answered Hersh pensively, "I supose that what must be, must be. Each of us must do what his heart tells him, and if his intent is sincere, than it is his right. I can only wish you well, and hope that all your dreams may be fulfilled. I suppose it won't be long before you leave for Memel. When you go, will you do a favour for me?"

"You are right, Hersh, I shall be leaving soon, as I have heard that my name is on the list of conscripts for the Russian army. What is this favour you ask? I shall certainly try my best to grant it."

"It has to do with my late grandfather, Chaim Nochum." said Hersh." Before he died he told me many times of a Dorbyaner by the name of Phillip Jacob who left almost forty-five years ago. Right up to his death he wanted to know what became of Phillip, but his wish was never satisfied. Somehow the curiosity has continued within me, and if I could find out something about him, I feel that I would be doing something for my grandfather......

".......Phillip too will be an old man, and perhaps no longer living. I believe he started out in Memel, then moved to the west where he settled in Holland. If you could just learn something about him, it would bring a lot of satisfaction."

"I shall start enquiring just as soon as I get to Memel, Hersh, and one thing more, that I forgot to mention."

"And what is that?," said Hersh.

"I have been so occupied in telling you about my own plans and my dreams that I forgot to wish "*Mazel Tov*" to you and Chana Eta."

CHAPTER 3

David Wolff left Dorbyan a short time later, for Memel, to work for a period in his family's lumber business, his plans going very much as expected.

For Hersh Jacob, however, things did not happen as he wished, and he did not manage to marry as soon as he had hoped. His love for Chana Eta was as strong as any which had ever existed, but their young ages proved to be a barrier. Although they were accepted as a suitable pair by both families, there was resistance to an early wedding from all quarters. Hersh's parents, Joseph and Riva simply believed that they were too young, and that waiting a few more years would do them no harm. On Chana Eta's side, Leiba Zup and Shora Hinde had other considerations. Their elder daughter Mere Gita was still unmarried, and they considered the marriage of Chana Eta improper under the circumstances. They were adamant that Mere Gita should marry first.

Hersh reluctantly accepted the verdict, and secretly prayed that Mere Gita would find a lover quickly, but at the same time prepared himself for a lengthy courtship. He knew that his love for Chana Eta would sustain him through the wait, no matter how long it lasted.

In many ways Hersh was more fortunate than others in the village. Several years earlier a Dorbyaner had made his way to that most distant of lands, America. He had prospered and sent for others of his family to join him. Some of these had been already married, and had found it necessary to leave their wives and children behind until they too could become established and send for them. Hersh found it difficult to conceive of a separation such as this, and yet it was happening. There must have been something special in America which made it worthwhile for people to endure such privation.

He only knew that he himself would never leave Dorbyan. He had found happiness with his horses, and was beginning to make a good living from them. Most of all, he had Chana Eta, and although not yet married, he knew that they would be eventually. In fact Chana

Eta's sister Mere Gita had recently become friendly with Mordechai Kveril, who ran a sawmill with a partner on the outskirts of town. Their relationship appeared serious, and surely they would announce their marriage before long. If only they would hurry up!

From time to time he received a letter from his friend David Wolff, to which he always replied without delay, uncertain whether his answers would reach their destination, as David never seemed to remain in the same place for long. David had now been gone from Dorbyan for several years and was no longer in Memel. His letters had come from various parts of Germany and even France. Along his journeys he had encountered many people influential in the *Zionist* movement, and had seen his convictions, if anything, strengthened.

In 1881, some eight years after David Wolff had left Dorbyan, Hersh received the following letter from him:

Cologne,

March 11. 1881

My Dear Friend Hersh!

I hope this letter finds both you and Chana well. Not knowing your situation I cannot wish you Mazel *Tov* except in a general way. It is sometime since I last heard from you, and I cannot be sure if you are married yet. Probably you are, and you may even be parents by now.

I know that I should write to you more often, but writing letters is a luxury when one is as busy as I have been. I hope that you will be a better correspondent than I have been, and I am enclosing my present address. No matter where I may find myself, I shall always be interested to hear about you and the happenings in Dorbyan.

But my main reason for this letter is not to tell you of what I have been doing, but to let you know that I have finally had word of your grandfather's friend Phillip Jacob, or Phillip Jacobson, as he is now known. He is still living, and I am certain that what I have found out will interest you. By all accounts he has led a most interesting life, and now he is well-to-do, very healthy, and still very active, even though he must be close to eighty.

Phillip made his way from Memel westward, working wherever he could find work, doing everything that could be imagined. No job was too trivial for him to attempt. If there is a trade that Phillip has not done, then I have yet to hear of it.

Eventually he found his way to Holland and worked in several cities. Finally he found employment in Eindhoven, a large city, where he is still to be found, and where he is well known.

It was not his intention to stay there, but fate can cause strange outcomes. He met Johanna Andries, a *Shiksa* from the nearby town of Bladel, and they married. Phillip began trading, and they did well. He seems to have a better head for business than most of our people, even though he seems to have the sentiments of a *goy*. He has traded in everything that one can think of, and still does. I have been told that if one has problems in obtaining a certain item, then Phillip Jacobson is the one to ask.

He and Johanna have one daughter, Sophia, now married to a Louis Haas, and they in turn have three children. I understand that Louis Hass is Jewish, and that Sophia converted to marry him, and so the family has come back to Judaism.

The way Phillip is going he still has many years ahead of him. A most remarkable man.

When my contact in Holland told me this, I asked him to question Phillip about his connection with Dorbyan. He has told me that Phillip admits to no connection with Dorbyan.

His words were, "My family has forsaken me. They are no longer my family. The family that I have is here in Holland."

He asked about your grandfather Chaim Nochum, and when it was mentioned that he was no longer living, his eyes filled with tears, and he said, "I have but one regret in this life, and that is that I could not bring myself to keep in contact with Chaim Nochum. Many times I intended to write to him, but I could never find the courage to do it. I know that he would not have approved of my actions, but neither would he have condemned me and forsaken me. He was the finest man I have ever met, and the best friend I have ever known. I should have written to him while he was still alive. Now it is too late."

I am sending Phillip Jacobson's address along with my own. He is an old man with a heavy heart. Perhaps if you were to write to him it would ease his burden. I am certain that he would be most grateful to know that your grandfather remained interested in his well-being right up to the end.

And now, my friend, I must leave you. I pray you, write more often than I do. Even though I do not see myself returning in the near future, my interest in the place of my birth and happy childhood will never leave me.

Your Friend
Dodke (Wolffsohn) *

Hersh pondered over the letter, and reread it one hundred times. He would certainly reply to his friend without delay, and would write to Phillip Jacobson as well. David's signature puzzled him as well, why "Wolffsohn", and not "Wolff", the name he had been given at birth?

A strange phenomenon seemed to be taking place. People living in Dorbyan did not add the suffix "son" to their surnames, yet it seemed that whenever someone left the town they changed their name in this manner. Phillip Jacob was not the first to become "Jacobson", as most of those who had migrated to North America had done likewise. In addition "Avraham" had become "Avrahamson", "Mendel" had become "Mendelson", and so on. Where would it end?

He wrote to Phillip Jacobson shortly afterward, introducing himself and telling as much of life in Dorbyan as he felt would be of interest. His letter to David Wolffsohn would have to wait, for there were tidings that he wanted to include. At last, after eight years of waiting, his marriage to Chana Eta was now in sight. Mere Gita and Mordechai Kveril had set a wedding date, shortly after the harvest festival of *Succos*, and he was determined that his own wedding would follow not long afterward.

His heart sang. Eight years of successful horse trading had placed him in the position where he could look after Chana in style, and he had already made plans to build their home in the *Shkuder Gass*, where a vacant piece of land still existed, not far beyond the bridge and a bare five minutes' walk to the synagogue. He considered himself fortunate to have acquired the piece of land, even though the area available for horses would be no greater than he had been using at his parents' home. More space would have been a boon to his business, but still, one could not expect to have everything.

It was not until the spring of the following year that Hersh was able to reply to his friend David Wolffsohn.

Dorbyan, March 1882

Dear Dodke!

Please forgive me for taking a full year to answer your last letter, which brought me a great deal of happiness. Now my greatest fear is that the delay will cause my letter to miss you, as you may have changed your address.

Even though what I have to say may not seem exciting compared to the life you are leading, there is still much to tell you about the happenings in Dorbyan. Do you know, Dodke, that you are becoming well known outside as well as here? Visitors come to Dorbyan, and when they mention your name and tell of things you are doing, we are proud to be able to tell them that you are a Dorbyaner. Many outsiders do not realize this, and it makes us proud that one such as yourself has come from our town.

Shortly after receiving your letter I wrote to Phillip Jacobson[1] as you suggested. I did not expect an answer from him, nor did I receive one. I can only hope that my letter may have done some good, and given him some comfort.

In Dorbyan there is much to tell. Most important for me of course is that Chana and I are finally married! It does not seem like nine years since I first mentioned my intentions to you, but more like nine hundred! But it has happened at last, and now we are happy together in our new home on the *Shkuder Gass* . You will remember the spot,

---

1   *Phillip Jacobson died in 1896 aged ninety-three. He is said to have been buried at Vucht near the town of Bladel, in the Eindhoven area. Upon the request of the authour, two Dutch friends pedalled to Vucht, and spent an afternoon examining the cemetery, but were unable to find a monument to Phillip Jacobson. They suggested that his resting place may be a larger Jewish cemetery nearby. the Herstellenbosch. To date this possibility has not been investigated.*

it used to be the empty lot between Fraintel and Zimon just beyond the bridge. Of course you will know it, for sometimes we used to find mushrooms there.

We are busy making up for lost time, and should there be any new arrivals, God willing, I shall make sure that you are the first to know. Who can say, for such an occasion you might even find the opportunity to come back here to share in our *nachas*.

My business goes well. Horses are in many ways easier to deal with than *menschen*. Chana has even lost some of her fear of them. In fact she will even touch one on occasion, providing I am right beside her. But she is learning, and is now able to help with the feeding.

Other things are happening. More and more Dorbyaners are leaving to go to America, and now to Canada as well. It seems as if each time someone leaves, the rest of the family are not long in following. In some cases almost all the sons of a family have gone, and sometimes the daughters as well. I can only imagine the heartbreak that this must cause to the parents. We all recall how sad we were at the time you left us.

At the moment Dorbyan is still growing, but if this continues, the day may well come when our town becomes smaller.

I know that you will be interested to know that amongst us, a few are starting to talk of Palestine, although noone is ready to go at this time. Names like *Rishon L'Zion* and *Zichron Ya'akov* in Palestine are becoming known, and there is more and more interest in the subject. Sam Simon Jacob is talking of Jerusalem, and you will surely remember Shimon Zacharia Jacob, son of Yakov the glazier. He is married to Sara and is constantly talking of making *Aliyah* to Palestine. He has almost convinced Sara, although I doubt that she will ever be in full agreement. Still I believe that one day they will go, just as soon as their children are sufficiently grown to withstand such a change in their lives.

As for me, Dodke, there is no need to tell you. I shall remain in Dorbyan where I have found happiness. In fact, I do not even feel the need to travel to Krettingen or Memel on occasion, even though Chana is always willing to go. My parents Joseph and Riva are well, and grateful that none of their children are showing any signs of leaving, although noone can say what will happen in the future.

And so my friend, this is what is happening in the town of your birth. I hope that wherever our paths may lead us, we will always be able to remain good friends, and keep in touch from time to time. I know that you are very busy, but even the shortest letter from you will always be very welcome. In the meantime I wish you good health and every success. May God bless you in your efforts.

As Ever, Your Friend
Hersh

CHAPTER 4

At last, things were working out for Hersh Jacobs the way he had planned. After what had been a painfully long wait with seemingly never ending delays, the house was now finished and he and Chana were happily settled in it. Hersh kept his horses at the far end of the rear yard, while Chana maintained a chicken coop and a small vegetable garden closer to the house. Their home was by Dorbyan standards, comfortable, not large like the home of Elberg the chemist or the old Hessel homestead, but new and modern. Unlike most other Dorbyan homes , their outwarding opening windows were still new, shiny and completely weathertight. Shimon Zacharia Jacob, the glazier, and a cousin of the family, had constructed them, but not even his expertise in his trade could prevent window frames from ageing and warping within a few seasons. Hersh knew that the perfect fit of his windows was only temporary, and that after a few hot summers and sub-freezing winters, they would suffer the same stiffness and draughtiness as in every other home.

He and Chana were particularly proud of the wood stove they had been able to procure. It was of the latest design, and was efficient for both heating and cooking. Unlike older stoves, there was little wastage, and it was capable of a full hour's burning without refuelling. Even the smoke that was produced did not go to waste, but went to heat separate chambers which could be used to keep a kettle hot.

Next to the kitchen were two rooms, a storeroom on one side and a dining area on the other. From the kitchen the back door led to the garden area, the well, and the woodpile. The well did not pump water into the house, but rather into a rain barrel, from which it could be carried into the kitchen in buckets

The bedrooms, as was common practice, occupied the front half of the house.

Hersh and Chana had specified three bedrooms in anticipation of a large family to come. They had waited long enough, and now beginning a family was their first priority, but once again fate stepped in to thwart their plans.

Throughout its more than 150 years of history, the Dorbyan Jewish community had known not only prosperity, but also its share of misfortune. Fire had always been the major threat, and there was not a Dorbyaner who was not familiar with the crackling sound of unchecked flames. In 1824 and 1831 major fires destroyed large sections of the inner town. These were in addition to the minor outbreaks which seemed to be almost a yearly occurrence. There had been other disasters, outbreaks of disease, and a high infant mortality rate. The great cholera outbreak of 1848 had taken the lives of twenty-three from the Jewish community and a similar number from the Lithuanian peasantry. Such outbreaks, when they occurred, were invariably severe, and could be only allowed to run their course, for the lack of sanitation provided a fertile environment for disease, while the medicines then available were insufficient to prevent its spread. Children and the elderly and infirm were the usual victims, with other family members forced to stand by helplessly as their loved ones were taken from them.

The greatest catastrophe of all however, caused no known loss of life, yet affected the destiny of the entire town. It occurred later in the year 1882 on *Yom Kippur* eve, the holiest night of the Jewish year. It was a time when almost the whole town was crammed into the synagogue, with only the very young and the infirm remaining in their homes.

The reason for the attendance was the once in a year opportunity for every person, no matter what his station, to atone for the sins committed either knowingly or unknowingly over the past year. The prayer about to be chanted was *Kol Nidre*, an ancient Aramaic declaration of all oaths and vows made rashly in the past, but now to be rendered null and void. Although not strictly a prayer, *Kol Nidre* was considered the most solemn and sacred recitation of the Jewish faith. Recited prior to the actual service of atonement, its purpose was to allow the congregation to commence the service cleansed of its transgressions. In order that no member be left out of the participation, *Kol Nidre* was chanted three times.

Barely had the chanting begun, when the sexton interrupted the service with a message of urgency. A fire had broken out in the opposite end of the market place, and was being driven along the *Shkuder Gass* through the *Jewish Platz* by a strong wind.

Despite the solemnity of the occasion, the Rabbi halted proceedings, and told the people that the will of God had always been that people, their homes and belongings should be protected first.

A number of congregation members volunteered to carry the precious *Torahs* out of the synagogue to the safety of the *Shul Platz*. Hersh knew that his own home was directly in the path of the flames and ran directly out into the square without waiting for Chana. As he dashed along the street he could see that the whole street was already ablaze, and that even the old wooden church opposite the synagogue was threatened. He reached his burning home, and saw to his horror that any attempt to enter it was hopeless. His thoughts turned to the four horses at the back, and he ran around the house in time to see his beloved animals, crazed with panic, trying to break through the enclosure.

Making his way through the smoke he found a length of rope and tied it around the necks of two of the horses, which soon became calmer under his reassuring carresses. He led them around to the front and into the middle of the street, wondering what to do with them while he fetched the other two. Suddenly he gave a cry of anguish, and let the rope fall from his hands.

"Chana!"

Chana had arrived on the scene, and through the smoke he could see her trying to force her way into the house, her scarf wrapped around her face in a futile gesture. He screamed her name, then dashed after her just as she disappeared into the smoke filled doorway. He caught her just as she came up against a wall of solid flame, seemingly unware of the blistering heat that was searing his skin. He grabbed her around the waist from behind, picked her up and carried her back into the street, gasping for breath in the cooler air.

"Why, Chana? Why did you go back in?"

"Our china, our beautiful plates and dishes! I must try to save them! Please help me go back and save them!"

"Chana, we cannot go back in there. Nobody can save them. If you had gone but one step further you would have perished!"

"Our treasures," sobbed Chana brokenly, "They were the most beautiful things I have ever owned. They came from mother's mother, from Plugyon. They were so beautiful."

Hersh pulled her to him and held her tightly. "Chana, I'm sorry. Even if you had brought them out, they would have been damaged beyond repair. They are gone, but no matter how much we have lost, we still have each other. We are fortunate. Others have lost much more...

."......If I had lost you I could not go on living. I promise you, we shall find some way to replace the china. It will be the first thing we do, even if we have to sell all the horses to......"

"The horses! Hersh remembered the two out on the street, and turned around in time to see them bolting along the *Shkuder Gass*. He would have to let them go and try to collect them later, and hope that they were not discovered by anyone with thieving intentions, for it was firmly believed that many of the fires which plagued Dorbyan were deliberately lit by Russian Cossacks in order to create looting opportunities. At the moment the greater problem was the two remaining animals in the enclosure.

"Chana, come with me! We must try to rescue the horses out in the back!"

"I am afraid, Hersh! What if in their panic they turn on me?"

"I know that you are not comfortable with horses, but this time I beg you to forget your fear! We have no choice! You must come! I need you!"

They ran to the rear, where parts of the fence were smoldering. The screams of the horses through the thick smoke told hersh that they were still alive, but in their frenzied state, it would not be easy to lead them to safety.

"Wait here, Chana, while I fetch the first!"

Hersh groped and coughed his way through the smoke towards the screaming sounds. Within a moment his reassuring sounds and gentle touch had soothed one of the animals. With a rope he led it to Chana, telling her simply to hold the rope and to make gentle sounds. Chana, amazed at the docility of the animal, continued to soothe it while Hersh went back for the remaining horse.

A few minutes later, coughing and spluttering, he emerged with the remaining horse. He took the rope from Chana.

"You behaved perfectly," he told her, planting a kiss on her forehead. "Before long they will be preferring your company to mine. Now we must find a safe place to tie them while I look for the others."

Leaving Chana in charge of the two horses, Hersh followed the *Shkuder Gass* in the northward direction that the horses had bolted. Everywhere were scenes of confusion and destruction. Almost every house was ablaze, some like his own, almost totally destroyed, others through some stroke of fate suffering only minimal damage. In front of every house was a dejected looking family standing beside a pile of belongings rescued from the fire, most of the piles pitifully small.

Recognizing Hersh, and knowing that the horses could have only belonged to him, people pointed northwards as he passed. Following their directions, he continued the half mile until he reached the edge of town. There, to his immense relief, in the first open field he came to, were the two horses grazing contentedly, still roped together. As he approached them, they came at his first call, and he gently led them back toward the centre of the town.

It was now late in the evening, and the pall of smoke filled the whole town centre. The fire had burned itself out, but the damage had been done, and the heat and the charred embers would prevent any rummaging through the ruins for several hours. Looking past the remains of his house towards the town centre he could see that the old wooden church and its monastery had been gutted, the church beyond repair, while the synagogue almost directly opposite had suffered no damage.

He reached his home and a dazed Chana, still guarding the horses. As they gazed sadly at the charred shell that but a few hours earlier had been their new home, he kissed her and said softly.

"Do not worry, my love. It is terrible, but it could have been worse. We are among the lucky ones, and I do not envy those with large families. We will manage better than most. and with these horses we have a start towards a new home. We will replace the china with something we can be proud of, and like the old china one day it too will have meaning for us. I am but grateful to God that I didn't lose you in this fire."

"It was very foolish of me, wasn't it, Hersh?"

"I don't know. Who is to say? It is normal, and many others would do the same to save their treasures. I know that the china cannot be replaced, and how much it meant to you,.......but...if I had lost you as well.....

".....You know, it is said that Breina, wife of Leiba, the founder of Dorbyan, lost her life because she went back into a fire. This was told to me when I was very small, and suddenly it came back to me when I saw you amidst all the smoke. I could think of nothing else....What if you had perished, Chana?......, Everything I have in this world can be replaced,.....except you......"

The great fire of Dorbyan marked a turning point in the destiny of the town. It was counted that forty houses and thirty shops had been totally destroyed, with a far greater number suffering various degrees of damage. In all, more than half of the Jewish homes in the central area had been affected. Many of the townspeople had lost not only their homes, but their livlihoods, for in many cases a house was not only a home, but a workshop, a small factory, or a warehouse for the storage of merchandise to be peddled or transported. Many of the people were not only homeless, but destitute as well, and many of the families made destitute were those with newly born infants and young children.

Hersh and Chana were better off than most, despite the loss of their home. They still had their livlihood, and had money in the newly opened bank. They were still owed money from previous transactions, although debts owed them from people who had lost everything would have to be forgiven. One of Hersh's debtors was a Lithuanian carpenter who would be grateful for the chance to pay off his debt by working on a new house. They would manage, but the recovery would take time, and until they had a new home they would have to put off having a family. In effect, a period of two years had been snatched from their lives.

They agreed that they would prefer not to rebuild their gutted home, but would look for a larger piece of land elsewhere in the town.

When they had acquired what they sought and begun normal trading again, then they could afford to think of construction.

Taking stock of their charred remains on the following day, they could find very little worth salvaging. The china they had treasured was scorched and broken in a thousand pieces, some even showing signs of melting. Despite Chana's sifting through the ashes, she was unable to find even a single piece which could be retained as a keepsake. The main salvageable item was the stove, which had been designed to withstand heat. It required a good cleaning and many hours of scraping, but would eventually function as before. All clothing and furniture had been destroyed, not the disaster it might have been, for the house had been only partially furnished at the time. Otherwise, only a few cast iron pots were worth keeping. They too, like the stove, would require a great deal of cleaning to render them serviceable.

For the dispossessed people of Dorbyan, there was but one thing in their favour. The exodus of villagers to North America had left many of the homes in the town only partially occupied. For those seeking a roof over their heads, there would be no shortage of suitable accommodation.

At first Hersh and Chana considered staying with Chana's parents, Leiba Zup and Shora Hinde, whose home was located in an area of town which had been spared from the flames. Chana's sister Mere Gita had the same thoughts, and between them it was agreed that Mere Gita and Mordechai Kveril had greater need of the space. There was no shortage of accommodation on offer, and in the end they decided to move in with the family of Avigdor and Mailki Jacob, cousins of Hersh's father Joseph. It was a convenient move for many reasons.

The family of Avigdor Jacob was one of the poorest in Dorbyan, and one which had been dogged by misfortune at every turn. The contribution made by Hersh and Chana would be welcome. In recent years Avigdor and Malka had seen their eldest son Nathan migrate to North America, and then their daughters leave to work in neighbouring towns. Now only their youngest sons, Barney and Aaron remained at home, leaving a large empty room available. There was no doubt that they too would leave, just as soon as their age permitted them to do so.

Malka, or Mailki, as she was known, was the daughter of Rachmeal and Sara Turk, and had been one of the last to be born in the old village of Loigzim. Her father, a poor but pious tailor, had been forced to leave the village following a disagreement with the Baron von Loigzim. The story was that he had promised to have some garments finished for the baron for an occasion without reckoning that he would have to work on the Sabbath to do so. His devotion to the Sabbath ruled out any consideration of the consequences involved, and the result was that the baron, in a fit of drunkenness, expelled Rachmeal and his family from Loigzim.

Thus it was that Rachmeal, Sarah and their daughter Mailki came to live in Dorbyan. Their son, Moishe had been serving in the Russian army at the time and was not at home to assist in the move.

The departure from Loigzim had broken Rachmeal's spirit, and he died in the prime of his life, making no attempt to prosper in his new home. Towards the end he had insisted that when he died he be buried in the old Loigzim cemetery. His wish was carried out, and he is believed to be the last to have been buried there. Every year thereafter, on *Tisha b'Av*, his wife and daughter made the pilgrimage to Loigzim to shed bitter tears over his grave.

Mailki's husband, Avigdor came from an equally impoverished background, as his mother had been widowed at a young age and left with a large family. After reaching adulthood and marrying Mailki, Avigdor had met with further misfortune. Too poor to avoid conscription into the Russian army, he was forced to spend long periods of time away from his family. It was during one of these periods of duty that he suffered a head wound which caused him frequent fits of mental derangement, and made it impossible for him to earn a living after his release from the army. Somehow Mailki managed to raise their family, helped by three acres of land behind their rough cabin. Now, at last there were signs that their burden was about to be eased, for they were beginning to receive regular remittances from their son Nathan in America..

A portion of the rear yard would be available for Hersh's horses, which was not as much as he had hoped for, but more than had been available elsewhere. Two of the horses would have to be kept on another property, and he longed for the day when he and Chana could once again live in a home of their own, with space for as many horses as he wished.

Other families, particularly those with younger children, moved in with relatives knowing that they would never again possess the means to rebuild their houses. With nothing but a bleak future facing them, it was at this time that another alternative began to look more attractive.

The alternative was migration. With those who had already left Dorbyan apparently doing well, the conditions were now in place for others to leave.

Letters of desperation crossed the Atlantic seeking assistance, and those on the other side remembered their kinfolk. In a short time letters containing money and steamship passages began to arrive in return.

At about this time Canada was beginning to displace the United States as the preferred destination. Entry was easy, and anyone showing a certificate of good health was admitted if means of sustenance was shown. Even this amount, usually $250, could be waived if relatives could be found to take responsibility for the new arrival, and even this condition could be circumvented, for Jewish aid organizations had already sprung up in the major ports of entry to take charge of any Jewish migrant who arrived destitute.

The town of Saint John in the eastern province of New Brunswick became the major port of entry, and staging post for further migration elsewhere. Less developed than the American cities, but growing rapidly, it offered a good future, and many of those who landed there felt no need to travel further.

Migration did not enter the minds of Hersh and Chana, and from their refuge in the home of Avigdor and Mailki, they began to plan their new home. If they were ever to have the family they dreamed of, the sooner they made their start, the better.

It was now a year since the fire, and with winter approaching, they knew that any construction would have to wait until the following spring. They were determined that this was the longest that it would wait, and they began to make all foreseeable arrangements beforehand, that there would be absolutely no delay when the good weather arrived.

This time they would have more than enough room for Hersh's horses, for the more horses they could keep, the sooner they would be back on their feet.

Their families were surprised when they chose a piece of land on the Krettinger Gass on the outskirts of the other side of town, just across from the *Mikvot*, the baths where Jews cleansed themselves for both hygienic and ceremonial reasons. There were few homes on the street, none of them Jewish, and they were a five to ten minute walk to the synagogue. The main feature was the more than two acres of land, which was sufficient to keep horses and any other animals that Chana wished, while still leaving sufficient space to grow vegetables to feed themselves all year around.

A short distance beyond their land could be considered the end of the village, where the countryside became pastureland and forest.

Hersh spoke to the Lithuanian carpenter who owed him for a horse, and then to Mordechai Kveril, his brother-in-law. Mordechai's sawmill on the edge of Lake Darba about a mile from town produced many types of building timber, from almost unfinished logs for supporting framework to evenly sawn boards for furniture and flooring. He and Mordechai were fond of each other, and he would be given not only the best possible price, but ample time to repay.

The land had been obtained, labour and materials had been arranged, and construction could begin in the spring of 1884. Other essentials would be arranged as the construction neared its end. These included the glazing of windows, the refitting of their old stove, the building of shelves inside, the digging of a well outside, and the construction of a shed. Of course new furniture, eating utensils and crockery would be needed as soon as they moved in.

It was late in the summer of 1884 when Hersh and Chana moved into their new home on the Krettinger Gass. The layout was almost identical to the home they had lost, but the dimensions were slightly larger. The furniture was sparse, and most rooms remained empty, but three horses grazed peacefully in the large yard at the rear, and someday two more would follow.

Hersh watched Chana light the Sabbath candles, thinking to himself that it was the most beautiful sight he had ever seen. Chana had pronounced the new china to be *Milchiche*, and they sat down to a pre-prepared meal of bread, herring and cottage cheese.

It was with love in their eyes that they sat opposite each other in the candlelight, eating their first Sabbath meal there, on the fine new china that they had managed to acquire.

CHAPTER 5

It was a warm autumn afternoon in the year 1884, and everywhere the leaves were turning. Returning from a visit to the countryside with his horse and wagon, Hersh breathed in the fresh air and revelled in the blaze of colour which surrounded him. Earlier he had paid a visit to a Lithuanian farmer to discuss the sale of a horse, the same horse which now pulled his wagon.

The farmer, Rolandas Galdikas, had been Hersh's very first customer, and as such held a special place in his affections. With his young son Viktoras, Rolandas managed a living on a small property just three miles outside of town along the road to Polangen. The Galdikas family was poor, as were most farmers, but their struggle was no greater than that of many of the Jewish townsfolk of Dorbyan. They were honest and hardworking, and Hersh respected their integrity. As a result he always went out of his way to provide the very best for them, with the easiest possible terms of repayment. In return Rolandas Galdikas had directed Hersh to any of the district farmers who had foals to sell, for to most farmers, keeping a non-working animal was a luxury. A foal was better sold off as soon as it was born, and it made better sense to purchase at a later date an animal which could be put to work immediately.

On this occasion no bargain had been struck, a result which neither surprised nor dismayed Hersh, for he had become accustomed to the fact that the greater portion of his efforts would not result in sales. Hersh had expected that on this occasion the animal would be suitable, for he had a pretty good idea of Rolandas Galdikas' tastes, but he had been mistaken. He accepted the decision and promised that he would return the next day, this time with two horses from his stable, one of which he guaranteed would be ideal for its purpose.

As he came within sight of the beginnings of Dorbyan, Hersh was surprised to see a frantic young child running toward the road along a track coming from one of the farms. The boy was waving at him to stop, and his breathlessness suggested that he was in a state of terror.

Hersh recognized the youngster at once, who was no more than nine years old. He reined in his horse and waited for the boy to reach him.

It was Aaron Jacob, the youngest son of Avigdor and Mailki, the family which had housed them after the great fire, and whom he and Chana had only recently left to move into their new home on the Krettinger Gass.

"Aaron! What are you doing here at this time of day, and all by yourself?"

"Please, Hersh, sir,.. Mr Jacob,...sir, gasped the youngster. "Please.. You must help me! Something terrible has happened!"

Hersh listened as Aaron Jacob, a distant cousin, told his story.

Aaron's neighbour, Lazarus Levy Behrman, had invited Aaron to accompany him on a ride into the countryside earlier that afternoon. Lazarus Levy was well known in Dorbyan, slightly older than Hersh, but already considered prosperous because of his dealings as a moneylender. Despite his profession, he was considered an honest and generous person, and was well liked by everyone in the town. His dealings often took him to the countryside around Dorbyan where he likewise enjoyed a good reputation.

The reason for the trip that afternoon had been for Lazarus Levy to collect some money that was long owing him as an interest payment on a mortgage. Aaron had not understood what Lazarus Levy meant when he said that he would probably soon own the farm on a foreclosure.

At the farmhouse they had been met by the usual barking of dogs, and then by the Lithuanian farmer, who had welcomed the two of them warmly. Lazarus Levy had bade Aaron wait in the wagon while he went with the farmer to discuss their business. For what seemed a much longer than reasonable time neither man had returned to the wagon.

Eventually the farmer had reappeared, carrying a heavy axe on his shoulder. He approached the wagon and told Aaron that Lazarus Levy wished to see him inside. There was something about the farmer's agitated manner which did not seem genuine, and using his intuition, Aaron had jumped from the wagon and run as quickly as his legs would carry him, the mile back to the main road.

Aaron was certain that Lazarus Levy had come to grief, and his unfeigned terror convinced Hersh that the matter should be looked into, but not alone. If Lazarus Levy had indeed met with foul play, the Lithunian farmer could be dangerous. He headed back to Dorbyan as fast as his horse would allow.

In the town they had little difficulty in convincing others of the seriousness of the situation, and within a short time some twenty men were on their way back to the farm. As they reached the track from the main road they noticed a woman driving a wagon loaded high with hay. They continued on to the farm.

The initial search showed the farm deserted, with neither the farmer nor his wife at home. There was no sign of Lazerus Levy until the sharp eyes of one of the men spotted bloodstains on the ground near the rear of the house. A moment later a bloodstained cap was found, which Aaron immediately recognized as the cap that Lazarus Levy had worn earlier that day. There was now no doubt in the minds of the men that Lazarus Levy had been murdered, but where was his body?

It was then that Aaron had an inspiration. The wagon of hay! Could it have been used to hide the body? The men chased after the wagon, and overtook it just in time to see the woman leaving it with the team of horses she had unhitched. Ignoring the woman, they began removing the hay, and as expected, near the bottom, they found the body of Lazarus Levy. It was a gory sight, for the head had been completely crushed by the weight of a heavy blow from an axe. Aaron Jacob trembled as he gazed upon the bloodsoaked body, for he realized that he himself had come very close to meeting the same fate.

The body was taken to Dorbyan to be buried at the Jewish cemetery near the Wainaiker Forest the next day. Shortly afterward, Lazarus Levy Behrman's wife sold all the family belongings and took her two young children to South Africa where her brother, Lewis Nathanson had become a prosperous merchant. Thus it was that Dorbyan suffered the loss of yet another family.

The police questioned the farmer's wife, but could extract no confession from her. Her husband had disappeared, but before leaving had simply instructed her to take the load of hay to the forest and leave it there. The priest spoke to her, and received the same answer, and it was generally concluded that she was blameless in the matter.

The countryside was searched for several days afterward, but no trace of the farmer could be found. Then one day the farmer's body was found hanging from a tree not far from the farmsite. He had meted out his own punishment.

Although time would fade the memory of Lazarus Levy Behrman, his fate became a piece of Dorbayn folklore, for the town was generally peaceful, and incidences of violence, as everywhere, remained on people's lips for many years.[2]

---

2   *This episode has been taken from the autobiography of Harry A Jacobs, entitled "Across Three Oceans".*

CHAPTER 6

In the fall of 1885 Chana became pregnant, and in 1886 their first child was born. It was an occasion, and for several months Hersh could hardly contain his impatience for the event to occur. He was now thirty-one, and Chana one year younger, making them far older than anyone they knew without children.

The preparations were completed. A baby carriage was obtained from relatives whose children had outgrown it, clothes were purchased, and one of the empty rooms in the house was fitted out for the new arrival. Chana had secretly hoped that their first-born would be a boy, knowing that this was Hersh's wish.

"Dear, I know that you are wishing for a boy, but what if God should decide otherwise?"

"Of course I want a boy, so that I may pass on the teachings I received from my father, but if it is a girl this time, than my only wish is that she looks just like you, and is just as beautiful."

Their first child was a girl, whom they named Ida, but came to be known as Chaia, meaning 'life'. The baby was healthy, and pretty, and Hersh doted on her, snatching her from Chana's arms every day upon his return from morning prayers at the synagogue.

The following year their second daughter, Leah Feige, was born. Two years later, in 1889, Chana gave birth to Esther.

When their fourth child, Rachel, nicknamed Racha, was born, both parents were concerned. According to many traditions, a Jewish family could not be considered complete unless it had both sons and daughters. A worried Hersh spoke to his father-in-law, Leiba Zup Jacob.

"Tell me, Leiba, what has it been like being the father of a family without sons?"

Leiba Zup smiled at Hersh.

"Not as bad as I once thought, and not as bad as you might feel. I must be honest, and tell you that at first I did not believe it could happen that our family would not have a son, but now I know that it is impossible to dispute God's will...

"....When Chana Eta was born, we continued to expect that we would have more children, and that our wishes would be fulfilled. But for some reason it turned out that either Shora Hinde or I became barren, even though we were still young. Gradually we came to realize that no more children would be born to us."

"But Leiba, what were your feelings, not to have a son?"

"At first it was very painful, and we found it hard to face other people, and to talk about it. We felt deprived, but slowly we began to accept it as God's will, and to trust in His wisdom. We knew that we had two beautiful daughters, and we devoted our lives to bringing them up well-schooled, well-mannered and faithful to our traditions. Because of this they became attractive to men, and praise God, they were each able to find a fine man as a husband. You and Mordechai have been the next best thing to having sons of our own. In fact, you have become our sons."

Leiba placed his hand on Hersh's shoulder.

"I know that it troubles you, Hersh, but in your position I would be happy with the joys that I have, and let the future take its course."

As Hersh and Chana's family grew, the empty rooms became filled with life. The home was now furnished, and just in time, for the horse-trading business which had earlier provided for the two of them so comfortably now strained to support a family of six. Needless to say, business always seemed to be slack just at the time that something was needed, and Hersh took it upon himself to do more and more of the chores which he normally would have given to outsiders to do.

One of the front bedrooms had been specially designated for new arrivals, who would sleep there next to Hersh and Chana's room until old enough to join the others in the other room. Early one morning Chana led Hersh into the baby's room and pointed to the window.

"Dear, this window needs attention. It cannot be shut completely, and I am worried about the draught that is coming in. It may affect the baby, now that the cold weather is approaching."

Dutifully Hersh examined the stiff window. pushing against the outward opening sash.

"Chana, there is nothing wrong with this window. You simply haven't been pulling it shut strongly enough."

Hersh forced the window shut.

"There, a perfect fit. Now I'll open it and you can try."

When Hersh tried to open the window again, he found that it was jammed, and that with all his strength he could not budge it.

"Jammed, but not a problem," he said calmly. "It only needs to be tapped with something solid."

He took off his heavy boot and began to tap on the window frame, harder and harder. Suddenly the window flew open, shattering the glass into several pieces.

Chana glared at Hersh.

"Well, Mr *Hochum*, what do you say now? This time the window really needs attention! The baby cannot stay in a room like this. We shall have to move the children around."

"Do not be in such a hurry to move the children," said Hersh, remaining calm. "I shall remove a window from another room and swap it with this one until we can have it repaired."

"You will do no such thing!," stormed Chana. "If you do that we shall have two broken windows on our hands! I'll move the baby until this one is fixed!"

"Trust me, Chanele, it may not be necessary. I am going to the synagogue in a few minutes. I expect that Shimon Zacharia Jacob will be there. If we are lucky he will be able to come over to fix it today. Wait until I have spoken with him."

Later in the day Hersh watched as Shimon Zacharia first removed the window frame from its hinges, then shaved it down until it was a perfect fit in the sash. Hersh was awed at the way that Shimon Zacharia showed no fear of the broken glass, picking it up with his bare hands and then tossing it distainfully into the bucket he had brought with him for that purpose. He watched, impressed, as with the utmost of ease Shimon Zacharia cut the new pane from a larger piece of glass. A slight scratch with the tool that he called his "diamond', then a quick snap, and the glass was broken, with a perfectly smooth edge, and not so much as a splinter produced.

Shimon Zacharia was known as a craftsman, and a master at his trade, and was in constant demand in and around Dorbyan. Whether his work took him to humble farmhouses or the estates of the nobility, he was always treated with the utmost of respect. Like Hersh, he was easy going and fair-minded, and along with Hersh he was one of the few Jews who had made close contacts amongst the non-Jewish population. Hersh had been very fortunate that Shimon Zacharia had been available to make the repair that very same day.

"I'm always available to help my *Mishpoche*, "he said.

When asked how much payment he required, he answered, "In a day or two I shall need the use of one of your horses to carry out some errands. Apart from that, perhaps a cabbage from your garden. I don't know why, but Chana seems to know more about growing cabbages than does my Sara."

He raised his head suddenly.

"Oh, and by the way, Hersh, I have a few things to tell you. One thing I almost forgot to mention, is that a couple of days ago I did some work for a good friend of yours."

"Who?"

"Galdikas. Like you, he needed a window repaired. He says that he knows you well, and that you are good friends."

"Yes, Rolandas Galdikas. He is correct when he says that we are good friends.

In fact he was my first customer, and he still buys and trades horses with me. They are good people. They struggle, but they are honest."

"He had only good things to say about you, Hersh. He says that you are one of the finest people he knows, either Jewish or Lithuanian."

"That is flattering. We get along well. Sometimes they have difficulty in paying me, and then I will accept produce in payment. As long as I can sell to them without making a loss, I am happy to help them in any way I can. I hope that you will do the same for them."

"If they are friends of yours, Hersh, then they are friends of mine. They have been in the district for a long time, that is certain. Rolandas was telling me that his grandfather could remember when my great-grandfather used to visit the baron's estate to repair glass.

"I believe this," said Hersh. "These people cannot read nor write, but they have long memories of events that have been passed on through the generations. I don't know whether to believe it, but they have told me what it was like on the estate when the first Jews arrived in Dorbyan."

Shimon Zacharia nodded, "I think I would be inclined to trust their stories, for they are honest people, and would not change the truth knowingly,.......but there is one thing you must know, and that is that not all Lithuanian peasants are quite so friendly towards us."

"I have never met this," said Hersh, "But perhaps you have seen something that I haven't."

"Let me tell you something that happened to me on my last visit to one of the baron's estates," said Shimon Zacharia.

"For a long time my son Jacob Sender has been pleading with me to take him on one of my trips, and finally Sara agreed to it. At the baron's he watched me while I worked, but as there was more to be done on the next day, the baron gave us a place to sleep in the animal stable....

".......During the night Jacob was awakened by something hairy brushing across his face. He was terrified, but did not cry out. Finally, after it brushed over our faces several times, he woke me, and I too was terrified. We ran from the stable and pounded on the baron's door, who let us sleep in the kitchen....

".....The next morning we went with the baron to the stable and found a wooden cross with some animal skins fastened to it hanging from the rafters in such a way that it could be raised and lowered. The baron was furious with his peasants, and told us that we need never fear being treated like this again on his property. Of course after the baron was gone, the peasants only showed their dislike for us even more, and referred to us as "the baron's *Juden* ". I will not feel comfortable about going back to that estate, and if I do I shall make certain that I do not have to stay overnight. I am afraid that this experience will remain with Jacob for the rest of his life."

Hersh said, "It may be that the peasants who work for the barons still have the mentality of serfs, even though they no longer are."

"That could be," answered Shimon Zacharia, "It was a terrible time for them when they were serfs on the baron's estates. No human deserves a life like that, and it is easy to understand how the bitterness came about. Thank God, most of them now have farms of their own, even though they struggle."

"Yes, they certainly deserve a better life than they have known," said Hersh.

Then Shimon Zacharia pointed to his glasscutter and said, "I know what it was that I wanted to tell you, Hersh, but first, take a good look at this "diamond". You know, it's not so difficult, what I'm doing, not if you have a good tool like this one. Here, why don't you have a try on one of these pieces of scrap?"

He handed the glasscutter to Hersh.

"That's it, simply hold the "diamond" between your thumb and finger, like a pen, and scratch a line across the glass. After that, you simply break it."

Hersh did as instructed, but before he had finished his scratch, the glass shattered.

"Nothing to worry about, Hersh. You simply pressed too hard and went too near the edge. Here, try again."

This time the glass broke evenly along the line that Hersh had scratched. Although the edge was not perfectly smooth, and he had created splinters, he was still pleased with what he had done.

"You see, Hersh, it's not so hard, at least for the smaller pieces. Larger pieces are a different story, but at least you can see how it's done."

"If you do not mind, I think I will leave the glasscutting to you," said Hersh.

"I have shown you this for a reason," said Shimon Zacharia, taking back his glasscutter.

"A moment ago I said that there was something I wanted to tell you. Maybe you know someone who would like to learn the glazier's trade. You see, shortly I shall be needing someone to take my place."

"Oh no, Shimon! Don't tell me that you too are thinking of leaving Dorbyan!"

"Yes, Hersh, you have guessed correctly, but we are doing more than just thinking, for the time has finally come that we are able to leave. You know yourself for just how long I have been dreaming of Palestine, all the time wondering if it would ever happen. Well, the time has finally come that it is no longer a dream."

He continued excitedly.

"Last year when Sam Simon decided not to follow his brother to Saint John, but went to Jerusalem instead, it made me realize that there was no need to wait any longer. I thought to myself, 'If Sam Simon can do it, then why not I?' I began investigating all the possibilities, and now I can hardly believe it! Everything is now in place, and in a short time we shall be walking in the land of our ancestors!"

"What do Sara and the children say to this?"

"You know my Sara, she is cautious. What would you expect her to say? She does not like uncertainty, but she is prepared to do it if it is the realization of our dreams. As for the children, for them it is an adventure that they can hardly wait to begin."

"But where will you go? How will you live? What will you do for a living? There are so many questions."

"A Zionist organization is assisting us. The money for the settlement is being provided by the Rothschild family. The trip there will cost us almost nothing, and when we get there we will go to a new part of Palestine which has never been cultivated."

"Where?"

"The Huleh Valley, to a settlement called *Yesud Hama'alot*".

"I have never heard of it."

"And little wonder, neither has anybody else, but I promise you, one day it will be well known. At the moment it is a swamp, where not even the Palestinians attempt to live, and for that reason it is available to anyone who is prepared to settle there."

"But I don't understand," said Hersh. "If a place is so hostile, then why go there? When Sam and Riva Simon went to Jerusalem, I could at least see some reason, even though it is not my idea of a life."

"The Huleh Valley is a very historical area, and very beautiful. The tribe of Naphthali once occupied these lands. Today it is hostile, but tomorrow it will not be. With our efforts it will become the most fertile district in Palestine, richer than even the Jordan Valley or the Valley of Jesrael..... In time the Palestinians will come to realize the mistake they have made in not claiming the land for their own."

"And where will you live?"

"In tents, at least for the first year or two, until such time as we can support ourselves off the land. After that we will build permanent homes."

"And tell me, Shimon, just how does one go about draining a swamp?"

"Easy, Hersh,.. or rather, not so easy. The principle is very simple, but the work may take a lifetime before an entire swamp is drained. At first trees are planted in their hundreds around the edge. There are certain types which grow very quickly and soak up enormous amounts of water. I am told that one such type is known as eucalypt and comes from Australia, but there are others. As each area becomes dry, more and more trees can be planted until finally the whole area is reclaimed. The soil that is then available is the most fertile soil of all, and there is nothing that cannot be grown in it."

"But isn't a swamp an unhealthy place to live?"

"I cannot deny that, Hersh. There is always the possibility of malaria or yellow fever for the first few years. They are terrible diseases which can leave one unfit for work for weeks and even months, but from what I hear, most people who are young and healthy do not die from them."

"It still doesn't seem too attractive to me. Are you sure that you want to subject your children to this sort of life?"

"They want it as much as I do, Hersh, and one cannot allow himself to be distracted by the possibility of illness. Have you forgotten the cholera epidemic that plagued our parents? As the Huleh swamps are drained, the danger will become less and less, and finally disappear altogether."

"Well, Shimon, I'm glad that it is you who are going, and not I. I envy you for your courage, and I wish you every success."

"I cannot wait, Hersh! Just think, we will be in the land where our ancestors once lived, in the land of the Bible! After two thousand years, we will be a family returning home!......And do you know how all this is starting to become possible?"

"No, tell me."

"It is because of the work of people like our friend Dodke Wolff and people like Theodore Herzl. They have achieved wonders in a short time. They are tireless! Did you know that they are constantly seeking audiences with heads of state to make their cause known? They do not know the meaning of discouragement! More and more people are thinking of Palestine, and because of it people like the Baron de Rothschild are also becoming interested, and providing the money to make it possible.

"The Baron sees Palestine as a place for Jews to work on the land as they did in the olden days. Your friend Dodke sees Palestine as a Jewish homeland for only Jews, but the Jews working the land must come first. I only hope that I live long enough to see it all take place in my lifetime."

Within the year another family had left Dorbyan. Shimon Zacharia Jacob, the glazier, his wife Sara and their five children departed to Palestine to realize their dream. At about this time Chana gave birth for the fifth time, to a daughter, Ada. It was not until two years later that their sixth child was born, another daughter whom they named Mina. When in 1895 their seventh daughter, Breina, arrived, Chana could feel the dispair that Hersh was suffering, yet hiding so well.

As much as Hersh wanted a son, he was saddened to see the effect that the constant childbearing was having on Chana. Now close to forty, he felt that time was running out, and that it was God's will that they should have no son. In his eyes Chana was still the most beautiful woman on earth, but he could not help but notice the ageing of her body.

"Chana, we cannot go on having daughter after daughter. I worry that one of these times it will turn out to be too much for you."

"We shall continue to have children for as long as God, and you, are willing. It is my duty to provide you with as many children as I am able until you are happy, until you decide that our family is complete."

"You are wonderful, Chana, I have known it from the first day I saw you. I will always love you, son or no son. How can we be disappointed with what we have, when it is God's will? He has blessed us with the seven most beautiful daughters on earth. They will grow up to be well-taught, well-mannered and faithful to our religion. One day they will grow up to marry and bring sons into our family. With a wife like you, what greater blessing could I ask?"[3]

3   *The description of the visit of Shimon Zacharia Jacob's visit to the farm of a noble-man is based on an episode related to the authour by Sara Yablon, historian of the Hali-fax, Nova Scotia Jewish community, Shimon Zacharia Jacob was her paternal grandfa-ther, and Jacob Sender was her father.*

CHAPTER 7

March, 1890: It was a cold, damp morning as Hersh stepped out of the synagogue following the completion of the *Shah'ris* prayer. The snow was largely gone from the town, although it could still be found lying in the hollows of the countryside and the shadier areas of the forest. A thin layer of ice on the puddles attested to the fact that the temperature had fallen below freezing during the night.

It was Wednesday, market day, and already most of the vendors, mainly farmers from the countryside, stood beside their produce filled wagons, their breath forming a vapour in the still crisp morning air. Shortly the first Jewish traders would join them, bringing their home manufactured textiles, fish brought in from the Baltic, and their smallgoods obtained from Memel and the larger centres beyond. At the same time the Jewish shops lining the market square would open their doors.

Hersh would spend the morning in the market as he always did, finding plenty to keep him occupied. He would gossip with the Jewish traders, and sometimes he would see his Lithuanian friend Rolandas Galdikas with his son Viktoras standing beside a wagon heaped high with produce for sale. He would stop and have a chat with them, usually making a small purchase in the process. Later when Chana would join him, the two would try to purchase as many of their needs from Galdikas as possible.

He would always keep his eyes open for suitable horses, and sometimes he was successful. On this particular occasion it was urgent that he locate something, as recent sales had left his stable depleted. Galdikas had been unable to give him any leads, and he would go home on this day empty-handed, remembering ruefully the time but a few weeks earlier when there had been more horses on offer than he could put to use.

He would circulate about the market until noon, by which time Chana would arrive to make her weekly purchases. Then the two would return home for their midday meal, sharing the load between them.

As he walked about, examining the various stalls, a lady rushed up to him, calling him by name. It was Mailki Jacob, wife of Avigdor.

"Hersh! Look! I have something to show you", she gushed. "Look! It is my first letter from Aaron in America! 'Harry', they are calling him over there!"

She waved an envelope in front of Hersh's face.

"Mailki, how are you? I don't see much of you these days, since we left your home. How is Avigdor?"

"He is home at the moment, please God, and he is much better than he has been for some time."

"I am glad to hear that. Does this mean that he is no longer staying with the Lithuanian farmer?"

"For the moment he doesn't need to," beamed Mailki. "The treatment seems to be helping him, praise God. Each time he has a bad spell we send him to the farm, and each time he recovers more quickly and returns home improved from the last time."

"This is wonderful news, Mailki. I'm happy for you. Perhaps the time will come when he will be cured completely."

"This is what we are praying for, Hersh. The farmer is happy to have him, and no longer asks for payment. He says that the work Avigdor does now makes it worth his while to keep him."

"But what about the bad spells, Mailki?"

"They do not come as often. Now, when he has one on the farm, they simply put him outside alone in the fields until it passes. The peace and quiet and the healthy life are making his spells fewer and fewer."

"I'm happy for you, Mailki," said Hersh, "For you deserve an easier life than you have been having."

Mailki waved the envelope in front of Hersh's face again.

"And look at this!" She held out a handful of coins. "This was in my son's first letter. Actually it was dollars, but it was easy to change. Look! Five Rubles! Enough for Avigdor and me to live on for a whole month, and yet between my three sons, it was nothing! America must be a wonderful place!"

Then she sighed, and the pain showed on her face.

"...And yet, even though they are all doing well, I would still give anything to have them home with me. I miss them so,... our home seems so lonely, and yet what can I do? What can anyone do?"

"I know," said Hersh. "There is no doubt that Chana and I will face the very same situation when our children grow up. Everyone seems to be leaving."

"But what I really wanted to show you," exclaimed Mailki excitedly, "Was this letter, from Aaron. Here, read it, for in it you and Chana are mentioned."

New York

February 1990

Dear Mama!

I am sorry I have taken so long to write you, but as you will see, everything did not go as planned after we left Dorbyan, and we were longer than expected in arriving in America.

The boat from Memel was the most terrible thing I have ever endured in my life. The voyage was rough and cold and too uncomfortable to describe. The sailors on the boat were German ruffians who treated us like cattle, and their only interest was in getting to Kiel and off the boat. The only good thing I can say about this voyage is that it was the shortest part of our journey.

From Kiel to Hamburg the voyage was also rough, but still much better than the one we had just finished. At Hamburg the immigration wharf was crowded with thousands of others all going to America. Such a crowd I have never seen, all nationalities, all races, and all languages, and yet most of them seemed to be Jewish.

When Barney and I boarded the ship to America we were told that the half-ticket I had wasn't sufficient for a boy my age, and I was thrown off the ship. Barney would not leave me, and he jumped off the ship just as it was about to leave. But our baggage was on board, and we watched the ship sail away with everything we owned.

We didn't know what to do, but someone suggested the Jewish Aid Society for Immigrants, in Hamburg, so we went there, and were given food and shelter.

Then Barney remembered your cousin Mr Hirshman in Hamburg, and we were able to find his whereabouts, because he is well known. When we told him who we were, he believed our story and was very generous, giving us enough money to allow us to continue our journey. I promise you, Mama, that someday soon I shall repay him everything I owe him.

The next boat to America was sailing from Glasgow, so we took a small boat from Hamburg to Glasgow. This time the boat was British, and the soldiers a bit more pleasant, but the voyage was no more comfortable. The trip took five days, and we were inside for the entire time, without sight of daylight.

When we reached Glasgow, our ship, the Columbia, was ready to depart. It was the biggest ship I have ever seen in my life. Our steerage berths were not very comfortable, but still they were better than our previous voyages. The problem was that opposite our berth was an Italian family. From their bunks swung a huge sack of garlic, whose smell filled the entire cramped space. Between the garlic smell and the rough weather we were sick a large part of the time, and yet going on deck was no help. The weather was wet and freezing cold, and the spray breaking over the boat drenched everything in sight.

Every day was the same as the day before, until on the seventh day, the skies became clearer and the seas calmer. Then one day someone shouted from the deck, "LAND!", and we all rushed to the side to have a look. In the distance we could see a large statue of a woman with an outstretched hand and a crown on her head. The scene is hard to describe. People broke into tears, and families and strangers hugged each other, and everyone was shouting "AMERICA" in a thousand different accents.

I have since learned that the statue is called "The Statue of

Liberty", and it stands at the entrance to New York harbour to welcome new arrivals to America.

At the immigration dock Barney and I were almost the only ones not met by friends or relatives. We watched as others were joyfully reunited with their families, but Barney and I were alone, for we had been expected two weeks earlier.

We left the immigration area and walked into the streets. People stared at us in our east European attire, our pocketless coats, our knee-length boots, and our round black derbies.

We had just enough money to buy a loaf of bread, but I passed too near a standing taxi and the horse snatched it out of my hands before we had taken our first bite. Despite our loss, we were in good spirits, for we were in America!

In the east side of New York where we were, everyone speaks Yiddish, and we were shown the way to our uncle's address on Allen Street. When we got there we saw that the entire block of buildings was on fire, and our uncle was nowhere to be found.

We were directed to the Hebrew Sheltering Aid Society, where a Mr. Marcus loaned us the money for new clothes. We didn't even try to wash our old ones, just threw them into the rubbish bin where we knew they would be burned, for we looked too out of place in them. It was now *Sabbes*, and the services that were held were the happiest occasion we had known since we left Dorbyan.

After *Sabbes* , Mr Marcus helped us locate Nathan, who came and collected us. He bought us some more clothes and took us to a Mr Yudel, who introduced us to the peddling trade. For a while I peddled for Mr Yudel door to door, selling everything from chair bottoms to matchsticks.

Now I am no longer working for Mr Yudel, and I peddle on my own. I am beginning to do well, and now Nathan, Barney and I are able to send you this money order which will be worth five rubles. The time will soon come when we are able to send you more than this.

So this is what has happened to me. Give my love to Papa

and my sisters Sara, Rivki and Rachel, and tell them that America is a wonderful land. Give my greetings to my friends Chaim and Benjamin when you see them, and remember me to Hersh and Chana Jacob. They were good to us when they were staying at our house. I still remember with fondness the rides Hersh used to let us have on his horses, even after they left and moved to the Krettinger Gass.

I hope Papa is feeling well, and your life is not too difficult. We will try our best to see that life is easier for you from now on.

Do not worry about us, Mama. America is a wonderful place, and we are lucky to be here. Someday we will have enough money to bring you and Papa here to be with us.

Your son, Aaron
(Called 'Harry' in America)[4]

---

4   *Based on an episode related in the autobiography of Harry Jacobs entitled "Across Three Oceans."*

DORBYAN

PART 3

Moshe Bloch lay quietly on his simple bed in the sparsely furnished attic. The others were sitting and talking downstairs in wait for the evening meal., but as usual he preferred to remain where he could be in silence. The others understood his wishes, and he would not be disturbed until they called him for the meal.

He had become preoccupied with the notion that he must remember as much about Dorbyan as he possibly could, and tell what he knew to somebody in case something should happen to him, for his own survival was by no means assured.

Although he could remember his own experiences well, there would be a problem with things that had happened before he was born or old enough to remember.

His conversations with old Hersh Jacob came back, as did bits of conversation overheard between the older people in his family. Hersh Jacob had always been the oldest in the town, and it seemed that he had been an old man for as long as Moshe had known him.

The name David Wolffsohn, the renowned Zionist, was well known to every Dorbyaner, as he was the most famous person ever to have originated from the town. Yet, apart from Hersh and Chana Jacob, noone had ever met him personally, for he had left the village while still a very young man. Hersh had mentioned that the two had been friends, but had said very little more. If only he had asked Hersh more questions on the subject.

He remembered the discussions between his father and Hersh in the *Shul Platz*, with their neighbour Leiba Kashutsky often taking part. They discussed mainly religious matters and politics, but from time to time the subject would change to events in Dorbyan during bygone days. It was at this point that he tended to lose interest in the conversation and switch his mind to other topics. The folly of his lack of attention now struck him, as he realized how little he knew of the village's early history, and he racked his brain to remember the few things he could on the subject.

There had been talk of Dorbyan's many fires, the greatest one being in 1882. His own father had been born five years later , and only knew what he had heard from his own parents. Many of the village elders had been alive when the fire occurred, but most were too young to have memories of the event. Only Hersh and Chana Jacob would have been able to tell the full story.

There had been another fire, more recent, which was better known. Not as much of the town had been destroyed in 1909, but unlike the earlier fire, this one had caused the loss of the synagogue and *Beit Hamidrash* buildings. He remembered his father telling him with pride that every one of the *Torahs* had been saved, and that he himself had been responsible for the rescuing of two of them. He had taken one outside to safety and passed it to someone in the crowd before going inside for a second time. This time the heat had been searing and the smoke intense, but he and two others had been in time to remove the last of the *Torahs* from the ark. The synagogue could be rebuilt, but once a *Torah* was lost it could never be replaced, for each *Torah* was unique, and its uniqueness and craftsmanship made it just as irreplaceable as any masterpiece or work of art.

At the time he had not been curious, and he now regretted that he had never asked his father what the previous synagogue had been like. He only knew that it had been much larger than the present one, but apart from this he knew nothing about it. Hersh Jacob, or his father, or in fact anyone more than forty years old would have been able to tell him, but there was now nobody of that age from the village remaining. As far as he knew, at the age of twenty-seven, he was the oldest Dorbyan villager still alive.

He remembered the almost daily gossip about the people who were leaving Dorbyan, mostly to go to Canada or America. He remembered the relief felt by his family that somehow none of their number had chosen to migrate, making them one of the few Dorbyan families not to suffer the loss of loved ones.

Now the thought occurred, that perhaps the best hope for the memory of the village to be perpetuated was through those who had left their home for distant lands. Some had gone to Palestine, but their exodus had been recent, and in the few cases he knew the migrants had been young, no older than himself. He knew that there were Jews in Saint John, Canada and in Kroonstadt, South Africa who would be able to remember the village as it was, but he did not have addresses, for it was the older people who did the corresponding. In any case, there was now a war going on, and any attempt to communicate would be hopeless.

Most of all he knew that he must piece together the story of Dorbyan as best he could, for without it there would be no proof that the village had ever existed. In his mind he was now certain that the Germans would someday, possibly far into the future, lose the war, and eventually be brought to account for their actions. If there was no one present at the time to bear witness against them, it was possible that they would walk away from their crimes scot-free.

CHAPTER 1

As the nineteenth century progressed into its final decade, a major change was taking place in Dorbyan. For the first time since its beginning over one hundred and eighty years earlier, the Jewish community was no longer growing. For the moment the high birth rate was offsetting the increasing migration, but this could not last, as more and more of the migrants were younger people, taking their children with them.

It was inevitable that the birth rate would gradually decline, and along with it the population of the town.

The changed atmosphere was immediately noticeable to any visitor. Although there was still a measure of prosperity in the town, the feeling was that the best days had passed. The turning point had been the great fire of 1882, which had changed the ever-existing trickle of migrants into a flood. Now, as more and more families became established in the new world, there were more and more relations left behind who were being called upon to join them.

The fire of 1882 had had another effect, more psychological than real. The old wooden church dating back to 1620 had been totally destroyed by the blaze. It had been tiny compared to the *Shul* and the *Beit Hamidrash* opposite it on the marketplace. Now, through the assistance of the Titschcovitch family, a new church had been built. It was a magnificent structure of granite, with its steeple towering high above Dorbyan and the surrounding countryside. For the first time since longer than anyone could remember, the amenities of the Jewish community were inferior to those available to Christians.

As ever increasing numbers of Dorbyaners rushed to join their relatives in Eastern Canada and the United States , Hersh began to feel the effects among his own family. His sister, Esther, had married Israel Goldberg, who sailed alone to Saint John, Canada in 1892 to join relatives. His plan had been to send for Esther and their three young children just as soon as he was able to support them. Although he was able to send them regular remittances, he never seemed able to achieve the situation that would permit their reunion.

Hersh watched his sister carry on with the task of raising the three children alone for year after year, wondering what there could be to the new world which could possibly justify such an ordeal. It was not until 1899, after seven years of separation, by which time his children were no longer recognizable to him, that Israel Goldberg built up his junk business to the stage where he could send the money for four trans-Atlantic tickets to Dorbyan.

Separation of families for a period was not uncommon, but the time apart endured by Israel and Esther Goldberg had reached biblical proportions.

It was also about this time that a new destination for Dorbyaners appeared. From time to time a villager had made his way to South Africa, where the opportunities were considered just as promising as in North America. Now, more and more Dorbyaners found reason to follow the path of their relatives in this direction.

Every departure from the town was a tragic occasion, with families split, and with those remaining behind knowing that they were gazing upon the departees for the last time. One of the most tragic occasions for the Jewish community came however, not in the departure and subsequent loss of yet another family, but in the return of an earlier migrant, Shimon Zacharia Jacob, the glazier.

Shimon Zacharia's experience in Palestine had been heartrending, and as soon as Hersh learned of his return, he went to visit him at once. What he saw shocked him.

"Shimon, what has happened to you? Your colour! I have never seen anybody looking so pale and thin!"

"Hersh, believe me, I did not want to leave Palestine, but I had to! I have no further strength to carry on! I have lost everything!"

"I know, Shimon, I have heard stories, but I did not expect this. Tell me about it, How did it happen?"

Shimon Zacharia spoke as though dazed.

"It was the malaria!.....I never knew that a disease could kill so many people so quickly!"

"But how, Shimon? Were there no medications? Could you not take precautions?"

"What medications?....What precautions?...What can one do when one is in the middle of a swamp, and there are mosquitoes swarming about you every minute of the day, and even more so during the night?"

His voice wavered.

"....It started out as if it might work. For most of the first year everything went according to plan, and we remained healthy. There was very little sickness, and nobody died. We made good progress, and succeeded in clearing a portion of the swamp...

"....Then in the second year when the summer came, the weather became hotter than the year before, much hotter than anything I had ever known. The mosquitoes became worse, and gave us no rest, and even in our tents we could not be free of them....

..... Almost everyone of us, forty *chalutzim* , became sick at one time or another, but we all survived, little knowing that in a weakened state, we would fall ill again, for this is the way that malaria works."

Hersh looked into his cousin's tear-filled eyes, and could feel his own eyes beginning to water. The tragedy was too great to bear, and yet he felt that he had to know every gruesome detail.

"You probably know what is coming. Do you want to hear the rest?", asked Shimon Zacharia. Hersh nodded.

".....Somehow we managed to get through that summer, and when the cooler weather came, it brought relief. We thought we had survived the worst, but the next summer came, at least as hot as the one before, and in our weakened state we were struck down like flies. Not a person was untouched, and the only care the helpless could receive was from those less ill than themselves.......

"... I watched their suffering.... First it was my youngest two daughters, then my wife Sara,.... and then my other two daughters. There was nothing anyone could do for them......."

He held out his hands in a gesture of helplessness.

"Hersh, have you ever watched someone you love slowly die, and have no power to help them in any way?....This has happened to me five times......"

Shimon Zacharia wiped his brow, which was now wet with perspiration. He cleared his throat and continued.

"....You cannot begin to understand.....In the middle of the hot-

144

test summer possible, they were shivvering as though freezing to death, and yet their bodies were on fire. Giving them blankets was no help...

"....I was fortunate, for I was not struck severely enough to die. Also my son, Joseph Sender, but we have been weakened, and would not survive if we were to fall ill again...................

"....Still, I would have preferred to remain, for there is an inspiration in being in the land of our ancestors,....but our bodies had no strength to continue, and we would have only been a burden to those still able to carry on. I do not know what will become of them, but I know in my own heart that someday the Huleh will be fertile, and a joy to those fortunate enough to live in it. I will always regret that I am not strong enough to be the one to make it happen....

".....You know, Hersh, I would gladly give my own life, but I cannot bring myself to risk the life of my one remaining child. He too would have remained if I had wished it, but I could not do it to him.... and so, we are back in Dorbyan, while my wife Sara and our four daughters lie buried in Palestine...."

Shimon Zacharia buried his face in his hands, and whispered a prayer. Hersh placed his hand on his shoulder.

"Shimon, this is the saddest thing that I have ever heard. We all have our problems, and it makes me realize how trifling mine are, and how selfish I have been in resenting that I have only daughters, but no son. I cannot imagine anything worse happening to anyone than what you have suffered."

Shimon Zacharia nodded, but said nothing. Hersh continued through tear-filled eyes.

"What are you going to do now? I know that it is useless for me to say this, but if there is anything we can do to make your situation more comfortable, please tell me."

"Thank you, Hersh. You are a good man. You always have been, and it is a comfort to have people like you around me. Perhaps I shall need you, perhaps I shall need to borrow one of your horses on occasion, but first I need time to recover and to get my thoughts together. If you will only mention to some of the *goyim* that I am back in Dorbyan, it would help, for I am available for business just as soon as I can get some new tools."

"I shall certainly do this, Shimon, for you are remembered, and you have been missed. You have a good name. If you need help in purchasing your tools, there is a little money saved up. I know that Chana would agree to letting you have it. Whatever happens to you, I am sure that once word gets out of your return, you will find work to do again."

Both men were silent. After a moment's thought Hersh spoke again.

"You know, Shimon, what you have just told me makes me wonder just what it is that Dodke Wolff and his friends are doing. I know they are sincere, but can they be aware of the suffering they are causing to people like yourself? Surely they must bear some of the responsibility for what has happened."

Shimon Zacharia's sunken eyes blazed.

"No! Do not say that! Do not place the blame on them! I myself hold no blame against them. Like myself, they have a dream, and like myself, they are dedicating their lived to fulfilling it......

"......Nobody has said that the path would not be difficult or dangerous, but someday.....one day......there will be Jews in Palestine, living their lives in comfort and the safety of their own homeland, and giving thanks that people like David Wolffsohn and Theodore Herzl existed.......

"......I would surely go back again, if only I possessed the strength to be of use. Now I must find an easier way of life and leave the pioneering to others."

The year was 1896, a year after the return of Shimon Zacharia Jacob to Dorbyan. Chana gave birth for the eighth time, and this time the miracle took place.

The child was a boy, and the whole town knew of Hersh and Chana's *Nachas* . They named him Joseph , after Hersh's father who had died too soon to see the happy event that God had provided. Hersh and Chana rejoiced, for their family was now complete.

The following summer, in 1897, another event took place, which, although apparently unimportant at the time, was later to be recognized as one of the most significant events in the long history of the Jewish nation. The event had a connection with Dorbyan in a sense, although it would have been far removed from the town, and would have had very little or no effect on the lives of the townsfolk, if indeed it were even known to them.

Through the intense dedication and untiring efforts of Theodore Herzl, an Austro-Hungarian Jew with very little religious upbringing, a new force was emerging amongst world Jewry, the force of Zionism. Briefly stated, its belief was that there would be no future for Jews anywhere on earth until they achieved their own Jewish homeland and returned there to make their lives building a Jewish state. Their beliefs were not entirely unfounded, for they had the full weight of Jewish history to back them up, with a particularly virulent form of anti-semitism spreading through both eastern and western Europe at the time.

The homeland envisaged was not defined, and although historical Palestine was preferred, almost any land would suffice, as long as it belonged to Jews alone. Now for the first time, through Herzl's driving force, Zionists throughout Europe were gathered together in Basle, Switzerland for what was to become known as the First World Zionist Congress.

The obstacles were formidable, with educated English, German and French-speaking Jews debating issues with Yiddish speaking Russian and Polish Jews whose entire education was through their religion, and whose knowledge of western European languages was non-existent. Western European Jews possessing a degree of wealth and influence sat alongside the disenfranchised and the persecuted, the victims of the pogroms of the east. Those who saw the Jewish state as a future economic entity debated the issues with those who saw it only as a place to practice their beloved religion in freedom.

The driving force behind the gathering was Theodore Herzl, but the organizational genius behind Theodore Herzl was David Wolffsohn of Dorbyan, by now a wealthy man and destined to become Herzl's chief lieutenant. The arrangements of the Congress were due to his labours, while the communication between factions largely fell upon his shoulders. Alone amongst Herzl's colleagues, he possessed a non-secular education, for his Dorbyan upbringing had provided him with the capacity to bridge the gap between the progressive westerners and their tradition-bound eastern brethren.

The Congress achieved little apart from the election of Theodore Herzl as chairman of the World Zionist Organization, but it laid the foundations for the infrastructure of a future Jewish state, and it provided sufficient inspiration for the delegates to decide to repeat the exercise the following year. Apart from the creation of the Jewish Colonial Bank as its financial arm, it could point to little concrete achievement. What it did achieve could not be recognized at the time, but it served notice on the world that the Jewish nation no longer wished to remain homeless, a race of wanderers, and that it aspired to a homeland of its own, in its own historical land, in Zion.

CHAPTER 2

In most countries of the western world the beginning of the twentieth century was accompanied with an unprecedented wave of optimism. Throughout most of Europe and the English speaking world technological progress was taking place at a rate heretofore unimaginable. New machinery was being invented which would make the lot of workers easier. Travel was quicker, safer and cheaper. New methods of cultivation, fertilization and harvesting promised to make food shortages a thing of the past. Diseases which had ravaged entire populations were being conquered. More leisure was available, and the arts were becoming accessible to others than the very rich. Education was no longer the privilege of the gentry alone.

In the developed world at least, the coming century promised an era of comfort and prosperity such as had never been known.

There were still many parts of the world with little cause to rejoice. Many of the undeveloped lands of Asia and Africa still groaned under the yoke of colonialism, prevented from achieving their full potential. Other lands which should have prospered were in decline, notably the areas of eastern Europe under the Russian Tzarist regime. Here things should have been better, for wealthy soils and mineral riches were available in the same measure as in the progressive countries. The difference was a despotic and antiquated regime which stifled all inclination towards progress.

It was inevitable that once the world became open, regimes such as those of the Tzars would not be able to hold their people. The exodus included all races, but it was always the Jews who chose a new life in greatest proportion to their numbers.

Their wandering tradition since biblical days was one factor, but the greater reason was that they owed no allegiance to any country. A tradition of multilingualism meant that they held no fear of a new environment. In addition, the commercial prowess that they had of necessity acquired through the generations gave them the confidence to believe that they could succeed in any new situation.

As the twentieth century began in Dorbyan, there was very little optimism, and if anything the lethargy which had begun some twenty years earlier continued to increase. The exodus was now well and truly underway, and could not be stopped.

It was now a rare week which passed when a family member, or sometimes an entire family, would not announce an intention to join relatives in Canada or the United States. Usually the announcement would follow the receipt of a long awaited letter containing money or an overseas ticket. Once the decision was taken, departure was generally swift, and yet another family would disappear from the town.

The routes taken were varied, but always began with a short trip across the Prussian border to Memel, and then a short steamship voyage to one of the major European ports, Hamburg or Rotterdam. Often the voyage to North America was cheaper from Britain, in which case another short voyage was made to either Glasgow or Liverpool, after which a large ocean going steamship would be taken across the Atlantic. The destinations in North America were New York, Saint John, Halifax, or sometimes Quebec City, with the earliest migrants choosing New York, and sometimes Boston, while most subsequent migrants chose Saint John. Of the North American cities, New York and Boston were by far the largest, with New York poised to take its place as one of the world's major population centres. The Canadian centres were considerably less developed, with Halifax a strategically located port destined someday to assume importance, while Saint John could only be described as a quaint city, inconveniently located at a considerable distance from the mouth of the Bay of Fundy, and constructed largely of adjoining timber homes crowded tightly one against the other. Indeed, such was the layout of Saint John that a Dorbyaner would not have been too surprised at his first glimpse of the city. Saint John, however, had other physical attributes, which made it unique amongst the cities of the world.

As South Africa began to assume significance, the departure point was usually Rotterdam or the British ports of Glasgow or Liverpool. Landings were always at Capetown, with most migrants continuing to Kroonstadt or Johannesburg.

In the early 1880's a brother of Mailki Jacob had gone to New York. The following year he sent for Mailki and Avigdor's son, Nathan.

In 1888 John Simon left for Saint John in Canada. In 1889 the remaining sons of Mailki and Avigdor , Barney and Aaron Jacob, joined their relatives in New York. In the same year, the brother of John Simon, Sam, left for Jerusalem with his wife Rivka.

In 1890 Shimon Jacharia Jacob, his wife Sara, their four daughters and one son, left to work in the Huleh swamps in Palestine in a new settlement known as *S'deh Hama'alot*. In 1891 Meyer Whitzman left for New York, after which he continued to Saint John. Shortly afterward he sent for his wife Chava and his daughter Tamara.

In 1892 Israel Goldberg sailed to Saint John to join an uncle. In Dorbyan he left behind his wife Esther, and his children, Hyman, Jessie and Beckie, whom he was not to see again until 1899.

In 1894 the daughters of Mailki and Avigdor Jacob, Sara and Rachel, sailed to New York to join their three brothers. In December 1896 Mailki and Avigdor followed.

In 1897 or early 1898 Hyman Wolff Jacob and his wife Olga (nee Behrman) sailed from Rotterdam to Capetown, South Africa, whence they continued to Kroonstadt.

In 1898 John Simon sent for his brother Joseph, wife Estermary and five children to join him in Saint John. Arriving with them were two nephews, Morris Levy and Barney.

In 1899, after a seven year separation, the wife and children of Israel Goldberg sailed to Saint John to be reunited with him. In the same year Louis Jacob (known as Leiba Zup), the son of Nochum David, a brother of Hersh, arrived in Saint John. Leiba Zup was exceptional in that he returned to Dorbyan on several occasions, bringing out family each time, finally returning for the last time in 1920.

Shortly before 1900 Hoda and Sura Jacobson arrived in Saint John.

This is a very incomplete list of those who left Dorbyan in the years prior to the turn of the century. After 1900 the list increased tenfold.

In 1900 Morris Block left for eastern Canada. One year later

Phillip and Jack Simon followed. Eight of their nine children followed them, Baila, Sophie, Jack, Harry, David, Sam, Charlie and Irwin. Only one daughter, Hanna, married and remained in Dorbyan.

Also in 1901 was the arrival in Saint John of Sam and Rivka Simon, brother of John. Sam and Rivke had lived in Jerusalem where they lost four children to yellow fever before coming to Canada.

In either 1901 or early 1902 Srole and Bala Hodeh Jacobson also arrived in Saint John.

In 1902 Isaac Jacobson arrived in Saint John, where he subsequently married Jessie Goldberg, daughter of Israel and Esther. In the same year Sarah Jacobson arrived, and later married John Everett.

In 1903 Harry Jacob, son of Joshua Hessel Jacob, left Dorbyan for Saint John. In the same year Judal Jacob, the hawker, and his wife Malka arrived with their son Joseph Louis in Capetown. They had been married in Dorbyan two years earlier, giving birth to their son in the nearby port of Polangen.

Up to this point Hersh and Chana were largely unaffected by the exodus, although they had felt the loss of Israel and Esther Goldberg as well as that of several friends and distant relatives. The dismay of each departure had been bearable, but now the dismay turned to distress as a departure touched their immediate family.

Their eldest daughter Chaia had married another Dorbyaner, Leizer Bloom, in 1903 at the age of seventeen. Although Hersh and Chana had misgivings about her marrying at such a tender age, they were able to remember the ordeal of their own extended courtship, and they gave the new couple their blessing. One year later Chaia became pregnant, and in 1905 their first grandchild, Joseph was born. As it turned out they were to see very little of their new grandson, for Chaia and Leizer had decided to migrate.

Their destination was Harrisburg, Pennsylvania, where family members of Leizer were already established. As Hersh and Chana tearfully watched the departure of their eldest daughter, they knew the barrenness that had been felt by every family in Dorbyan, some many times over. They knew that they were gazing into the face of Chaia for the last time.

It was less than a year later when Hersh and Chana received

another, heavier , blow. Their third daughter, Esther had become friendly with Beir Dov (Barnet) Jacob, a son of Joel and Chia Bluma, distant cousins. Barnet's family already had members in Saint John, and were likewise related to Israel and Esther Goldberg, with uncle and aunt Morris and Sura Jacob also established, having been there almost as long. Barnet had decided that his future no longer remained in Dorbyan, and he had persuaded most of his family like-wise. Accompanying Barnet on this voyage would be his parents as well as other brothers and sisters.

Leah, Hersh and Chana's second daughter, decided to accompany them. She had the perfect excuse, for as Esther and Barnet had not yet married, convention made it desirable for her to go along as chap-erone to Esther.

This time Hersh and Chana and their remaining children had to farewell two family members at the same time. Not only were Chaia, Leah and Esther gone from them, but they were living away from home in different countries. As they looked into the faces of their remaining children they could not help but wonder which one would be the next to go.

The following year, 1906, Srole, Bella, Esther and Mira Goldberg, siblings of Israel Goldberg, left for Saint John.

In 1907 Shimon Zacharia Jacob, the glazier, who had returned from Palestine and remarried, to Elka Spitz, sailed to Saint John. With them they took their seven children, Jacob Sender from the earlier marriage, and Ethel, Lily, Hyman, Harry, Sam and Morris, born since Shimon Zacharia's return to Dorbyan.

In 1908 Jacob Morris Garson arrived in Saint John at the age of fifteen, having been sponsored by Leiba Zup Jacobson. Five years later he sent for his childhood sweetheart Mary from Dorbyan along with her family.

In 1909 Percy and Nathan Levine (Levi) also sailed to Saint John.

The following year, 1910, Motte Zelick and Fraida Goldberg ar-rived in Saint John. Accompanying them on the voyage were Motte's brother Shrolick Hershel and his children, Rose, Louis and Bertha (Breina).

In 1911 Harry Hains sailed from Hamburg to Quebec City, whence he continued to Saint John.

In 1912 Aron (Ork), Zelick, Ida and Rose Jacob sailed together to Saint John. Ork was later to marry Sara Cohen, daughter of Hersh and Chana's daughter Leah, who had arrived on the same boat as Esther and Barnet and subsequently married to Aaron Nathan Cohen, another Dorbyaner.

The abovementioned are but a very tiny sample of the Dorbyaners who chanced their lives to make a new start in North America and elsewhere in the early 1900's. The outflow was only stemmed by the outbreak of World war 1, which lasted from 1914 to 1918, after which the migrations resumed with an even greater urgency than before.

CHAPTER 3

Early in 1914, Hersh was surprised to receive a letter from his old friend David Wolffsohn. David had become famous throughout the entire international Jewish community for his work for the Zionist cause, and following the death of Theodore Herzl had succeeded him as the elected president of the World Zionist Organization. His office had taken him to such places as Russia, Hungary and Turkey to plead the case for a Jewish homeland. Hersh had not heard from his friend for several years and was amazed that he had found the time to write.

Hamburg

February, 1914

Dear Hersh!

How surprised you will be to hear from me after so many years, but the fact that I have not had time to write letters does not mean that I have not had the time to think about my past. The truth is that I have suddenly realized that it is now forty years since I left Dorbyan! I cannot explain it, but something deep inside me compels me to write.

It is strange that after all these years and the different paths our lives have taken, that I am still able to think of you as my best friend. I have visited the capitals of the world in pursuit of my dream, while you have never left Dorbyan. Yet despite the different ways we have gone, and the long separation, you will believe me, that when someone asks me who my oldest friend is, I can always answer without hesitation, 'Hersh Jacob, from Dorbyan'.

How wonderful it would be if I could return to visit you and other friends and *mishpoche* , to meet your lovely family, and to see the places where we grew up, the river where we used to skate and swim, the *shul platz* where we used to play, and the forest where we used to collect mushrooms. In a world that is changing unbelievably quickly, it is good to think that there are some places that do not change.

Perhaps I shall yet manage a trip to Dorbyan, but at the moment I see no chance of it. Ever since Theodore Herzl died, the burden falling on my shoulders has become greater than ever, and I suspect that this will be my lot for as long as I live. Even though some of it has been removed, it requires all of my energies. It is only my faith in God which has given me the strength to carry this burden

Although I have never had children, fate has caused me to become a father. Before Theodore died he nominated me as the guardian of his children, and since that time I have been doing my best and learning as I go along. I now realize that people with children have experienced life in a way that those who are childless cannot know. Perhaps it is you to whom I should be turning for advice when things do not happen as planned.

Now in recent years, my health has become poor, and prevents me from moving to Palestine and learning the Hebrew language. Whether I have little time left, or many years still, only God knows. I only know that every moment that I am able to give must be spent in pursuing the cause.

And yet I cannot deny my debt to Dorbyan, for my happy childhood, for my precious religious upbringing. Many times I resented that amongst Theodore's colleagues I was the only one without a university education. Yet as I look back upon him I am now able to realize my good fortune, for he and the others were denied a religious education, and whenever a religious matter arose, it was my advice that had to be sought. Because of my background I was able to be of assistance every time it was needed.

It is with a heavy heart that I have to tell you that the clouds of war are gathering over Europe. Perhaps where you are you do not feel it, but from inside Germany the signs are all too clear. What troubles me is that the Germans, whom I consider to be the most intelligent of people, seem to be the most eager for it. I cannot see it being avoided, and now I fear what the effect will be on our search for a homeland. Sometimes events can hasten the fulfillment of a dream; sometimes they can push it beyond reach. Although many of our people already live in Palestine, they still live in a land that is not theirs. I do not know what the outcome will be, but I continue to pray that the dream will be fulfilled. I no longer expect that I shall witness a Jewish homeland in my lifetime, but I am more than certain that our children will see it come to pass.

If you are able, please write to me without delay. Let me know what has happened with your family, and others that I know. Write to me about the little things in Dorbyan, and if they have changed; the river, the forest where we used to collect mushrooms, the shops, the *Shul Platz*, anything that you feel that I may be able to remember. Something within me has created this urge to hear about my birth-place.

I look forward to hearing from you soon.
As ever, your friend
Dodke

Hersh read the letter silently, then took it with him as he went to the rear of the house to feed and water his horses. When he did not return after a reasonable time, Chana went outside to look for him. She found him leaning on the enclosure fence, a bucket of water in one hand, the letter in the other. His eyes were filled with tears.

"Chana, this letter from Dodke Wolff, it is very sad. The more I read it, the more it tells me that he doesn't have very long to live.

"I have always hoped that somehow he might manage to come back to Dorbyan for a visit. Now I know that I shall never see him again."

In 1914 David Wolffsohn died, mourned in Europe, North America and Palestine. His prophecy of impending war in Europe proved all too accurate, and in August of that year the conflict began.

With the advent of modern weapons, the war was bloodier and more devastating than any other in history. Rumour was rife in Dorbyan. The Germans would certainly fight the Russians, in which case the district could well become a battleground. The Russians would have need of large numbers of conscripts. Anyone of military age was under threat, including Hersh and Chana's three new sons-in-law.

Fortunately the issue was settled with a speed which took everyone by surprise. A short time after the outbreak of war, a major battle was fought at Tannenburg, southwards along the Prussian-Lithuanian border. Here the German General Hindenburg crushed the main Russian army, to the extent that within five days Lithuania was cleared of all Russian influence. Dorbyan had emerged unscathed throughout the episode, although a few minor skirmishes took place in nearby Krettingen.

As the German columns entered the district in triumph, both Jews and Lithuanians rejoiced. The Russian yoke which had strangled the country since 1795 was broken. For the Jews it would mean the beginning of a new prosperity, such as had always been enjoyed by the Jews in Germany proper. If the successes of the Jews in Memel could be taken as a measure, there would now be little need for Jews to migrate in search of a better life.

DORBYAN
PART 4

CHAPTER 1

It was a damp, cloudy day in the spring of 1918. The thaw had begun, turning most of the earthen roads in the surrounding countryside into a quagmire. It was a time of reduced business activity as the condition of the roads made the peddling of merchandise to the peasant farmers of the district an impossibility. Trade with Krettingen or Memel could only to be carried out via the railroad, where trains stopped at the station just outside of town several times a day.

It was mid-afternoon and Hersh had finished his chores for the moment. He stood on the stairway at the front of the house staring at the deserted street, muddy and laced with potholes and wheel ruts. Looking along the Krettinger Gass towards the town centre he could see the tall steeple of the church above the trees which obscured his view of the rest of the town. At the beginning of the street at the junction of the Polanger Gass he could see the large concrete house of Elberg the chemist, the only non-wooden home in the town.

He now had an hour to spare before he and his son Joseph would meet in the *Shul platz* before entering the synagogue for *Mincha* and *Ma'ariv* prayers. Then he and Joseph would arrive home after dark, feed and water the horses for the last time, take their evening meal, and retire for the night.

In the distance he could see a small figure making its way from the centre of town and entering the Krettinger Gass. It slowly came closer, making its way carefully between the water-filled potholes and ruts, and Hersh was able to recognize a well dressed young man who had recently become a familiar sight around his home.

"Aah, Elior! Good afternoon! Good to see you, although I think I can guess the reason for your visit! You will find Breina inside with her mother in the kitchen."

Elior and Breina had become Dorbyan's latest couple, and there could be no doubt that their relationship was serious. With six previous daughters all married off, Hersh and Chana had become expert at reading the signs, and visits from Elior were always greeted with knowing winks to each other.

Hersh and Chana made very little mention of it to Breina, knowing from experience that during a courtship phase a daughter could be less than reasonable when approached on the subject. Secretly they were overjoyed, for Elior was the son of one of Dorbyan's most respected businessmen, a textile manufacturer whose operation, unlike most others, enabled him to employ workers outside his own family.

Elior thus had become one of the town's most eligible bachelors, well-mannered and well taught in religious matters, and Hersh and Chana were flattered that it was their daughter who had attracted his attentions.

"Good afternoon, sir. Yes, of course it is Breina that I want to see, but before I do, is it possible to have a word with you and Mrs Jacob at the same time?"

Hersh took Elior inside and showed him to a chair, then went off to fetch Chana. He had a good idea what was to follow, and he gave her a double wink, which had been their signal for something extra special. After all, this same ritual had been experienced on four previous occasions. As Chana left the kitchen, Breina smiled knowingly, for she too knew what was coming.

"Well,.....", Elior started off hesitantly, "....Mr...Mrs Jacob, your daughter Breina knows what I am about to say,.........We have talked about this many times.....and we are in agreement...."

Then he blurted out, "...There is no need to delay! We are unable to wait any longer! I wish to ask you for Breina's hand in marriage!"

He looked earnestly at Hersh and Chana.

"We love each other!.....We cannot live without each other!"

Hersh replied, Chana nodding in agreement with every word he said.

"Elior, there is no need for you to feel so uncomfortable. This should be a moment to treasure. We are not blind. We both have been expecting this moment, and if anything have been impatient for it to arrive. We too have talked this over, and the two of you have our blessing, for you will be the type of husband that every parent wishes for a daughter.

"We are overjoyed that you two have chosen each other, and that your family and ours will become *mishpoche*."

Elior smiled, then sighed in relief. He had been expecting this answer, but the thought of failure had been in his mind nonetheless. Despite the chill weather his forehead had broken out in perspiration.

"Thank you,...both of you. I promise that I will be the best husband possible for Breina, and I shall devote my life to bringing her happiness. I am the luckiest of men, for she is the most beautiful girl in the world."

Hersh thought back to the days when he had courted Chana, some forty-three years earlier. He looked into Chana's eyes, which despite the ageing of the rest of her body, still glistened. Of all his daughters, Breina most resembled Chana in her youth. Breina was taller, but unlike her other sisters, she had the blond hair and grey eyes of her mother.

"Wait a moment, Elior, and I shall fetch Breina, for this is a moment we should all share together."

As Breina entered the room, the look on Elior's face told her all that she needed to know. They embraced immediately, then stood hand in hand as Hersh questioned Elior.

"Does your family know of this?"

Elior looked at Breina, then they both blushed.

"Yes sir, we have mentioned it together to my father and my mother. They know you well, and were certain what your answer would be, but agreed not to speak to you until after you gave your final decision. They are happy for us."

"I see," grinned Hersh. "So, Chana and I have been the last to be told. Well, I suppose that's the way it must be with parents of a daughter....

"...The last to be told perhaps, but not the last to know,... for there have been signs, which the two of you do not hide so well. We have been waiting for this to happen, and hiding our impatience with difficulty."

He turned to Elior.

"And now we can let the women get back to the kitchen, so we can talk a little.

I'm sure they also have things to say to each other that are not for our ears."

He brought out a bottle of schnapps, which the ladies declined before leaving. Then he filled two small glasses, handing one to Elior.

"*L'Chayim!*," he said.

"*L'Chayim!*," answered Elior, and they raised their glasses .

"There is much to think about in the way of your plans," said Hersh, "And I would like to get to know you better."

Elior waited for the barrage of questions which he knew would follow.

"Elior, am I safe in assuming that you have no plans to leave Dorbyan?"

Elior nodded.

"You see, the greatest fear that Chana and I have is that someday you will decide to take our daughter to Canada or some other place. I suppose this is the greatest fear of any parent. Although we are fortunate to have most of our family still with us, the three daughters we have lost are three too many, and the pain it has caused us cannot be measured. We would like to think that we will have Breina near us for the rest of our days."

"I think I can ease your mind on this question, sir", replied Elior. "Nobody can predict the future, but I think we are as sure of remaining in Dorbyan as anybody. Our family is well established here, and comfortable. We would not improve our lot by moving to any place I can think of. I only want to give Breina the best of everything, and I know of no better place to do it than Dorbyan."

"Good," said Hersh. "I am happy to hear this. I believe that your position is as secure as anyone's can be, and will probably become safer when this war is over and we become a part of Germany. Then there will be better times, and we should all prosper."

162

Elior grimaced. "I am not so sure of this," he answered.

"What!", exclaimed Hersh.

"I only know what I have learned from my father, who follows these events very closely. I know that he is not so confident about what the future holds for us. He mentions it often."

"How can this be, Elior? I thought that with the Germans here, things could only improve. After all, look at the difference in the way we live and the way that the Jews of Memel are living."

"Papa's concern is that the Germans will lose the war, and that we may not have them around for much longer."

"What! Germany lose the war!" Hersh looked at Elior in shock.

"How could this happen, Elior? The Russians could never come back and drive the Germans out of Lithuania. Their country is a shambles, and they are in the midst of a revolution."

"It is not the Russians that the Germans need to fear," said Elior.

"But even in the west," argued Hersh, "The French and the English are not defeating them. Sooner or later the Germans, the French and the English will decide that they have had enough of this war, and that nobody can win. Then they will come to an arrangement, the map will be redrawn, and Lithuania will almost certainly become a part of Germany."

"Papa is becoming more and more certain that Germany cannot win," replied Elior. "The English have their whole empire behind them, and can carry on the war for longer. The Americans are now taking the side of the English. This is no longer just a European war. Sooner or later the tide must change against the Germans."

Hersh's jaw dropped. He had just been told something which heretofore had not even entered his mind. The mere suggestion of a German defeat had been unthinkable.

"I can only hope that your father is wrong, Elior, but even if he is correct, we won't have to worry about the Russians again."

"No, but it won't be the Germans either."

"Then who?", asked Hersh, then answering his own question. "If the French or the English wish to administer this country, then this is also fine by me. Believe me. they will be an improvement on anything we have known from the Russians.".

"Papa doesn't think it will turn out as well as this," said Elior. "He cannot imagine the allies having much interest in such a poor and distant land. He believes that an independent Lithuania is the most likely result."

"Well," replied Hersh. "Would this be such a bad thing either? After all, the Lithuanians have been waiting to have their own country for a long time. Like ourselves, they have not had an easy time of it under the Russians."

"Yes, in many ways they have had a harder time than we have," agreed Elior, "And Papa has sympathy for them. In some ways we Jews have been lucky, as we only wanted to practise our religion, whereas the Lithuanians had ambitions of having their own country. The Russians saw them as the greater threat, and suppressed their language and customs even more than they did ours."

"Therefore it can only be a good thing for the Lithuanians to regain their independence," argued Hersh.

"A good thing for the Lithuanians, but not for us," answered Elior. "Papa says that when independence comes, our lot will become more difficult."

"How can this be?," asked Hersh.

"As I understand it," said Elior, when Lithuania becomes independent, they will look after their own people. We Jews have always had an advantage in trading because the Lithuanians have never been schooled. Once they start to receive an education, they will no longer be our customers, but rather they will become our competitors."

"I do not see this as a good reason to deny people an education," said Hersh, "Besides, Jews have always been able to meet any competition in trade, no matter where they have lived."

"You must speak to Papa someday about this, for he feels very different than you. He says that once the Lithuanians are in charge, they will become like any other nation which has gained independence, and they will favour their own. They will make certain that their laws give advantage to Lithuanians. This is only natural. If we should one day have our own nation in Palestine, I am certain that the laws we make will be arranged to give Jews an advantage over *goyim*."

Hersh was thoughtful.

"You have certainly given me many things to think about that I hadn't considered," he said. "What you say doesn't sound too hopeful, but this is the very worst that could happen. I respect your father's opinion, but Germany hasn't lost the war yet, and at the moment doesn't look like losing it. Even if she does, who is to say that an agreement will not be reached? At the moment I prefer not to burden myself with what may or may not happen. I would much rather think of the happy event that will happen between you and Breina."

Hersh rose from his chair, pulling his watch from his pocket.

It is time for me to meet Joseph at *shul* to *daven Mincha* and *Ma'ariv*. We will all go together, for after we have finished we can have a word or two with the Rabbi."

"Joseph will be happily surprised to hear the good news," said Hersh.

Then he looked at Elior sternly.

"I don't suppose that Joseph already knows about this."

Elior blushed.

CHAPTER 2

The wedding day of Breina and Elior in the summer of 1919 was a day of joy, or *nachas*, as the inhabitants of Dorbyan would say. It was particularly a time to be remembered, for weddings were becoming a rarer and rarer occasion, as more and more families left the town taking their children with them. Gone were the days when a wedding in the *Shul platz* was a joyful monthly occasion.

For Hersh and Chana, it would be their last chance to celebrate such a *simche*, as they had now run out of daughters to marry. Joseph remained unwed, but when his time came it would be the responsibility of the family of his bride. Any future festivities would have to be for a different reason, such as the birth of a grandchild.

Prior to the wedding day, Breina had been prepared for matrimony by Chana and her aunt Mere Gita, according to the orthodox traditions which had prevailed in the community thoughout its history. Amongst the rituals was the close cropping of Breina's blonde hair, which would be replaced by a wig.

On Friday morning, the wedding day, the relatives began to arrive in the house on the Krettinger Gass, spilling out into the street at the front and into the yard at the rear. In effect these relatives included almost every Jewish person in Dorbyan, and many others from further afield. There was no Dorbyaner who did not make an appearance.

The house was noisy, and the sounds of music could be heard halfway to the centre of town. Only the bride and groom abstained from the feasting, for tradititon dictated that they fast the entire day leading up to the wedding.

In mid-afternoon the party left the home of Hersh, and in noisy mood, escorted the bride and groom along the Krettinger Gass, over the bridge and along the market street to the *Shul platz*. .

The Rabbi and the Cantor were already there, standing under a canopy in the square, which in turn was surrounded by a sizeable crowd. The crowd parted for the *Unterfirers*, the parents of the bride and groom, who led their children to the canopy. The ceremony itself consisted of an hour of vows and benedictions, at the end of which a glass was broken underfoot to symbolize the destruction of Jerusalem. The crowd then dispersed, and the newlyweds proceeded to the home of the bride.

With the arrival of the Sabbath, the festivities ceased, but as darkness came on Saturday evening, they were resumed. The dancing, singing and feasting continued at Hersh and Chana's home throughout the night and for the entire following day. It was not until late on Sunday night that the party began to break up, as sheer physical exhaustion began to overcome the desire for further merriment.

The wedding of Breina and Elior would be remembered by the townspeople for many years as the last of the old-time weddings. Recent weddings had of necessity become smaller, as the size of the community had shrunk. What were intended to be joyful occasions had often been tinged with a touch of sadness because of the absence of family members, but this had been the exception. Because of the widespread connections of Elior's family, the numbers had been swollen by guests from many points distant. The Sabbath services following the wedding had seen the synagogue crowded in a way it had not been for almost twenty years.

Hersh and Chana could not contain their pride at the event and the complements that had come their way. The wedding would bring them happy memories for as long as they lived.

The young couple were now on their own, "until death do them part." There was little doubt that they, like every other couple who had married in the Dorbyan *Shul Platz*, would abide by their covenant, and love and honour each other for the rest of their lives.

CHAPTER 3

In May,1920, the letter Chana received from her daughter Esther in Saint John was longer than usual.

Main Street
Saint John
May 29, 1920

Dear Mama!

Chaia and Leah told me that they have written to you. Now it is my turn to tell you what is happening to us. As you will see, I have much to tell.

Our Sammy Shimmy is now twelve years old, and studying very hard for his *Bar-Mitzvah* . It is hard to believe. He is a very good boy and learns his lessons well, both at school and in *cheder*. We know that you would be proud of him if you could meet him.

Ever since Sammy was born we have been sad that we could not provide a younger brother or sister for him. Now at last we have happy news. Chaia and Leah promised not to mention it to you so I could have the joy of telling you myself.

Two months ago a Hersh Hershmann from Poland landed in Saint John. He was sent to Canada by one of the Polish Jewish welfare organizations, and with him he brought a group of Jewish children aged between five and nine who were orphaned during the Great War. Mr Hershmann was here to find families to adopt the children, and Saint John was his first landing place.

For Barnet and me, and for Sammy too, it was a dream coming true, for there have been many times that Sammy asked why he had no brother or sister, and how is one to answer a question like this?

We agreed to adopt one of the children, but listen to this! When we arrived to accept the child allotted to us, Sammy's eyes fell on another child, the youngest and smallest, a girl. Such a fuss I have never seen! He cried and screamed the way he used to when he was

168

a three year old! In the end everyone agreed that we should adopt this girl, and so we now have Celia (Tsipporeh Malka) as our child. It is our hope that the love we give her will erase from her mind some of the horror that she has suffered.

Other things have happened to us. Barnet has opened a store on Main Street, and we now live upstairs from it. The store is doing well, and we are prospering. Although he did well at peddling in the Annapolis Valley in Nova Scotia, he agrees that the time has come to settle down. When his father Joel died last year, it made up his mind, for he had no one to accompany him on his journeys.

Here in Saint John, Sammy can have Jewish friends and the best possible Jewish education.

Chaia and Leah have probably told you about their lives. For Chaia it is a struggle. Leizer peddles, and does reasonably well, but they have a large family, and it is not possible to live as simply in Saint John as in Dorbyan. But they raise their children well, and all of them have a good Jewish education.

Their family has certainly grown. Their youngest son, Bernie, is already a year old, and the others have become *menschen* already!

Leah's husband, Aaron Nathan Cohen, also has a store, and he makes a reasonable living. I'm sure that Leah told you in her last letter about the birth of their fourth child, Leibe, just two weeks ago. Such a beautiful baby! You would love her, Mama!

I have asked you this before, and Barnet makes me ask again everytime I write. Do you ever think of coming to Canada yourselves? It is something you should do. You will be well taken care of here, with three families looking after you, and Barnet has promised that you will want for nothing. He says he can easily make the immigration arrangements, and will send you the tickets just as soon as you wish.

We Dorbyaners stick together and meet in friends' homes at every opportunity. When we are together there is one thing we always talk about,- other Dorbyaners! We speak in Yiddish except when the children are around, for we want them to speak good English, which will help them in this country. Celia, of course, speaks Yiddish, but a little different from the way we speak. Sammy speaks and understands it well, although he prefers English. He would certainly have no problem in speaking to you, Mama.

Chaia's three oldest children. Joe, Mary and Rose, speak very good Yiddish, and also Leah's son, Bennie. You would find it very easy to speak to all your grandchildren.

You would also not feel out of place in our home. We still eat the same food we ate in Dorbyan. We have our omelettes, coffee and rye bread for breakfast; for dinner it is meat, chicken or fish, and our own home made salami or smoked meat, while for supper it is usually smoked herring with rye bread, schmaltz and a salad. So you see, nothing has changed, not even the big pot of borsht that I make every *Pesach* and give to the others, just as I remember you doing. Are you still making the borsht, Mama?

If there is any difference between the food here and in Dorbyan, it is that we believe that the vegetables are better here, even though yours are home grown. Maybe it is the soil, or maybe it is the climate, for although the winters here are about the same as in Dorbyan, our summers are hotter.

Even the *shul* here is a copy of the Dorbyan *shul*, although it is not as big. The men sit on the ground floor, while the women sit on a balcony at the rear. Barnet says that most of the *shuls* in eastern Canada are built this way, wherever there are Dorbyaners to be found.

Barnet also says that Saint John now has almost as many Dorbyaners as there are remaining in Dorbyan. He says that if we count the Dorbyaners in Saint John, Halifax, Moncton and Glace Bay, there will be many more Dorbyaners here than where you are.

There is only one thing that you would find strange, and that is that motorcars are beginning to become common on the streets, with many people preferring them to horses. Barnet has been thinking of buying one, but he has not yet made up his mind. I hope he never gets one, for they frighten me, but once Barnet gets an idea in his head....

There is another thing about Saint John which is hard to describe to you, and which you will find hard to believe. I have never mentioned it before, but I promise you that it is true. Saint John has its harbour in the middle of a bay called the Bay of Fundy, which is very long and narrow. Because of this, we have here the highest tides in the world, sometimes as much as fifty feet! Not at all like we know at Polangen! The high tides cause another wonder that cannot be found anywhere else in the world, a waterfall that falls in both directions at the mouth of the Saint John River. Yes, what I am telling you is true, the waterfall falls in two directions!

When the tide is low the water from the river flows into the sea over a waterfall, but when the tide rises the sea is higher than the river and the falls flow in the other direction. It is called the Reversing Falls, and it is a beautiful sight, and for a short time twice each day there is no waterfall and the water is as calm as the *Prud* of Dorbyan.

Because salmon are usually found at the mouths of rivers, our Saint John Harbour has the biggest and best salmon in the world, and we eat it often. Your grandson Sammy Shimmy loves it fresh, but the rest of us prefer it smoked.

One reason Barnet wants the motorcar is that there is a beautiful spot twelve miles from Saint John along the river where the Jews are beginning to go in the summer. It is called Pamdenac, and when we go there the children can play in the river, while the adults can sit and talk about old times. Sometimes the men catch pickerel from the river, which is wonderful for making *gefilte fish*. Some people are even thinking about building small cottages there so they can move there for the summer months.

And so, Mama, goodbye for now. Once again, try to think about coming to Canada, even though I know it will be hard to convince Papa of it. Canada is a wonderful country, and I know you would be very happy here. I would also invite my sisters to come here, but I do not wish to be the one to take them away from you. I believe Joseph has been talking about leaving Dorbyan too. Tell him that if he makes the decision, he will have all the help he needs from us.

In the meantime I am enclosing a little something for you. Buy something for yourself or Papa, or use it to give something to the *Kinder* . Whatever you do with it, I hope it brings you pleasure.

And now I have left a little space for Sammy to say something to you. He is very anxious to show that he can write in Yiddish.

Your Daughter,
Esther

Hello, Bobe;-

I can now write in Yiddish. I have been learning it in *cheder*, and sometimes Papa and Mama speak to me in it. Next year I will be *Bar-Mitzvah* , and I am already going to the Rabbi's house to study. Maybe you and Zeide could come to visit me when it happens. It will be in August, 1921.

Give Zeide a kiss for me.

Your Grandson
Samuel Simon

CHAPTER 4

In 1920 the inevitable happened. Joseph Jacob, only son of Hersh and Chana, decided to migrate. There was no work for him in Dorbyan, and his sole activities had been in helping his father with the horses and in attending the synagogue as often as possible. The days were past when Memel could offer employment, and reluctantly he came to the conclusion that there was no future for him in Dorbyan. He wrote to his relatives in Canada, and the replies were encouraging. He would leave Dorbyan as soon an suitable arrangements could be made.

As the time approached for Joseph's departure, Hersh began to feel very gloomy, knowing that before long all he would have left of Joseph would be memories. The thought of it played on his mind, giving him no rest. Chana knew what he was experiencing, and did her best not to mention the subject, but eventually could prevent herself from speaking about it no longer.

"I know what you are feeling, Hersh, for I too am feeling the same thing."

"I am sorry," said Hersh, "To be behaving like this, but I cannot help it. I cannot be very good company for you and the others."

Chana said, "I have had a thought. It will be a small consolation, but at times I wish we had done it long ago, before the others left."

"And what is that, Chanele?"

"Why don't we have some family photographs made, of all of us, before Joseph leaves, so at least we can remember our family as it is now? It is now ten years since the last time we did it."

Hersh thought for a moment, and then smiled for the first time in several days.

"What a wonderful idea, Chanela! You're right, we should have done it while Chaia, Leah and Esther were here, and we should do it while Joseph is still with us, and before anyone else decides to leave.

"I know exactly what we'll do! There is a bit of money saved up.

This won't be cheap, but it will be for a lifetime, and it will be worth it! I shall speak to Govsa Yankel Kveril and tell him we want to have a full family sitting!

The following day Hersh paid a visit to the house of Govsa Yankel Kveril, one of the few Jewish homes on the church side of the market place. Dorbyan had two photographers. *Foto Bruchus* had been operated by members of the Bloch family for more than a generation. The Blochs were *mishpoche* of Hersh, as was almost every other Jewish family in Dorbyan, but the relationship with Govsa Yankel Kveril was closer.

Chana's sister, Mere Gite, had married Mordechai Kveril, and had had four children. Hoshe, the eldest, had married Basha, and had worked with his father in the sawmill on the outskirts of town. After the death of his father he had taken over the operation on his own.

Sam had recently migrated to the United States and had found work in a motorcar factory in Detroit.

Chana had married Rachmiel Attis from a family of Dorbyan butchers, and Govsa Yankel, the youngest, had spent a year in Memel learning the photography trade. There he had acquired a German made Voigtlander studio camera which he proudly boasted was of the latest design. With his acquisition and other paraphernalia he had recently returned to Dorbyan and set himself up in the photography trade, calling himself *Foto Zion*. As one of Chana's nephews, there could be no question that the business should be given to him.

Hersh's request to Govsa Yankel was detailed, and entailed a major operation for the young photographer, and would be expensive despite the favourable terms that would be provided. Hersh wanted individual photos of each of his daughters, as well as a complete family portrait, which would show Chana, himself, his son Joseph, his four daughters, their husbands, his first and only Dorbyan grandchild, and Chana's mother, Shora Hinde, who, although in her late eighties, had insisted in taking part in the sitting. It would require the full skill of Govsa Yankel to compose such a menagerie into a pleasing and interesting family portrait.

"Are you certain that you want everybody in the same photo, Hersh? It would be much more presentable if it were broken into subject groups."

"I shall have this done also, Govsa, as I want the best, but I want at least one photograph of the entire family as it is now, before we suffer further losses. As you know, Joseph will be leaving for Canada shortly, and who knows who may follow him?

"Yes, I understand," answered Govsa Yankel Kveril. "We have already seen Sam leave for America, and we now worry that Rachmiel Attis may also leave, and take Chana and the children with him."

"Yes," said Hersh. "This is why we feel that it is so important, and why we are sorry that we didn't do it years ago before our three daughters left."

"Right then, Hersh. It shall be done. I shall think about the composition of the family photo. It will be more difficult than the others. A single person can remain still for a sitting while the picture is being made, but to expect everyone in a large family to remain motionless at the same time is impossible. Unless the light is exceptionally bright on the day the photographs will have to be made using the light of magnesium flash powder."

What is magnesium flash powder?", asked Hersh.

"It is a powder that we ignite to make a flash of light while the camera lens is open. Because it produces so much extra light it is not necessary to keep the lens open for so long, and so there is less chance of movement from the subjects."

"Then why not use the powder for all photographs?", asked Hersh.

"There are reasons," answered Govsa Yankel Kveril. "The powder is not cheap, and adds to the cost of the work. The flash can also create shadows on the photograph, which are not always pleasing. In addition there is a certain danger to using it."

"If there is a danger, then maybe we shouldn't be using it at all," said Hersh.

"If the powder is not misused, there is no danger of injury to anyone, Hersh, but it is messy, and can sometimes soil clothing. When the powder ignites there is usually a small explosion, or rather, a pop, which spreads the unburnt powder all about the room. It can land inside the lens and ruin the pictures, and it can soil the clothing for the next photographs."

"But," he added, "This should not happen, and to date I have been able to avoid all but the tiniest amounts of powder being thrown into the air."

"I see," said Hersh. "I suppose you know these problems better than I do. I will leave it to you to do what you consider is best."

There is another problem, Hersh," said Govsa Yankel Kveril. "This will be for you to resolve. The sitting will take about two or three hours, and you will have the task of organizing your whole family to be here in my studio for that time. My own idea is that the best time is before *Sabbes* when everyone is already cleaned for the occasion, but it may be that there is too much to do in preparing for the Sabbath for the time to be spared. You will have to work this out between yourselves and let me know, and I shall arrange a sitting when you are available. If you do not wish to use your own *Sabbes* clothes, I have formal clothing here that I keep for the very purpose, although I doubt that I have enough for your entire family at the same time."

"When the time comes, I think we shall wear our own clothing," said Hersh.

Hersh left the photographer's home, knowing that he has been placed in a dilemma. There was no way that he could arrange for everyone in his extended family to be present at a sitting. The problem lay with his four sons-in-law, all of whose livlihoods involved their being away from Dorbyan for lengthy periods of time. Elior, Breina's husband was presently away on a business trip, and would be gone for at least a further two weeks. His increasing involvement in his father's textile business had made him the driving force, with his father now mainly managing the financial matters. His task was to locate and secure the supplies of raw materials to be made into yarns and then into cloth, then to visit customers, mainly tailors in towns as far afield as Memel, Plugyon and Libau, to show samples of his latest wares. Often he would make deliveries of finished cloth at the same time as he accepted forward orders. It was common for him to be away for two or three weeks, returning to Dorbyan before the Sabbath only to leave again after but a two or three day stay with his family.

The others, Michel, David and Hatzah, the husbands of Ada, Mina and Rachel, were all in the peddling trade, and had found themselves likewise going further and further afield for longer periods of time to compensate for the declining economic activity in the town itself. Trips away from home of two weeks were commonplace.

He could not wait for the return of Elior, as there was just enough time to complete the operation and have the photographs finished before Joseph's departure. In addition David was about to leave on a trip in the next few days. There was no way to arrange the sitting before he left. Elior and David would have to be missing from the photograph.

The day came for the sitting, and eleven members of the Jacob family, wearing their finest attire, converged on the home of Govsa Yankel Kveril. It was a sunny day and as they approached their destination townspeople waved to them knowingly, for to wear such finery on a midweek day could only mean one thing.

Govsa Yankel Kveril's studio was a converted shed at the rear of the building. One wall, the only one without a window, was unfinished in brown timber beams. A black curtain was bunched up in one corner which could be extended to cover the wall. The walls on either side of it were equipped with black curtains which could be drawn over the windows. A portion of the ceiling had been cut away and was now fitted with a window in order to allow overhead lighting, which was deemed to be closest to natural sunlight and therefore the best.

Facing the plain wall was the Voigtlander studio camera, a large, heavy box-like affair with a large lens protruding from the front. It sat on a massive wooden tripod. At the rear was a large black cloth shroud, sufficiently large to cover the head and shoulders of the photographer. One by one the subjects entered the room, pausing to admire the instrument with interested yet puzzled expressions.

Govsa Yankel Kveril gave a brief explanation of his camera and how it worked.

"You will be facing the lens which will be at sufficient distance to include all of you in the photograph. When the lens is open it allows light to enter the camera through the lens which falls on a screen at the back. If anyone is interested, you may place your head inside the shroud and see what I mean, as the lens is now open."

A few of the family members placed their head in the shroud and saw the scene as seen by the camera through its lens.

"The picture is upside down, Govsa."

"Why so it is, what a surprise!"

He smiled. "But I have a way of correcting this! When the picture is finished and comes out upside down, I will simply turn it around so it is right side up. That way we don't all have to stand on our heads to look at it."

There was laughter. Govsa Yankel Kveril had obviously told this joke before.

"First we will do the family photograph. That way after it is finished if anyone needs to leave sooner than the others we can do his or her picture first. Now first I want you all to look at the birdie."

He pointed to an elaborate model of a yellow bird, possibly a canary, which he held directly above the camera.

"When I say, 'Watch the Birdie' I want you all to smile and to become very still.

You will have to remain that way for maybe a half a minute. At that moment I am going to open the lens, so any movement will spoil the photograph. I will then ignite the flash powder, and after the flash I will close the lens. Then I will tell you that it is alright for you to relax."

He then arranged his subjects in the order he had decided upon earlier. Seated at front were Hersh and Chana, with Chana's mother Shora Hinde between them. Standing in the rear were the five children two of them with their spouses, one couple also displaying their latest addition to the family. When he was satisfied with the composition he went to the back of the camera.

Govsa Yankel Kveril then buried his face in the shroud, emerging a few times to motion to one or other of the subjects to change their stance, before finally deciding that the arrangement was to his satisfaction. He closed the lens, removed the back from the camera, and replaced it with a photographic plate.

"Watch the birdie!," he instructed.

As one the subjects smiled and stared at the yellow bird, remaining motionless.

A few seconds later there was a blinding flash of light accompanied by a small pop and a bit of dust given off. There was slight movement from the subjects, but it did not matter. Govsa Yankel Kveril had closed the lens.

"Now I will make one more of the same picture, just to be certain, and then we can begin the individual photographs. But this time we are going to do it without the flash, for I believe there is enough light in this room."

About an hour later the session was finished, and everyone went home to carry on with their day's work. Hersh remained behind to discuss the remaining details with Govsa Yankel Kveril. The photographs would require between one and two days for development in his own darkroom, after which proofs would be made for his examination. When the proofs were accepted and the photographs produced, several copies would be made, enough for everyone of his Dorbyan family to have one and his Saint John *mishpoche* as well. Hersh was relieved. They would be finished quicker than expected, and in time for Joseph to take them with him to Canada.

One week later Hersh collected the finished photographs and was completely satisfied with the result. The entire family appeared smiling and happy. The photos were on non gloss paper as recommended by the photographer. The faces were all clear and recognizable, unlike others he had seen elsewhere. It was with great respect for Govsa Yankel Kveril's craftsmanship that he willingly parted with what was the equivalent of half a week's earnings. He had received value for money, and his nephew had certainly learned his trade well in Memel.

CHAPTER 5

Chana received Esther's letter some five weeks after it was written, and immediately began to write her reply.

Dorbyan
July 19, 1920

My Dear Daughter Esther!

Thank you for your wonderful letter and your gift. As you might have guessed, I spent it on candy and gifts for your nieces and nephews. I told them where it came from, and they were all grateful and send their thanks.

There are many things to tell you, as so much has happened here of late, Ada and Rocha have both given birth again, to boys, but I will leave it to them to tell you the happy news.

First of all, your brother Joseph has now made his final arrangements to leave Dorbyan, and he will be going very shortly. He told me that he had been in touch with you, and that you were helping him, but we did not expect this to happen so quickly. He will be on the S S Polangen, the same ship that many others sailed on before the war, and he will be arriving in Saint John in October. Please keep watch for this ship when it lands, for your brother will be on it.

Needless to say, your father and I are distressed that this is happening, and I fear that it will break Papa's heart. He hides his feelings well, and he realizes that it is God's will. There is nothing for Joseph to do here in Dorbyan except help his father with the horses. We had been hoping that he would meet a nice Dorbyan girl and find work to do, even in Krettingen or Memel, but it was not to be. Even though we are heartbroken, we know that for his sake, going to Canada will be the best thing for him.

Ever since Lithuania became independent, our lives have become more difficult. The Lithuanians are now going into business for themselves, and doing things that only Jews used to do, making it harder for Jews to make a living. Your Papa says that it is their right to do this, but they receive help from their government that we do not receive.

When Joseph arrives in Canada he will be able to tell you about this. He has tried in vain to find work anywhere, but none exists. Even in Memel, it is the same since Germany lost the war. The situation is the same everywhere in Lithuania, we are told, and everywhere Jews are suffering.

Now there is talk that Memel will be given to Lithuania as a punishment to the Germans for losing the war. At the moment there are French soldiers there, but they are expected to leave shortly.

As I said, sometimes Joseph helps his father with the horses, but even this is not a living anymore. We usually have two horses, sometimes only one, and that is all that is needed. I can remember a time when we had five, and your father was selling or trading one almost every week.

Now there is nothing for Joseph to do except go to *shul* and then spend most of the day in the *shul platz* sitting and talking with friends. This is no life for a twenty-four year old, and most of his friends are in the same situation. Many of them have plans to leave as well.

You ask why we ourselves do not move to Canada. I will tell you. Your father and I have talked about it, and no doubt after Joseph is gone we will talk about again. But half our family is in Dorbyan, so no matter where we are, we will still be away from half our family.

Your father loves his work of caring for horses, and believes he can keep on doing it for the rest of his life. Unless you have horses for him to tend, he would feel useless in a very short time.

As for me, the horses I could live without, but I would not be happy away from my grandchildren, even though I would leave if it was Papa's wish. I have watched them grow up since birth, and now there are the new arrivals, and more to come, for Breina is expecting her first child at the beginning of next year. I have grown so used to having children about the house every Saturday after *shul* that I do not think I could live without it.

There is other news! At last, after almost thirty years, we are no longer the only Jewish family living on the Krettinger Gass. Your aunt Mere Gita, now lives further along the street, less than ten minutes' walk from us. Now we are able to visit each other as often as we wish. Ever since your uncle Mordechai passed away, she had remained in the same house with her children. Now that your cousin Hoshe has married to Bashe and has children of his own, he has built his own home on our street.

It is the newest and most up-to-date house in Dorbyan, and larger than ours. This is not surprising, for Hoshe has been running the lumbermill ever since his father died. It was a very sad thing when Mordechai Kveril died, for he was still so young, and he left your aunt Mere Gita with a growing family. But, thanks to God, everything has turned out well for her, and now her lovely children are all grown, and we are able to be closer than ever.

The migrations from Dorbyan are starting again. The war put a stop to it for a time, and for awhile we thought they might stop if this country became prosperous. Now it seems that more people than ever before are planning to leave, and more and more are starting to go to South Africa, where it is said that the life is good.

Also, more are going to Palestine, and there are Zionist organizations which help them, and train them in agricultural work before they leave. No doubt you are aware that David Wolffsohn came from Dorbyan, where he was known as Dodke Wolff. What you probably didn't know is that your Papa and David were good friends in their childhood days before David left Dorbyan.

Your cousin, Sam Kveril left not very long ago, and Mere Gita tells me that he lives in a city called Detroit, in America, where he works in a motorcar factory. Is Detroit very far from you?

Motorcars are something that we do not have in Dorbyan yet, although I am told that they can be seen in Memel, and on occasion in Krettingen, where the baron Tytschcovitch owns one. As for me, it is not important if they come here or not. I think your Papa's horse business will be safe in Dorbyan for a long time to come.

Your sisters are well, and their husbands are secure in their businesses. I do not think they will be leaving, even though it is harder to make a living. Breina's husband Elior tells us that their business is not what it used to be, but I cannot see that they are suffering. Dorbyan is still a good place to live. I remember that during the war, when you worried so much about us, and when much of the country was hungry, we used to say in Dorbyan that we ate better than either the Germans or the English.

Every home has a vegetable garden, and some of us have chickens and cows. Most of us produce more than we need, and we share it, so there is no need for a Jew to go hungry.

Dorbyan has been lucky. Even when the Russians deported so many Jews to their slave camps at the beginning of the war, Dorbyan was spared. We have been blessed with a good life here. If only there was enough work to do, then our young people would not find it necessary to leave.

This is all the news for now. Give our regards to regards to Chaia and Leah, and tell your Sammy that I gave his grandfather a kiss just as he asked. I quietly approached him as he was standing on the front steps, and then suddenly kissed him. He was surprised, and when he asked me why, I asked him in return, "Am I not allowed to give my husband a kiss?" Then I showed him your letter and the part that Sammy wrote.

You know, your father is sometimes jealous that the letters from you, Chaia and Leah are always addressed to me. Perhaps when Joseph is living with you, your father will start receiving letters addressed to himself.

Goodbye for now, and health to you and your family.

Your Mother

P.S. Your father says to give Sammy a kiss from him.

CHAPTER 6

In the year 1926 Hersh celebrated his seventieth birthday. The occasion was celebrated as part of the usual Saturday afternoon gathering of the family at the house on the Krittinger Gass. The four daughters, Rocha, Ada, Mina and Breina were all in their thirties, all married and all had children. Chana's sister Mere Gita came as usual, bringing with her several of her grandchildren by her sons Hoshe and Jankel Govsha.

After the main meal, which was as usual a bean dish called *Bab*, the children cavorted merrily about the street in front, and around the side and back of the house, returning inside from time to time to fetch one of the sweets. The adults sat and stood around the front steps while the children could be counted on to make their way to the back where Hersh's two horses were kept.

For the occasion Hersh had produced a bottle of schnapps, and was happily circulating among his guests filling up small glasses.

"Not only is this a happy occasion because it is my birthday," he beamed, "But it is the time of another happy event. I have received a letter from our Joseph and I have been saving it until now to read to you. There is also news that will please the Kveril side of our family, although I expect that by now you will already have heard it from Sam."

Pontiac
Michigan, USA
June, 1926

Dear Papa!

I am writing this letter to wish you well on your seventieth birthday. May you have *Nachas* on this day and on many more birthdays to come.

I also have wonderful news to tell which I hope will make your day even happier.

As I have told you and Mama, it was Sam Kveril who first convinced me that I should leave Saint John and come to Detroit. He and his wife Ruthie have been wonderful to me, and because of them the sorrow of having to leave my sisters in Saint John has been easier to bear. As I mentioned, life for me in Saint John wasn't very good. Business there is down, and it is hard to make a living. I peddled with Leizer for a time, but I never seemed to do well, and I believe that I was becoming a burden to him, as his business wasn't big enough to employ me. Barnet also offered to employ me, but even though he could afford it, I could see that I wasn't really needed. Thus it was that when Sam Kveril told me that things were better in Detroit, I decided to try it out.

Sam's wife Ruthie is also a Jacobson, also from Saint John and Dorbyan, and you will know her parents of course, who are Nathan and Rose Selick Jacob. For my part, I believe that I bring them happiness that they now have another Dorbyaner nearby. I cannot describe how much they have done for me, and I spend almost as much time in their home as in my own.

It was Sam who arranged for me to become a painter, and for a time I did very well, earning much more money than I could at peddling in Saint John. Then the painting came to an end, but Sam was able to get me another job at a new motorcar plant in Pontiac, working "on the line."

The assembly line of a motorcar factory is an amazing thing, and I must tell you more about it sometime, if I can get you to believe me! Motorcars are becoming a big thing in America, and some are saying that the time will come when almost every family in the country will have one.

The new car I am making is called the 'Pontiac', and my job is very easy, simply tightening screws on parts of the car as they pass by on a moving belt. Sometimes it is monotonous, for I may tighten one thousand screws in a day, but I am well paid, and it makes me proud to see a finished Pontiac driving along the road, and I know that the day will come when I will be driving one myself. I could not imagine myself doing this job for the rest of my life, but in a few years' time I believe I shall have enough saved to begin a business of my own. This part of America is growing very quickly, and there are many possibilities to do well.

Now I come to the exciting and happy part of my story. In order to work on the assembly line I needed a new outfit of work clothes. I found a store nearby which carried them, but the complete outfit was too much for me to buy at one time. Each payday I went to the store and bought one more item until finally, after several weeks, my outfit was complete. The shopkeeper and I became friendly, and he found it hard to believe that your blonde, fair-skinned, grey-eyed son could be Jewish. He began to invite me home for dinners on *Sabbes* , and on each occasion his wife's younger sister was there. Their names are Saul and Sara Mones, and the sister is Rebecca, whom everybody calls Rae.

As maybe you are guessing by now, I have become very friendly with Rae.

Rae's family name is Remocker, and it is named after a small village in Poland where her grandparents were born. She herself was born in Leeds, England, but grew up in Glasgow, Scotland, in an area known as The Gorbals, where most of the *Yidden* live. She and her sister left Glasgow for the same reason that I left Dorbyan, no opportunity. She and her whole family are very religious Jews.

It took very little time for us to realize that we were meant for each other. Saul and Sara are overjoyed at the part they played in bringing us together, and they have asked if they may be the ones to give us away at the wedding, that is, unless you and Mama come for the occasion.

But we are not quite ready to marry. We have planned that if we are able to work separately for perhaps another year, we will be in a very good position to begin a business and start a family. We are very happy whenever we are together, which is just as often as we can manage, and the thought of waiting does not bother us. We only have to think of you and Mama, and the stories you have told of the time the two of you had to wait before your marriage.

Only one thing could make me happier than I am now, and that would be to hear from you that you will come to the wedding. There is some money, and I could send you tickets. When the time comes, we shall invite the whole *mishpoche* from Saint John, and of course Sam and Ruthie Kveril will be here, so there will be Dorbyaners at this wedding.

186

This is the news that I couldn't wait to tell you. I hope it makes a good birthday gift for you along with the other gift I am sending.

Regards to Mama, Rocha, Ada, Mina and Breina and the rest of the *mishpoche* and *mazel tov* to yourself.

Your Son.
Joseph

Hersh happily put the letter back in its envelope, taking care to fold it exactly on its creases. With a flourish he placed it in his pocket, then lifted his glass.

"So you see, wonderful news! We could not have asked for more! She sounds like a fine Jewish girl, the type that any parent would be happy to have as a daughter-in-law. This is a very happy day for Chana and me."

He reopened the bottle of schnapps.

"This is naughty, but why not finish the bottle while we are all here? It is not often that so much *Nachas* falls on the same day."

Meanwhile the children had tired of playing at the back of the house and had come around to the front. They crowded about the adults and poked at the sweets that Chana and the other women were serving. Hersh was always the centre of attraction, and they clustered around him, tugging at his clothes.

"Will you let us ride on the horses, Zeide?"

"Please! Please!"

"Will you tell us a story, Zeide?"

"Zeide, can we ride on the horses?"

"Can I be the one to feed the horses?"

"Tell us again about the great fire of 1882, Zeide!"

"Please, Zeide, please!"

Despite the stern warnings of their parents, the children could not be driven away from Hersh, and he, as usual, would weaken. He excused himself from his guests and, accompanied by a horde of adoring children, made his way around the house to the backyard. The smaller ones he would lift one by one onto the horses' backs, sometimes two to an animal, and he would walk alongside as they made their way around the perimeter of the yard. He would allow the older children to mount themselves, and taking care not to offend, would offer a subtle hand only when absolutely necessary. Then he would stand back and watch approvingly as they made a loop around the yard at a somewhat quicker pace. Finally, when each child had had several turns at each horse, he would call an end to the proceedings.

"We have all had a good time, but now we have work to do, for we cannot expect the horses to perform for us unless they are fed."

He soon had the children organized filling up buckets and pouring them into the horses' trough just inside the fence. At the same time the older children were tossing forksful of hay through the fence into a pile. For some reason the children did not seem to look upon this as a chore, although he suspected that they might if it were to become a daily routine. Although he himself sometimes found the task onerous, the reward of seeing his beloved animals contentedly feeding always outweighed the physical effort involved.

The feeding now completed, he paused for his usual Saturday afternoon reflection. Who had outsmarted whom? Had he gained by having the better part of his afternoon's feeding and watering done for him, or had the children received the better part of the bargain?

"There, Zeide, we have finished. Now, will you tell us a story?"

"Now, now, my children, I had better be getting back to the others, or they will be wondering what has happened to me."

"Zeide, how old is Shora Hinde, Bobe's mother? Why is it so hard to speak to her, and why does she only sit in the kitchen all day?"

"If I answer these questions for you, will you promise not to ask me any more, for today at least?"

"Yes, Zeide, we promise."

Hersh led the children to the shed which housed the woodpile and assorted tools. It was a tumble-down wooden structure, barely providing a shelter, its ancient timber roof warped and split from an unknown number of hot and cold seasons. Three of its sides were enclosed by similarly weathered boards, the cracks between them large enough to poke several fingers through in places, while the fourth side was completely open to the elements apart from the weathered uprights which supported the roof.

Hersh moved to a large stump used as a chopping block, sat down and lit his pipe.

"Well, first of all, as we all know, Shora Hinde is the mother of both Bobe Chana and Bobe Mere Gita, and she is the oldest person living in Dorbyan."

"How old is she, Zeide."

"For some reason, nobody really knows. In fact, she isn't sure of her exact age herself."

"How can that be, Zeide? We all know how old we are. Everybody knows their age. Why doesn't she?"

"I shall try my best to explain, children, but it may not be easy to understand. When our Shora Hinde was born, Dorbyan was a much different place than it was today. Even Libau and Plugyon, where they lived were not as we know it now. Today, when a child is born, records are kept. Many years ago they did not keep records all the time, and those which were kept were often lost. So it became necessary to depend upon people's memories, which as we all know are not always to be trusted.

"With Shora Hinde, the problem is not that noone knows her age, but that many people think they know, but cannot agree.

"Shora Hinde believes she is ninety-one years old, but says that her mother always told her that she was one year older. Yet both your Bobe Chana and your Bobe Mere Gite are certain that they remember her celebrating her seventieth birthday twenty years ago. So who is right? Now you can see the problem when there are no records to settle an argument."

"Which do you believe, Zeide?"

"I have no answer, my children, for I paid no attention to her age when she was younger. I find it hard not to agree with Bobe Chana and Bobe Mere Gite, but yet I cannot bring myself to disagree with Shora Hinde, even though she herself is not as certain of things as she once was."

The children were pensive, until one of the youngest changed the subject.

"Why cannot Shora Hinde tell us stories like you do. You too are old, *Zeide*, yet you do not sit around the kitchen all day and watch the others working. Will we all be like this when we are old?"

Hersh smiled at the innocence and audacity of the question.

"You have asked me several questions at once, my child. I shall try to answer them as best I can.

"....Someday, my children, you will find out what it is like to grow old. Yes, I too am old, but not nearly as old as Shora Hinde. You will find it hard to believe, but once Shora Hinde was young, and had at least as much strength as you any of you...

"I know that I am growing old, even though I once thought that I would remain young forever. Until not too many years ago Shora Hinde was fit and healthy, but now she is not well. Her hearing is not good, and so it is not easy for her to speak to you and answer your questions. Also, she can no longer see well, and so it is difficult for her to do any work. She still likes to sit in the kitchen, so she can be near her daughters and granddaughters when they are preparing the meals. This is her pleasure, and I think that after all she has been through in her lifetime, she has earned the right to have a rest."

"What has she been through, *Zeide*, that you have not?"

"It is a pity that she is not able to speak to you, my children, for she has much to tell, much more than I, for she can remember things that were only told to me as a child.

"When she and her husband Leiba Zups came from the town of Plugyon, Dorbyan was a much smaller place than now, but growing very quickly. She has seen Dorbyan grow, and then become smaller again. The things she remembers were before my time, or at a time when I was too young to remember, for example, when the Tytschcovitch family owned almost all the lands in and around Dorbyan, and the Lithuanian peasants were their serfs."

"What is a serf, *Zeide*?"

"You should know this, for I'm sure you have been told. A serf was a person who was almost a slave, who worked for someone else on land which was not his, but who was not allowed to leave the land. He was not allowed to marry or have children without the permission of the landowner, or to move to another home or to live with people other than agreed to by the landowner. Sometimes the landowners were kind and decent people, but all to often they were of the type that mistreated their workers. The problem was, that there were no laws which decreed that landowners must treat their serfs fairly."

"Why did people become serfs then, if it is such an unpleasant life?"

"Aha! The questions you ask me! ......

"......Nobody wishes to become a serf, or becomes one voluntarily, but perhaps many years ago these people were conquered in battle, and so lost their freedom; perhaps they needed protection, and offered their services to the landowner in return for this; perhaps they became indebted to a landowner and could only repay their debt by working for him, little realizing that they were condemning their children and their children's children to the same servitude.

"Who knows the exact reason? All we know is that once one became a serf there was no escape from it either for himself or his descendants."

"But *Zeide*, this is unjust! Why did the people stand for it?"

"The people did not accept it, just as we did not accept our bondage to the Pharaohs, but they did not have the power to change it. The landowners possessed all the wealth, and they could hire armies to put down any rebellion."

"Then how did they defeat the Tytschcovitches, *Zeide*? They must have, for there are no serfs today."

"This is where Shora Hinde could tell you better than anyone else, for she is the only one living who was old enough to remember it at the time. I know what has been told to me, and I have also asked her to tell me what she saw. In 1831, before she was born there was a rebellion which failed. It was led by by Berek Joselovitch whom you may have learned about in *cheder*. Berek Joselovitch was once well known here because he was born in Krettingen, and was Jewish. In the end he lost his life when the rebellion was crushed, but now he is looked upon as a hero.

"Then, in 1861, the revolts began again, for the serfs had never lost their desire for freedom. This time the revolts took place all across Lithuania and in Poland and Russia as well. It happened in so many places that the landowners could not fight it everywhere at once, and finally the serfs succeeded in enough places that they were able to break the hold of the landowners. New laws were made, obliging the landowners to pay their workers fairly and to treat them decently. Workers were now allowed to leave the landowners' employ

191

if they wished, and as a result many landowners suffered."

"Is this what happened to the barons of Loigzim?"

"Yes it is, how did you know that?"

"I once heard my father mentioning it to someone else."

"You are a very observant child, and I wonder what other things you have overheard, ..but yes, what you heard is correct.

"The barons von Loigzim were always known as very cruel task-masters, who mistreated their serfs at every opportunity. When the workers were no longer forced to work there, they left at once, and not even the baron's promises to pay them well could make them stay. With no one to work it, the baron's estate became overgrown very quickly. It was at this time that the last of the Jews living there had a disagreement with him. In his madness he forced the Jews to leave as well, and soon found himself left with nothing. He and his family went to live with other family members on estates elsewhere, and today, as you all know, there is nothing at Loigzim except a few peasant farmers making a living from a small piece of what used to be the baron's land.

"What happened to the Loigzimers may someday happen to us, and therefore, it is necessary that we be well educated in case we are ever called on to leave. It is also a good idea, no matter how poor one is, to have a bit of money saved up so he can make his way in the world.

"There still remains the old Jewish cemetery at Loigzim, but for more than fifty years no one has had cause to visit it. It is badly over-grown and becoming difficult to find. Someday, it will be forgotten altogether.

"And now, my children, I can see that you wish to ask me more questions, but this will have to do for today, for I must get back to my guests."

DORBYAN

PART 5

It was evening and the time of day Moshe Bloch dreaded most. Without the day's labour to partially occupy his mind, there was nothing for him to do but ponder over his experiences during the past few months.

He lay quietly in his bed in the attic of the old farmhouse. His room in the attic was for a practical reason, for if unwelcome visitors should appear his room would be the last to be searched, allowing him the chance to flee if necessary. The liklihood of this happening had decreased considerably of late, and the isolation of the farm added to his security, but care in every action he took was still an integral part of his life.

He lay quietly, listening for any unusual sounds, but as usual there were none to be heard. The whole house was darkened as everyone had retired for the night. These people, like farmers everywhere, retired early almost every night, knowing that their next day's work would begin at the break of dawn.

He too would begin work at the break of dawn, but not for him was there the luxury of sleep. Despite the pitch blackness of his room, and the fact that his eyes were shut, he continued to remain awake. This happened every night in fact, for every night his troubled mind would be overflowing with thoughts. Eventually he would lapse into sleep, but the process always took several hours before it happened.

His thoughts raced back some twenty years earlier, to the day he had first heard the name of Adolph Hitler. It had only been mentioned in passing during a conversation in the *Shul Platz*, and it had been some time before the name had been mentioned again. Apparently this man was making a name for himself in Germany and achieving notoriety through his denunciations of the Jews. Nothing unusual, as anti-semitism had existed in almost every corner of Europe for as long as anyone could remember. The strange thing was that it was happening in Germany, where anti-semitism had generally been held in check, even if not totally eradicated from German society. Most eastern European Jews had looked upon the German Jews as fortunate in the citizenship they possessed. On the whole they were more affluent than Jews elsewhere, and appeared to have the same freedoms in society as all other Germans. If there was a downside to their situation, it was that their affluence and assimilation into German society had caused them to forsake many of their traditional Jewish ways.

As Hitler had become more prominent, Moshe Bloch could remember the differing opinions of the people of Dorbyan concerning him. His father, Mordechai, had been one of the earliest to sound the alarm bells, proclaiming that the man was evil, and would eventually lead Germans both Jewish and gentile to disaster. Others, old Hersh Jacob in particular, believed that Hitler would eventually change, that once he gained power, he would no longer see the need for a platform based on anti-semitism. Their neighbour, Leiba Kashutsky, tended to agree with his father about Hitler's true colours, and many was the argument they had had with Hersh on this point. Others believed that although Hitler was evil, the inherent intelligence and decency of the German people would prevail, and that he would never achieve any great measure of success.

In hindsight his father had been totally correct in his assessment of Hitler. As the years passed and his power increased, the measures he instigated against Jews had also increased, to the point that Jews were virtually excluded from German society, and unable to earn a living. It was at this point that the first of the German Jews, the foresighted ones, started leaving.

He remembered the night later to be known as *Krystallnacht*, when synagogues and Jewish businesses throughout Germany were destroyed, with the number of Jews injured in the process running into the hundreds. The German police had stood by as the damage was done, and ordinary Germans had cheered as it had happened. It was at this point that old Hersh Jacob was finally forced to admit that Hitler would not change, and that the German people, rather than disapprove of his actions, actually welcomed him with enthusiasm. It was unusual for Hersh Jacob to lose his faith in the good of people, and Moshe suspected that he had secretly hoped that some change in Hitler might still be possible.

He thought back to the days when Hitler had annexed Memel, and how some two hundred displaced Jews from that city had chosen Dorbyan as their refuge. They had been shattered, and he would never forget the shock and despair amongst them as they arrived in Dorbyan, most of them carrying with them very little in the way of personal belongings. He had wondered at the time if Dorbyan would ever suffer the same fate, but had been reassured by his father's opinion that it was unlikely, as Dorbyan had no German population which could be a temptation for Hitler to integrate it into the greater German Reich.

He remembered the Russian occupation of Lithuania in June 1940 and the hardship it had brought to his hometown. Many businesses had been closed, others had been confiscated by the Russians, and word had been that institutions such as the market would be closed and all commerce would eventually become state owned. His father and uncle had been spared the loss of their businesses as they had not been large enough to attract the attention of the Russians, but all knew that it was but a matter of time, as the elimination of all private business was a major philosophy of the communists.

He also remembered the damage done by the Russian occupation to the relations between Lithuanians and Jews, with many Lithuanians blaming the Jews for the situation and making them scapegoats for their misfortunes.

By now Hitler had invaded Poland and was known to be persecuting Jews there.

The horror stories escaping from that country were being told with increasing frequency and had become too blatant to be overlooked. If anything, the Polish Jews were enduring even greater injustice than their German counterparts, and stories of organized murder and torture were becoming commonplace. There could be no doubt about the fate in store for Jews in any country Hitler chose to conquer.

Although Hitler was now at war with England and France, and appeared to be conquering everywhere, there was no war happening in Dorbyan. The Russians were not desirable occupiers, but at least their presence meant that Hitler was not likely to invade in their direction............or so the people had believed.

CHAPTER 1

Chana waited on the front steps in the mid-morning sun for Hersh to return from the synagogue. She had not expected him home imediately, for he had told her that after *Shaharis* service he would wait around the *shul platz* until the mail arrived at the post office. A letter from one or another of their children was well overdue, and he had a strong feeling that one would arrive on this day.

On mail days the post office had become a focal point of the town almost as much as the synagogue. The Jewish community was now far outnumbered by family members living overseas, and incoming mail far outweighed the letters written by the townspeople. Everyone could be found there, the elderly, the down-and-out, the mothers with infant children, the men who had taken leave of their work, all of them hoping that on this day their lives would be lifted. Sometimes their expectations would be met, with the arrival of a package or letter containing money or tickets. Much more often, hopes were dashed as people turned sadly away from the office to wait for the next delivery.

Chana watched, and sure enough, at the expected time, Hersh appeared at the beginning of the Krettinger Gass, making his way rapidly towards home. What was strange was that he appeared to be running, or at least trying to, inasmuch as his heavy clothing and heavy boots would allow a seventy-year-old to run.

"Chana! Chana!", he panted. "They're coming! They're coming!"

"Stop running Hersh! You're not a young man! Do you want to kill yourself?"

"They're coming, Chana! They're coming!"

"What on earth do you mean, they're coming?"

"Just read this!", gasped Hersh, wiping the perspiration from his face. "Just read it, this letter from Joseph!"

Pontiac

April, 1928

197

Dear Papa!

It is with great *simcha* that I write this letter. Rae and I have been married, just a few weeks ago, on the date that we planned, and as we told you. We are now husband and wife living happily together.

The wedding was a wonderful affair. Esther and Barnet came from Saint John, and of course Sam and Ruthie Kveril were present, so we were not without Dorbyan *mishpoche*. Rae was not alone either, as her sister Sara Mones attended, together with her husband Saul. Everything was perfect. After the ceremony we had a reception in the basement of the *shul* . Not quite like the celebrations we used to have in the *shul platz* , but things are done differently here. It was a lovely affair, and one that will bring us happy memories for the rest of our lives.

And now for the best news of all! *Rae and I will be coming to Dorbyan to visit you in about three months' time!*

Can you imagine? In my next letter I will be able to give you the exact date and details. I cannot believe it! I will get to see my family once more, and you and Mama and the *mishpoche* will be able to meet my beautiful wife!

How did this happen? In America there is a custom that immediately after a wedding, the newly-weds take a wedding trip somewhere, just the two of them. It is called a 'honeymoon'. As Rae and I were discussing our honeymoon before the wedding, she said to me, "Wouldn't it be wonderful if we could travel to Glasgow so that you could meet my mother. I know that she would love you. She is old and unwell, and I would love to see her one more time."

I answered her, "And wouldn't it be wonderful to continue on to Dorbyan for you to meet your new *mishpoche* !"

We began to talk about it, and we realized that it could be done. America is prosperous, and it is always possible to earn back the money we will be spending. This would be our honeymoon, and the money we had put aside for other purposes would be used for this journey. Our other plans would have to wait, for this was something that could never happen again!

I have been told that when I return I will be able to work in the same place as before, if I wish. Rae will work for a little longer when we get back before we think of starting a family. We will not look for a home of our own, but will live with others for a time.

But it will be worth it! I can hardly wait to see you again! After eight years! Chaia, Esther and Leah will be giving us things to bring when we come, and we shall be able to spend hours telling you about them, and how they are doing in Canada. Rae is even more excited than I am, and I am looking forward to meeting her family.

Our plans will give us about ten days in Glasgow and ten days in Dorbyan, although this is not yet exact. I know that this is not enough, but I only thank God that it is possible. If there is anything special that you would like me to bring from America, just let me know, and I will do what I can.

My love to you and Mama, and also to Rocha, Ada, Mina and Breina. Tell them that I will be seeing them before long!

Your Son.
Joseph

Hersh threw his arms around Chana's waist, lifted her off the ground, and swung her around in a circle.

"They're coming! They're coming! This is my happiest moment, what I have always prayed for! I shall see my son again! They're coming!"

CHAPTER 2

It was well past midnight, and Hersh lay sleeping in his bed, Chana curled up cosily beside him. In his dream he could vaguely make out a tapping sound which seemed to increase in intensity. As it became louder and more insistent, he came to his senses, and realized that there was a frantic pounding at the front of the house. He rose without waking Chana, lit a candle, and padded his way to the front door.

At the door stood a young child, nine , perhaps ten years of age.

"Jonas Galdikas! What brings you here, child? And at this time of the night! Something is the matter! Tell me about it!"

"Ponas Jacobas!," panted the lad, "My father has sent me!"

"And it looks as if you have run all the way too, almost three miles!"

The boy nodded.

"It must be very serious, or your father would not have sent you at this time of night."

"It is our horse, he is very sick, and nothing that father can do seems to help. We are afraid that he might die. Father said that if anyone could help, it would be you."

"I am not a doctor," answered Hersh, "But I know a little about horses. If I am able to help, I will. Come inside."

Hersh gave the boy some candy from the jar kept on hand for his grandchildren, then went into the bedroom and woke Chana.

"Chana, I must go out. I have been asked by Viktoras Galdikas to help with a sick horse. They are good people, and the horse is one that they bought from us. I'll try not to be too long, but I cannot be certain, so don't worry."

He led the boy to the rear of the house, went to the old shed and wheeled out a seldom used wagon. Then he removed a bar from the fence, and called one of the horses, which came immediately to his call.

A few minutes later the horse was hitched to the wagon which then creaked its way into the night. Once they were underway, and Hersh was certain that all was in working order, he handed the reins to the young boy, whose eyes lit up at the faith that was being placed in him.

The horse clopped its way to the beginning of the Krettinger Gass, then at the junction, instead of continuing into town, turned sharply towards the left and continued along the road to Polangen. Some two miles and thirty minutes later they reached the small Galdikas farm. Hersh hitched his horse while Jonas Galdikas ran towards the barn.

Inside the barn a small candle burned inside a lantern, giving off a pallid light.

On the floor covered by straw lay the horse, spread out awkwardly. Jonas' father, Viktoras knelt by the side of the horse, cradling its head, wiping its brow with a rag dipped in a bucket of water alongside.

"Thank you for coming, Hersh," he said. "I knew you would. This horse has been sick for most of the day, but suddenly he has become much worse."

Hersh bent down and stroked the horse he once owned. The horse's ears pricked up at the memory of a former loving master.

"You have kept this horse in fine condition, Viktoras."

"It is my son Jonas, Hersh. He worships all animals, but this horse most of all. He is the best horse we have ever had.

Hersh looked into the horse's mouth, then went to its rear and examined its droppings.

"Viktoras, I don't know how this could have happened, but somehow this horse has managed to eat something poisoned! The first thing we must do is get him back on his feet. In this position it is harder for him to breathe, and the poison will take longer to pass through his system. Do you have any rope, also a few blankets?"

Viktoras Galdikas sent his son to fetch the items that Hersh had requested.

"Is it serious? Do you think he will live?"

"If we can get him to his feet, he stands a good chance. Otherwise his chances are not so good."

Tieing the rope around the horses neck and lifting with all their strength they managed to pass the blankets under the horse's body and make them into slings. Then they tied the ropes to the bunched ends of the blankets and began to lift, but to no avail, for the weight of a heavy draught horse was too much for the strength of two adults and a child.

"Jonas, go to Vlacovas, and bring back help," Viktoras Galdikas ordered., and Jonas dashed off.

Twenty minutes later Jonas returned with an elderly peasant farmer whom Hersh knew vaguely, and his two strapping sons. Viktoras introduced them, and then in reasonable Lithuanian laced with a heavy Yiddish accent Hersh explained what was to be done.

"We must bring the horse to his feet, and then make sure he stays there. This will mean tying the ropes to the rafters."

The horse was slowly raised, and the agile Jonas Galdikas scampered along the rafters and fastened the ropes according to the tension that Hersh wanted. When he had finished, the horse was standing in an erect position, its feet on the ground, yet unable to drop more than a fraction of an inch.

Hersh nodded approvingly.

"Good," he said. "Now the thing to do is to see that he drinks as much water as possible. It is impossible to give him too much. The water will help flush the poison from his system."

The three neighbours remained, interested and anxious to learn as much as possible, for Hersh Jacob had a good name when it came to dealing with horses.

"May I have a bit of salt please."

Hersh held the salt to the horse's mouth, and forced a few grains between the teeth. The mouth opened slightly and he gave the horse a larger dose. He repeated the proceedure several times.

"Now, Jonas, hold the water bucket up to him," said Hersh.

Jonas held up the water bucket, and the horse drank.

"This is a good sign. I did not expect him to drink so easily," said Hersh.

"Give him as much water as he wishes, but do not force food upon him. The more you can make him drink, the better. Tomorrow, when he may feel like eating, do not give him hay, give him green grass at first. In this way he will be getting moisture as he eats."

"Do you think he will get better?", asked Viktoras Galdikas.

"As I told your son, I am no doctor," answered Hersh. "I only know from the things I have seen in my own horses. I cannot be certain, but from what I see, there are good signs. I believe he will recover quickly, and that by tomorrow you will see a big difference in him. If there are any problems, let me know, and I shall come again after I have been to synagogue."

"Is there anything I can give you in payment, Hersh?"

"Viktoras, we are friends. I have incurred no expense in coming here. You owe me nothing."

"...But, Hersh!"

Hersh looked at the Lithuanian sternly.

"We have done business before, and in fact you have bought this very horse from me. I am sure we will continue to do business in the future. You owe me nothing."

"Then perhaps I can offer you a bed for the night."

"I have told Chana that I would be home before the night is over. If I am not, she will worry, and then when I get home I shall face a very difficult scene." Hersh winked mischievously.

The serious face of Viktoras Galdikas showed a faint trace of a smile, then became serious again.

"Then perhaps I should accompany you home. It is not right that you should have to travel alone at this hour."

"What's the problem, Viktoras? I am a big boy, and am able to travel in the dark. The roads are safe. You were not afraid to send your son out alone. There is nothing to fear. It is better that you and Jonas remain by the side of your horse, for tonight at least."

"No, Hersh." Viktoras Galdikas was insistent. "I will ride home with you. Jonas can look after the horse from here. It is a long time since I have had the chance to speak to you, and we will be able to have a few words together."

As they rode into the night, Hersh spoke. "How are things going on your farm, Viktoras? It was a very sudden thing when your father died a few months ago."

"Yes, we were all shocked. For although father was old, he was healthy, and appeared to have many years left. Yet he died as he would have wished, fit and active, and able to do a full day's work until the end."

"There is a lot of work to be done on a farm," said Hersh. "Do you not struggle without him?"

"Yes, it has been difficult without him," admitted the Lithuanian, "But my older children come to visit me often and help. And Jonas is wonderful. He goes to school, and then when he comes home he works as hard as any man. I don't know what I would do without him.

"By the way, Hersh, thank you, for coming to father's funeral."

"How could I not come to Rolandas Galdikas' funeral! Do you know the part your father played in my life? He was my first customer, and then through him I made my next sale to Vlacovas. I can still remember the day I learned that he was interested in buying one of my horses, and how I went with the horse to visit him.

"....I was never so terrified in my life, that he may not like the horse, that he may not like the price, or that he would force me to sell it at a loss.

"....But when I went to him, he treated me like a friend, and made me feel comfortable, and gave me the encouragement I needed."

"Yes, my father has told me this story, but he also told me another thing which I have never forgotten."

"What else did he tell you, Viktoras?"

"...He said that when he asked you what you were going to do with the money, he expected you to say that you would buy another horse, but he was surprised when you told him that the first thing you would do would be to pay back your debt to your father.

"...He told me that if all Jews behave like this then they must be a fine race indeed, for he always considered the honour of one's parents the most important thing of all. He told me that I should never have any fear in dealing with you."

"It is a strange thing," said Hersh, "That this should be mentioned now, for what your father never found out was that my father would not allow me to repay the debt. He told me that he and Mama gained their greatest pleasure from seeing their children do well. I could not get him to accept the money at the time, but I made him promise to accept it after I sold my next horse. After your father pointed me in the direction of Vlacovas, and I made my next sale, he had no choice but to keep his promise. Believe me, I have a debt to your father. He was a very fine man."

"I know all this," answered Viktoras Galdikas, "And that is why it is hard to tell you something which disturbs me. You and your son-in-law Elior, I believe, out of all the Jews in Darbenai, were the only ones to come to the funeral. I cannot understand it. Our family has dealt with Jews for generations."

Hersh squirmed uncomfortably on his seat.

"I know how you must feel, Viktoras, for it distressed me also at the time. I cannot explain it. Many Jews knew your father and felt very kindly towards him, but for some reason they felt uncomfortable about attending the funeral, and stepping inside a church. It is almost as if they didn't belong.

"It is the same with your people. Although they have nothing to fear from entering a synagogue, I know that there are very few, if any, who would do it, even for the funeral of a friend. It seems as if there will always be a barrier between Jews and Lithuanians."

Viktoras Galdikas answered with deliberate slowness.

"My son Jonas tells me that amongst the Jewish children he has no friends, and he knows of no other Lithuanian child who has. This cannot be a good thing....

"I know that they go to different schools, but after school almost every child in the district of Darbenai is in the market square. The Christian children play in the church yard, while the Jewish children play near the synagogue. They play the same games, hop-scotch and throwing and kicking a ball. Why can they not play together?"

Hersh replied, "This is a good question, Viktoras. Maybe something could be done to bring them together, for children are always quick to make friends. It might make things better for them when they become adults."

"Do you think it is because it is always you who must speak our language, while we are never able to speak to you in yours," asked Viktoras Galdikas.

"No, not at all," answered Hersh. "I don't think this has anything to do with it. We accept that we are all living in Lithuania, and when we are all together it is only right that we speak Lithuanian. If we wish to speak our own language when we are by ourselves, then that is our affair. This is exactly what my daughters in Canada tell me happens there. They speak their own language when they are amongst themselves, and English everywhere else."

"Your daughters in Canada," answered the Lithuanian. "I don't know whether to feel happy for you, or to offer you sympathy. You tell me how well they are doing, but they are so far away, and you will never see them again. Our family is poor, but at least all my children live close to me."

"We are happy that our children have a good life," said Hersh, "But having them leave and knowing that we will never see them again has been the most painful thing that has ever happened to Chana and me. When they left it was almost as if a part of my own body had been cut off. The feeling has never left me. And then, to lose our only son Joseph, was the hardest blow of all.."

Hersh then stamped his foot excitedly, jolting the horse into a sudden spurt.

"But what I almost forgot to mention, Viktoras! There is a blessing, one that I never expected to receive! Joseph has married, and he has written that he is coming back shortly, for a visit! Can you believe it? He is bringing his wife here to meet us! It is the most wonderful thing to happen in our lives for many years!"

"It makes me feel happy for you," said Viktoras Galdikas. "It is good to see you in such a happy frame of mind."

"And I have just had a thought," said Hersh. "Why don't you come to visit us when he is here? We have invited many people, and I am sure that you will find it interesting to hear what he has to tell about life in America."

Viktoras Galdikas looked at Hersh in shock.

"...You, a Jew, are inviting me, a Lithuanian, to visit you in your home?"

Hersh answered, "Not quite. I, a friend, am inviting you, a friend, to visit my home."

"It is a wonderful thing, but it wouldn't work," said the Lithuanian flatly.

"Why not, it was not very long ago that you offered me a bed in your home for the night."

"This is different, Hersh, I would be visiting when you had other guests, and I would be different from the others, and out of place."

"You need not worry about this, Viktoras, for every Jew in Dorbyan can speak Lithuanian, and in any case I will stay by your side for as long as you care to stay.

".....And I had another thought, Viktoras, bring Jonas! My grand-children will be there, and they can play together, and like your Jonas, they also enjoy the horses."

"I cannot see it happening, Hersh, for Jonas and I cannot both be spared from the farm."

Hersh was insistent.

"Then let Jonas come over after school. When he has had enough I will bring him home myself. But a few moments ago we were talk-ing about this very thing. This is the chance to do something!"

"It is a wonderful thought, Hersh, but perhaps it is not as easy as I thought. Maybe the only way is to wait for the next generation, and hope that they will mix."

"My invitation still stands," said Hersh. "All I can ask is that you think about it."

"I will do that," answered Viktoras Galdikas, "And thank you."

Hersh knew that his friend would not visit, and although his in-vitation had been genuine, he felt a sense of relief. Should Viktoras Galdikas enter his home, all the normal topics of conversation would cease immediately, and Yiddish would turn into Lithuanian. There would be very little of common interest to discuss, for most Jews were not well versed in things agricultural. Most Jews drank very sparingly, and when they did, it was usually schnapps in small quan-tities. Viktoras Galdikas, like most Lithuanian peasants, preferred beer, and in appropriate quantities when the occasion demanded. Every Jew in Dorbyan had received a school education, which Viktoras Galdikas and his generation had been denied.

When they spoke again, Viktoras Galdikas changed the subject.

"I don't blame you, that you many of you are leaving," he said. "I know that it will be sad for you a second time, when your son has to leave again."

"Of course it will be sad," sighed Hersh. "But what are we to do? It is not like with your own children, who are living in their own country. For us it is different. Maybe someday if we Jews too have our own country, we will not be so eager to keep searching for a better life elsewhere."

"I don't blame you for leaving," the Lithuanian repeated. "I can see plainly that things have become much harder for you of late. There have been many changes since Independence, and I am not sure that I like all that I see. Perhaps I am old-fashioned."

"I suppose that after we reach a certain age, we are all old-fashioned," said Hersh.

"My son, Jonas," continued Viktoras Galdikas, "He is a different person than I was when I was his age. I cannot read or write. Jonas now goes to school just as your children have always done. Everyone tells me that this must be a good thing for him. Perhaps I am too blind to see, but I cannot see that there has been any improvement."

"Viktoras, the world is changing. What you and I are able to do may not be good enough in the future. A little learning can do no harm to anyone. Jonas is a very bright child. Someday he may be able to use his knowledge to make life better for your family."

As they approached the junction of the Polanger and the Krettinger Streets, Viktoras Galdikas asked Hersh to stop the wagon.

"Here, Hersh, we are at the Kretinga Gatve. You are almost home. If you will just let me out, I shall walk home from here."

"No," said Hersh, bringing the wagon to a halt. "It is I who will walk, for it is but a few yards to my house. You will drive home in the wagon, and bring it back to me tomorrow. "

"I cannot accept this," answered Viktoras Galdikas.

"In that case," said Hersh, "I have a better idea. Let Jonas bring it back to me when he comes to school in the morning. I am sure he will agree with this."

"Bless you, Hersh."

As Hersh crawled into his bed just before the first light of dawn appeared, Chana awoke.

"So, tell me, what happened?," she asked sleepily.

"Galdikas's horse swallowed some poison and became very sick, but I believe that everything will now be all right."

"They have a nerve, calling you at this time of the night. You are not even a doctor, and it is not your job to be doing this. Did they pay you?"

"They offered, but I could not accept. You see, the horse is one they bought from us four years ago."

"You are too kindhearted, my love," she said.

Then she hugged him. "But that is the very reason that I love you so. Never mind, someday you will be rewarded for all the kind things you have done."

CHAPTER 3

In July of 1928 Joseph and Rae arrived in Dorbyan. Joseph was one of the very few Dorbyaners to return to his birthplace, and the first since Leiba Zups Jacob from Saint John came to collect the last of his relatives some eight years earlier. The small town held no secrets, and there was not a soul within a five mile radius who was not aware of the visit. For a ten day period the house on the Krettinger Gass became the social centre of the town, with a non-stop stream of visitors dropping in to pay their respects, but more importantly, to glean whatever news they could of their relatives and life in North America.

Virtually every family in the town was related to every other in some way, and by now there was no family without relatives overseas. The visitors crowded around Joseph, each patiently awaiting his turn to ask him the countless questions on his mind. No Dorbyaner was omitted, and each and every person who had ever left the town was mentioned. For his part, Joseph was up to the task, and surprised everyone by being able to answer the most obscure of questions.

This should have been no surprise, as Joseph had always shown a fascination with family connections, even before leaving Dorbyan. Upon his arrival overseas, his interest had only increased, and he had made it his solemn duty to maintain contact with as many Dorbyaners as possible, visiting those within easy reach, and corresponding with those further away. Those whom he had not contacted personally, he had made it his business to find out about, by asking those who knew.

Rae was at first out of place, but not for long. The friendliness of the townsfolk and the hospitality of the family soon put her at ease. Her dress, ordinary by American standards, was elegant alongside the Dorbyan peasant costume, but was the cause of curiosity rather than envy. Yiddish, spoken by her mother, but barely learned by herself and not needed on the streets of Glasgow, was a problem. But, as the days passed she was able to remember more and more from her early childhood, and gradually she found herself able to understand a large part of what was said, even though she was hard pressed to express her thoughts. Fortunately Joseph was always on hand to act as an able and efficient translator, which was essential, as no member of the community possessed the ability to communicate in English.

The ten days sped by like a flash. Between twice daily visits to the synagogue, visits to family members and childhood friends, parties at home, and a visit to the cemetery, the time was filled completely. Long after Chana and Rae had retired for the night, Joseph and Hersh would sit up talking, Hersh lighting his pipe several times over during the conversation. They would talk about any topic in existence, but most importantly they would simply talk, savouring the opportunity to be alone with each other.

As the day of departure neared, it was inevitable that gloom appeared on the faces of Hersh and Chana.

"You know, that this is the last time we shall ever see you, my son, for we are old, and for all we know, we may not have much time left."

"I know, Papa, there is no point in pretending that we shall see each other again. Rae and I have our lives to return to, and we wish to begin a family of our own just as soon as we can manage it. I am already thirty-two, older than you were when Chaia was born, and we cannot wait much longer. Once we have children, I don't see how we can ever travel again."

"Of course, my son, we have known this all along, but just having you here this time was a blessing that we never expected to receive. We are grateful that God has allowed us to see you again, and to meet your lovely wife. You have made a wonderful choice, and Chana and I rejoice that we have lived long enough to see it."

"It seems strange, Papa, for of all the family, I am the only one who has not married a Dorbyaner. In fact it seems as if most Dorbyaners in North America have also married other Dorbyaners."

"It does not matter," said Hersh. "What matters is that you have made the best choice anyone could make. Your Mama and I know that you will be very happy, and we are very proud of our new daughter."

"You know, Papa, this is exactly what Rae's mother said when we had to leave her. We shall see her again on the way back, but for only part of a day. Leaving her will be difficult too, but still we leave knowing that we have done the right thing. Just to meet the *mishpoche* on both sides has made the whole journey worthwhile, and we shall both have something to remember for the rest of our lives."

CHAPTER 4

Life in Dorbyan became progressively more difficult with each year that passed. The world had slipped into a depression.

Although the simple needs of Dorbyaners made them largely immune from the economic ruin which had engulfed the western world, the effects were felt nonetheless. Perhaps the most noticeable effect was the slowdown of remittances from family members overseas, particularly in Canada and the United States where business conditions had become appalling. Most Dorbyaners transplanted into these countries had since their arrival chosen to become their own masters and open their own businesses. For more than a generation they had almost without exception, prospered. Now for the first time, they were faced with financial difficulties unlike any they had known in the place of their birth.

One day Hersh happened to notice a large tear in Chana's left shoe, in the area where the upper was fastened to the sole. He asked Chana to remove the shoe, and he examined it closely, expecting that he would be able to mend it himself with little effort. After puzzling over it for several minutes, he finally came to the conclusion that the problem was beyond his abilities, and he asked her, "Chana, how long has this shoe been like this?"

"For a week, maybe two," she answered.

"We should have had it mended before it became so serious," said Hersh sternly.

"I know, but I didn't have the money for that purpose at the time."

"You didn't think it would get better by itself?", Hersh persisted.

"No, but I was waiting until I had a little bit of money to spare."

"We have a bit of money put away."

"Yes, but our children's families are having so many problems. They need it more than we do, and when I have money, I prefer that they have it."

"I hope it is not too late for this shoe. Tomorrow I shall take it with me to *Shul* and show it to Shrolick Chaim Simon when I am finished. You will either have to wear your old uncomfortable shoes or go barefoot for the morning, but if we wait any longer, you will be needing a pair of new shoes."

"I prefer to go barefoot", said Chana.

The next morning, after synagogue service, Hersh accompanied Shrolick Chaim Simon back to his home on a small street off the Wainaiker Gass. Shrolick led Hersh through his modest house to his shoemaking workshop in the rear. It was little more than a large shed-type building with a long, low table in the centre which served as his main workbench.

On the table were several boxes filled with nails of assorted sizes and mysterious wooden spikes, a bin containing a dozen different sized knives, and two cans of oil. Hanging from the wall were various sized pieces of leather and hide. Behind the table on the wall were shelves containing unopened boxes and several pairs of unclaimed shoes. Beside the table was a chair in front of several short planks which had been fashioned together to form a sort of foot stand.

"Let's have a look at this shoe," said Shrolick Chaim.

"I hope it can be repaired,' said Hersh. "Chana does not wish the expense of new shoes."

"I understand the problem perfectly," smiled Shrolick Chaim grimly, as he sat down on his small footstool and started to separate the leather upper from the sole.

His forehead then wrinkled into a frown, and he held the shoe close to Hersh's face.

"Look, you can see the problem. This shoe is old, and the leather is tired, It has perished in the places where the nails have been holding it together."

"Can it be repaired?", asked Hersh anxiously.

"Yes, I can mend it, but the problem will come back sooner or later, and next time it will not be repairable. "

Hersh nodded.

"There is just enough leather there for me to put in a few new nails, but it won't last for much longer. There is not even place for me to stitch new leather."

"Please fix it, and we shall use it this way for as long as we can. I shall tell Chana to be gentle with it," said Hersh.

"I don't blame you, Hersh. Everyone in Dorbyan is doing the same thing, and I do very little business anymore. When I walk on the street I notice people's shoes, and almost all of them need repair or replacement. But people have no money for this. Usually when a shoe is brought to me it is because it is beyond the point of repair."

Shrolick Chaim pointed to the upper shelf, where several pairs of unclaimed shoes rested.

"Look, Hersh. Some of these are shoes people can't afford to reclaim, but usually when this happens I let them take the shoes and pay me later. Most of the shoes were brought here for repair and left behind when their owners left Dorbyan. They are of no use to me, but I cannot sell them, even at a very low price. Nobody wants an extra pair of shoes anymore.

"I also have some new shoes here. Years ago I used to order in shoes for people and was always able to sell them. It is more than three years since I last sold a pair, for nobody can afford them. If only I could sell them, I would be prepared to take no more than I paid for them three years ago, for my family and I need the money very badly."

"I never realized that things were so bad for you," said Hersh. "What about your sons, Jossel and Jankel in Canada? Do they not send you money from time to time?"

"They do," answered Shrolick Chaim, "But not as much as they once did, and what they send is not enough. They are now struggling in Canada to support their own families, and we feel the difference here. As you know, our garden is not as large as yours, and the food we grow does not feed our family."

"Do you ever think of leaving Dorbyan?", asked Hersh.

"All the time,........all the time....", murmured Shrolick Chaim.

"We talk about it every day...... but as you know, the doors have been closed in Canada and the United States. The only way to go there now is if to have relatives who are able to support us completely, and even this is not certain. Jossel and Jankel certainly cannot do this, so there is no chance.

"To be honest, Hersh, I don't know what we are going to do. Sometimes we have very little food on our table, and it can only get worse. My youngest son Mordechai has no future here. He certainly can't follow me into this business. The only thing I can think of is to leave for South Africa, where it is still possible to go."

"But you have nobody in South Africa, Shrolick.."

"I have some distant *mishpoche* there, Hersh. I have written to them, and they think they can help me. If they can help me with the passage, then we will go there ...... but it will not be easy, going to South Africa, knowing that my oldest two sons are in Canada...."

"......In the meantime, we still have to manage until this happens.....

"But......enough of my problems, Hersh. Mine are probably no worse than anyone else's. I will fix your shoe for you while we talk, and it will cost you very little, just the price of a few nails and some glue."

He pointed to one of the shelves.

"But I am serious, Hersh, when I say that Chana will need new shoes before long. No matter how careful she is, this one won't last much longer.

"There is a pair of new shoes on the shelf that will fit Chana perfectly. Why don't you take them home to her, and if she likes them, they are yours for less than I paid for them. They are of no use to me, and if I leave, they will be of no use to me at all."

Hersh grimaced.

"Chana won't like this, I know it," he said, "It will be dangerous, but I'll show them to her. Don't be surprised if you see me bringing them back to you tomorrow."

Shortly before noon Hersh returned home and fearfully showed the new shoes to Chana, knowing what was to come.

"*Bist Du a Meshugganeh? How could you even consider it? You know we can't afford a luxury like this!*", Chana snapped angrily.

216

"Chana, please listen to the whole story. When I have finished, if you do not want the shoes, I will take them back, although I would rather that you took them back yourself, as I do not have the heart to do it."

"Very well, I shall take them back myself!", snorted Chana, "But one thing is certain, we are not keeping them!"

When Hersh had finished his story, he noticed that Chana's eyes had become misty, and she spoke in a subdued tone.

"I had no idea that things were so bad for the Simons," she said. "I see very little of Shrolick Chaim and Dvorah these days. It makes me realize just how fortunate we are."

"Yes," said Hersh. "We have been the lucky ones. Although Chaia and Leah struggle, Esther and Barnet do well and are very generous, and Joseph has always been very good to us."

"You know, Hersh, tomorrow I was planning to take two chickens to the Kverils' slaughtering shed. They are slaughtering an animal there, and the *shochet* will be there. Some other women are also bringing chickens, and the man who plucks them and keeps the feathers will also be there.

"It seemed so perfect. I had planned a chicken meal for the whole family, and most of the work would have been done for me while I went inside and spent the morning with Mama and Mere Gita.

"Now I feel guilty. I have been thinking of a chicken meal when Shrolick and Dvora Simon do not have enough food for their table. Are there others like this?"

"I am certain that there are," answered Hersh.

"Hersh," decided Chana. "Right now you will go back to Shrolick Chaim and pay him for these shoes! Tell him that I have fallen in love with them...

"...And you will pay him a little more than he is asking. Tell him that it is only proper that he make a profit on them.......And wait! I am not yet finished! If you will give me just a few minutes, I shall go out to the garden and find a few ripe vegetables for you to take to them."

A few moments later, Chana appeared with a large box filled to everflowing with fresh produce. Hersh winced when he saw it.

"How am I to carry this? It will break my back!"

"You will find a way," said Chana firmly.

"Are you sure that we can spare this much for them?", asked Hersh.

"If we could not spare it, I wouldn't be giving it to you to take!", snapped Chana, leaving no doubt that matter was closed.

A moment later she smiled, and Hersh saw that her mood had changed.

"You know, Hersh, we shall need to rub some mud or earth on these shoes. Whatever happens, I don't want to be seen in the town with new shoes on my feet!"[5]

---

5   *Based on a description related to me by Sol (Sliomas) Gilis of Yarmouth, Nova Scotia. Mr Gilis had relatives in Dorbyan named Simon (Zimon). One family operated a hardware store, the other were shoemakers. When I submitted this chapter to him his comment was : "The Simons were poor people, but I don't think they were that poor."*

CHAPTER 5

The departure of Joseph and Rae back to America marked the end of a happy period in the lives of Hersh and Chana. Times had changed, celebrations were fewer and less boistrous. Their daughters had passed the age of childbearing, and no longer would there be new arrivals to celebrate. Their youngest grandchild Natan Beir, born to Breina and Elior late in 1926, would be the last. It would be several years before the next generation came along, an event that would probably beyond the lifespans of both of them.

The daily life of the Jews in Dorbyan had become progressively more difficult, and there was little cause to expect improvement. The effects of the new Lithuanian regulations had been detrimental, and now a worldwide economic depression was affecting the fortunes of Jew and gentile alike. The new decade could only promise more of the same, and everyone of Hersh and Chana's daughters, even Breina, was experiencing hard times. The business of Elior had once been large and lucrative, but years of adverse business conditions had reduced it to the point where it barely provided a living. The other spouses fared no better, managing a sustenance through the petty trading of virtually any item which could be bought and sold at a profit. Such items included flax, saccharine, pelts, grain, hides and textiles.

The only bright spot had been the regular news from the family members in Saint John, and from Joseph in Pontiac, Michigan. Most letters from Esther and Joseph contained a remittance, which was always welcomed. Chaia and Leizer's older children were now grown up and making a living, thereby easing the burden for that large family.

Leah had married Aaron Nathan Cohen, a Dorbyaner, and their family had now grown to five children. Aaron was a shopkeeper, and although he never operated on a large scale, he always managed to support his family despite the hard times which plagued Canada as much as any other country.

Joseph had gone back to working at the motorcar plant, but had decided that his fortunes lay elsewhere, and had opened a *kosher* butcher shop. The reports he sent told of a living being made but very little more, for the boom times of previous years had become a thing of the past.

Esther and Barnet continued to prosper, despite the hard times, and their family had increased to three children with the birth of Julia Jean (Shaine Yudel), born in 1927, some nineteen years after their son Sammy. They had found the money to send Sammy to university, the first of the family to do so, and a source of amazement to other family members. Sammy was bright, and would do well. A fine future was predicted for him.

Hersh and Chana welcomed the remittances from Canada, but their need was not as great as that of others, many of whom depended upon remittances for their complete existence. They had no debts, and the horse trading still provided the occasional payday, although Chana suspected that Hersh kept the animals more as a hobby and as a means of entertaining the grandchildren. The backyard was large by Dorbyan standards, and had become a blessing, as it was spacious enough to grow vegetables to feed the whole family throughout the year. The chickens and cows they kept meant that the family never wanted for poultry, eggs, milk or cheese.

The migrations from Dorbyan had never stopped, but merely ceased to increase, due to the smaller number of people in the town eligible to migrate. The population had become heavily weighted towards the aged and ageing, with a further segment of the very young, whose parents hesitated to make a move. With each year that passed, more and more of these younger families finally gave up the battle and left to join their families overseas.

The children of Hersh and Chana were the exceptions, middle aged parents with grown children who somehow had managed to remain in Dorbyan.

In the late 1920's another change took place. Canada and the United States began to restrict the number of immigrants they would accept, and began to "close their doors". As the economic situation worsened, the entry regulations gradually became more and more stringent, until in effect the doors were closed altogether. South

Africa, still desperate to increase its white population, continued to welcome immigrants, and now became the prime destination for Dorbyaners. Palestine, long the goal of the Zionists and idealists, now overtook North America as the second choice.

In 1933, Shora Hinde Jacob, Chana's mother, died. It marked a turning point in Chana's life.

When Shora Hinde died, her passing had meant the end of an era, not only for Chana, but for all of Dorbyan. She had been by far the oldest inhabitant of the town, and was but a year or two short of her hundredth birthday.

Her lifetime had stretched back farther than anyone else could remember, back to the days when Dorbyan was growing rapidly, back to events which were no longer even taught in the schools. When she and her husband arrived in Dorbyan, a young couple eager to better themselves, they had been but one of many families attracted to the town because of the opportunities it offered. Dorbyan at that time had yet to reach its peak, and its future had seemed limitless.

She had lived through the second half of the nineteenth century, when the town was mature, and able to boast many of the amenities that were available to Jews of the larger cities. Dorbyan had possessed separate synagogue and *Beit midrash* buildings, both with plumbing. There had been a Jewish school, Jewish library, Jewish theatre, a Jewish sporting association, and much more. These institutions still existed, but their activities were restricted by lack of patronage, and were but a shadow of their former glory.

She had witnessed the first beginnings of decline, unrecognizable at the time, as the first brave villagers chanced their futures in the new world. She had seen the early trickle of migrants from the town turn into a steady stream, and then into a rushing torrent.

Her greatest comfort was that her two daughters had taken husbands who would remain in Dorbyan, allowing them to remain close to her during her entire life.

Upon the death of Shora Hinde, Mere Gita, who was herself in poor health, confided to Chana that she would not survive the death of her mother for very long. Chana was devastated, and her worst fears were realized when Mere Gita died in the following year.

As was the case with weddings, funerals in Dorbyan were no longer a regular occurrence. So many of the townsfolk had left, and would die and be buried in distant lands. These were now including the elderly, formerly the most reluctant to leave. Voyages had become shorter and more comfortable than before, and the closed door policies in North America did not apply to aged family members who could be supported by already established relatives.

Thus it was, that when a community member passed away, the funeral signified more than the passing of a single individual, but rather another chapter in the inevitable slow death of the community itself.

Now for the second time in less than a year, the community horse-drawn vehicle arrived at the home of the Kveril family on the Krittinger Gass, where the crowd of mourners had already gathered. Because of their proximity to the house and their relationship to the deceased, Hersh and Chana had been the first to arrive. With tearful embrace they comforted the brothers Hoshe and Yankel Govsha Kveril over the loss of their mother, and then they were in turn comforted by the other mourners as they arrived.

There was silence as the members of the *Chevra Kadisha* carried the communal coffin into the house, and in the privacy of a bedroom covered the body of Mere Gita with a white shroud before placing it inside the coffin and shutting the lid. Amidst sobs for the deceased they carried the coffin to the hearse, then allowed the horse to set off at a pace sedate enough for the mourners to keep up with it on foot.

The procession made its way along the Krettinger Gass towards the town, crossed the bridge into the market street, and continued through the town square past the synagogue with its open doors. When it reached the Wainaiker Gass it turned to the right for the final mile of its journey to the cemetery.

The horses reached the gates of the cemetery and stopped. Outside the cemetery walls stood the small concrete building where the body would be taken for its final preparation before its burial. When this preparation was completed, once again by the *Chevra Kadisha*, the body would then be fit to be taken inside the cemetery proper to be buried.

The pallbearers carried the body of Mere Gita through the iron gates to a freshly dug pit not far from the resting place of her mother, Shora Hinde. This was co-incidence, as tradition did not permit families to be buried together upon request, but rather each new burial was to take place next to the one which had preceeded it.

The grave had been dug and lined with timber planks on the bottom and along the four sides. To the accompanyment of prayers the body of Mere Gita in its white shroud was taken from the coffin and gently lowered to rest on the bottom planks. Then the uppermost of the side planks were turned down to form a covering over the body.

One by one the mourners filed past the body, each picking up a pebble and placing it inside the grave, a ritual which signified the participation of the entire congregation in the burial of one of its members.

As the mourners dispersed, some to make their way home, others to linger over the graves of departed loved ones, the *Chevra Kadisha* began its final task of filling in the pit with earth.

Chana returned home physically and emotionally drained, for she knew that with Mere Gita's passing, an important part o f her life was gone forever.

No one could forsee it at the time, but Mere Gita Kveril was to be the last immediate family member to be buried in the old Dorbyan Jewish cemetery.

CHAPTER 6

Main Street
Saint John, N B
January 28, 1935

Dear Mama,

Just a little letter to tell you the latest news. What a story we have to tell! Our Sammy is now married, but the story is not so simple, and it happened very suddenly!

Since Sammy has been working in Halifax he has met a young girl named *Ruby Zwerling*. She is a *Shaine Maidele*.

It did not take them very long to realize that they were perfect for each other, and they decided that they would get married. Ruby is two years younger than our Sammy and has a college degree as a dietician. We did not know what this meant either, until Sammy explained it to us. A dietician is someone who has been trained to prepare meals in hospitals and other places where proper diet is necessary.

Ruby's family is prominent in Halifax. Her father *Charles (Chaim) Zwerling* came to Canada in 1892 from Ternapol in Galicia and later sent for *Cecelia Fruchtmann* from Krakow who arrived to become his bride. Like ourselves, his first job was peddling. Then he worked in a bank, and finally opened what was to become a successful menswear store in Halifax. They have five children, three sons and two daughters, of whom Ruby is the youngest.

Charles Zwerling is very well respected in Halifax. He has been active in the *Shul*, donates generously to charities and was particularly active in assisting Jewish refugees who arrived in Canada after the war. We had met Ruby in the past and had no doubt that she would make the perfect wife for our son. We could not think of a better family for Sammy to marry into, except for one problem.

Charles is a very cultured man. Unlike the people of Dorbyan, he received not only a strong Jewish upbringing but a secular education in Ternapol. He seems to have managed to learn English without any accent, even though like ourselves, *Yiddish* is the *Mama Loschen*. He also speaks Hebrew, Polish and German, so you can see, like most Dorbyaners he speaks many languages. Unlike the Dorbyaners however, Charles and Cecelia have refused to speak *Yiddish* in their home, with the result that their children have grown up knowing hardly a word of it.

The problem is that Charles Zwerling believes that his daughter has lowered herself to marry our Sammy. He seems to feel that Dorbyaners are uneducated peasants, and that his daughter should be able to do better. When they went to him to ask his blessing for their marriage he refused to give it to them, and forbade Ruby to marry our Sammy.

Of course they were shattered, but they were determined that they should be for each other, and they did not obey Charles' wishes. They eloped secretly to Montreal, and after a few days they returned as a happily married couple, very much in love with each other.

On the way back they stopped in Saint John and we gave them the *Nachas* they were denied in Halifax. It was not the wedding we dreamed of when it came the time for our son to marry, but they are both very happy together which makes Barnet and me very happy also.

Whether what they have done is a wise thing or not is not for us to say. Barnet and I believe that eventually Charles would have come to see the good in our Sammy and had a change of attitude. Now we fear that there will be bitterness, and that this will be a long time disappearing, if ever. We do not know Cecelia's feelings about this, but it probably would not matter, as Charles is master of his family, and what he says is law.

We pray that one day Charles will have a change of heart and realize that his daughter has done well to marry Sammy, for in all other respects he is a very fine man. In the meantime there are many others who share Charles' attitude. They are always of the Jewish community who arrived earlier and are now well established. For some reason they look down on the newer arrivals who have not yet had the chance to make their mark.

This is something that could not happen in Dorbyan, and is one of the bad features of Jewish society in almost every large community in North America. I am told that in big Jewish communities like New York this is very common, where established German Jews will have nothing to do with those who come from farther east.

This is the reason for this letter. As you can see our lives have been very exciting. We are now blessed with a beautiful daughter-in-law. The rest of us are all healthy, and we wish health to you and Papa and *die Schwestern und die Kindern.* There is a little something in this letter for you to buy something for them.

Ihre Tochter
Esther

Main Street
Saint John, N.B.
CANADA
August 29, 1935

Dear Mama and Papa,

Just a little letter to tell you that everyone is healthy in our family and also with Chaia and Leah. We hope that all is well with you and the rest of the *mishpoche* in Dorbyan.

Our family is now shrinking. Sammy is now working in Halifax, and when you read the rest of what I have to say you will agree that he will probably remain there.

Celia is now twenty years old and is now thinking of going to Halifax to work as well.

The time has passed very quickly, and it only seems like yesterday that we adopted her (or rather Sammy adopted her!). Yet it is now fourteen years that she has been with us.

Jean is just turning eight and so we won't lose her for a long time to come. She does well at school, has many friends, and is a joy to everyone.

As I told you before, Sammy finished college in Halifax, and then went to a university called Harvard in Boston to do further business studies. Last year he finished his degree and went to Halifax where he found a position as an accountant in a department store called

Klines. He has many times told us what a good business it was and that someday he would like to run a business of his own just like this one.

A few days ago he provided us with a surprise when he told us that the owners had offered him the chance to buy the business from them. The problem was that they wanted five thousand dollars for the business, which of course Sammy doesn't have.

When he asked us for the money we were shocked. It is a very large sum, but Barnet has managed to save this amount over the years. From time to time he told me he was considering to invest it, possibly in a house which he could rent to others, or possibly in a second store in the new part of town known as King Square, but to date he never made a decision and simply kept the money in the bank.

Five thousand dollars is a lot of money and it has taken us most of our lives to save it, and we were very troubled when Sammy asked us for it. We stayed up the whole night agonizing about it. What if Sammy's judgement was wrong, and the owners were selling because the business had no future? Or should we trust Sammy's judgement as, after all, he is better educated than we are, and he knows the business from being there as an accountant?

In the end we decided that if we didn't give Sammy this opportunity we would never be able to live with ourselves. Barnet told Sammy about the other investment plans he had been considering, but told him that the best investment we could make would be in our own son. I have never seen anyone as grateful as Sammy was at that moment. He was in tears, and he promised us that we would never regret our decision.

As I said earlier, the only problem now is that Sammy will almost certainly make his life in Halifax. We were hoping that he might find something in Saint John and that we would have him near us, but Halifax is not so bad. When I think of what you and Papa went through when we moved to the other side of the world I realize how fortunate we are.

So that is the news from our family. We don't have as much money in the bank as we used to but we have a very happy son, and we still lead very comfortable lives.

I am enclosing a little something for you to use as you wish. Give our regards to my sisters and their families. Health to all.

Ihre Tochter,
Esther

DORBYAN

PART 6

CHAPTER 1

The years following the first world war brought little change to Dorbyan. More Dorbyaners now lived in distant lands than in the town itself, which was gradually shrinking. Letters from abroad told of amazing advances in living standards with a degree of comfort and affluence possible which would have been unimaginable but a generation earlier. The motorcar had become popular, new gadgetry was making the lot of the housewife easier, education was available to all, the radio, the railways, the telegraph systems were improving communication and making isolation a thing of the past. These changes were taking place in Canada, the United States, and South Africa, and the migrants from Dorbyan were amongst the first to share in them.

In Dorbyan no such changes had occurred. The daily life of the villagers consisted of the same routine that their parents and grandparents had known. Apart from the railway built some fifty years earlier and the telegraph system, both little used by Dorbyaners, it was difficult to point to any change that had occurred in the village. The menfolk, almost to a person devout, rose every day to perform their morning prayers in the synagogue, returning again for the same ritual before sunset of the same day. In the hours between they earned their living in much the same fashion as their forebears had always done. Trading had been the Jewish way of life and would never change, possibly because it provided the freedom to maintain one's devotion to his daily religious duties.

The women generally rose at the same time as their men, to provide them with a meal before they went off to synagogue, then turned their attention to the children, who likewise had to be fed before going off to *cheder* classes. These duties taken care of, their lives then became easier for those without infant children, with housework, cooking and shopping easily fitted into the day. The exception was those with infant children, or those who were pregnant, a group which constantly seemed to include most of the married women of childbearing age.

For the children, *Cheder* classes began as early as three years of age, and seldom later than four. The *cheder* classes were a full-time occupation, taking up most of the mornings and afternoons. Both sexes received equal training at the beginning, with greater stress placed on the males as the age of *bar-mitzvah* approached. Education was a serious matter, and was considered the key to the future of any individual. Children's tastes were simple, of necessity, and so were their methods of amusing themselves. Swimming in the river after *cheder* in summer and skating on it in winter were two favourite pastimes. Amongst the younger ones hopscotch was a favourite game, played in the *Shul Platz* or in any other area where the appropriate squares could be drawn. Older children practised kicking a ball in preparation for the days when they hoped to win a place on the Macabee soccer team.

In the summer every Friday afternoon the men and women congregated on opposite sides of the lake of Dorbyan known as *The Prud*, where they bathed in preparation for the coming Sabbath. It was not unusual for the men to be accompanied by their horses.

In the winter the bathing was done at the *Mikvah*, or technically speaking, the *Mikvot*, for Dorbyan was unusual in that the bathhouse was in fact two small buildings, one for each sex. At the entrance of the buildings could always be found an attendant available to heat water for a fee.

There was very little in the daily life of a Dorbyaner which would have seemed out of place to his grandparents, and in fact very little had changed since the earliest days of settlement in *Loigzim*.

The Dorbyaners who migrated to other lands began to have less and less in common with those they had left behind. While ties remained strong between those whose birthplace had been the town and their families remaining there, it was inevitable that with the passing of time the ties would weaken. As the first new generation appeared in the new world, the process became evident. Most Dorbyaners placed the greatest importance on adjusting to conditions in their new country, and did everything within their power to pass on the advantage to their children. Less and less was Dorbyan mentioned in their conversations, less and less was Yiddish spoken in the presence of children, and more and more the emphasis was placed on succeeding in the new world under the conditions which existed there.

A new generation appeared in Canada, in America, and in South Africa, with little knowledge of Dorbyan, a place accasionally mentioned by their parents, and to all purpose having little more meaning than any other distant and foreign land.

CHAPTER 2

As the world watched the actions of Hitler in Germany, reactions elsewhere were mixed. Needless to say, Jews throughout Europe and America reacted with alarm, having seen and experienced it all before. Amongst the gentile communities there was little sense of urgency, and reactions ranged from total indifference to mild but ineffective condemnation. Many countries refused to accept what was happening to the Jews as fact, and those which did, considered the matter grossly exaggerated. Some believed that the problem was an internal matter to be sorted out by the Germans themselves, while others agreed with British prime minister Neville Chamberlain's generous statement that, although he did not find the Jews a particularly likeable people, he could nonetheless not condone the pogroms against them.

Thus it was that very little attempt was made to dissuade Hitler from his policies of anti-semitism, and it became obvious as time passed that western governments would do nothing to intervene. At this point, Jewish communities began instead to lobby their own governments to open their doors to the thousands of German Jews who were desperate to flee their country. Once again their efforts were frustrated, and the number of refugees allowed into western countries did not appreciate to any degree. By now most German Jews were destitute, and did not possess the qualifications which made them desirable immigrants. The number of German Jews who were able to find sanctuary in the west remained pitifully small.

Of all the western countries, only Holland came to the rescue in any meaningful way. Small, overcrowded, and less able to accept refugees than almost any other country, its doors remained open to any German Jew who was able to make it across the border. The Dutch, to their everlasting credit, accepted German refugees far in excess of their capacity to accommodate them, and continued their gesture right up to the moment when their own country was overwhelmed by the Nazi onslaught.

It was to the east that the greatest number of German Jews fled. The Baltic countries and the areas administered by Russia had long been considered undesirable, but now offered the only escape route. German speaking districts became the favoured destinations, and in the Memel area alone the Jewish population trebled from 3,000 to 9,000 in the short space of three years.

Dorbyan, less than twenty miles from Memel, was not unaffected, and the rise of Hitler was taken seriously. The Russian pogroms had spared the town, but had been near enough to be well known, and now the same thing seemed to be happening again. The puzzling thing was that the perpetrators were not primitive and illiterate Russians, but Germans, whose country was the land of Bach and Beethoven, the land where such barbarities could never happen.

In 1937 Hersh and Chana opened a letter from their daughter Chaia in Saint John which left them stunned and speechless. After more than thirty years of happiness in the new world the good fortune of their family had come to an end. The tragedy occurred in the family of their second daughter Leah, married to Aaron Nathan Cohen, himself a Dorbyaner.

Aaron Nathan had been tending his dry goods shop on a typical weekday afternoon. Business had been only so-so, which was probably normal in a still partially recessed economic environment. The forty-four dollars in his till would have probably seemed considerable to an outsider, but after allowing for the cost of the merchandise sold and other expenses, would have been less than sufficient to provide for his wife and five children. When a robber armed with a gun appeared in his doorway, it was not surprising that Aaron Nathan Cohen refused to part with his day's takings without a fight.

He had in fact given the money to the robber, but then had made the mistake of chasing the man as he fled down the street. He managed to catch the fugitive, but in the ensuing struggle he was shot and killed. The whole story had been written by Chaia to save her sister the agony of writing about it.

The family had helped Leah in the traditional manner, and although life would never be the same for her, she would manage. Son Bennie, twenty-four years old, took over the running of the store, Daughter Liebe, who had been working in Halifax in a store owned by cousin Sammy Jacobson, returned to be at her mother's side. Likewise, daughter Sarah returned home and youngest daughter Minnie was able to complete her education.

In a sense, it turned out that Aaron Nathan Cohen and his family were not the only victims of the incident. The killer, a Catholic, was a victim as well, a victim of a misguided anti-semitism which has never been succesfully eradicated from any society on earth. Later, in the court, he told that his motivation for committing the crime came from what he had heard from the pulpit of his church, where the priests had constantly lamented the fact that "The Jews had all the money." He was acquitted of murder but eventually convicted of manslaughter.

As Hersh numbly read the letter that Chana had handed to him, his hands trembled and his head shook in disbelief.

"Chana, how is this possible? What is this world coming to? Just what is it that we have done to make the rest of the world treat us so?"

He continued, "Who would believe that this thing could happen in Canada, which everyone has told us is the justest and freest country in the world?....

"......How can anyone explain this? Look, look, what is happening in Germany! Our people there are being mistreated to the point that the only thing they can do is to flee the country! Why Germany?..... the country where Jews have always felt at home, and were appreciated and treated according to their worth?"

He swallowed, and cleared his choking voice. Chana looked downwards , placing her head in her hands.

"Oh, Leah, my poor daughter! What have you done to deserve this?....Your family is so young!....Why?......If only I were nearer to you, perhaps I could be of some comfort, but what can I do from here?.....I feel so helpless...!"

Hersh continued.

"First Germany, and now, who would believe that this could happen in Canada, a man dying simply because he was a Jew? In Germany it took only one man, yes, just one man, to change the people from decent human beings into a nation of beasts. Can it be possible for one man alone to do this, or is it something that was already in the people before he came along?"

Chana did not answer.

"And now, can it be that in Canada, it is no different, that the people there are the same as *goyim* everywhere, hating us, yet keeping it hidden until the right man comes along?

"...When I think of my friend Dodke Wolff, I can now see what a wise person he was, and how far ahead of his time. He seemed to know, he had a vision, that no place on earth is safe for Jews, and that we must always keep wandering to preserve ourselves, until the day comes that we have a homeland of our own.

"How can anyone disagree with him now? And what would he say if he were alive to see the things that are happening now? I only know that I have more respect for those who are leaving for Palestine than I used to have.

"Chana, look at us! We are both past eighty, we are old. How much change have you seen since we were young? Can you not remember when Dorbyan was growing, and the Lithuanians were happy to have us because of the prosperity we created? I sometimes wonder if they still feel the same about us, even though they do not show it. Things are not the same anymore, not even in Lithuania. Do the people here still want us, or would they rather be rid of us?"

Chana shook her head in resignation.

"At last you ask this question, Hersh, to which I have known the answer for many years. Of course the people here would like to be rid of us. Everyone knows this but yourself. I am surprised it has taken you so long to realize this."

"Chana, I ask the question, but I am not sure of the answer. I am sure that there are those who compete against us and would prefer to see us gone, but I still believe that most Lithuanians are decent people who accept our right to live amongst them."

"Then you are blind, Hersh, for I do not believe that there is a single Lithuanan who would be the friend of a Jew if a Hitler were come here."

She continued, "But for us, this is not important. We are both old. How much time do we have left? I worry about our children and our grandchildren, who are now growing up. What future do they have? What will become of them? I used to think that they were better off in Canada, but now that this has happened......

"......I have never felt so helpless! Is it not a parent's duty to help her children when they need help? Yet how can we help, when we are so far away, when it is we who must seek help from them?"

"Chana, there is nothing that we or anyone else can do, but place our faith in God. It seems that the whole world is against us, and that as in our past, noone is prepared to come to our assistance. Perhaps it is something that we Jews must suffer every thousand years or so. Who knows?

"...Our lives in Lithuania have become difficult, but it is nothing like what is happening in Germany. And now, it makes me frightened to have to think it, but for the first time I feel that the same thing can happen some day in Canada and America."

"But why, Hersh? Can the world not see that something evil is taking place? Why does the world allow this to happen?"

"The world does not care about Jews, Chana, so long as it can continue to do business with the Germans. Perhaps if it were *goyim* who were the victims it would be different, but who can say?"

"Perhaps," answered Chana. "It is a good thing that we are old, and will not have to live through what is coming. But still, it makes me feel selfish, for we have had long and happy lives. Why should our children not be able to have the same?"

"I have no answer, Chana, but I am worried, exactly like you. Maybe they should be going to Palestine. Even in Palestine the life is hard, and the land has to be fought for, but at least most of the world seems to agree that we should be there. Maybe this is the answer. I know what Dodke Wolff would say."

CHAPTER 3

As a tactician, Hitler had shown himself to be a master, and success followed success for him in Germany. The campaign against the Jews and other minorities had diverted public opinion away from the real economic issues, and yet there had been sufficient economic gain to keep the people happy. The great depression was coming to an end, national prestige was rising, and Hitler and his party were in the position to take credit for it.

He had been equally successful in the international sphere, playing one nation against another with uncanny skill. The French occupation forces had long departed, Germany had reclaimed the Rhine district. He had masterminded the *Anschluss* with Austria, a union through which Austria became the inferior partner and effectively a province of Germany. He had formed an alliance with the Russians, formerly his hated enemy, through which his eastern frontiers had been made secure. He had threatened and bluffed the western powers into allowing him to sieze the Sudeten area of Czechoslovakia on the grounds that the German speaking population there rightfully deserved to be reunited with Germany.

Six months later he occupied the whole of Czechoslovakia, causing disquiet amongst the western nations, who were finally showing signs of alarm at his actions. This time he was warned that similar actions, particularly against Poland, could lead to war.

In March of 1939 the people of Dorbyan were shocked to find that their buffer against Hitler had disappeared. Using the same tactics he had used to sieze the Sudeten area of Czechoslovakia, Hitler announced the annexation of the Lithuanian district of Memel, which he claimed had been German speaking and Prussian territory for centuries before the Great War.

The operation was sudden, the western powers were caught unprepared, and without warning the 9000 Jews (20% of the total population) of Memel found themselves in deadly peril. Independent Lithuania was powerless to prevent the takeover, and when the German army arrived the Jews were given but a few days to leave, during which time they suffered the same personal assaults, the same looting of homes and businesses and the same burning of synagogues that their brethren had suffered in Germany proper.

North America was available to only a fortunate few. Some crossed over the Baltic to the Scandinavian countries, a few managed to make it to England and Scotland. For most, the only direction to flee was eastwards, into what remained of independent Lithuania.

Some of those who fled were doing it for the second time, for they had been refugees when Memel had seemed a safe haven from the persecutions in Germany itself.

In the space of four days, the last two Jews in Memel, a Mr Sliomas Gilis and a Ms Katz had left the city. A prosperous and influential Jewish community, which dated its beginnings in Memel back some four hundred years, had disappeared from the map without a trace.

Yet, whatever hardships the Jews of Memel had suffered, they could count one thing as a blessing, for they were the last of Europe's Jews to be given the option of fleeing.

Kretinga, some eight miles from Dorbyan, became the new German-Lithuanian border, with German troops stationed but a few hundred yards beyond the outsksirts of the town. Refugees flooded into Kretinga, although many considered that it was not distant enough from Hitler. Dorbyan's Jewish population, which had declined steadily to the point where it numbered little more than five hundred, suddenly increased by more than half. Some of the refugees had managed to bring money or valuables, but most arrived with little more than the clothes they wore. Even those who had salvaged some of their belongings were distressed, for they had lost homes and livlihoods, and could see nothing but destitution in their future.

In more prosperous times the sudden influx of refugees into Dorbyan might have caused accommodation problems, but the town now abounded with semi-empty homes.

Surprisingly, despite the exodus from the town, very few if any homes had become empty, the migrations simply allowing remaining families to spread out over greater space. Yet almost every home could point to an empty room or rooms, and the newcomers were quickly made to feel at ease. Despite the economic hardships known by the village, feeding itself had never been a problem, and most homes were close to self-sufficient. Whatever might arise in the future, there would always be enough to eat in Dorbyan.

The morale of the refugees was a different matter. In most cases up to a short time earlier they had enjoyed a life of affluence, members of an established and influential community dating back to the sixteenth century. Like many German speaking Jews, they had become assimilated into the local society and had felt themselves a part of it. Unlike the pious people of Dorbyan, their Jewish religion had been secondary, and had never featured prominently in their dealings with the greater community. Now, in the short space of but a few days, they had seen their places of worship desecrated, their property vandalized and stolen, and their friendships and connections with the Christian community count for nothing.

What had been hardest of all to bear was that the people in whom they had trusted and considered their friends had turned against them upon the first arrival of the German soldiers.

All this had taken place in Memel, a city well known to Dorbyaners and long a destination for personal and business visits. Less than twenty miles away, it was now separated from from Lithuania by nothing more than a barbed wire frontier guarded by heavily armed German soldiers.

In September 1939 Hitler made the first major miscalculation of his political career. For months he had been threatening Poland, on the grounds that Danzig, a Polish city with a large German speaking population, should be treated in the same manner as the Czech Sudeten and Memel, and rightfully become a part of Germany. This time the French and British held firm, and warned Hitler that an attempt to sieze Poland would lead to war.

Based on his past experience, Hitler had little reason to take the warnings seriously, and upon a flimsy pretext, he sent his armies into Poland in a full scale invasion. Now, for the first time, he found that the warnings were real. He was given an ultimatum to withdraw by the French and British governments, and when he refused, he found himself at war with them. The Second World War had begun.

CHAPTER 4

Hersh Jacob, now eighty-three years of age, but still rock solid on his feet and mentally alert, tried to learn as much as possible about the events in Memel in the hope that it would help him understand the madness which was taking place throughout the entire world. He spent his time in the *Shul Platz* after prayer, seeking out refugees and speaking with anyone who would spare the time to speak with him. Many of the refugees were reluctant to discuss what had been a tragedy in their lives, others were too polite to refuse, but gave little away. Others simply didn't know the answers to the numerous questions that Hersh asked.

Why was this happening? Could anyone have prevented it, or even forseen its coming? Had there been any change in the mood of the German people in Memel before it had happened, or had the change in peoples' attitudes ocurred only after Hitler had arrived? What would have happened to the Jews had they stood their ground and refused to flee? What about close gentile friends and neighbours, how had they reacted? Had they offered any support at all?

No matter how may people he questioned, Hersh could make no sense out of the answers he received, and found himself unable to draw any conclusions. Most of the Memel refugees seemed to be just as puzzled as he was, their puzzlement compounded by shock. Until the announcement of the German arrival all had seemed normal, although there had been apprehension in many quarters. Then suddenly, as though a signal had been given, everything had changed. The welcome given to the entering German soldiers had been ecstatic, with flowers thrown at their feet as they marched into the city. The joy and celebration had been unprecedented, matched only by that of a few days later as the Jews were leaving. The refugees could remember crowds jeering and mauling the Jews, then cheering as each succeeding Jewish shop front had been smashed or set alight. Most shocking of all were the expressions of sheer hatred on the faces of those who had once been their friends.

Each night Hersh told Chana the result of the day's conversations, and each time he inevitably began with the same puzzled question.

"Why, Chana? How can it be that people can change their behaviour so completely in the space of but a few days? Can it be that all this was arranged beforehand? I don't see how. It almost seems as if this Hitler *mamser* has everyone in the world hypnotized."

"Nothing has changed, Hersh. People do not change from day to day. They have always felt this way about us, but until now they had no opportunity to show it."

"But why, Chana? If people feel this way about us, why don't they simply tell us? Do you mean to say that the same thing could happen here in Dorbyan if, God forbid, Hitler should someday decide that he wants all of Lithuania?"

"Of course it would happen here! Why do you thing that the *goyim* here should be any different from those in Memel?"

"Chana, I cannot believe this. We live in a small village, not a large city. I know many of these people, and I am even close friends with some of them."

"You think you know them, and you think you are close friends with them, my dear, but you fool yourself. Maybe I have become bitter, but unlike you, I am realistic."

Hersh continued stubbornly, "Not so, Chana. Many of these people I have been dealing with for years. We have helped them, and on occasion they have been of help to us. If their mood has changed, I would notice the difference at once."

Chana smiled knowingly at Hersh. "I will never convince you, my dear, for you have always put your faith in the good in people. But times have changed, and the people have changed with the times."

"Chana, I cannot accept this. I know these people. Apart from a very few, I can not imagine them turning against us, even if Hitler were to come."

"Then you are not awake to the times, Hersh. Everyone talks about it, and we all agree that the only person a Jew can trust nowadays is another Jew. If Hitler were to come I don't believe you would find a single *goy* in or around Dorbyan to stand up for us. Our only hope is that Hitler will not come."

"Who knows what that *mamser* will do?" Mused Hersh. "Reason says that he should not be interested in us as we are not Germans, and have never been. But since when has reason played a part in anything he does? Once we were too far away for him to bother us, but no longer. All I know is that if he decides to come here, nothing will stand in his way. The Lithuanians could not stop him from taking Memel. The Russians would do little better than they did in the last war. The French and the English have very little reason to care what happens here in Lithuania."

Chana did not answer. Hersh continued.

"What wories me is that Hitler will soon realize this, and then decide to have Lithuania too. Then, Chana, where would we flee? Where? Eastwards, perhaps, into Russia?"

"I will not flee anywhere, Hersh. Here I was born, here I have always lived, and here I will die when God wills it."

"For us it is easy Chana, but what about the others who still have their lives ahead of them? Our children, our grandchildren, where would they go?"

Chana was silent.

Dorbyan
December 6, 1939

Dear Joseph!

I write this letter to wish you a Happy Chanukah, and to tell you a bit about our lives in Dorbyan.

Since the Germans came into Memel everyone has been very worried, but now it is beginning to look as if nothing will happen to us and we will be safe. Most of us believe that Hitler made his first mistake when he invaded Poland. Until then he had no reason to believe the warnings of England and France were serious, but now he finds himself at war with them. When the fighting starts I believe he will find himself in trouble very quickly, for fighting England and France is not the same as fighting Czechoslovakia or Poland. For us it can only be good news, as he will not be thinking of taking over Lithuania, or particularly Latvia, where many Germans are living.

This is happy news for us, for many feared that our fate would become the same as the Jews in Germany. As you probably know, the Jews there have lost their jobs and their businesses, and are now having their homes and possessions taken away from them. They are hounded by gangs of thugs who assault them and destroy their prop-

242

erty, with the permission of the state. These things are told to us by Germans who first fled to Memel, and later to here. How the German Jews are expected to live, who knows? And now, it has become impossible for them to flee their country, for they have no means, and no other country will have them.

Now we learn that the same thing is happening in Poland. Many believed that the Germans would not treat citizens of other countries like they did their own, but for the Jews of Poland it is even worse. We hear stories that many of them are being killed. We can only hope that Germany loses the war quickly, before it is too late to save these people.

It is times like this that we realize how lucky we are to live in a country like Lithuania. Even though life is difficult and nobody makes a good living anymore, we are not subject to pogroms, and we are still better off than Jews in most other European countries. We are not prevented from practising our religion. Chana and I eat well, and have enough left over in our garden to help the rest of the family. We do not need much to live, which is just as well, as I now keep only one horse. It is now very rare for me to buy or sell one, and the last one I sold to a friend for no profit. But I love horses, and I shall try to keep one for so long as I live, even if it costs me money to do so.

I am healthy, but at times I worry about your mother. She is beginning to look frail and shrunken, even though she complains of no illness. Perhaps at our age this should be expected. I said that she does not complain, but this is not quite the truth. She does complain quite a bit, but it is only about her concern for her children and grandchildren, and what kind of future they can expect. One of the reasons that I am still so healthy is that she has always sacrificed herself to look after me, as she has for everybody else. I can honestly say that I have been well taken care of.

So you see that your worries about us being in danger are not necessary. Things could be better, but they are not as bad here as in other places. Keep healthy, both you and Rae, and tell your children Betty, Alvin and Shirley that their *Zeide* wishes them a *Gut Yuntif.*

Your Father,
Hersh

Dear Papa!

I received your last letter, and I hope this letter finds you and Mama in good health. Be sure to make certain that Mama takes care of herself as she does for everybody else.

We are all relieved to learn that life in Dorbyan is not as bad as we thought.

What is happening to the Jews of Germany is horrible, and it is hard to imagine that what is happening in Poland is even worse. It seems that Hitler's plan is eventually to murder them all. When will it all end......when there are no Jews left?

I am sure that you know as much as we know here, but now we are hearing that Germany will allow the Russians to take over Lithuania. It will be again like the Lithuania I grew up in, except that this time instead of a Tzar there will be communists. Who knows if this will be better or not? I don't remember the Russians ever being very nice people, but maybe it means that Hitler will leave Lithuania alone. We would all like to know what you think about this.

Here in Pontiac we hardly know that there is a war going on. Many Jews want to fight against Hitler because of what he is doing to our people, but America is not at war. Some go to Canada, where they can fight for the British Empire. I can tell you that the people of America hate Hitler and would like to help the British, and I believe that someday this will happen.

Rae and I are healthy. The children are growing up. Betty is now almost twelve, Alvin is eleven, and even our baby, Shirley, will soon be eight. I gave up trying to be a butcher and have now opened a dry goods store, where I sell surplus army and navy clothing and equipment. It seems to be a good business, and so far I am doing well at it, and making a better living than I have ever done before.

Chaia, Leah and Esther are always writing to me, and I answer them as soon as I get their letters. Leah seems to be managing quite well after the tragedy to Aaron Nathan, and Bennie is doing a good job of running the store. The girls are all doing well.

Whenever Esther writes to me, all I hear about is Sammy's son Danny, whom they adopted two years ago. Esther and Barnet are proud to become the first to be grandparents, and I am sure that they

244

have sent you photographs by now. It is hard to imagine that you and Mama have become great-grandparents. I hope it happens to you many more times.

There is no more news to tell at the moment. Give my love to my sisters and their children. Good health to you and Mama.

Joseph

Dorbyan
June 18, 1940

Dear Joseph!

Just a letter to let you know that all is well in Dorbyan even though the Russians have taken over. It is still too early to say what will happen, but for the moment there is no change to our lives. They tell us that the mail we send will be posted just as before, so we are about to find out if this is true.

For us the Russians may be a good thing, as we keep hearing that Hitler is winning in the west, and we worry that he may turn his attention in this direction if he is successful. No matter how bad the Russians may be, they cannot be as bad as Hitler.

I cannot but feel sympathy for the Lithuanians. For hundreds of years they have wanted a country of their own, and now after only twenty years of having it, they have lost it, and only God knows for how long. They made things difficult for us in many ways, but they did not deserve this, for now it is likely that their treatment at the hands of the Russians will be even more harsh than ours. I wonder how many years it will be before they can have their own country again.

Sometimes I find this hard to believe, but there are many Jews who actually welcome the Russians. The communist underground of Lithuania contained many Jews, and they have been just waiting for the day that the Russians would come. Of course the Lithuanians do not like us for this reason, and they seem to blame all Jews for the loss of their country. They seem to think that all Jews are communists, which makes me feel very uncomfortable. I do not sell many horses to Lithuanians these days, but there are one or two that I speak to, and they do not like what is happening. They are not happy with the Reizman family, who have been very active communists. I try to tell them that most Jews are religious and have no use for communism, and I tell them that many Jews are businessmen who will lose their businesses under the Russians, and suffer like the rest of them, but they cannot accept this. I also tell them that it might not be a bad thing if the Reizmans of Dorbyan have influence with the communists, as it might cause the Russians to go easier on the people of the town.

Who knows what will happen next? All I know is that Hitler seems to be winning in the west. Who would have believed that he could defeat every country in Europe, especially France? Now it is beginning to look as if he will defeat England as well. Our only hope is that this will not happen, for as soon as he is successful there, he will come in our direction, Russians or no Russians.

This is all I can say now. Our lives go on as before, and apart from our worries for the future, we are not suffering, certainly not as much as the people who are fighting against Hitler.

I wish you and Rae good health. Love to our grandchildren.

Your Father
Hersh

Pontiac, September 1, 1940

Dear Papa!

I hope this letter reaches you in time for *Yuntif.* Health to everyone in Dorbyan. Your last letter reached us without trouble. It took a little longer than usual, but with war in Europe, what can one expect?

We are all well here in Pontiac. Rae and I are healthy. The children are growing very quickly.

It is impossible for us not to worry about you in Dorbyan. We keep asking ourselves if there is any way for you to get out. It seems as if Hitler has won the war, and many people believe that England will shortly be forced to surrender. Even if America were to join in the war against Hitler, we would not be able to help in time. It may be possible for you to get a boat from Polangen, or maybe Libau, that would take you to Sweden. If there is any way to do this, and if it requires money, let me know, and we will find it for you at once. Everyone now believes that it is only a matter of time before Hitler turns his armies in your direction. If the English have not been able to stop him, then what chance do the Russians have? What frightens us most of all is the knowledge that Hitler is not only persecuting Jews, but murdering them.

Sam Kveril, who now calls himself Karel, gets letters from his brother Hoshe in Dorbyan, and what Hoshe tells is not encouraging. He does not seem to be the optimist that you are. I hope that you are the one who is correct.

Here we will all be celebrating *Rosh Hashanah* together, our family, the Mones family and the Kverils. It is lovely to have so many *Mishpoche* and friends together, but the occasion is spoilt everytime someone mentions the danger you are facing. We hope that all of you enjoy a *Gut Yuntif* on the *Krittinger Gass,* and we will be thinking of you. Even though America is a wonderful place to live, I often feel homesick that I cannot be with you to celebrate.

This is the news from here. Health to you and the rest of the family.

Please write as soon as you receive this letter, as we are all worried about you, and wait anxiously for every piece of news.

Joseph

Dorbyan

January 27, 1941

Dear Joseph!

I am writing this letter as soon as I am able, but it is not easy now, as the war is having an effect on the mail, and your last letter took a month longer than usual to arrive. Still we should be grateful that we are receiving any mail at all while this war is going on.

Your mother is well and keeping very busy with her letter writing. Her job is three times greater than mine, as she has three daughters to write to. I think she enjoys it all the same, and nothing brings her greater happiness than when the mail arrives and amongst it is a letter from one of our daughters in Saint John.

The Russians are now beginning to behave just like the Russians of old, except that the communists have different ideas from the Tzars. When the Tzars ruled it was possible for a Jew to do business in Lithuania provided he paid money to the right people. Now it doesn't seem to matter what we do, and even if we had the money to pay them it would make no difference, for business is a bad word with them. They have begun to confiscate the businesses of people and turn them over to the state. Thus far it has happened only in the larger cities, and Dorbyan has been spared, but it must also come to us someday. In this the Lithuanians suffer perhaps more than we do, for they were the ones who pushed us out of many of our businesses, which they now operate. Now the Russians are taking over the businesses, and for this they still seem to find some reason to blame the Jews.

Still we cannot complain too much, for we suffer less than the countries that are at war, and we always eat well. The Russians take some of our food, but we are still left with enough. We do not do much, and we need very little money.

You say that we should leave, but this is not so easy. Most countries will no longer accept Jews, and even large amounts of money cannot change this. Chana and I would not leave what has been our home since birth, and we could not leave our family behind in any case. Others who have tried very hard to leave have had no success. For the moment we feel safe here in Dorbyan.

With the people from Memel, the *Shul* is now very crowded every day, just as it used to be when you were growing up. There is not much for people to do in Dorbyan, so we all go to *Daven* and sit around the *Shul Platz*. The children continue their lessons as they have always done. Rabbi Isser Weissbord is a fine man and a very good teacher, and the children all love him.

Your Mama and I are well, although as I told you, she is showing signs of her age. I suppose that I am ageing as well, but at the age of eighty-four it must be expected. I still get pleasure out of keeping a horse, and I even think that it has become part of Chana's life as well.

Keep healthy. Love to Rae and our grandchildren.
Your Father

Hersh

Dear Papa!

I write this letter with much worry in my heart. Although you write that you are well and healthy, we are afraid that this will not last. We are all hoping against hope that we are mistaken, and that you and Mama and my sisters and their families will be safe.

As we begin to think of *Pesach* in two weeks' time, our thoughts are with you more than ever. I still remember the wonderful *Seders* we used to have in the *Krittinger Gass,* and I try to make our own *Seders* just like the ones I knew. I still remember the borsht that Mama made for everyone, and although we make borsht here too, I still tell people that it can never be the same as Mama made.

But even these happy memories cannot stop us from thinking about your danger.

It now looks as if England will not surrender to Hitler. This must be a good thing, as they are getting more and more help from Canada and their Empire, and slowly , from America as well. If the English can stand up to Hitler, then perhaps he will not be able to move in your direction, but many people believe that he will do so in any case.

Even without Hitler, life cannot be good for you under the Russians. I can remember from my own childhood how cruel they were. All we can do is hope that nobody from our *Mishpoche* is suffering. It must be very difficult for the younger ones.

I ask again about the chances of getting out. I can understand that you and Mama do not wish to leave, but what about my sisters and their families? There must be someplace they can go, at least until the war is over. As I have said, if the problem is money, let me know, and it will be taken care of. The only thing on our minds at this moment is that you are safe from danger.

The five of us in Pontiac are healthy and doing well. It is you that

249

we worry about. Please write back as soon as you receive this letter, as we cannot help thinking about you.

Love to you and Mama, and love to my sisters and their families.

Joseph

Dorbyan, June 17, 1941

Dear Joseph!

Your letter arrived just a few days ago, and now I write to let you know that we are all alive and well. Although our lives are difficult, we are perfectly safe for the moment, as you can see from this letter. There is talk of the Germans fighting the Russians and coming into Lithuania, but none of us believe that this will happen. Hitler is no longer winning the war against England, and he does not need more *Tsores* by fighting the Russians as well. He may be a very wicked man, and a *Mamser* as well, but an idiot he is not.

It is our lives under the Russians that cause us the most worry. They have taken over the businesses of thousands of people, both Jews and Lithuanians, and sent many of the owners to Siberia, just because they protested at the loss of their property. In Dorbyan there are not so many businesses for the Russians to take over, but still we have suffered. Elior's business has been taken over, and now he has no means of supporting his family. The children, except for Natan Beir, are grown, but also unable to find any means of helping. We help them where we can, with food, and we all survive, but there is no future. Elior takes it well and smiles, but we know he is hurt inside. He says that his business has been so bad of late that the Russians are welcome to it.

Your cousin Hoshe Kveril has also lost his business, the sawmill. One day the Russians came and told him to go home, that the sawmill was now the property of the state. They said that they might offer him a job there later on. Hoshe's business was one of the few good businesses in Dorbyan, and they lived very well in their home just up thr road from us. Now we do not know what his future will be. He argued with the Russians when they came, and we consider that he

250

was very lucky not to be sent to Siberia.

So far not one Dorbyaner has been sent to Siberia or imprisoned, and we believe that Leiba Reizman may have had something to do with this. He has now become general secretary for the Communist Youth Party for all of Lithuania. Many people are beginning to become proud of him, even those who are religious and not communists. The problem is the Lithuanians, who cannot seem to realize that people like Leiba have helped to make our lives less difficult.

Many Lithuanians firmly believe that Leiba Reizman and other Jews were the ones who invited the Russians in to take away their country, and they seem to think that we have all benefited from their presence How we managed to invite them, they cannot tell us, but they blame us just the same. It would do them good to have a word with Hoshe Kveril.

Just a few days ago the Russian secret police raided many homes and arrested hundreds of people, both Jews and Lithuanians. The raids are continuing even as I write this letter. As usual Dorbyan has been spared, probably again because of Leiba Reizman, but this time the Lithuanians are arming into partisan groups top fight the Russians. Many of them believe that the Germans will soon come, and that they will regain their country and take revenge on those who wronged them. Of course we do not expect this to happen, but we worry just the same. There are many people in this country who are very confused.

That is all for now, Joseph. Things are not very good here, but I hope you will believe me when I say that we are safe. I shall mail this letter today along with the three letters your mother wrote to your sisters in Saint John. I wish you and Rae and the children much health and happiness.

Your Father
Hersh

DORBYAN

PART 7

CHAPTER 1

It was mid-morning of Sunday, June 22, 1941, when Hersh arrived home from the morning prayer, breathless and excited.

"Chana! Turn on the radio! Have you heard? Have you heard?"

"I know what I have been hearing all morning, hundreds of airplanes flying overhead, and the sound of distant explosions every few minutes!"

"Chana, they are coming! They are coming! Hitler is attacking and coming into Lithuania!"

He continued excitedly, "And they said that he would never do it! He must be a complete *meshuganeh*! Now he is not only fighting England, but Russia as well!"

He paused as another explosion rumbled in the distance.

That one seems to be coming from the direction of Krettingen! They must be suffering a bombardment! We have been lucky here. So far only a few shells have struck Dorbyan, and they were probably by accident."

"Will we see the German army marching through Dorbyan, Hersh? What do the people in town think?"

"I don't think they will be coming here. I'm told that the two main German armies are to the north and south of us."

"Will this make any difference to us?", asked Chana soberly.

"Probably not. It won't change anything except give us a bit more time, answered Hersh. Everyone now agrees that we are doomed. Once the Germans take over a country, we know what happens to

Jews. The *roitzchim* will come in and kill some of us, and put the rest of us to work in some German slave labour camp. Someone has already heard on the radio that Hitler has announced that he has no quarrel with the Lithuanian people, and that he has come into Lithuania to liberate the country from the communists and the Jews."

He put his arm around Chana.

"It is terrible. Maybe not so bad for us, but I feel sick at the thought of what will happen to our children's families. They are so young, and now, what future do they have? There is nothing anyone can do. I'm going inside to listen to the radio."

They went into the house, and into the kitchen and dining area where the radio was kept. Hersh fiddled with the dials, and moved the wires about which connected the radio to its glass storage battery. For a full minute there was silence, then a dull hum as the radio began to warm up. Then came a crackling noise which gradually became recognizable as human speech. They both hunched as closely as possible to the radio to catch the flickering announcements.

An announcer came on, and Hersh immediately continued his fiddling with the dial.

"Hungarian, maybe Rumanian, who knows? There must be something in German on somewhere, or maybe Russian or Lithuanian."

Then he stopped short as an announcement came on in a recognizable language.

"This is a joke!", he exclaimed. "Did you hear? Stalin earlier announced to his armies not to engage the Germans in combat until the situation has become clarified? The idiot! Just how must clearer must it become before he sees what's happening?"

He laughed ironically.

"Perhaps he should listen to the German broadcasts! Too bad he is not here himself to find out what it's like to have German airplanes dropping bombs on him!"

He fiddled the dial again, then hushed quickly as a crackling voice turned into a German bulletin. German armies were achieving their objectives everywhere along a front of 1800 miles, stretching from the Arctic circle in Finland to the Black Sea in Rumania.

The Russian armies won't do us much good now," said Hersh resignedly. I never did have much confidence in them. Before today is over, the only Russians still to be found in Lithuania will be prisoners of the Germans."

He continued, "In fact, it would not surprise me if the Lithuanian partisans are already fighting against the Russians as well. For sometime they have been insisting that this day would come, and that when it did, they would play their part in driving the Russians from their country. Something tells me that all this was known to them for quite some time."

"I suppose that after the Russians are gone, we can expect the partisans to turn against us," said Chana without emotion.

"Who knows?", answered Hersh. Who knows what the Germans have organized for this country....Shh!....I think another announcement is coming!"

Both strained as they moved their heads closer to the radio.

"Listen!", said Hersh. "The Allies have condemned this invasion by Hitler, and they say that they will help Russia in this fight."

He laughed again.

"Another joke! What can the Allies do to help us, or the Russians, or anybody else at this moment? They are barely able to help themselves!"

Hersh continued to fiddle with the dial. Another announcement came on, this time from another part of Germany, describing a communique issued from Berlin. He groaned as the communique proceeded to list the successes of the German armies thus far.

"Listen! The German armies under Von Kuechler have now passed through Krittingen and have followed the coastal road past Polangen, and are now on their way towards Shkud and the Latvian border. They say that the Russians are now in full flight, and the only thing limiting the German advance is the speed of their vehicles. They are advising the people of Libau and Riga that their liberation is but a short time away."

He turned to Chana.

"Liberation! Liberation! Hitler should buy a dictionary!"

He turned off the radio.

"If it is all right with you, Chana, I don't wish to listen to anymore of this. It is too depressing. I wonder how long it will be before the first German secret service *mamsers* appear in Dorbyan."

Chana was engaged in thoughts of her own. Her eyes were distant as she spoke.

"This is what we have been fearing all along........and now it has happened.....there is no need to ask what our fate is going to be. The only question is whether our murderers will be Lithuanian or German.

She raised her head, and turned to Hersh.

"If we have so little time left,..........then is it not better at least to spend as much of it as possible with the *mishpoche*? Do you think we should walk over to Rachel or Breina's house and perhaps stay with them?"

"I don't think the situation is quite so gruesome as that, at least not yet," answered Hersh. "Surely it will take the Germans at least a few days to occupy this district, and even then there are many towns much more important than Dorbyan which will have to be occupied first. If we are lucky we may even have a few weeks before anything happens."

"Hersh, I know that we have talked about this before, and that we have agreed that we ourselves cannot flee, but what about our children and grandchildren? Is there no place that they could go? We have a bit of money saved up, could we not use it to help them get out?"

Hersh shook his head.

"If there is any place left for them to go, I don't know of it," he answered sadly. "Many of our younger people have been willing to leave for sometime. We have been talking about it in the *Shul Platz* just this morning. It is simply too late, not even Palestine is open to them anymore. Tell me, just where could they go?"

"To the east, I suppose."

"Maybe yesterday, Chana, but not anymore. It's now too late for even this now. By now the German armies are miles in front of them. They would somehow have to manage to reach the front and then cross over it, or else they would still be in territory controlled by Germans. They might as well remain right here in Dorbyan."

"Could they not make their home and hide in the forest? It is a big place."

"Yes, I suppose they could, and I suppose that some will try it, but for how long? What would they do? How would they eat? How would they survive when winter comes? They would be hunted down like animals. I suppose a few could get away with it, but if any large number tried it they would soon be discovered. You must remember that the Lithuanian partisans used the forests when they fought the Russians. They know the forests well, and they would now be on the side of the Germans....

"....I can see only one hope, and a very small one. If it is possible to find Lithuanians to hide our families in the farms and the small villages, they might eventually find the opportunity to escape. It is a very small chance. The Germans are here for years to come, and it is a very long time to remain hidden with another family."

"I wouldn't trust the Lithuanians to hide any of our people for five minutes," answered Chana bitterly. "From what I know of these people, they would turn us over to the Germans the moment we turn our backs."

"Don't say that, Chana! I know how you feel, but there are many good Lithuanians whom I know personally. Some of them hate the Germans almost as much as we do, and would not hesitate to help us if a way could be found. Perhaps I shall have a word with someone tomorrow. I'm thinking mostly of Natan Beir. He is our youngest grandchild, and the only one who is not yet grown up. Perhaps there is someone who will hide him for us if it becomes necessary."

"Of course it will become necessary, but I'll believe it when I see it!," answered Chana.

Hersh went to the doorway at the front and stood at the top of the stairs.

"I want to have a look at the sky. Earlier I thought I saw smoke coming from the direction of Krettingen, but it seems to have gone, and now there is some coming from farther north......

"Look, Chana! I believe we are going to have company, just like on a Saturday afternoon!"

Chana joined him on the steps, taking his hand in hers. As they looked along the Krittinger Gass towards the town they could see the party of people rounding the corner and making their way into the street. The party moved quickly in their direction, about twenty-five people in all.

"They are all there, Chana! Rachel, Ada, Mina and Breina, with their families! It will be good for us all to be together at once, even though we were together only yesterday. But I don't think the conversation will be as cheerful today."

"Hersh, you must excuse me. I wasn't expecting this. It is almost mealtime, and I will have to go into the kitchen to prepeare something."

Hersh smiled. "I'm sure that you will have help, my dear."

The four families reached the front steps, and soon the house was alive with earnest discussion. Chana was greeted by each of her daughters with a tearful embrace and a "What will become of us?", while the men behaved more stoically, agonizing over the reasons for the latest calamity, and recounting the effects it would have on various people they knew in the town and elsewhere. The only child amongst them was Natan Beir, Breina and Elior's youngest, *Bar-Mitzvah* little more than a year earlier. Hersh was proud of his youngest grandson, and admired the way in which he took interest in the proceedings, showing an intelligence far beyond his fourteen years.

Hersh took Natan Beir aside.

"I suppose your father has told you what all this is likely to mean for us", he said.

"Yes, Zeide, Papa wants to send me away. He says that I am now old enough to manage on my own with other people, and that it would be possible to hide me."

"Perhaps your father knows what he is talking about. There may be people who could be trusted to look after you, and perhaps you would be safer with them."

"I have told Mama and Papa that I will not go anywhere without them. If they are in danger, then I want to be with them. I could not bear to be without them. I will leave only if they leave too!"

"You are *Bar-Mitzvah* , Natan, and that makes you a *mensch* . By law you now have the right to make your own decisions, but I don't think it would be possible to hide your entire family. Your parents, brothers and sisters are older and better able to manage for themselves. You are still young, and it is you that we worry about most of all."

"I know what is going to happen, Zeide. Papa has told me about what is happening in Poland, and how the Jews are dying there. He says it is certain to happen here too. The only thing he couldn't tell me is *why* it is happening."

"I don't think there is a sensible person in the world who could tell you *why*," answered Hersh.

"Then," said Natan Beir, "If we are going to die here, I want to be with Mama and Papa when it happens. Perhaps if we pray hard enough, something will happen to save us."

"You are a good boy, Natan, and I can see that you have a strong mind. I can see that I am not going to make you change. Tell me, how would you like to go around to the back and spend a little time with Yoiphi?"

"May I ride her, Zeide?"

"Yes, if you promise not to go too fast, and if you will feed and water her when you are finished. The saddle is just inside on the wall of the woodshed."

As Hersh watched the excited youngster dash off, he thought to himself, "....Still very much a child, ...but how much will he have to grow up in the time he has left?"

He then circulated from group to group, adding whatever he could to the conversation. As usual the family split into two groups, females in the kitchen, males on the steps and in the space to the front.

"I know that this is no time to celebrate," he announced. "But I have some schnapps here. We may as well finish it off. If we don't drink it, then I will pour it into the ground before I"ll allow the Germans or the Lithuanian partisans to wet their lips with it."

He began to pass out the drinks. The conversation continued.

"Shmuel Kagan has said that as soon as the first German forces arrive he will be setting fire to his house."

"Isn't it easy enough for a house to catch fire without setting it alight deliberately?"

"If he does that, I expect that the Germans will be even harder than usual on him and his family."

"He says that he will set it on fire then leave. What can they do to him that they have not already done to the Poles?"

Kveril has made arrangements for someone to hide his daughter Esther."

"I know, it is Vladas Jashinskas."

"Jashinskas, is that such a wise choice?"

"Who knows? Is there any such thing as a wise choice left to us? What choice does anybody have?"

"I don't trust Jashinskas, he never cared much for Jews. Why is he suddenly willing to help?"

"Foolish question! He may not care for Jews, but he cares for our money!"

"Even if Jashinskas is to be trusted, and does help, it cannot be a good thing that everyone knows what he is up to. It won't be long before the Germans find out as well."

"Some families aren't waiting for the Germans. Marjampolski the doctor, some of the Shatelis family, Shubitz, and a few others are already getting ready to leave."

"And what good will that do them? Where will they go? You can ask my sons Chaim and Leizer. They will tell you that they have been wanting to leave for weeks, but with the war going on the only direction possible was eastwards into Russia. Now not even this is possible."

"Who would wish to flee into Russia? The Russians aren't exactly the nicest of people either. You might just manage to survive for a short time longer, but the life there would be just as bad as death."

"Perhaps Leiba Reizman would be welcome in Russia. I only know, that if I were Leiba Reizman, I would be the first to leave Dorbyan."

"I didn't know he was in Dorbyan."

"He has been here with the *mishpoche* for the last week. You didn't expect to see him in *shul*, did you?"

"Where could Reizman go? He is known everywhere. I don't think there is a Lithuanian anywhere in the country who would be willing to hide him."

"I don't know about Reizman, but I"ll tell you what I intend to do this evening, just as soon as it is dark, and I would advise everyone here that they do the same."

"*Nu*?"

"I am going to dig a hole in my yard, and bury everything that is of value and small enough to hide. Who knows, we may be taken as slaves to Germany, but some of us might live to return someday. It's better than letting the *mamsers* have it. I intend to keep only enough money to pay for help if it exists; anything else can rot in the ground before it falls into the enemy's hands"

"How will you know how much money to keep on your person? How can anyone know how much is needed to pay hor his safety?"

"If someone is willing to help us, and is of good intention, then he will not try to rob us. If someone hates Jews, or is afraid to help, then no amount of money will change his mind......Maybe if someone is kind to me, and I feel indebted to him, I will tell him about the valuables which are buried."

Hersh interrupted, "It will soon be time to *Daven Mincha* and *Ma'ariv*. I think we should all go today. There may not be many more chances to go to *shul* left for us."

"There's not much else we can do. About the only thing left for us is to pray."

"Rabi Weissbord has said that the services will continue for as long as there are ten of us alive and able to *daven*. Germans or no Germans, nothing must be allowed to come between us and God."

The conversation ceased suddenly as the frantic clopping of a horse's hooves sounded in the street. Shouting and waving as he sped past was Natan Beir, riding high on the back of Yoiphi, his arms around the horse's neck.

Elior's face turned red with anger.

"Why, that disobedient little.............! I will not tolerate such behaviour! He has been told not to ride the horse out on the street, and he should know better than to ride without a saddle! He is in trouble! Just wait until he returns!"

Hersh spoke gently to the irate Elior, and placed his hand on his shoulder.

"Please, Elior, do not be too hard on the boy. This may well be the last moment of pleasure he has in his life."

A short time later Chana was left alone, as the women followed their menfolk back to the synagogue and their homes in the town. Hersh would be gone for little more than an hour, but the wait would be as long and lonely as any she had ever known.

CHAPTER 2

Since the rise of Hitler, North American Jews had beheld the plight of their German bretheren with concern. Early efforts to ease the burden were in the form of aid by Jewish welfare societies sent to those left behind in Europe. Parcels to overseas family members had always been the norm, but these now took on greater urgency, for they often amounted to the sole means of support for families persecuted to the point of losing their livlihood.

Canadian and American Jews desperately lobbied their governments in an effort to accept more of the displaced refugees as immigrants. The gestures were largely ineffective, and despite the affluence and influence of many Jewish communities little effect was had on the policies of their governments. By the outset of the Second World War in September, 1939, most German Jews were still to be found in Germany, destitute, subject to persecution, and helpless in the face of the greater evils yet to come.

With the beginning of war and Hitler's march into Poland, Jewish fears changed from concern to outright fear, heightened by the certainty that their families and relatives were living on borrowed time. The reports coming from Poland during 1939 and 1940 described systematic slavery, torture and even murder of Jews. These were too consistent to be ignored, and yet, despite the pleas from the Jews themselves, they were given little notice by other sections of North American society.

The invasion of Poland had changed another aspect of the issue. Jews with Polish connections outnumbered German Jews by more than ten to one, and their arrival in North America had been more recent, with strong ties still remaining between the old world and the new. It was a rare synagogue service where the Rabbi's sermon did not contain some mention of the plight of Poland's Jews, with special prayers frequently offered on their behalf.

Hitler's attack and invasion of Russia on June 21, 1941 increased the stakes a further tenfold. Apart from a small community of

Spanish and Portuguese Jews, and the Germans, virtually every Jew in North America had his original roots in eastern Europe. Hitler's push to the east had suddenly placed some five million additional Jews at risk. It was a rare North American Jewish family which was not affected.

From the most influential and powerful Jewish families to the most impoverished, the concern and fears were the same. Their loved ones were in mortal danger. Hitler played no favourites, and no amount of wealth or influence could now assist those under his control. Rich or poor, powerful or destitute, every Jew in North America shared the same feeling, that of utter helplessness.

What everyone feared, yet what noone actually believed would happen, had now taken place, although the knowledge of it had not yet reached the outside world.

Early in 1941, in anticipation of his invasion to the east, Hitler had authorized the implementation of a new policy towards the Jews. An *Endlosung*, or final solution to the "Jewish Problem" had been decided upon, and he had ordered his subordinates to devise the mechanics of carrying it out.

The policy of persecution was not having the desired effect of eliminating Europe's Jewry, and the coming push to the east would bring several million more Jews under his control. The only way to rid the continent of its Jews would be through a policy of extermination.

In June,1941, less than one month before the invasion to the east, Heinrich Himmler"s assistant, Reinhard Heydrich, held a meeting with the captains of his special task force, the *Einsatzgruppen*, and gave them their instructions. Their duty was to follow behind the conquering German armies and neutralize all opposition and undesirable elements in the occupied areas. The "undesirables" to be "neutralized" included the communists, the intellectia, the demented, and the gypsies, but by far the largest category was the Jews. Only in Nazi Germany could a word such as "neutralize" have been invented. In any other language in the world the word used would have been "murder".

The communists were to be eliminated because their philosophies conflicted with Hitler's beliefs, and could conceivably pose a threat. The intellectia were likewise seen as a potential threat which could likewise render the occupation more difficult. Likewise the demented and the physically handicapped, who must be reomoved from society because of the burden they created for others. The Gypsies and the Jews were to be eliminated for a different reason, and a simpler one, simply because they were Gypsies and Jews.

The small town of Gorzd[6] in Lithuania lay just across from the Prussian border, and was one of the first towns to be overrun. It contained an ancient and influential Jewish community which comprised a substantial proportion of the town's population. This was to be the first test for the *Einsatzgruppen* as they cut a swathe through eastern Europe in the wake of the German armies.

The *Einsatzgruppen*, totalling several thousand men in four major groups each allotted a territory, would be divided into smaller groups known as *Einsatzkommandos*.

These in turn would be subdivided into smaller units comprising of between twenty and seventy men, known as *Sonderkommandos*. The number and size of the *Sonderkommando* units in operation would depend upon the size of the community to be liquidated, and the degree of opposition that could be expected. The organization was carried out with typical German thoroughness, with very little left to chance, and when things were running smoothly several *Sonderkommando* units could be in operation in different locales, carrying out their tasks simultaneously.

In Gorzd the *Einsatzgruppe* operation was carried out to perfection, all targets being being eliminated with ruthless efficiency with very little loss to the Germans. Reports were sent to Berlin, and the German leaders were pleased at the results. The operation would continue with very little modification.

Dorbyan, some twenty miles to the east of Gorzd, was overrun in the first day of fighting, as were Krettingen and Polangen. Less than a day's journey from Gorzd, and now under German occupation, these towns could now expect to receive the direct attention of the *Einsatzgruppen* in the very near future.

---

6   *Garzdai in Lithuanian, Garsden in German*

In June of 1941, Halifax, Nova Scotia was a busy Canadian port of almost one hundred thousand inhabitants, its population swollen by the influx of military personnel gathered there for the fight against Hitler. Roughly a thousand miles northeast of New York, it was the major port and naval base of Eastern Canada, due largely to its unique geographical position, for the province of Nova Scotia jutted out into the Atlantic like a giant pier, making Halifax the nearest mainland North American city to Europe.

Britain and its empire still held out against Hitler, alone. Although the worst days had passed, and Britain was gradually strengthening to the point of being a match for Germany, the issue was still very much in doubt. Britain's defeat no longer seemed likely, but neither did the possibility of Britain someday mounting an invasion of Europe and liberating the countries under Hitler's yoke.

America was not yet at war, and any assistance it offered to Britain in its life and death struggle was channeled through Halifax, rather than through its own ports. The Canadian war effort likewise poured through Halifax, choking its harbour and adjoining Bedford basin with ships being readied to sail in convoy across the U-boat ridden Atlantic to beleagered Britain.

In its almost two hundred year history Halifax had never known such importance and frenzied activity as had occurred since the outbreak of war. For the first time in living memory, Bedford basin showed no signs of freezing over in the winter, and it was jokingly said that even without the ice it was possible to cross the basin by stepping from ship to ship.

Samuel Simon (Sammy) Jacobson, the grandson of Hersh and Chana Jacob, was a successful up-and-coming young businessman who operated two large clothing stores in Halifax. Klines Limited occupied a prime location in the newer business district of Gottingen Street , while Hudsons Limited on Barrington Street was located in the heart of the original Halifax business district. Barrington was Halifax's longest street, and was a fascinating area where virtually anything could be found. It was the main point of attraction for merchant sailors, naval personnel and new arrivals, in fact anyone who had taken leave of a recently berthed boat.

Samuel Simon (Sammy) Jacobson, son of Esther and Barnet had become a highly successful businessman, a pillar of the Jewish community and one of Halifax.s most prominent citizens, thereby fulfilling his parents' trust in him in every respect.

In the comfortable study of his newly purchased large home, Sam Jacobson read the daily newspaper, with its headlines telling of Hitler's latest push to the east. In the background the radio gave bulletins of the same activities at regular intervals. He was unable to concentrate on either, for since returning from work that evening, he had been interrupted every few minutes by the ringing of the telephone. When the telephone rang yet again, he called to his wife.

"Don't bother, Ruby, I"ll get it myself. I know what it's going to be."

He picked up the phone for the seventh or eighth time that evening.

"Hello! Hello!.....Uncle Joe! Nu? Wuss machst Du?"

He whispered to Ruby, who had come to stand by his side, "Shh! It's not a very good line. It's Uncle Joe from Pontiac."

"Yes, yes! I hear you , Uncle Joe, just speak up."

"No need to tell you why I'm calling, is there, Sammy."

"No, it's in all the papers in the world, and on every radio station in the country. Everyone else has called. I've been on the phone all evening long, first to Mama and Papa for almost an hour, then to Uncle Laizer, then Tante Leah, then Uncle Jake Cohen and half the Dorbyaners in Halifax. Wuss gaiht? Wuss waisst Du? Do you have any news at all about Dorbyan?"

"Gornisht, Sammy. Only what I can guess myself. By now the German *mamsers* are well and truly past Dorbyan on their way to Russia."

"Will they actually be in Dorbyan, Uncle Joe?"

"Maybe not, from what I remember, the roads they are taking do not pass through Dorbyan."

"Maybe they will be too occupied to bother with Dorbyan for the time being."

"Maybe, but for how long?....Before too long it will be too late.....

We must do something while there is still time!"

Sam Jacobson could hear his uncle's voice thickening as he continued.

"I'm trying to think of everything I can, something we can do to help. I've spoken to just about everyone. Nobody has any ideas. I only know that no matter how hopeless it is, we have to keep on trying. Maybe you can think of something."

"I think that every Yid in the country is trying to think of something, Uncle Joe. The way Hitler is behaving, I don't think anyone in the world can help. Even if America were to declare war on Hitler tomorrow, it wouldn't make any difference.'

"Sammy, we should have declared war on him years ago, when you did. Perhaps if we were all fighting him together, he would have had a harder time of it in the west, and he wouldn't be able to do what he is doing now."

"I don't even see how that could have helped," replied Sam. "He's hellbent on conquering Russia regardless of the consequences. Even if it were the families of King George or of President Roosevelt trapped in Dorbyan, it wouldn't make any difference."

Joseph's voice choked.

"Sammy, you don't know how it is.......It's my father,......Mama.... my *Schwestern* and their husbands,........the *Kinder*....I know them all!.......They have never left me....When I visited them, Natan Beir was only a year old.....just last hear he was *Bar-Mitzvah*...."

Joseph's voice stopped, and Sam waited patiently . He knew that on the other end of the line Joseph was crying into the telephone. After a few moments his uncle composed himself and continued.

"Sammy, you know people. I don't expect miracles, but maybe you have some idea, anything, so so long as we are doing something."

"Uncle Joe, here in Halifax I may have a little pull, but I don't see what I can do. Everyone in Halifax is doing everything they can think of, and the big people like the Bronfmans in Montreal, too. Don't forget, nearly every *Yid* in North America has *mishpoche* in Russia. There's not a person anywhere whose family is not in danger."

"Maybe that's why, if everyone can be organized to protest at once, it might do something," answered Joseph.

"Maybe," answered Sam. "I'll speak to whoever I can. I'm going on a business trip to Montreal tomorrow. There are some people it might be worth talking to."

"Thanks, Sammy. I called because I had another thought. You deal a lot with the *Goyim*. Maybe you know someone who has connections with the Red Cross."

"The Red Cross? How can they help?"

"I don't know, Sammy, but maybe, just maybe,...they can find some way to put some observers into the battle area."

"Can you imagine Hitler allowing observers into an area where he is murdering Jews, Uncle Joe?"

"No, I can't.......," answered Joseph, his voice again choking, "But we must keep trying. We must try everything until there is nothing more to try."

"You're right, Uncle Joe. Even if it's hopeless, we can't give up. This is exactly what Papa and Mama said. Maybe something will happen. I know someone in Halifax who has to do with the Red Cross. I'll give him a call just as soon as we're finished. In the meantime about all we can do is to go to *shul*."

Thanks, Sammy. It's always good to talk to you. If nothing, it makes me feel a bit better. I've been telephoning everyone, ...*Yidden*.... *Goyim*...anyone who will listen to me and who might have an idea. Maybe I'm wasting my time, but I have to keep on trying...........What else can I do?"

"I don't blame you, Uncle Joe, anything we do is better than nothing. I'll call you later tonight, after I've spoken to a few people. Regards to Rae and the kids, *Zait Gesundt*."

After Joseh Jacobson had hung up, Sam took a long deep breath, then turned to Ruby who was sitting nearby.

"With Uncle Joe from Pontiac, that makes everyone of the *mishpoche* I have now spoken to. Everyone is speaking to everyone else. Maybe we should be buying shares in the telephone company!

"For some reason they all seem to think that I can do something. But noone can help, noone. I have never felt so helpless in my life."

"I know, Sam. Pa has just told me the same thing when I spoke to him earlier.

Even though he has no connections with Tarnopol, it breaks his heart to know what is going to happen. Even fifty years here isn't enough to make him forget where he came from. He said he was grateful that Ma is no longer alive to find out what is going on in Krakow. He thinks Myer might be able to help, because he has connections with the Liberal party."

"Everyone is grasping at straws," answered Sam.

"It's happening everywhere, isn't it, Sam? Where will it end"

"Who knows? Perhaps when there are no Jews left."

"Is there noone that can stop Hitler?", asked Ruby.

"He will be stopped!", answered Sam firmly. "Of course he will! He is going to lose this war....!"

Sam's voice then trailed off.

"....The trouble with this *Mamser* is that he doesn't seem to care if he loses the war or not.... All he seems to care about is killing Jews........."

CHAPTER 3

The wait for Hersh to return home was even worse than Chana had expected. The distant rumblings had ceased, the sound of airplanes could still be heard, but coming from a distance and of no consequence to Dorbyan. There was no traffic on the streets, and the air was strangely silent, although earlier she thought she had heard the sounds of drunken Lithuanian hoodlums coming from the town centre. After the crowded afternoon, the silence of her home was depressing, and she longed for the reassurance of company. Perhaps she should make the five to ten minute walk to the home of Hoshe and Bashe Kveril further along the Krettinger Gass. She knew that Hersh would not approve, for there was no way of knowing if the streets had become dangerous for Jews. If not, how long before it started? Would Hersh encounter hostility in the town, especially on his journey alone back to his house? She thought about everything she had heard about Memel, and the hostility towards Jews that had always been held in check, which had finally erupted into an orgy of hate and destruction within a matter of hours.

For some reason the afternoon's gathering had seemed almost festive. Although the talk had been about their predicament, there seemed to have been little depression, or little that had shown. As always, the chief concern had been the economic hardship facing the community, and now it seemed as if even this did not matter anymore.

Now as she lit a small candle to ward off the coming darkness, she suddenly felt threatened.

"Poor people," she thought, "What will happen tomorrow when they wake up and realize exactly what has happened? Do they really know what is coming?"

She herself wondered if anything could have been done to cause things to turn out differently. At one time there had been ample opportunity for the entire family to leave Dorbyan and migrate to Canada, although not so much in recent years. Until 1928 it would

271

have been a simple matter for her and Hersh, all their children and their families to sail to Saint John. They would have received all the asistance they needed from their daughters, who had in fact pleaded with them to come. Even at a later date Joseph in Pontiac, Michigan in the United States had tried to convince them to join him and his family. Their answer had always been the same. In her case, she might have been persuaded, particularly if her children had also gone, but Hersh's answer had never changed, and had simply been, "What would I do there?"

Needless to say, she had always followed Hersh's wishes, not only because it was the done thing, but because she in her own heart did not need much convincing to remain. Joining one-half of her family only to leave the other half behind was no solution. The easiest way out had always been to make no decision at all.

She remembered how grateful she had been that four of her daughters had married and remained in Dorbyan, forgoing the opportunity to improve their lives in doing so. She thought of them now, in their homes, apprehensively waiting for the return of their menfolk, their doors locked, wondering if the townsfolk would become hostile towards them. With hindsight it was now obvious that they would have been better off in every way had they left, but she could not deny that the presence of the four families had brought twenty-five years of pleasure into her life.

If only one or more of them had made the first move, then perhaps there would have been reason for the rest of the family to follow, as had happened in so many other cases. Perhaps if she and Hersh had gone, others would have followed. It was too late for any of this now, but perhaps she and Hersh were in some way to blame for their family's present circumstances.

She heard the familiar footsteps of Hersh and moved to the door as his shadowy figure came up the front steps.

"Chana, has anything happened here while I was gone?"

"No, it has been deathly quiet."

"Well, keep the house locked from now on. Already in the town Lithuanian gangs are breaking into Jewish shops and homes and taking things."

"What did you expect, Hersh? You know that as of today we Jews will no longer have any rights or protection."

"I think we are safer here than in town, Chana. There are only two Jewish homes on the Krettinger Gass, while there are a hundred in the town centre. But sooner or later they will get the idea to come here. Perhaps it is a good idea after all to bury our valuables while we can. I shall do it tomorrow morning before daylight."

"We cannot possibly bury everything we own, my dear."

"I know, I know, but some of our smaller valuables, some money, our good cutlery, the candlesticks, our family pictures, these can be hidden. Who knows? Maybe the time will come when someone in our family can get them back. Once they are stolen, then they are gone forever."

"Our china, Hersh. This is my greatest treasure. Is there anything we can do about it?"

"I don't see how we can bury it. It would take a very large hole to hide it, and it would probably get broken in any case."

"Then I shall break it myself, piece by piece," replied Chana. "This is better than seeing it fall into the hands of the Germans or Lithuanians. Perhaps I shall start on it tomoorow."

"No, don't do that! It may not be necessary. I'll ask around tomorrow. Perhaps we can find someone who will keep it for us. It has been part of the family since the great fire, almost sixty years ago. We have feasted and celebrated on it since before Chaia was born, and each of our children has grown up using it. If the Germans must have it, then it is God's will, but I could never bring myself to destroy it with my own hands."

"Well I could!", stated Chana firmly.

Hersh changed the subject.

"Enough of this, we'll see what tomorrow brings. Now let us have something to eat, on our good china. The events of today have not yet caused me to lose my appetite. Perhaps an extra helping of the herring on the salad will help. I want to listen to the radio for awhile, although I can't imagine anything good coming of it."

A short time later, they sat opposite each other, a small candle burning between them on the table. Their eyes were moist, their voices were silent, as they looked at the fine china and thought back to another time almost sixty years earlier when they had shared their first meal in their new house on the same china.

Yes, sixty years had passed. Besides themselves, there were very few in the town who could remember the great fire. Their house was now weatherbeaten and needing repairs, with floorboards that creaked, and windows and doors that did not close evenly. But the house had been filled with love and memories, and had seen the birth and growth of their eight children. Only the china seemed not to have aged, with the patterns as clear and vivid as they day it was purchased.

Also untarnished throughout the years was the love felt by Hersh and Chana as they looked into each other's eyes across the dim candlelight that evening.

CHAPTER 4

The following morning before the break of day Hersh was awake and digging a hole in the backyard. He first chose a spot which appeared the least obtrusive and likely to be discovered, and then started digging. When it was approximately eighteen inches square and two feet deep he felt he had done as much as his back would allow him. His original plan had been to line it with timber planks, in the manner of a grave site, but this would have required a larger hole. He no longer performed heavy labour with the same ease he had done as little as ten years earlier, and the hard ground had meant that after removing the topsoil, the work had been a struggle. Two weeks of warm dry weather had turned the soil to stone, and burying the china was out of the question.

He lined the bottom and sides of the hole with an old oilskin, and then proceeded to wrap towelling around the various parcels. He looked longingly at each family photo as he wrapped it before setting it down in a pile at the edge of the hole. There were photos of his daughters, his grandchildren, and his favourite, the family portrait taken more than twenty years ago, copies of which he had given his son Joseph to take with him when he migrated to Canada. His favourite prayerbook, a small wine cup, the silverware, some money, the Sabbath candlesticks and the *Chanukah minorah* all received the same treatment. He then took each parcel and wrapped it again with oilskin before kissing it and lowering it gently into the hole, wedging the cavities with more towelling. When the last package was in the hole, filling it slightly more than halfway to the top, he crammed more towelling around it and then folded the oilskin on the sides over the top. He laid his last piece of oilskin over this and began covering it with earth, trampling it flat after each shovelful. When the hole was filled to ground level, he poured a bucket of water over it and allowed it to settle, then added earth and trampled it for the last time. He then placed some loose soil over the scar and covered it with turf taken from another part of the yard. He carried the excess soil in buckets to the horse's enclosure where it would be quickly trampled. Noting to his satisfaction that the scar was almost invisible, he made careful note of the location to mention to his sons-in-law. Should the cache ever be retrieved, it was far more likely that it would be by one of them than by Chana or himself.

"Chana, I am going to *Shul*. I shall try to learn what I can."

"Please be careful on the street, and please hurry. You have no idea of what it is like to be left alone at a time like this."

"I shall be home just as soon as I can, my dear. I too worry about you being alone in the house if the wrong type of visitors arrive."

As he left and looked back at Chana standing forlornly on the front steps, he wondered if he was wise to leave her alone. She had always been known for her fiery disposition, and recent events had, if anything, only inflamed it. In the event of a visit by German or Lithuanian looters, her ability to provoke would not be a blessing.

Nonetheless, the synagogue and its prayer services had to come first. He would *daven shaharis*, go to the post office, speak to one or two people, and return as quickly as possible.

As he had expected, Chana was watching for him anxiously as he returned along the Krettinger Gass.

"How has it been, Chana? Has anything happened while I was gone?"

"Basha Kveril was here with the three children. She did not like to be out on the street, but like me, she just felt she had to get out of the house, if only for a short time."

"Did she mention anything about sending her daughter Esther to Vladas Jashinskas?"

"Yes, when the children were out of earshot, she mentioned that Hoshe had spoken to Jashinskas. The whole thing seems strange to me, and I'm not sure that I trust it. They were going to send Sara Rivke, the youngest with him, but he insisted on Esther who is older. He said that the older girl would have a better chance of escaping."

"It sounds reasonable to me," said Hersh.

"Well, to me, and to Basha as well, it seems that the thing to do is to save the youngest. Esther is fully grown, and has a better chance of saving herself without Jashinskas' help. Anyway, the matter is settled. Jashinskas will take Esther or noone.

But this is for the moment, as Jashinskas has already changed his mind more than once."

"When you tell it to me this way, it does seem strange," said Hersh seriously. "But I'm glad that you had the company, although I don't know if it is wise for Basha and the children to be seen on the street, even though things seem to have improved since my last time in town."

"In what way have things improved?"

"There are now Germans in town. Not many, so far I have seen only six, but their presence has made a difference. They seem to be keeping things in order. They have told the Lithuanians that there is to be no loooting, and suddenly, the looting has stopped."

"They are clever, these Germans, aren't they," snapped Chana. "They stop the Lithuanians from looting, only so they can do it themselves at a later time."

"Perhaps, but isn't it better that our homes are safe, if only for the moment?

They have shut down the post office. On the door is a notice that for the moment there will be no letters either in or out of Dorbyan."

"Well, I suppose, you are right Hersh, we are better off for the time being. I suppose it could be worse. Maybe we will be lucky, but I still cannot help but wonder how long it will be before they start butchering us."

"Who knows? Perhaps for the moment they have more important things to do, and all they want is order. But if we look at the things they have done to Jews in other lands, we must expect that our time is soon up. There are certainly a lot of people who believe that it will come sooner rather than later."

"And what do you believe, Hersh?"

"I know no more than anybody else. Our hope is that the Germans will not have such an easy time of it during their invasion, and that they will be too occupied to think of us."

"I cannot see that," answered Chana. "The Germans are too strong for the Russians, and will defeat them in very little time."

"Maybe,' said Hersh. "Certainly many people think this way. Did you know, that in *Shul* today I could see a big difference. There were many missing faces, many empty seats. I would say that the congregation was only half its usual number. That would mean that half of the Jews of Dorbyan have fled the town, although only God knows where. I cannot imagine where it would be possible for over four hundred people to hide."

"Hersh, while you were gone. I cannot believe how quiet it became on the street. Apart from the Kverils, there was not a single person passing by. There are no longer any explosions, and the airplanes that fly overhead are distant. If they are dropping bombs, then it must be too far away for us to hear it. I listened on the radio, and it seems that the Germans are now well into Latvia and entering Estonia."

"May God help the poor Latvians and Estonians, although their plight may be a help for us in some small way. Perhaps the Germans will be too occupied to think of small places like Dorbyan. Perhaps that is why they only want to see order here for the time being."

"For how long?", ashed Chana. Since when have the Germans shown any interest in law and order?"

"Not since before Hitler," answered Hersh sadly.

That evening after the *Ma'ariv* prayer, Hersh returned to Chana with more news.

"There is a letter posted on the *Shul* door."

"And what does it say? That we aren't allowed to pray anymore?"

"No, Chana, nothing like that. It is a letter telling the Jews to return to Dorbyan, that they will not be harmed if they come back. The letter tells all Jews in Dorbian to remain here, and to make contact with their relatives and urge them to return."

"Would you trust such a letter? Why should it matter to the Germans if they return or not? What is it to them if they are here or somewhere else?"

"A good question," answered Hersh. "I hadn't thought about it. I suppose they feel that it is easier to control us if we are all in one place."

"Or easier to kill us all at one time," replied Chana bitterly.

Hersh gently kissed Chana on the forehead, then put his arm around her and walked her into the house.

"Chana, it is so easy to be bitter, we have every reason to be, but it does not help. Is it not better to be positive, and pray for the miracle that may yet come? If we are to have any chance at all, all we can do is keep aware of what is happening and to keep up our strength by not losing our faith in God."

"Forgive me Hersh, I do not mean to be unpleasant to you, but I keep asking myself by what right these Germans have to be doing this, and I have no answer. I know we have enough to worry about without my mentioning it all the time. I shall at least try to appear cheerful, although I do not feel that way. You are right, only God can save us."

"There is only one thing that troubles me," said Hersh. "It seems strange, but since the Germans came into Lithuania, there has been no word from any of the towns that they passed through first. They must have been in Gorzd, and by now probably Polangen and Krettingen as well, as they are on the main roads. Why is it that there has been no word from these towns?"

"I'm sure the Germans have closed the telegraph," said Chana, "And they are probably not allowing anyone to leave."

"It's still strange, Chana. People have left Dorbyan and fled to the next towns.

Surely someone has fled from Gorzd who would have arrived in Dorbyan, or someone from Krettingen or Polangen. I cannot understand it."

CHAPTER 5

On the following morning, Tuesday, June 24, Hersh returned from the synagogue with further news.

"Chana, Kagan has done exactly as he said he would! He has set fire to his house and fled Dorbyan with all his family!"

"I wonder just where all these people are going to," said Chana.

"It is strange," answered Hersh, "For just as Kagan was leaving some of the families who went away earlier have started to return.'

"What made them come back?"

"They could see no choice, Chana. It's not that they trusted the Germans. In fact, none of them even knew about the letter on the *shul* door. Many of them went to Gruslakis, and they could find no help there. In fact, the villagers there drove them away, and beat them with sticks and stones to the point where some of them began fearing for their lives. Only a Catholic priest stopped the people from harming them. They knew that it was pointless to remain there, as they would not be hidden from the Germans. I can see no way of hiding anywhere, and I think that sooner or later, all must return, even Kagan."

"Kagan will not be very welcome here after what he has done," answered Chana. "If the Germans make it harder on the rest of us because of his actions, he will not be very popular."

"I don't know what else he can do, except come back," said Hersh.

"Do you know what I think?", answered Chana. "I think the Germans are just trying to keep things quiet, and just waiting until everyone is back in Dorbyan, either that or waiting until they have more soldiers. This morning two Germans passed our house here in the Krettinger Gass. They walked towards the Kveril home, then turned around and walked back into town. Maybe they were making a note of which homes belong to Jews."

She added, "Actually, they seemed quite pleasant, and even waved to me as they passed. They looked so young.....barely adult."

"I have heard another thing which is disturbing," said Hersh.

"The Germans are now recruiting the Lithuanian partisans to help them, and they are marching together. Already I have seen a group of Lithuanians in uniform marching alongside the Germans in the market square."

"The Germans must be a very clever people if they are able to train Lithuanians to do anything at all," answered Chana mischievously.

Hersh ignored the attempt at a joke.

"What bothers me," he answered seriously, "Is that amongst these collaborators I saw someone I know. It was Jonas, the son of Viktoras Galdikas....

"....It shocked me, for I know the family well, and I cannot imagine Galdikas allowing his son to do anything to help the Germans."

"You thought you knew the family well!", snapped Chana. "Did I not tell you that the moment the Germans came we would have no Lithuanian friends? There is no such thing as a Lithuanian who will not turn against us when the moment is right!"

"I do not believe this, Chana. The Galdikas family are decent people, and Jonas Galdikas has always been a lovely child. His parents always saw to it that he was God-fearing, well-mannered and polite. Like his father, he loves horses, and is always gentle with them. Over the years I have learned that it is always possible to judge a man by the way he treats his animals, and Galdikas is not a cruel type."

"Then why is it that he joins the collaborators who help the Germans? Answer this question if you can."

"I wish I knew," answered Hersh. "It doesn't make sense. I only know that Jonas Galdikas cannot have his father's blessing."

On Wednesday morning, June 25, market day, Hersh emerged from morning prayer at the synagogue and stepped into the market square, where most of the traders and farmers had already arranged their wagons laden with produce into display stalls. He saw his good friend Victoras moving from wagon to wagon, examining the goods on display and having a word with some of the farmers.

He went straight to his friend, who excused himself from the stall holder and greeted him cordially. Yet Viktoras Galdilas seemed ill at ease.

"Hershas, my good friend. It is good to see you about. We do not know what is happening, and we are starting to worry for you."

"We are all safe for the moment, but knowing the Germans, who can say for how long?"

He looked into his friend's face, which had broken into perspiration. Behind his friend he could see one of the farmers in the background motioning him to leave.

"What is the matter, Viktoras? You seem uncomfortable."

"It is terrible, Hershas, what is happening, but what can anyone do? Now I am told by my friends that it is not wise for me to be seen speaking to Jews, that it may cause problems later. Why? What reason is there for me to feel ashamed to speak to you? And yet they are trying to make me feel that way."

"Viktoras, I do not wish to cause problems for you. If we are unable to speak to each other, then so be it. No matter what happens, I will always know that you do not agree with what is happening."

"No, Hershas, damn the Germans! Why should we not be allowed to speak to each other? I shall be happy to speak to you anytime until such time as I am forced to stop! I know that I cannot fight them, but neither am I obliged to do anything that will make their dirty work any easier."

"There may be a way that you can help me, Viktoras."

"How, Hershas? As long as it is something that is within my power, I shall do anything I can."

"You know, Elior, my son-in-law, Viktoras. Our family is worried about his youngest child, who is called Natan Beir. Nobody knows what will become of us, but we can guess, and we want to be prepared for the worst. He is my youngest grandchild, and we worry about him. as he is only fourteen years old. We want to ensure his safety, if the time comes that we cannot look after him."

"You are asking me to look after him, are you not?", said Viktoras Galdikas.

"Yes, Viktoras, that is my request to you."

Hersh's voice turned into a plea.

"Perhaps you have a place to hide him, or you know of someone else who can. I will pay you everything that I have if you will do this for me."

His voice became husky.

"Viktoras, I know that what I am asking of you is much more than I have a right to ask of anyone. Nothing I have ever done for you has involved risk to my life, and yet I must ask you to risk your life on my account. Yet I can see no other way."

Viktoras Galdikas's eyes became misty, and he placed his hand on Hersh's shoulder.

"Hershas, you cannot know how sick in the heart it makes me to see you having to ask this of me. You are a good man, and you do not deserve to be in this position. I want to help you if I can, and I would also like to help Elior. You will remember, that apart from yourself, he was the only Jew to come to father's funeral. I would dearly love to help you, but I don't know how."

"You must, Viktoras, there must be a way. I shall pay you for everything."

"Hershas, believe me, if I can help you, I will, and I will be proud to take the risk on your behalf. And I would feel insulted to take money from you for doing what any Christian ought to do. The problem is that your grandson would not be safe in my care."

"I don't understand, Viktoras."

"It is my son, Jonas. I don't know what has become of him, but lately he seems to worship everything that the Germans do. They have become his heroes. He has now joined the collaborators who help the Germans, and even marches with them. He makes no secret of this."

Viktoras Galdikas continued, "I have tried to tell him that what he is doing is wrong, and that what the Germans are doing is a sin against Christ, but he does not listen."

He removed his hand from Hersh's shoulder, and gestured helplessly.

"What can I do? He is a changed boy, not at all like the wonderful child he used to be, and at times I am even afraid of him. He is so intense in his feelings. He and his wife live with me on the farm, and it would be impossible to hide your grandson."

"I understand," said Hersh resignedly. "..And I do not blame you that you are unable to help. In fact I saw your son yesterday, marching, and at first I thought that it could not be Jonas, that it must be some mistake."

"It is no mistake," answered Viktoras Galdikas sadly. "It is a terrible thing to see what is happening to you and your people, and to know that my son is involved. And it is a terrible thing to be afraid of one's own son. I feel sick in the heart that I cannot help my oldest friend. You have no idea how hard it is for me to look into your face and tell you this."

He paused, and wiped his sweaty brow with the back of his hand.

At that moment Hersh felt a rough hand against his shoulder, pushing him away from his friend. Two Lithuanian youths, perhaps in their late teens or early twenties, had forced their way between the two men. One of them continued to shove Hersh while the other shouted at Viktoras Galdikas in a rude voice.

"What's the matter with you? Don't you know you are not supposed to talk to Jews? Don't waste your time with them if you know what's good for you!"

Viktoras Galdikas stood his ground. He brushed past the youth and came to Hersh's side, forcing himself between Hersh and the other youth.

"Listen, you two! I know who you are! My name is Galdikas, and my son marches with the Germans! If you do not leave this moment, I promise that there will be trouble for you!"

The youths backed off in surprise, then left, but not before one of them had spat directly into Hersh's face.

"This is terrible, Hershas!", said Viktoras Galdikas, as he pulled a soiled handkerchief from his pocket and began wiping Hersh's face. "Why should someone ike you have to put up with this sort of thing?"

"Thank you", said Hersh. "That was a very brave thing you did, Viktoras."

"Perhaps it was not clever, Hershas, but it made me very angry. Those rascals do not know it, but if Jonas were here, he would be taking their side, not ours."

He replaced his handkerchief in his pocket.

"But Hershas, I now understand better what is happening. I am certain that you will be in great danger before long."

"This sort of thing is nothing, and I can handle it. It is what the Germans may do before long that worries us, and that is why I must find a safe place for Natan Beir."

"You are right, Hershas. We must do something. Maybe, just maybe, there is something to be done."

He thought for a moment. "My own farm would be no good. Vlacovas's farm would also be unsafe. It is too near ours to be safe, for my son visits him often and knows what is happening there. There is Zavueras, who is farther away, who could hide your grandson safely, but he is not to be trusted. I know that he does not feel kindly towards Jews, and has said that the coming of the Germans is a good thing...

".......I don't know what it is with these people. They seem to think that the Germans will free us from the Russians, but we are only trading one master for another.

".....There is one other, Lekasius, and they may be the answer. They are far enough away from us and have enough space to hide your grandson easily. And they can be trusted, I am sure of it.

"I would be evergrateful to you, Viktoras, if you would speak to them. We have yet to convince Natan Beir that the best thing for him is to hide from the Germans. But if we are able to convince him, and if he agrees, then I will rest easier if I know that there is a safe place for him. Tell Lekasius that I am willing to pay whatever they ask."

"You will pay nothing, Hershas. I have a feeling that before long you will need every lita you have to protect your own lives. If the boy can do a little work around the farm when he is needed, that will be payment enough. I would be happy to have him on my own farm for that very reason, if only it were safe."

Hersh's eyes filled with tears as he slapped his friend on the shoulder.

"Thank you, Viktoras. I knew that you wouldn't desert me. I feel confident that something will be done.....

".......And don't worry about Jonas. What you tell me about him is very sad, but don't lose hope. He is a very clever boy, and he has been brought up to know what is right and what is wrong. Sooner or later he will realize the mistake he is making."

"Thank you for the kind words, Hershas. I hope you are right. Now how much time do we have? It is not easy for us to meet without Jonas knowing or suspecting something. I shall speak to Lekasius as soon as possible, and if necessary, to others as well. Do you think we can wait until next market day to meet again, or is that too late?"

"I don't think next Wednesday is too late, Viktoras. So far the signs are good. They haven't really started to bother us yet, although I suspect that before long they will......"

"From what we just saw a few moments ago," said Viktoras Galdikas, "It could happen at any time."

"...It's better that you do not cause suspicion," answered Hersh, "Better for you, and better for Natan Beir. In any case we still have to convince him that this is best for him. Surely it will be at least a week before anything happens. Next Wednesday will be fine."

On the 25th and 26th of June more and more Jews returned to Dorbyan, and by Friday, the 27th, the second day of Tammuz by the Jewish calendar, practically everyone who had fled earlier was back in the town.

As if on cue, the German behaviour towards the Jews suddenly changed, and the attitude of the occupation forces became clear. To the townsfolk, the German occupiers were simply regarded as a portion of the German army. In fact, the unit now stationed in Dorbyan was a *Sonderkommando* division of the dreaded *Einsatzgruppe 'A'*, which had recently completed tasks in Gorzd and Polangen, and one of whose sister divisions was at that very moment carrying out its objectives in nearby Krettingen.

At noon of the 27th the Jews were instructed to assemble in the market square, where a new list of regulations would be read out to them.

Milling out the square. confused, and apprehensive of the armed Germans and Lithuanians surrounding them, the Jews gasped collectively as they heard the new measures which would henceforth govern their lives. They were now considered to be 'enemies of the state", and as such would be treated accordingly.

All of their property was to be confiscated for the state's benefit, as a form of repayment for past injustices committed by them. In the meantime nothing was to be removed from any home. Jews were to be allowed to remain in their homes for the time being, but no door was permitted to be locked, and no German or uniformed Lithuanian was to be refused entry.

No Jew was permitted to have any dealings whatever with any Lithuanian. The synagogue was to be closed for prayer, and anyone found entering or leaving the premises would be shot on sight.

The Jews were then sent to their homes, and forbidden to leave them until the next assembly in the market square, at noon on the following day.

CHAPTER 6

That evening, Friday, June 27, Hersh watched glumly as Chana lit the Sabbath candles without using the candlestick holders for the first time that he could remember. His voice choked as he recited the ancient passage from the Book of Genesis which welcomed in the Sabbath,...."*Va'yehi erev va'yehi voiker, yoim hashishi........*" (And it was evening and it was morning, the sixth day....)

A moment later he finished the recitation with the blessing,....."*Boruch Atoh Adoinoi Eloihenu Melech Ho'oilom boireh pri hagofen*", and together he and Chana sipped from small glasses of wine.

"How many more times will we be able to celebrate *Sabbes*? ", he mused. "Will this be our last *Sabbes* together?"

Chana could read the depression on Hersh's face. For so long he had remained steadfast, and had hidden any fears he had, but now the events were starting to take their toll.

"Do you know, Chana", he said despondently, "That this is the first time since before my *Bar-mitzvah* that I have missed a synagogue service."

"It is not your fault, Hersh."

"I know, I know, but still I have the feeling that I am betraying God."

"God knows what is happening, and must surely understand, my dear."

"What possible reason can they have for not letting us go to the *shul* to *daven*? In what way does it cause any harm to them?"

"Do they need a reason?", replied Chana.

"Tomorrow morning I shall rise earlier than usual. It is *Sabbes*, and it has been whispered that there is to be a *Minyan* at the home of Elberg, the chemist. I shall go there before daybreak."

"Is this not dangerous? What if you are spotted?"

"The danger is far greater for those who come from the other side of town. I have only to go to the corner of the Krettinger and Polanger

288

Gasses. There are not many Germans about and very little risk. Even the Germans must sleep, you now."

"But what about Lithuanians? They cannot be trusted."

"The Lithuanians must sleep too," said Hersh.

"And when the service is over, and it is daylight, how will you get back?"

"I can go from backyard to backyard without setting foot on the street, but I admit, for some of the others it will be harder, and I don't know how they are going to manage it. Still, they are younger and able to move more quickly. If they are willing to risk it, then the least I can do is to go too."

He looked into Chana's eyes earnestly.

"The important thing is that we must continue to pray together for as long as we possibly can. There is nothing else we can do. Can you understand this?"

Chana nodded. Hersh's face clouded over as another thought came to him.

"Chana, I mentioned to you how Viktoras Galdikas said he would try to find a safe place for Natan Beir. We were going to meet in the market place next Wednesday. Now, I don't see how I am going to be able to speak to him. We aren't even allowed out of our homes anymore."

"Don't worry about it, Hersh. Galdikas will not help us, even if he could. He is a Lithuanian, and no different from any of the others, including his son."

"Do not say that, Chana. Viktoras Galdikas is a kind, gentle person. Whatever his son may do, he is our friend, and he will help us if he can."

"Do not place too much trust in him," repled Chana, "I don't want to see you disappointed."

"I will not be disappointed," said Hersh adamantly. "I think I know him better than you do."

"What does it matter, anyway?", answered Chana. "Natan Beir has said a thousand times that he will not leave his father and mother, no matter what the danger."

"When the danger is actually upon us, he may think differently." said Hersh.

As darkness surrounded them, Chana brought out the lamp which had been lit before the Sabbath fell. She placed it on a shelf on the other side of the room.

"Bring the lamp here, Chana, and place it on the table near you," said Hersh.

"But why?"

"I want to look into your face, and see it in the lamplight."

"We have little fuel left, Hersh. Maybe we should put it out for now and just have the candle light."

"It makes no difference. We have little fuel, and probably little time. I would rather let the fuel run out than let the Germans have a drop of it. They have now shown their true intentions."

"Do you think that they are about to start killing us?," asked Chana.

"I don't think, I know . What astounds me is that all this has happened so suddenly."

"It is exactly as they planned, isn't it? They were just waiting for everyone to return to Dorbyan, weren't they?"

"It certainly seems so, but it seems as if everything was planned beforehand, in fact a long time ago. And now that they have us all together in the town I don't think we have much time left."

"Will they torture us, Hersh?"

"I'm sure that if we make a nuisance of ourselves, they will, but I believe they will try to get as much work out of us as they can. From what we have learned about Poland, they will work us until we drop, and then when we can work no longer, they will dispose of us."

"Then why work for them? Why not let them kill us now?"

"Chana, life is a wonderful thing that only God can give, although it can easily be taken away by others. As long as we live, we have our sacred gift from God, and some hope, however small. We must show our respect to God by treasuring his precious gift for as long as possible."

Chana was not convinced.

"Then how is it that the heroes of our history gave their lives so willingly on so many occasions? And how is it that there are eight hundred Jews in Dorbyan, and yet it takes but a dozen Germans and a few dozen Lithuanian collaborators to do this to us......?

".....Is there nothing that eight hundred Jews can do against such a small number?

"The dozen Germans we see are not many, yet they represent a force which is too powerful for us to resist."

"But if we are going to die in the end, would it not be better to resist, and possibly cause them some damage before we die?"

"I know that it makes sense, Chana, but to each of us life is precious, and not to be wasted. As long as there is life, there is some hope of a miracle."

"But Hersh, this is not our history! Can you imagine Joshua, or Saul, or David, or Sampson, or Shimon Bar Kochba yielding without a fight simply to prolong their lives for a few extra moments?"

"You have just mentioned something that I have been thinking about a great deal lately. You see, the heroes that you mention were all living in their own land, the sacred homeland given to them by God., and they were fighting to keep it. When one has a sacred homeland to fight for, then giving up one's life is not such a waste."

"So you think that because we are not in our own homeland, then we have lost some of our spirit."

"Yes, Chana, I am sure of it. We don't really belong in this land. We have nothing more than our own lives to fight for, and God will take care of these in any case."

He paused, then continued thoughtfully, "You know, I can remember the very discussions I used to have with Dodke Wolff before he left Dorbyan. I often argued against him, but time has proven that he was the correct one, not I."

"In what way was he correct? That we should all go to Palestine and die of malaria instead?"

"No Chana, nothing like that. Dodke's thinking went much deeper than that. It is now twenty-seven years since he died and almost seventy years since I last saw him, but everything we talked about is still very clear. Even then I believe he could see what was coming and what would someday happen."

"How could anyone forsee Hitler?"

"He couldn't forsee Hitler, but he could forsee that there would always be a hostility against Jews until we had a homeland of our own to live in, just as there is always a hostility towards outsiders in any country.

"But Hersh, what is happening now isn't simply hostility, nor is it just a pogrom against the Jews of some Russian town or village. This is murder, the murder of all the Jews of Europe. Whenever the Germans come into any land the same thing happens, and all the Jews die."

"Yes," conceded Hersh, "What Hitler is doing is worse than anything Dodke ever imagined, and worse than anything that has ever happened before in our history. Still, Dodke's ideas are correct. If we were in our own homeland we would fight fiercely, and die before being conquered, like the heroes of Massada, or like Bar Kochba."

"But what about the malaria? Can you not remember the suffering of your cousin Shimon Zacharia Jacobs?"

"I will never forget the suffering of Shimon Zacharia as long as I live," said Hersh, "For it made a terrible impression on me. He and his family paid the highest price, but no less than the price that is being paid by hundreds of Jews in Europe every day, and there is a difference."

"I can see no difference. If one dies, then one dies," said Chana.

"No Chana, that is not correct. Those who went to Palestine gave their lives willingly, and would have done it ten times over if possible, for like Bar Kochba, they believed in their cause. They knew that their lives were not wasted, and that they were making a future for those who followed. Now, we in Europe are losing our lives with nothing to show for it. Is it any wonder that very few of us are of the will to fight?"

He continued, "Like everyone else at the time, I saw the future differently than Dodke Wolff......If only more people had listened to him.....

"........It is strange. We looked on those who gave their lives in Palestine as *meshuganim*, yet we do not look on the heroes of old in the same way. Yet they all had the same purpose, to die for the sake of their own God-given homeland."

"But what about the Dorbyaners living in North America?", persisted Chana. "Have they not done better by being where they are?"

"Perhaps, for the time being, but who can say for how long? This is what Dodke was trying to tell us, that no place can remain safe. It is not that long ago that the Jews of Germany were prospering, and considered themselves lucky to be citizens of that country. I remember how the German Jews used to be the envy of the rest of us, but what happened?

"It is also not that long since we ourselves prospered in Dorbyan, and that most Lithuanians were pleased to have us. The same thing that has happened here can also happen in North America. Think of Leah's husband in Saint John, and the reason that he died. Aaron Nathan should not have died, but he did. Can you tell me with certainty that what happened in Germany cannot happen in Canada too? All it takes is a single Hitler to rise, and the Jews become the victims. The only place it will not happen is in a land that we Jews ourselves own."

He smiled, "I remember when Esther Jacob and Zalman Cohen left for Palestine in 1933, and then Shevah Bloch in 1935. I thought to myself, 'What *meshuganim* are these!', but now I can see that their thinking was ahead of mine."

Chana made no reply, and after a lengthy silence Hersh changed the subject.

"Draw the lamp closer to you, Chana, so that I can see the light in your eyes. For some reason it reminds me of the way you used to look when we were both young. Do you know that your eyes have not changed? You are just as beautiful as you were when I first set eyes on you more than seventy years ago. I knew then that I had to have you, and it was the best thing that I have ever done in my life."

"I am old and shrunken," said Chana.

"You are old, and so am I, but you are beautiful. You always have been."

He moved beside her and placed his arm around her shoulder. He moved his head close to hers, and she snuggled into his arms cosily. They both allowed their eyes to close dreamily.

They were interrupted by a noise outside the front of the house, followed by the sound of footsteps and heavy boots coming up the front steps. As Hersh got to his feet he could see three Germans at the front door, two of whom entered while the third remained at the entrance, his pistol drawn from its holster.

"Good evening, gentlemen, what may I do for you?"

One of the Germans brushed past him, then motioned for Chana to stand. The other went from room to room shining his flashlight in every crevice. After checking all the rooms he returned, his eyes falling on the Sabbath candles on the shelf, sitting on plain saucers.

"Nothing here! Just like everywhere else! Everything of value has been removed!"

"We are not wealthy people," pleaded Hersh. "We have never owned very much. We have nothing of value in this house which would be of interest to people such as yourselves.'

The Germans ignored him. One of them stopped suddenly and cast his eyes on the contents of a shelf.

"Aha! At last, here is something worth having! This will be mine! My mother has been wishing for some good china for years. This will make a good gift to her. She deserves it."

He reached out and took a large plate from the shelf, gazing at it knowledgeably.

"Yes, very good quality, my mother will be very happy indeed!"

"Put that down, you German *chazzer*! "Chana flew at the surprised German, her eyes blazing. "You will not touch this china as long as I am alive!"

The German stepped back, momentarily shocked, while his comrades managed to suppress grins. Then he recovered, and his lips curled in the trace of a smile.

"Then perhaps you should not be alive."

He slowly drew his pistol from its holster and deliberately levelled it at Chana's breast. Chana stood her ground defiantly, while Hersh looked on in horror.

Then Hersh jumped between the German and Chana.

"Please sir, pay no attention to my wife. She has been ill lately and does not know what she says. Of course you may have the china if you feel it would make your mother happy, and if you will but give me a moment, I will find you a box to carry it in."

He bustled Chana with him into another room, and told her to remain there while he returned to the Germans with a wooden box.

"There you are, sir, please take whatever you wish, then leave my wife and me in peace."

As the Germans left Hersh went to the front door and looked into the street. Two wagons driven by Lithuanians were moving away, laden with the booty of many Jewish homes.

Later that night they lay in bed, Hersh wringing his hands helplessly as he listened to his sobbing wife. He reached out and put his arm around her, but was shocked when, for the first time in their marriage, she moved away from him.

"How could you?", she sobbed. "I was ready to die for our china!...........It has been a part of our family since before Chaia was born.....I wanted to give it to Feige, Mina's daughter......they seem to have so much less than the others......and now it will go to some German home where they will eat *chazzer* off it! Don't you care about it? ....Why did you let it go so easily?....."

Hersh's voice choked.

"Please, Chana, don't be ashamed of me. I had to......I had to.... something made me do it......The china was just as precious to me as it was to you, but there was only one thing I could see in my mind when that German was about to shoot you.....

Chana continued to sob, and he made no attempt to touch her.

".....I could see only one thing.....I remembered how you tried to save our old china from the great fire.....You almost lost your life then, just as you almost lost your life tonight......The china on both occasions was precious, but nothing is as precious as your life....."

"My life! And how much longer do you think that will be?"

"Who knows, but every second of it is priceless, far more than any belongings we may own. As long as I have you, my belongings mean nothing, and with you, my life is priceless too. Without you it means nothing, and may as well end tomorrow. If we must die, then my only hope is that it is together, that neither of us have to suffer the agony of being without the other."

Chana's sobbing slowly subsided.

"You are right, Hersh. Even if I had died, they still would have taken the china. Still, I cannot bear the thought of somebody eating *trafe* off it. It makes me ill to think of it. Perhaps they will choke on it."

Then her tone changed, and she sat up in bed, pushing away the covers.

"I suppose this same thing is happening in every Jewish home in Dorbyan. What about our poor daughters?"

"I wish I knew," answered Hersh. "I only hope that nobody has been injured or killed during the night. The fate of all of us in in God's hands. Everything that happens must be for a reason, part of some greater purpose."

They snuggled back under the covers. He put his arm around Chana. This time she did not draw away.

"Ever since I have known you my life has been happier than I could ever have dreamed. With you our sixty years of marriage have flown by so quickly that it is impossible to describe. And now,..... even if we should die tomorrow, I shall die knowing that God has blessed me more than any other man on earth."

CHAPTER 7

The following morning , June the 28th, was Saturday, the Sabbath, and the third day of Tammuz, the tenth month of the Jewish calendar. Hersh left his home before daybreak, checking the street carefully before he left his home. He saw no need to avoid the street, as it was completely deserted, but still he made his way carefully from tree to tree as he made his way towards the home of Elberg the chemist. He was determined that on this day at least, no obstacle would prevent him from attending a service, as he knew full well that future opportunities might not exist. He felt no sense of danger from the Germans, but rather from the possibility of Lithuanian collaborators, who were the Germans' eyes and ears.

He needn't have worried, for at that hour the street was deadly quiet, and no sound came from any of the Lithuanian houses on the street. He watched for the signs of movement, the parting of curtains, or a shadow behind a window, but there was no indication that he was being watched. There were not many houses on the Krettinger Gass, but of these all but his and that of the Kverils were Lithuanian.

He approached the home of Elberg the chemist from the rear, the sound of his own careful footsteps the loudest thing that he could hear.

What it was like in the centre of town was another matter however, and it might well be that some of the congregants would be deterred by the presence of German or Lithuanian patrols.

Elberg's house seemed quiet, but this did not surprise him, as he expected to be the first to arrive.

It was but a short time later, and still partially dark, when Hersh returned to Chana. She was shocked to see him trembling and ashen-faced.

"Chana, I don't know what we are going to do," he said. "It is *Sabbes*, and now it is not possible even to pray! We waited and waited, but it became obvious that we had no chance of forming a *Minyan*."

"How many of you were there?"

"Only six, including Elberg's two *Bar-mitzvah* sons. Apart from myself, there was only Rabbi Weisbord and Shmuskavitch from the Polanger Gass. What are we going to do, Chana? How are we going to celebrate *Sabbes*?"

"The people are too frightened, Hersh, and after what happened last night, can you blame them?"

"I knew that Rabbi Weisbord would come, even if the centre of town was guarded, and I thought that some of the others would also."

"Even if they came, how would they get home again after the service when it is daylight? Did anyone think of this?"

"This must be the reason that noone came. For me, it is possible to get home by going from backyard to backyard. For the others it would mean waiting around for the assembly at the market square, and then going there as if nothing had happened. I suppose nobody was prepared to do this, for they all want to be with their families at a time like this.

"I am also surprised that Elior did not come, and with him Natan Beir. It can only mean that the area around their home was too heavily guarded."

"How will Rabbi Weisbord get back to his home in the centre of town?"

"I don't know, Chana. Both Shmuskavitch and I offered to accompany him home, but he would not hear of it. In any case, when we realized that there could be no service we all left while it was still dark."

Hersh paced the floor like a caged animal, and Chana knew that his mood would not be pleasant. It was the Sabbath, and he was prevented from praying. He would be confined to his home for the entire morning, and there would be no possibility of visitors. Like every other Jew in Dorbyan, they could do nothing except wait until the assembly at noon and ponder over what new and harsher regulations would be read out against them.

He could not guess at what was coming, but he had decided to prepare himself for the worst. There remained no further belongings worth burying, but there were some things that he had decided the Germans should not inherit, intact. He did not mention it to Chana, but he had a strong feeling that they would not be returning home after this assembly. Where they would be transported to he did not like to contemplate, although he felt that this would be part of the German plan. He suspected that the Jewish community would be herded into some enclosure for the rest of the day and night while the Germans and their Lithuanian assistants helped themselves to the larger items, such as the furniture. Allowing the Lithuanians a portion of the spoils would no doubt be a German tactic to ensure their continuing loyalty.

For some reason the Germans had not taken the radio the previous night, eventhough it had been in plain sight. Perhaps they had better ones for their own use. Just the same, some Lithuanian would appreciate it. He would not allow this to happen. He went to the shed and fetched his axe from alongside the woodpile.

One blow was enought to smash the radio beyond repair, and a second blow rendered the glass battery useless, with acid spilling along the floor. The spare glass storage battery received the same treatment a moment later. Chana, attracted by the noise, came into the room and watched silently as Hersh attacked the solid wooden table that had been the foundation of their kitchen and eating area. When three of the four legs were hacked off at different heights he splintered the top in a dozen places before placing his axe on the floor while he caught his breath. He then went to the bedroom.

"You feel as I do, don't you," said Chana, "That after this assembly we won't be coming back to our homes."

"Yes," answered Hersh, "I believe we are near the end. You were right when you wanted to smash the china, and I am sorry that I didn't let you do it. I should have listened to you and helped you do it myself."

"Why don't we do as the Kagans did, and set fire to the house just before we leave?"

"I have thought of this also, and I am very much tempted, but when I think of it,I don't think it is such a good idea."

"If they are not going to let us use our home, then why not destroy it? After all,it is our home to do with as we please."

"Chana, we have our fears, but we do not know for certain that we are not coming home tonight. I suppose we could stay with one of our families, if the Germans would let us, but everyone else has enough problems of their own without us on their hands."

"I would rather be with our families than here alone in this house," said Chana.

"I too." said Hersh, "But what if the Germans decide to make reprisals against us or others because of the fire? They don't seem to care whom they punish, anyone will do, and I don't want our action to be the cause of somebody else's misfortune."

"We are all going to suffer misfortune in the end, Hersh."

"Yes, I know. but there is another reason for not making a fire that disturbs me most of all."

"Tell me."

"You mightn't understand, Chana, for you do not have the same feeling for horses that I do, but I am frightened of what the effect of a fire would be on Yoiphi. She has always been a nervous animal, and if we were to leave the house on fire just as we were leaving, I don't know what would happen after we left. I only know that it would destroy me if I were to find out later that I was responsible for Yoiphi's death."

"I think I do understand," said Chana. "But what is going to happen to her after we are gone?"

"This does not frighten me," answered Hersh, "Although I am sorry now that I did not find a good home for her earlier. The Germans appreciate good horses, and take good care of their own. Someone amongst them will be pleased to have her, and who knows, with a little *mazel*, they might even fight each other over her possession."

Hersh then went to the rear yard and the horse's enclosure. He had given extra feed and water to Yoiphi the afternoon before, for he had suspected that the *Shabbes goi* would no longer come around to look after her on the Sabbath. He was tempted to give the horse an extra ration of hay and water for the following day, but he decided against breaking the Sabbath. He climbed through the fence into the trampled enclosure. Yoiphi came to him at once, lowering her head to receive the accustomed caress.

"I'm sorry, Yoiphi, but I'm afraid I won't be able to take care of you for much longer. You are a fine horse, and I know that you'll make somebody very proud of you, even if it is a German."

He stroked the horse's sleek mane, and his thoughts drifted into the past. A lump came to his throat, and his eyes misted over as he looked into the horse's face.

"If only I had been clever enough to forsee this, I could have found you a good home. Now it is too late, for I am not even allowed to leave this house. All we can do is hope."

He thought about his childhood, when he had first realized how much he loved the animals. He remembered his timid, trembling request to his father for permission to buy his first horse. He remembered the early good years, when he had kept as many as six horses at a time, and had never wanted for customers.

He found himself thinking of every horse he had ever owned, most of them nameless, but still vivid in his memory. He thought of his earlier horses, and particularly the ones he had named according to perceived human traits he could see in them. His first was *Malamed*, whom he had sold to Rolandas Galdikas, then *Shlefrig*, whom he had sold to Zavueras a month later. After that names had been superfluous, but the horses themselves had stuck in his mind.

Then, as his children were growing up, naming the horses had become their pastime, and for a period of several years most of the horses had been named. A smile came to his face as he remembered some of the outrageous names which had resulted, with each child trying to outdo the others in humour and originality......*Chutzpah. Shiksah, Boombaleh, Knaidlach,Trumpeldor, Koyach,......*

Those were the days when he could turn over more than fifty horses in a good year, and yet he could remember everyone of them, for each had somehow become a part of him, even those whose stay was short.

In more recent years his horse trading activity had declined drastically, especially since the days of Lithuanian independence, and the increased competition from the local population. It had then become common for horses to spend as much as six months in his care before finding a buyer. The few he named no longer received outlandish names, reflecting his own conservative tastes.....*Tante, Mamela, Shnee, Shaine,Honik, Maidele.......*

Then the next generation had come along, his grandchildren, and once again the names given the horses were imaginative, but not as numerous, as the number of animals to be named had declined....
Shimshon, Baksheesh, Zoyerkraut,Schmaltz, Fingerhut...

Inevitably there had been fewer and fewer horses, and in recent years it had been a rare event for Hersh to make a sale. The market amongst the Lithuanians had been effectively lost to him for a generation, and the decline in the population and economic activity of the Jewish community, meant very little demand for his product. He had not been bothered by the loss in trade however, for his advancing years made it difficult for him to muster the ambition to pursue his business properly. He and Chana no longer needed much to live on, and they were taken care of by remittances from abroad, which for the most part they were able to donate to their children and their familes. Why else would the last of his horses have been riding horses rather than the more readily saleable work animals? He knew the answer, the last horses he had kept had been only a hobby, and had been more for the benefit of his growing grandchildren, with their possible sale being but a minor consideration. Yoiphi, his present horse, had been with him for almost two years. Natan Beir had chosen the name, and had she been sold, Hersh was not altogether certain that he would have replaced her, although he suspected he would.

"Everyone of you has been wonderful to me," he whispered hoarsely, "And everyone of you has helped make my life the *Gan Eden* it has been. I can think of nothing else I would rather have done with my life."

He caressed Yoiphi one more time before climbing back through the fence. As he went back to the house he turned one last time to the horse, and asked gently, "Why is it that human beings cannot have the same dignity towards each other that you horses have?"

CHAPTER 8

As the Jews came from all directions, making their way towards the market square, they were jostled, jeered and struck by the Lithuanian villagers who lined the streets. German soldiers and Lithuanians in unform stood by, openly encouraging the vengeful crowd, and smiling with each new attack on the Jews.

Hersh and Chana approached the square, unable to find their children in the throng. They kept to the centre of the street as much as possible, hoping that by being part of a larger crowd they would receive some protection from the sticks and stones that were flying their way. Hersh tapped Chana on the shoulder as he motioned in the direction of a uniformed collaborator nearby.

"Look, there is young Jonas Galdikas! I must try to have a word with him!"

"And what good will that do?"

"I don't know, but I must find out what is happening."

"You are wasting your time. Can you not see that he is on their side, not ours?"

Hersh made his way towards the uniformed figure.

"Jonas, it is Hersh Jacob. Your family know me well. Can you tell me what is going on here? Why is this happening?"

When Jonas Galdikas turned around and faced Hersh, the hatred in his face shocked him.

"Of course I know you, you old Jew!," he snarled. "You do not need to ask me why this is happening! For years you Jews have been robbing and cheating us! Now, at last, things are about to change!"

"But Jonas, your father and I are good friends, and we have done business with horses for years. We have always been satisfied with the bargains we have made. How can you say this?"

"My father is an old fool! He does not agree with all of this, but when we are rid of you, he will be grateful for the change! Now move along, before I help you along with my rifle butt!"

Hersh moved back alongside Chana, the two of them shielding

their faces from a hail of stones.

"I cannot understand this, Chana. Jonas Galdikas is not the same boy I once knew. Perhaps it is his new wife who has brought about this change in him."

"Now are you satisfied, my dear? Now will you believe me when I tell you that we have no friends among the *goyim*?"

As they entered the market area, they could see the remains of a recently doused fire, crudely lit, and obviously placed so as to cause no damage to any building.

The German soldiers and their Lithuanian assistants then began herding the crowd into one corner of the square, using their rifle butts freely to speed up the process. When the last Jew had been herded into place the German commander, a man somewhat older than his assistants, began to speak.

"Jews, you have been called to this assembly for a number of reasons, but first I must mention something serious that has taken place here not very long ago."

The crowd hushed in curiosity and apprehension as the commander pointed in the direction of the recently doused fire.

"Why you did it we do not know, but one or more of you disobeyed orders to remain in your homes in order to light this fire in the square. Fortunately it was spotted before it could do any damage.....

"This sort of behaviour is dangerous, and I give you notice that it will not be tolerated! You are about to learn that because of this action you have brought greater hardship upon yourselves. Does anyone amongst you wish to confess to lighting this fire?"

The crowd remained silent. Finally after several minutes of waiting, the commander spoke.

"It will go easier with you if the guilty person confesses. Otherwise everyone of you will be punished. As I have said, we do not tolerate this sort of action!"

Hersh whispered to Chana, "He knows that nobody will confess, for he knows that we didn't do it. He only wants the opportunity to punish us all. I am going to confess."

Before the shocked Chana could react, Hersh stepped forward towards the commander, raising his right hand.

"I am the guilty one, sir. It is I who lit the fire. I do not know what made me do it."

The commander stepped forward and looked coldly into Hersh's face for several seconds. Without warning he struck Hersh with full force in the face with the back of his gloved hand.

"You lie, you old Jew!"

Hersh rocked backwards, but remained on his feet.

"You could not have lit the fire! I watched you arriving just a moment ago!"

He struck Hersh again, harder, knocking him to the ground.

"This is a serious matter!," he screamed. "Do you think I am from yesterday? You lie to protect the others! If I thought for one moment that it was you, I would shoot you on the spot! Now go! Get out of my sight, before I change my mind!"

Hersh went back to Chana, who examined the small cut above his eye.

"I tried, Chana, it is the best that I could do."

The commander was about to speak again, when one of his soldiers tapped him on the shoulder and pointed to a figure approaching the market square.

"Who is that man? Bring him to me!," screamed the commander.

The soldiers went forward and intercepted the approaching man. He was middle-aged and obviously Jewish. They grabbed him roughly by the arms and dragged him before the commander, as the crowd looked on with apprehension.

"It is Motte Bloch," whispered someone in the crowd. "I wonder what they will do to him."

His wife Rose, who had been waiting for him with four of their seven children, fidgited nervously with her blouse. Arieh Leib and Gershon, her grown sons, supported her. Her adult daughter Zelda took the hand of thirteen year old Chia, as they waited for the beating of their father which would surely come.

"What is your name!," barked the commander.

"Mordechai Bloch, sir."

"Bloch! Were you not told to be here at assembly at noon? Do you think we give our orders just for pleasure? I am going to make an example of you, as to what happens to people who do not obey our orders!"

He spat into the face of the man who was still held tightly by the two German soldiers.

Without a word he walked around to the back of Mordechai Bloch, then removed his pistol from its holster. Deliberately he raised it and pressed it hard against Mordechai's neck.

A second later he pulled the trigger. The German soldiers released their grip and allowed Mordechai Bloch to fall to the ground where he lay without twitching. As the pool of blood beside the shattered head grew, the commander took out a handkerchief and wiped first his pistol and then his bloodspattered gloved hands.

Thus it was that Mordechai Bloch, fifty-five years of age, son of Chaim Wolfa and Heine Bloch, husband of Rose Frankel, and father of Moshe, Shevah, Zelda, Arieh Leib, Gershon, Lipman and Chia, became the first Dorbyan Jew to die at the hands of the Nazi Germans.

The crowd looked on in stunned silence, unable to comprehend what had happened. Then the first few started to weep. Rose Bloch began to sob hysterically, leaving Zelda to comfort Chia. Helplessly Arieh Leib and Gershon glared at the Germans, hatred in their eyes.

"And now, Jews, you have seen what happens to anyone who does not follow our orders! We are Germans, and we have not become masters by allowing people to disobey us! From now on, when a German orders you to do something, you will do it! I hope, for your sakes, you understand!"

After allowing a moment for the effect of his words to sink in, the commander spoke again.

"And now, where is your Rabbi? It is time that I spoke to him!"

Rabbi Isser Weisbord's wife and two young daughters paled, for the Rabbi was not with them. It was the Sabbath, and the assembly would have to wait until he had finished what he considered his religious duties. Synagogue or no synagogue, Germans or no Germans, the Lord would still be honoured on His day.

"Where is he?", screamed the commander. "Does anybody here know?"

The crowd in the square remained silent as the commander glared at them, waiting for an answer.

Finally one of the Lithuanian collaborators spoke to a German soldier, who approached the commander with the words, "I believe you will find him in his home, sir."

The commander called two German soldiers over to him and whispered a few words in their ears. He then asked the collaborator to show the soldiers to the Rabbi's home, which was no more than one hundred yards away. Rabbi Weisbord's wife and daughters stood in silent dignity, although after the treatment meted out to Mordechai Bloch, they could be in no doubt as to what his fate was likely to be. When several moments passed and no shots were heard from the direction of the house, their hopes began to rise. Then the two Germans returned to the square dragging the body of Rabbi Isser Weisbord.

At the sight of their beloved Rabbi, the crowd wept. The younger of his daughters began to cry for her father, but her mother gently hushed her. The Rabbi's body had been beaten to a pulp, his face almost beyond recognition. One side of his beard had been shaven off, removing a large section of skin in the process. The hands of the two Germans were bloodied, and their uniforms stained with blood in several places, in a manner resembling a butcher's apron.

Thus it was that the people of Dorbyan had their first experiences with the methods and the dealings of the master race.

"Now, perhaps you understand that when we say something, we mean what we say! Just how many examples does it take for you Jews to learn a simple thing?"

The commander turned to the two soldiers.

"Take five of these Jews with you to bury this rubbish!"

The Germans collared the nearest five able-bodied Jews, and sent one of them off to fetch shovels. These were gratuitously provided by one of the Lithuanian collaborators, eager to see that as little time as possible was lost. One of the Jews carried the two shovels, while the other four carried the still warm bodies of Mordechai Bloch and Rabbi Isser Weissbord. The two German soldiers followed behind, their pistols drawn.

307

They walked in the direction of the intersection of the Krettinger and Polanger Gasses to where the wooden bridge crossed over the River Darba. Then on the instructions of the Germans they turned left, following the river bank for two to three hundred yards. The Germans chose a suitable location alongside the river bank, then ordered the Jews to put the bodies down and start digging.

As the bodies of Mordechai Bloch and Rabbi Isser Weissbord were laid to rest, each of the men picked up a small stone and laid it reverently on top of the two murdered men. A prayer could be heard on their lips as they covered the bodies with earth.

"*Shmah Yisroel, Adoinoi Eloihenu Adoinoi Echod* ....."

In the market square the crowd milled about not knowing what would follow, terrified of doing anything which would provoke the Germans to further atrocity.

Hersh muttered to Chana in a choked voice, "Poor Motte, we must offer condolences to Rose and the children before the *mamsers* demand our attention again."

They found Rose Bloch, already surrounded by a number of townspeople, offering their sympathies to her and her children.

"Wait here, Chana, while I try to find the Weissbord family. This is a terrible blow, first they have taken our synagogue from us, and now our Rabbi."

He thought for a moment.

"You know, Chana, without a Rabbi we cannot exist. Someone from amongst us will have to take his place."

"If you are thinking of yourself," guessed Chana correctly, "You realize that you will be the target for the next bullet."

"I am no Rabbi, but I am the oldest member here, and I know the religion and the procedures fairly well. If someone is to take Rabbi Weissbord's place and lead the congregation, then it is better that it is an old man like me. People as old as I am have little to lose, and little to fear from the Germans."

At that moment a shot was fired into the air and all conversation ceased at once. The commander's face broke into a triumphant smile when he saw how quickly the crowd had become hushed, and he nodded approvingly. Beside his feet were six wooden buckets which had been brought to him by the Lithuanian collaborators.

"Jews, you will now form into six rows! It is not important who is in which row, just do it now! Lithuanians, would you please hurry the Jews into their formations!"

Using their rifle butts with enthusiasm, the Lithuanians herded the Jews into six lines of approximately equal length, each containing somewhere between one hundred and one hundred and fifty people. At the head of each row facing the line, stood a German soldier. The commander gave each German soldier a bucket.

"And now, Jews, you will come forward, one at a time, and you will remove all personal belongings, rings, necklaces, bracelets, watches, money, and whatever else you possess, and put them into the bucket. When you have finished you will move to the opposite side of the square."

The first items began to thud into the buckets under the watchful eyes of the Germans and supervised by the commander. The Germans were thorough in their examination of each person, and if they suspected that a person was hiding anything then a nod was given to one of the German soldiers or Lithuanian collaborators standing by, and that person was dragged aside to be strip searched. Pockets were turned inside out, blouses were ripped open at the neck in search of chains and lockets, Rings were wrenched from fingers, tearing the skin when they would not come off easily.

As Hersh and Chana approached the head of their row, Chana gazed nostalgically at her wedding ring, the only piece of jewellery she wore.

"Do you know how long ago it is since we exchanged these rings, Hersh? It breaks my heart to part with them."

"The loss of our rings will make no difference to the way I feel about you, my dear," said Hersh.

The German relieved Chana of her ring, and two Lithuanians frisked her for further belongings. Satisfied that she had been left with only the clothes she wore, they allowed her to move on.

When it was Hersh's turn, he had already removed his ring, which he handed to the German.

"Not to me, old man, in the bucket!"

Hersh dropped the ring into the bucket, while the Lithuanians slapped his body in several places in search of further articles. One of the Lithuanians was familiar to Hersh, and Hersh thought he could sense a gentleness in the man's probing. He pointed to Hersh's pocket, and the German glared at him icily.

"What is in your pocket? Take it out!"

"Just my watch, sir. Also in the bucket?"

The German nodded.

With a flourish Hersh let the watch drop into the bucket, noting with satisfaction that the solid thud upon impact had probably destroyed the works. The German was too concerned in the next victim to notice, and waved Hersh away impatiently.

Chana waited for him to catch up to her, and noticed that he was smiling.

"Are you a *meshuganeh*? What do we have to smile about? We have just lost our wedding rings that we have had since we were married."

"It is not the rings that I am smiling about," said Hersh. "It is the watch. Those *mamsers* do not know it, but they have done me a *machayah* by taking it from me."

"I believe all this is making you *meshuganeh*!," snorted Chana. "I thought I knew you, but sometimes I can't understand you at all! What do you mean, a *machayah*? You have had that watch for many years. It was a good watch."

"I am grateful to be rid of it." Hersh smiled at her mischievously. "It was made in Germany!"

When the last of the Jews had been relieved of their possessions, the six wooden buckets had been filled to overflowing. These were then emptied into a large wooden chest which was closed and sealed with a padlock.

"The fatherland will make better use of your ill-gotten gains than you have made of them," said the commander coldly. "The chest will be taken to our administration centre at Tilsit, and from there it will be sent to Berlin."

Two Lithuanians lifted the heavy chest and staggered with it towards a waiting army truck at the edge of the market square. There two more Lithuanians assisted them in lifting it on to the rear of the truck, which then drove slowly away.

"And now, Jews, for the first time in your lives you are going to have the opportunity to do something useful! And at the same time you will provide some entertainment for our officers and soldiers."

With this the commander ordered that four groups of the most able-bodied young men be formed, ten to a group. At once forty young men were herded to the street side of the square where four heavy wooden wagons stood. The horses were then released from the wagons and tied to the hitching posts that lined the street.

"We are going to have a wagon race from here to Krettingen and back!", announced the commander, "But instead of horses it is you Jews who will provide the power. Unlike you Jews, horses work hard for most of their lives. It is only fair that they should have a rest....

"You will pull the wagons in teams of two at a time, while the reserves ride in the wagon. To make sure that you complete the race and do not become lazy, a German soldier will ride in each wagon!

"I shall review the reports of my soldiers upon your return. Should any of you misbehave, then you and your families will receive special treatment."

The commander smiled knowingly.

Two men were harnessed to the front of each wagon. The eight remaining Jews and the German soldier climbed into the wagons. The commander examined each wagon as it was about to leave.

"Too light!", he decided. "There is room for three more people in each wagon."

He went back to the crowd and selected twelve older men to sit in the wagons.

"Don't worry, old man," he told Hersh. "You will not be required to pull the wagon. Your job is just to provide extra weight to give it balance."

He smiled to himself as he savoured and repeated the word, "Balance."

The wagons creaked to a start and set off at a snail's pace, with the German in each wagon urging on its human beasts of burden. As they drew out of sight at the bend at the beginning of the Krettinger Gass he turned to the crowd.

"And now, Jews, the rest of you are going to perform some useful work. You are going to do something which should have been done years ago. You are going to clean up this town, which you have been filthying for as long as you have been here. The time has now come for you to start repairing some of the damage you have done."

The Jews were then set to work cleaning the streets, the church areas, and the homes of any Lithuanians who wanted work done. Special attention was given to toilets, outhouses and latrines. The Lithuanians who watched were encouraged to jeer at them and beat them with sticks upon the slightest pretext. The supervision of the work was carried out by the Lithuanian collaborators, who seemed determined to show their German masters that they could outdo them in cruelty and enthusiasm.

Chana watched her daughters dodge a hail of small stones thrown by Lithuanian children as they left to perform their appointed tasks. She and a few of the other elderly ladies had been assigned to remain in the square to mind the infants and children up to the age of four or five, those too young to be of help to their parents, and too young to understand what was happening. The German soldier in charge seemed quietly amused as he watched the children running around, and playing their favourite game, hop-scotch.

"This German seems almost like a pleasant fellow who likes children," remarked Chana to one of the other women. "Perhaps he has children of his own. By himself he might even have the makings of a decent human being, but amongst others of his kind he is a *chazzer!*"

"They are all *chazzers!*," said the other woman bitterly. "There is no such thing as a human being amongst the Germans. You saw what they did to Motte Bloch and Rabbi Weissbord."

"And there is no such thing as a decent human being amongst the Lithuanians either," added Chana. "I don't know how they can be this way, but they almost seem to take delight in our plight."

"I think the Germans have planned it this way," answered the other. "My husband has been saying that the Germans always try to involve the people of other countries in their dirty work. Everything they do is part of a plan, and the plan was made long before they came here. The work we do is not for the Germans, but for the Lithuanians. We clean their streets, their yards, their houses, and their latrines. By using us, the Germans are trying to gain the favour of the Lithuanians."

As the creaking wagons strained slowly along the Krettinger Gass, Hersh stared anxiously at his home, trying to get a glimpse of Yoiphi as he passed. He could not see the horse, and assumed, or at least hoped, that she was simply out of sight behind the house. The German in the wagon noticed his interest in the house.

"What is it that you find so interesting about that house, old man?"

"That is my house, the house where I live," said Hersh.

The German laughed, then spoke matter of factly.

"You mean it *used* to be the house where you lived, don't you? Jews do not own houses anymore. It belongs to the fatherland now. In any case you will have no need of it from now on."

A few moments later they passed the only other Jewish house on the street, the house of Hoshe and Basha Kveril. It was a fine house, one of Dorbyan's best. Although it was now some twenty-five years old, it was still one of the newest in the town, as there had been little new construction since it was built. Hoshe Kveril had always possessed the means to keep his house in good repair. Unlike most of the other homes in the town, the Kveril house was covered by a fresh coat of paint.

They passed the outskirts of the town into forest and farming country, and continued along the hard packed road, made dry and dusty by the hot summer weather. Hersh anxiously watched the two men pulling the wagon, soaked in perspiration and groaning as their energies faded. Their wagon was slightly in the lead, which served to keep the German in good spirits. A change in manpower was made, and the two young men collapsed into the wagon. They were told that they would receive water when they reached Krettingen.

As they passed each Lithuanian farm, men women and children came to the side of the road to stare at the procession. Most stood silently, until goaded on by the Germans in the wagons.

"Look, peasants, Jews! Let them know what you think of them!" And the jeering, spitting and stone throwing would start.

Four hours later they reached the outskirts of Krettingen, and

313

the Germans ordered them to halt in a grassy field. Hersh's wagon had finished slightly behind the leader in second place, but the Germans in all four wagons appeared to be in good humour. In fact they seemed to have enjoyed themselves throughout, and the few snippets of their conversation which Hersh was able to overhear indicated that they welcomed the change from their normal gruesome duties. What these may have been Hersh did not know, but he assumed that these men had seen previous action on the battlefield.

Still in good spirits, the Germans gave the Jews water and then surprisingly,bread with butter, and allowed them half an hour's rest before they began the return journey to Dorbyan.

It was late afternoon before the procession started the return trip, and it became obvious that they would not make it back before nightfall. As the twilight approached, the Germans selected a suitable field about halfway back to Dorbyan and ordered the wagons to halt there. The Jews would sleep closely together on the ground for the night, surrounded by the wagons. Two of the Germans would sleep in a wagon, while the other two kept guard over their prisoners.

As darkness fell in Dorbyan, the Jews were herded back into the market square. Men, women and children realized that the hard ground would be their bed for the night, and set about making themselves as comfortable as they could, the children snuggling closely against their mothers' bosoms. A few managed to sleep, but apart from the children, most could not drive the murders of Mordechai Bloch and Rabbi Isser Weissbord from their minds. Constantly present was their fear for the safety of the men on the wagons. Were they being taken somewhere to be slain? Stories of this sort of behaviour by the Germans had been heard before.

Children and adults alike slept on the ground, without covers, their minds dulled by the first pangs of hunger. They thought about the *cholent* meal that most of them would have been eating on this day, prepared prior to the Sabbath, and resting in pots and vessels in their homes.

For the first time since they were married more than sixty years earlier, Chana went to sleep without Hersh by her side.

Night fell, and the Sabbath came to a close. In the more than two hundred years of Dorbyan's history, the Jewish community had never known a blacker day.

Saturday, June 28, 1941, or Tammuz 3 of the Jewish year 5701, had been its blackest day ever, and yet, to a person everyone agreed on one thing - there would be blacker days to come.

CHAPTER 9

Sunday, June 29, 1942, the 4th day of Tammuz by the Hebrew calendar, and St Peter's day according to the traditions of the Catholics of the village: the sun rose,and in the Dorbyan market square those who had been unable to sleep, Chana amongst them, gazed enviously at those who were still sleeping. German and Lithuanian guards had maintained a vigil through the night, and a small number still stood guard at the outer corners of the square.

The first of the Lithuanian villagers began to approach the square on their way to early morning Mass, just as the last of those asleep began to awaken and look around them.

What they saw was a crowd of more than seven hundred men, women and children lying and sitting on the hard ground of the square, surrounded by a small number of armed German and Lithuanian guards. There was no way to approach the church except by passing through the crowd, which upon the orders of the guards parted, leaving a pathway to the church. The people arriving made their way through the crowd carefully, skirting the bodies on the ground, and trying their best not to meet the gaze of the Jews, lest recognition cause some embarrassment. They seemed to be a different type, more sympathetic than those who had mistreated the Jews the day before, and many felt shame that they were going to prayer in such circumstances. They were under no illusions as to what would become of the Jews eventually, and no doubt they would hear more of this from the pulpit.

The cries of the children increased as the morning wore on, and consoling them was difficult, for who could explain to them why they had not been allowed to eat since the morning of the previous day?

How could it be explained to them that their predicament was entirely due to the fact that but a week earlier, without warning, without reason, they had suddenly become "enemies of the state"?

Throughout the morning more and more Lithuanian villagers arrived for the later prayer services. Again they were of a different nature to those who had tormented the Jews earlier, and many of them gazed at those on the ground, showing as much sympathy as they dared. On no occasion was any effort made by either of the groups to make conversation.

One of the churchgoers passed closely by a huddled group of Jews, and as she passed she allowed a crumpled piece of paper to fall from her hand.

"Give this to Ponas Hershas Jakobas," she whispered, as she continued on her way without breaking step.

The paper was picked up from the ground and quickly passed from person to person in the direction of Chana. When Chana received it she was puzzled, but did not dare open it for fear of attracting attention. She tucked it inside the bodice of her dress,to give to Hersh when he returned.

Shortly before mid-morning the creaking sound of wagons was heard, and relief was felt, for shortly after, the four wagons appeared, pulled along by their human locomotion. Despite the exhausted condition of the men, spirits rose, for they seemed to have returned unharmed. When the German soldiers gave the word, the men were unhitched from the wagons and those inside allowed to climb down. Hersh went straight to Chana.

"Are you all right, Chana?"

"We have not been harmed. We are hungry, but safe. It was you that we worried about."

He looked towards the German commander, who was speaking to the soldiers and smiling. His plan had been simple, and as he looked at the utterly exhausted figures which had collapsed on the ground he knew that he could expect no resistance from them, the youngest and strongest of Dorbyan's manhood, during the events which were to come.

"It was not as bad as we feared. Of course I didn't have to do any work. Those who did the pulling are completely exhausted, and stiff and sore, but unharmed."

"That is a pleasant surprise," said Chana, "For many of us thought that you might in some way displease the Germans, and be killed."

"Nothing like that, Chana. For some reason the Germans seemed to enjoy the excursion, and were in good spirits. They even shared some of their bread and butter with us."

"Then you have eaten more than we have," replied Chana. "None of us has had anything to eat since we left our homes, and the small children are constantly crying. It is impossible to explain to them why this is happening."

"It is impossible to explain to any human being why this is happening," said Hersh. What possible explanation can there be?"

Every German soldier known to the people had now arrived at the market place, and a detachment of new faces as well. Amongst these was an another officer of at least equal rank to the commander who had killed Mordechai Bloch the day before. He stood before the crowd and raised his hand in the Nazi salute.

"Sieg Heil!"

He was answered in rousing fashion by the same salute from the German soldiers in the square.

"Sieg Heil!"

He then motioned to the regular commander, who stepped forward and spoke.

"And now Jews!", he shouted, "You are to be divided into two groups."

A murmur arose from the crowd, as he pointed towards one side of the square.

"The men will go to this side, where they will be under the direction of Gruppenfueher Bohm, and the women and children will go to the other side, where they will remain under my direction. All boys who are sixteen years and older will go to the same side as the men."

Hersh kissed Chana goodbye, and she embraced him tightly.

"I think this will be the last time we shall see each other."

Their eyes filled with tears, for both had their suspicions as to what was coming. The term 'selection process' was no longer secret, and invoked fear in all those who had heard about it. Word had leaked out of what had been happening in Poland, and now the situation in Dorbyan appeared identical. The Jews of a village or group would be split into two sections, one usually to die immediately, the other to remain alive for so long as it pleased the Germans, or could be in some way put to use. It was their preferred procedure, and usually it meant that the males would be killed first, as they were the ones most most likely to offer resistance.

"The men will come over here, *now*!", shouted Boehm. "You will be leaving at once for a camp where you will be labouring for the benefit of the Fatherland!"

Spirits rose again, for the men were not to be killed, at least not immediately. Life in a German labour camp would be hell on earth, but it would be life. Where there was life there was always hope.

From his side of the square Hersh watched as Elior gave Breina a final embrace, unaware that he was being followed by Natan Beir. Breine called after her son, alerting Elior's attention.

Elior turned around, saw Natan Beir, and gently said to him. "Natan, go backto your mother, she needs you."

"I want to go with you, Papa."

"No, go back. I have a feeling that it will go better for you if you are with your mother."

A German soldier came up to Elior and asked, "What is going on here?"

"My son, he wishes to come with me to be with the men."

The German appeared puzzled, as though unaccustomed to being called upon to make a decision. Finally he asked, "How old is he?"

"Sixteen," answered Natan Beir.

"Fourteen, not yet fifteen," answered Elior.

The German scowled, then decided.

"Back with the women, child!" He gave Natan a kick to his backside to help him on his way.

"Thank you," said Elior to the soldier, and watched with pride as Natan Beir scurried back to his mother.

The women and children in the square watched with tear-filled eyes as their menfolk were lined up in the semblance of a formation, some three hundred in all. When the German commander was satisfied with the formation he barked an order, and the motley crowd moved away.

Herded by Lithuanian collaborators on the sides and led by German soldiers at strategic intervals, they left the market square in the direction of the Polanger Gass and the outskirts of the town. Women and children craned their necks for a final glimpse of their loved ones, then turned sadly away as the group passed from sight. Although most believed that the men would not be killed, they knew in their hearts that they would not see them again.

As the men disappeared from view Chana could contain herself no longer.

"German *chazzers*!", she screamed. "Why do you take my husband? He is an old man and too old to work in your slave camps!"

At that point she was knocked to the ground by a vicious blow from the pistol butt of a German soldier. As she fell the other women and children looked on in horror.

Strangely enough, it was the German commander who came to her side. With a gesture he waved aside the German soldier who had struck Chana.

"Please, old one, do not make a difficult situation any worse than necessary.Where your husband is going there will be something for everybody."

"Take your hands off me, you German murderer!", she shouted. "You are lying and you know it, you German *chazzer*!"

The commander froze, shocked by the ingratitude.

"Filthy old Jewish whore!", he muttered under his breath as he aimed a heavy kick at the fallen woman's body. He strode off in anger, pushing people aside as he went.

Chana's daughters huddled around her in tears. Natan Beir knelt beside his grandmother.

"Are you all right, *Bobe*? Can you get up?"

Chana nodded, and he helped her to her feet. Breina removed her kerchief and dabbed at the trickle of blood at the side of her mother's face.

"Mama, why do you provoke them? It does no good, and only causes you injury."

"What can they do to me?", snapped Chana. "I am an old woman. What can they do....... take away the little remaining time I have left? You are the ones I worry about, not myself. I have no fear of them, they can do nothing to me!"

"Mama, you do not realize what these animals are capable of! If they wish to punish you, it will not be by killing you. Rather, they will take some small child and put it to death before your eyes, for this is how these beasts behave."

Chana's shoulders sagged.

"And they call us Jews *Untermenschen*," she growled. "Just who are the real *Untermenschen*?"

As Hersh marched away from the town along with the others he thought he could hear a commotion coming from the market place. He tried to steal a glance backwards as he walked, but the square and its people were already out of view.

He walked alongside Elior, the only one of his sons-in-law not himself accompanied by an adult son. They walked silently, making little effort to speak. Although the men tended to cluster in family groups, there was little attempt at conversation from any quarter. The Germans and Lithuanians continually shouted orders, goading the group to maintain its loose formation.

He spied Jonas Galdikas slightly in front of him, smartly dressed, and performing his task of maintaining order as he walked. He gradually made his way to the young Lithuanian and spoke to him. Jonas Galdikas glanced back at him, and then started to quicken his pace in an effort to move away.

"No, don't leave, Jonas. All I ask is that you listen to me. You don't have to answer. Just nod if you understand."

Jonas Galdikas continued, face forward, without showing any acknowledgement of Hersh's presence.

"Jonas, in the backyard of our house is a very good horse. I know that I shall never see her again, and it worries me what might become of her. I want you to go there and take her for your own, for I know what you are like with horses, and I know that in your hands she will be well taken care of."

Jonas Galdikas's ears pricked up, for old Hersh Jacob was well known as a master of horses. Any horse of his would have to be of the finest quality, for no one knew more about their care and maintenance. A wonderful opportunity was presenting itself.

The plans of what he would do began to circulate in his mind. He would visit Hersh's house and collect the horse in the evening after he had done his day's duties. His father would probably disapprove of the manner in which he had acquired the horse, but this was unimportant. He had, after all, been offered the animal, and it would be for the best if he took up the offer. Hersh and the other Jews were about to be sent away, and if he did not sieze the opportunity, it would be only a matter of time before the horse became the property of some small time looter or thief. It would then probably appear in a neglected state at the market on some future Wednesday.

"She will be hungry, and nervous. If you approach her with food, and allow her to eat, she will then be friendly to you. Otherwise she may show some temperament, but you know all of this anyway. She will answer to the name *Yoiphi*,yes, *Yoiphi*. Please nod your head if you have understood me."

Jonas Galdikas nodded, then quickened his pace, marching forward and repeating the horse's name in a whisper. As he thought of the horse that would be his, he tried not to think of the man who had been its owner. Hershas Jakobas was one of the few Jews who had had dealings with his father. Although contact had not been as frequent in recent years, they still considered themselves friends. He found himself trying to drive sympathy for the Jew from his mind. Perhaps old Hershas Jakobas was not such a bad person after all. He had certainly always been willing to assist the Galdikas family whenever it had been within his power. There was only one problem as far as Hershas Jakobas was concerned. He was a dirty Jew.

A German soldier appeared out of nowhere, and began to question Jonas Galdikas.

"What was that all about?"

"The old Jew is worried about his horse," answered Jonas Galdikas.

A smile broke across the German's face.

"His horse!", he exclaimed, and he began to laugh, and slapped Jonas Galdikas heartily across the shoulder.

"His horse!"......Ha! Ha!.......You know," he giggled, "That sometimes even this *scheiss* job has its funny moments!"

Jonas Galdikas stared at the German with a puzzled expression.

"*Scheiss* job?"

"*Ja, scheiss* job!"

"I don't understand."

"Don't worry, wou will understand before the day is finished."

He then started to giggle again, leaving Jonas Galdikas more puzzled than ever.

"His horse!", he snickered. "His horse!"

He broke out into uproarious laughter. "Ho! Ho! The old Jew worries about his horse, of all things! Does he not know that it is his own life he should worry about? His horse has a better future than he has, and I might add, greater value to the German Reich!"

He strode off, still chuckling to himself, leaving Jonas Galdikas puzzled over his words. A moment later he returned, this time his face serious.

"This horse, where is it kept?"

Jonas Galdikas hesitated, then answered.

"In the Kretinga Gatve, sir. The first house from the corner of Palanga Gatve leaving town on the right hand side."

CHAPTER 10

As the men disappeared from earshot, the crowd of women and children milled about the market place, wondering what would come next. There seemed to be no direction for the first few minutes until the commander spoke a few words to the dozen or so German soldiers who had not accompanied the men on thei march. The Germans then passed on the message to the Lithuanian collaborators who had remained behind. Then the commander addressed the crowd.

"And now, Jews, your synagogue is going to be your home for the time being, but before you are to be allowed to move in there is a large amount of garbage to be removed! We will go now to the synagogue and I will explain what is to be done!"

Watched by a crowd of onlookers standing a safe distance away, the Jewish women and children were marched across the market square and into the area in front of the synagogue known as the *Shul platz*. The two large doors at the front of the building were thrown open revealing a corridor which passed through the classroom area and ended some twenty-five feet later at the further two doors which provided entry into the synagogue proper. Strictly speaking the building was a *Bet Midrash*, as it provided both prayer and learning facilities.

"And now Jews, you will enter the synagogue a few at a time and you will each come out with as many books as you can carry. You will bring the books here and place them in a pile next to where I am standing. From time to time one of my officers will enter the building to see that you are carrying out your task. I don't think I need to warn you of the consequences if I receive a bad report ."

He smiled, then continued.

"A portion of you will go up the side stairs to remove all books from the upstairs section. When this area has been emptied of all its rubbish it will be sealed off. I expect that in a very short time there will be no books left in this building, and I am usually correct in my expectations!"

324

As the second set of doors swung shut behind them, Natan Beir spoke quickly to his mother.

"They are going to burn the books, aren't they, mother?"

"Yes, Natan, they have done this in other places," answered Breina.

"And the *Torahs* too?"

"Yes, and the *Torahs* too, "answered his mother resignedly.

"Then, we must try to save the *Torahs*!"

"How?"

"I think we can save one," answered Natan Beir, "But we must be quick, and you must help me!"

"Nathan, no! If we are discovered, we will be shot!"

"Then we must act quickly, so that we are not discovered!"

He ran to the ark, opened the door, and reached for the smallest and lightest *Torah* inside. He gently removed it, kissing it as he cradled it in his arms.

"Hold this *Torah*, mother, even though it is forbidden. Give it back to me when I climb onto the Rabbi's chair."

He closed the doors of the ark and climbed onto the back of the chair alongside the ark. Reaching out, he was just able to reach the shelf on the top of the ark.

"Pass me the *Torah*, mother, quickly!"

Straining to lift the heavy scroll above his head, he pushed it to saftey behind the carved timber front. He then jumped down, took a look upwards and satisfied himself that it could not be seen. Quickly he gathered up an armful of prayer books and handed some of them to his mother and grandmother. Then they made their way back to the exit.

"Poor child," said Breina to Chana. "They will probably discover it in the first five minutes."

"Maybe not," answered Chana. "In any case you should be proud that you have a son who cares so much for the *Torah*, and is even prepared to risk his life over it."

"Does it really matter?", asked Breina.

"Of course it matters!', retorted Chana impatiently. "Did your father and I waste our time bringing you up? Where is your schooling?"

She continued to chastise her daughter, who had become red faced with embarrassment.

"Why do you think this is happening to us? It is because we are Jews! Whatever happens to us, we must remain Jews, and let them know that all their evil cannot break our devotion to God. No matter what may happen to us today, there will always be Jews, even long after there are no Germans."

The procession of women and children in and out of the synagogue continued, and after several minutes the first began to return empty handed. They were pushed back into the synagogue and told to continue searching. When person after person returned empty handed the Germans went inside to satisfy themselves that no further books remained. Then came an obscene shout from inside, and one of the Germans came outside and beckoned to a Jew to come inside. He had discovered a book in a crevice, and did not wish to soil his hands in touching it.

There was now a large pile of books in a heap near the commander's feet. Amongst these were daily prayer books, some in Hebrew only, others translated into Yiddish, and other books of commentary and interpretation relevant to the prayer services. The number of books in the pile could not have been less than fifteen hundred.

The classroom areas had been similarly scoured. Removed from classroom number 1 were the books which taught mathematics and languages using non-Hebrew script. These books were no different than those used in many German schools, but the Germans took no notice of this. Every book was to be removed from every classroom and placed in the pile. One by one each classroom was emptied of the books teaching its specialized subject.

Then a German rushed to the door and asked for a Lithuanian to bring him either some sacks or a carton, for he had opened the holy ark and discovered the treasure inside.

As the Lithuanian collaborator brought a sack into the synagogue he could see a German pair at work. One was removing the *Torahs* one at a time and flinging them from the ark. The other was removing the velvet and silver decorative ornaments and then, with a laugh, tossing the *Torahs* as far from him as he could. noting with satisfaction the damage done to the scroll posts from the impact.

He called out to the Lithuanian.

"Over there, in the centre, on the platform, more treasure!"

When the last *Torah* had been removed from the ark and stripped of its ornament, The Lithuanian and one of the Germans left the building with the laden sack. The German then moved into the crowd and pulled twenty-two of the more robust women out, shoving them in the direction of the synagogue door. He herded them inside, and oblivious to their tears and gasps of shock, pointed to the pile of desecrated *Torahs* on the floor and motioned for each woman to carry one away.

"Worthless junk!", he said. The real treasure had been the ornaments that had been removed and placed in the sack.

"Take them away! Place them on the pile with the books!"

When the last *Torah* had been placed on the pile, the commander entered the synagogue. A moment later he emerged smiling. There were no books nor *Torahs* to be seen within the building.

A moment later he nodded, and a German soldier brought a cannister of gasoline and emptied it over the pile. dousing it completely. Then he stood back, dipped a stick of wood in the gasoline, lit it, and threw it onto the pile.

The crowd screamed, and then surged forward, to the extent that the Germans and their Lithuanian assistants were forced to club several to the ground. One woman who had burst forward and almost reached the flames was clubbed senseless, then her body picked up and flung back into the crowd.

"The commander screamed, "Jews, you will stop this at once! I give you one minute to come to attention or I will give my men the order to fire!"

The surging crowd subsided, and almost five hundred women and children sobbed as silently as they were able, as they watched four thousand years of their heritage go up in flames.

Like the others, Chana watched the scene with misted eyes. Older than the others, she felt greater emotion than most, and she was grateful that Hersh was not present to witness the scene. She could remember the acquisition of many of the scrolls, and Hersh's joyful announcement on each occasion that the community had been able to muster the funds to make the purchase. It had been several years since a *Torah* had last been acquired, and none of the children had ever been present at the blessing of a new addition, yet everyone had been taught of the care and toil that went into the production of each one. Like many of the other older women around her, the thought had entered her mind that she would be better throwing herself into the flames rather than witness the sight before her..

She remembered the many times in the past that the *Torahs* had been saved from fire, often at great personal risk, and she thought of the irony of their present fate. Many of the Torahs had been purchased during her lifetime, others were of undeterminable age, and could have been as old as the community itself. Almost every one had been at one time or other endangered by fire, but to date none had ever perished. In the great fire of 1882, scores of homes had been destroyed, and the synagogue had been under threat, yet no *Torah* had suffered damage. In the fire of 1909 which had burnt the previous synagogue to the ground, the *Torahs* had been the first to be rescued. There had been little time to spare, and many of the congregants, Hersh included, had risked their lives in ensuring that all *Torahs* had been removed before abandoning the building. A few congregants had suffered burns in the process, but no *Torah* had suffered damage.

Now it appeared that the fate of the *Torahs* had been pre-ordained, and that they had finally succumbed to the fate which had always hovered over them.

"And now Jews, you have seen enough! Into the synagogue!"

Thus it was that the culture of an ancient civilization was wiped out, that laborious craftmandhip carried out to perfection over a period of several years was destroyed. Artifacts with the same craftsmanship as a grand master's painting or classical Greek sculpture were desecrated, in brutal fashion, then destroyed, by the very nation which in its arrogance considered itself to be the most culturally advanced and civilized on earth.

The crowd was herded through the synagogue doors. When the last person had been forced inside, the doors were bolted behind them.

When the flames and heat had subsided, the Germans and their Lithuanian assistants prodded and poked at the pile of ash with shovels and pitchforks. Large portions of the rolled up *Torahs* and tightly closed books had survived the inferno and were relatively intact. The pile was stirred into a new position, doused again with gasoline, and rekindled. The proceedure was repeated several times, until finally the Germans were satisfied that nothing large enough to be recognizable could be salvaged.

As the synagogue doors closed behind them, some of the women and children, still weeping, remained in the classroom area, where they collapsed onto the hard wooden benches, allowing their heads to fall forward onto the wooden tables which ran the length of the room. The majority continued through the second set of doors into the synagogue proper, which offered greater comfort and somehow seemed more secure.

It was with a feeling of unease that these women entered the synagogue, for the place of the women was upstairs, and none of them would have ever entered the synagogue proper from any other direction.

As he entered, Natan Beir whispered to his red-eyed mother and grandmother.

"You see, they did not destroy all the *Torahs*! We still have one! We must return it to its proper place in the ark!"

"I am sure that they will discover it before long if it is there," answered his mother lifelessly.

"Not if we hide it properly," answered Natan Beir enthusiastically.

"How can we possibly hide it?," asked his mother.

"Breina, listen to your son!", interrupted Chana. "I believe he knows what he is doing. You do not notice these things, but he is a *mensch* already. Let us trust him."

"I know what we must do," said Natan Beir. "We will make a false front inside the ark, and the *Torah* can hide behind it, out of sight. I will move the cloth lining at the back closer to the front. Whatever may happen to us, it is still better if we have a *Torah*."

Chana felt a wave of pride surging within her, relieving her momentarily of some of the misery she had experienced during the day. The strict upbringing Natan Beir had received had not gone to waste. It had successfully traversed the generations from Hersh to Natan

Beir through their daughter Breina and her husband Elior.

Natan Beir was intelligent too, and resourceful, for of all the nearly five hundred people in the synagogue, he and he alone had forseen the possibility of rescuing the *Torah*. If Hersh had been here to see this, she knew that he would have been very proud.

"Yes, yes," she told Natan Beir. "We shall find a way to protect it, for it is precious, more precious than all our lives put together."

It was then that she remembered the message which had been passed to her in the square, and she felt under her chemise, relieved to find that it was still there. She had forgotten to give it to Hersh, but even if she had remembered, there would have been no opportunity. She opened the crumpled bit of paper and her aged eyes fell upon the blurred handwriting in Lithuanian with its unfamiliar Latin script, which she had never learned to read. She puzzled over it for a moment, then called Natan Beir over to translate the passage.

Natan Beir read the message easily.

> Ponas Hershas Jakobas
> You have asked about hiding your grandson from the Germans. There are Lithuanians in Darbenai who hate the Germans and who wish to help as many Jews as they can.
> We cannot give names, but if you will trust us, bring your grandson to the old watermill at midnight. We will wait there every night until you are able to come.
> We pray for you. May our Saviour protect you.

Natan Beir looked into his grandmother's face.

"Bobe, why are you crying? There is no need to cry. I know that it is me that they are talking about. You don't have to worry. I will never leave you and Mama!"

Chana continued to sob uncontrollably into her kerchief.

"You do not understand, Natan. These are not the same tears that I have been crying during these last two days. You do not understand these tears. They have to do with your *Zeide* Hersh.

"You see, for a long time your *Zeide* has been asking Lithuanian friends to help us, and I have never had any faith that any

Lithuananian would lift a finger to do anything for us.........I was wrong, and now I am ashamed.....Your *Zeide* knew a lot more about people than I,........ and he knew what he was talking about,........and now I shall probably never see him again to tell him how wrong I was.....

".....He was right, there are good Lithuanians....I am certain that this letter is honest...."

"But *Bobe*, I don't want to go, no matter what happens here. My place is here,with you and Mama!"

He looked into his grandmother's eyes pleadingly.

Chana hugged her grandson, who seemed to tower over her shrunken frame.

"It's all right, Natan, we have already realized this, and know how you feel. We would all feel better if you were safe somewhere, but you are a *Mensch* now, and old enough to decide your own future. Your *Zeide* was only thinking of you, and trying to do what he thought was best, but it is you who must decide what to do, not others."

She pulled out her kerchief again.

"......But it brings me joy just to think that there are good people who would take a risk to help us. I should have listened to Hersh when he told me this."

Outside the synagogue the German commander spoke to one of his officers.

"A very strange thing has happened here today, and I must make a report at once to send to headquarters. I am certain that the men in Berlin will be very interested to learn what has happened."

"I do not understand, sir."

"Did you not notice, Hans? What happened today was something that our instructions told us would never happen with Jews. We have been assured that once the menfolk are taken away, and that once their religious material has been destroyed, we can expect no resistance from the women and children. Yet these women and children came very close to resisting today. The people in Berlin should be made aware of this so they can plan their future *Aktions* accordingly.

"You know, Hans, we are still new at this business, and still learning. Thus far there has been no resistance in Dorbyan and we have suffered no casualties, but I have learned that already we have lost men in the operations around Polangen and Krettingen. In fact in Polangen it was a woman, Chaia Benjamin, who led the resistance. It is my job to see that it does not happen here, and that every last Jew is liquidated without cost to ourselves. Until our job is done, we must be constantly on our guard.

If you see or hear of any sign of resistance, no matter how trivial, I want you to let me know at once. The people in Berlin must be made aware of all developments as they happen."

CHAPTER 11

The first night passed uneventually, if uncomfortably, in the synagogue. The building had been designed to seat about four hundred worshippers in the main area with perhaps a further one hundred seats in the six classrooms. The five hundred inside were able to find seats, but sleeping required more space, and involved lying on the floor and on the benches. At times of the major summertime festivals, when the synagogue had on accasion been filled to capacity, the heat and stuffiness had always been a problem, but the problem had never been more than of a few hours' duration. Now, with the hottest part of the year approaching, and the building packed for the forseeable future, the discomfort was greater than any experienced in the past. Few had been able to sleep for any length of time although lack of food and water over the past two days had left them with strength for very little else. The moans and cries for water became more frequent, particularly amongst the younger children.

Early the next morning two German soldiers entered the synagogue and informed the prisoners that they would be allowed to file to the latrine fifty yards away once each day in the morning. In the event of any needs beyond this, one of the classrooms was to be used as a latrine. There would be little need for this, emphasized the Germans, as rations would be kept to the bare minimum for their subsistence. Each person would receive a bowl of soup per day, which was to be given out late in the afternoon.

As the women and children filed to the latrine under German and Lithuanian guard they could see a group of village children attracted to the area where the *Torahs* and books had been burned. They were playing in the ashes, and had found articles of interest in the charred remains. As they passed closer they could see that the children had been picking out small scraps of leather which had earlier been the bindings of books. Some of the children had fashioned the scraps of leather into drums which they were gleefully tapping to make a sound. Others innocently waved the scraps at the Jewish women and children as they filed past.

As noon approached, conditions in the synagogue worsened. The day was hot and the late June midday sun beat down mercilessly on the dark slate roof. There was little that anyone could do except to remain inert and conserve whatever energy still remained. Conditions were unbearable, and it was obvious that they could not be endured for long, yet there was no doubt that the hottest part of the summer was still to come.

"So this is the way they intend to treat us," said Breina. "How do they expect us to live under these conditions?"

"I don't think they expect us to live," answered Chana."

Yet the situation remained unchanged, and the prisoners somehow survived it, for almost a full month. The daily visit to the latrine had been stopped by the Germans after only two days, as they had considered it unnecessary. The soup which they had spoken about turned out to be a cauldron of boiling water placed at the entrance, with a shovelful of grass thrown in. Nutritionally its value was non-existent, but it at least provided a drink of water for each person once a day. Pleas for better conditions to the Germans providing the soup fell upon deaf ears. On the rare occasion that a German chose to reply, his words were invariably, "We are working on it. Something will be done."

It was late in July when two German officers not previously seen by the prisoners entered the synagogue. The officer appearing to be the more senior addressed the women and children.

"You have been complaining for sometime of overcrowding in this building. As I look around I have to agree with you. Until now there has been no place to move you. Now, we have decided to remove a group of about one-quarter of you from the building to work in the fields. We will select the fittest of you to work in a labour camp outside."

The puzzled prisoners looked on in silence, unable to decide whether this was a good thing or not. Although there was little ground to trust the German's motives, any change would be welcome. The month of undernourishment and unbearable living conditions had left them too mentally and physically exhausted to show any reaction.

"Very well, then, said the German. "We shall begin the selection at once."

The youngest and fittest of the women were directed through the door to the outside where a group of German soldiers stood waiting. Some one hundred and twenty young women were selected, including everyone of Chana's granddaughters.

"What will become of them?", she asked one of the Germans.

"Nothing that concerns you," he replied coldly. "Just be grateful that this place will no longer be so crowded!"

As the Germans left the synagogue, Chana could hear one German remark to the other.

"Phew! I am glad to get out of here! This place stinks!"

"What did you expect?", the other had replied. "These people live like vermin! Now do you see why we call them *Untermenschen*?"

For almost a week no word was heard of the women who had been taken from the synagogue. Deprived of information, rumour and conjecture had been the only avenues of information open to the prisoners. Families and remnants of families sat and lay in groups talking amongst themselves, occasionally circulating to join in other conversation. Voices were kept low, as any conversation which became too loud attracted angry warnings from the guards outside.

Amongst the people Chana most often spoke to was Rose Bloch, widow of the murdered Mordechai.

"What do you think has happened to our children who were taken away?", she asked.

"From what I have come to know of the Germans, they are all dead by now," answered Rose Bloch without emotion.

"Do you think that the Germans will first try to get a bit of work out of them?"

"They were not interested in getting work out of my Motte, or out of Rabbi Weissbord", she answered bitterly, "And I don't think they are interested in getting work out of the other men either.

"And I think they are only interested in killing every Jew in Dorbyan," she added

"Mama, it is still possible that they are alive," interrupted Rose's daughter Zelda. "Life can't be pleasant for them, but the Germans are fighting a war, and do not have enough men. I believe they are being made to slave for the Lithuanian collaborators.as a favour to them from the Germans."

Zelda Bloch was twenty-four years old, and despite her emaciated state, still exhibited good looks under her soiled and smelling peasant dress. For some reason thus far the imprisonment seemed to have sapped her energies less than those of many of the others. She had deliberately positioned herself in the crowd when the working party was selected, not out of fear, but as a means of remaining close to her mother and thirteen year old sister Chia. She knew that eventually she would be separated from them, but her plan was to avoid it for as long as possible.

Chana looked her directly in the face of Zelda Bloch.

"You say the men are safe because they are working", she said. "And my husband, Hersh, and the other old men, just how much slaving can they do for the Germans? When they are no longer able to work, what happens?"

Zelda Bloch could only shrug her shoulders in helplessness.

CHAPTER 12

With the departure of the work party conditions in the synagogue had improved, but only marginally. There were still almost four hundred women and children in the building. The days were still stifling, but the nights had now become mercifully cooler. On August 3 the Germans were surprised to find that the vat of soup placed inside the synagogue doors was largely untouched. For in the year 1941 that day was *Tisha b'Av*, the ninth day of the Jewish month of Av.

Tisha b'Av was traditionally the most sorrowful day of the Jewish year. For a race whose history recounted tragedy after tragedy, this day denoted the greatest tragedy of all, the destruction of King Solomon's Temple in Jerusalem by the Babylonians, the event which was to mark the beginning of the wanderings of the Jews throughout history, and which was to lead to the words known to every Jew who has ever lived, words taken from the ancient 137th psalm which described the plight of the Jews in their exile in Babylon.

"Im eshcahaich Yerushalaim, tishcach yimini, tidbach leshoni.............." (If I forget thee O' Jerusalem, let my right hand forget its cunning, let my tongue cleave to the roof of my mouth..............).

"*Tisha b'Av* signified other tragedies, such as the second and final destruction of the temple by the Romans, and in time came to commemmorate every other tragedy which befell the Jews, even if the event did not occur on the date. It became a day of praying and fasting for those Jews who considered themselves devout. In Dorbyan there were very few who did not fall into this category.

To the people in the synagogue the day they were mourning was a cruel parallel to their own trials, and none amongst them who had passed the age of thirteen would break the fast day and touch the soup.

Twelve days later the Germans made another selection of approximately one hundred and fifty women. Once again Zelda Bloch managed to avoid the selection which almost claimed her mother, for this time the Germans were taking middle aged women who appeared sufficiently robust. Chana watched silently as her four daughters Rocha, Ada, Mina and Breina were led off. She tried to comfort Natan Beir as he stared futilely at his mother's departure, holding back the tears as he waved. Whether the women were to be killed or not, nobody knew. What they did know was that they would not see or hear of them again, just as had happened to the previous group.

"Natan, we must be strong. There is nothing else we can do."

"Don't worry, *Bobe*, Mama will be safe, I just know it. You'll see. God will watch over her."

Chana did not believe her grandson's words, but she was grateful for his efforts. She was so proud of him, as she had always been. He was her youngest grandchild, and had always been her favourite, but how much more time did he have? Could it be that God had decided that fourteen years was all that he should live? Perhaps this was so, as other children had been known to die at a younger age.

Natan Beir was still fit and somehow energetic, and must surely before long be selected by the Germans. On occasions she had noticed the Germans eyeing him curiously when they entered, but she suspected that it was for another reason. Like his mother, Natan Beir's fair complexion, blonde hair and grey eyes meant that he could walk through the streets of any German city and pass for a pure Aryan.

On the twenty-eighth of August the Germans made a selection of a further one hundred and twenty women, leaving slightly more than one hundred people still in the synagogue, older women and children only. One thing noticed by the people was that this time no Lithuanians had taken part in the operation. It had been carried out by Germans only.

This time Zelda Bloch had been unable to avoid the selection, leaving her mother Rose with only thirteen year old Chia at her side. Of the Bloch family of nine, Moredchai was dead, Arieh Leib and Gershon had been marched away by the Germans on June 29, and now Zelda had just been taken away. Her sons Moshe and Lipman had been visiting the coastal town of Polangen at the time of the German invasion and had not been heard from since. There was little reason to believe that their fate had been any different from anyone else's.

Only her son Shevah was known to be safe, for he had had the foresight to migrate to Palestine some six years earlier.

Chana did not know if she was worse off than Rose Bloch or not. Rose still had her daughter Chia, and her sons Moshe and Lipman might still be free. In her own case, she had lost Hersh, her four sons-in-law, and her grown up grandsons, all of whom she suspected were no longer alive. Her granddaughters had been taken away in the first selection and her daughters in the one which followed. Of her large extended family, which had always been such a source of joy to her, the only person beside herself that she could say with certainty was alive, was Natan Beir.

Yet as she looked about the synagogue, she could see other women, and children, whose situation was worse, and who could not point to a single living family member.

The next morning one of the women entering the classroom used as the latrine noticed a folded piece of paper crammmed between the window and the sill. It had not been there the evening before, and could have only been placed there during the night.

When the note was read to the others, there were gasps of amazement, and tears gushed from the eyes of Rose Bloch. The note had been written by her son Moshe, who had avoided capture by the Germans, and who was still at large. He asked that the window where he had left his note be left slightly ajar that night, as he planned to enter the synagogue.

Later that night, when the German guard was at its lowest, the prisoners waited expectantly. Rose and Chia Bloch braved the unpleasantness of the latrine, maintaining a constant vigil. Shortly after midnight their patience was rewarded, when the window was pulled open from outside, and the stealthy figure of Moshe Bloch climbed in, shutting the window immediately behind him.

The embraced him, ignoring the shock in his eyes when he observed their emaciated and disheveled condition.

"It's alright, Moshe. We are *gesundt*, it's not us we have to worry about."

They led him to the synagogue proper where everyone lay, most still awake, but some having yielded to the release given by sleep.

Understanding the need for silence, each of the prisoners greeted Moshe Bloch in turn, as he urged them not to rise on his behalf. He went to where each was lying and gave each of the women and girls a kiss, followed by a hearty handshake for the older boys, with the whispered words, *"Boruch Hashem"* (Blessed be His name).

By the time he had finished, all but the infants were awake. They moved closer to him and listened to the story he told.

"I have much to tell you, but first of all, Mama, Chia, I want you to know that Lipman is safe. He is being hidden by good people who can be trusted, and who hate the Germans as much as we do.

"Now, for the saddest thing that I must tell you, although I suspect that you have been told by now, is how the men were put to death....

".....Our men are all dead, everyone of them.... There is nobody left, not a soul...

"...When they were marched from the square on *Tammuz* 4. they were taken along the Polanger Gass to a spot neat the old water mill, where they were made to dig a long trench. When the trench was finished they were made to stand at the edge in small groups, and they were shot in such a way that they died as they fell in. As soon as one group was shot, another was made to stand in its place, and when they died they fell on top of those who were already shot. It was all over very quickly, and it was so sudden that nobody expected it and nobody was able to escape. I am told that there were one or two who tried to flee, but that they were shot before they could cover any distance."

"I am also told that many were still living when the pit was filled in with earth."

He looked at the others, and was shocked at the horror on their faces.

"My God!", he whispered. "You did not know this! Nobody has told you! You have been thinking that somehow they were still alive!"

It was Rose Bloch, his mother, who spoke first.

"Don't torture yourself, Moshe. We didn't know, for there was nobody to tell us,but I think we all knew in our hearts that this was so. Still, you can understand that we continued to hope."

"It is not only Dorbyan where the men have been murdered,"

340

said Moshe, "But in every other Jewish community in the Krettinger district. On *Sivan29*, it was the men of Gorzd,, on the 30th, it was Krettingen, and on *Tammuz 2*, it was Polangen. Since then the murderers have visited every single town where Jews have been living."

He moved towards his mother, bent down, and embraced her again.

"I'm sorry, Mama, but I swear that I shall avenge the deaths of Papa, Leiba and Gershon even if it takes me the rest of my life. There is not a person in here who is not *Mishpoche* of mine in some way, and the same is so of every man who was murdered. Someday these *mamsers* will suffer, and know the same misery that they have brought to others."

One of the women looked up at him and asked, "Moshe, what of the women, our daughters. the ones who were taken away from here to work for the Germans. Has there been any word? My three daughters are amongst them."

He looked sadly at the woman.

"Yes, I was coming to this. There has been word of them, but it is not good news. You see, there is no good news, anywhere, to tell.

"The women in the first group are dead, and those in the second group are now believed to be, for when the Germans select a new group, it is because they have killed the previous group. There have been no survivors as far as is known. The women just recently taken are probably still alive, but their days are numbered, for there is no possible way to rescue them.

"Those taken first were put to work day in, day out, in the fields of Lithuanians who were sympathetic to the Germans. The work that they were given to do was more than any beast of burden could be expected to do, and yet for this they were given almost no food and very little water. As each one collapsed on the fields she was beaten to death by the Germans or Lithuanians with farm tools, in order to spare ammunition.

"Then it was the work of those remaining to bury them. Finally, when the group was too small and too weak to be of use to the Germans, the remaining women were beaten to death together and taken by wagon to somewhere in the Wainaaiker forest to be buried.

"It is believed that the same thing happened to the second group, but a day or two ago.

"I have asked, and as far as I can learn. the last group, which includes our Zelda,is still alive, and still has some time left. But it is hopeless. They are being moved to different locations, and always under heavy German guard. Nobody seems to know where they are at the moment, for the Germans no longer use Lithuanians to help them. All I know at the moment is that there is no sign that they have been murdered.

"But what hope have they? For how long can a human continue under such a heavy load without food or water in this hot weather?"

Moshe Bloch then asked, "Does anyone know the whereabouts of Basha and Sara Rivke Kveril? I thought that they might be here, but I do not see them."

"They were taken in the last group. The Germans only wanted Sara Rivke, as Basha has not been well, but she insisted on being with her daughter, so they both went."

Then perhaps it is a good thing that they are not here to learn what has happened", said Moshe Bloch.

"The man Vladas Jashinskas, whom they paid to help their daughter, Esther escape, is a murderer, and worse! May his soul burn in *Gehennah*!

He went with Esther at night to take her to Libau, where there is supposed to be an organization which tries to help Jews cross the Baltic. I am not sure that this organization even exists, but this has nothing to do with what took place....

".....When they reached the Wainaiker Forest he turned on her and raped her. Then to cover his crime, he murdered her and buried her body in a shallow grave. Later that night he returned to his wife with blood on his hands. After he had too much to drink she was able to get the truth out of him. It also seems that his action was witnessed by a forester at Wainaiker.

"Since that time he drinks more than ever, and boasts to the Germans of what he has done, as if to prove to the Germans what a good fellow he is."

After a long pause he added, "I suppose that Basha will never learn of this. Perhaps it is better this way."

Moshe Bloch then turned to Chana.

"Chana, I have had news about Hersh. Perhaps it is better if we are by ourselves when I tell you. If you wish, you can tell the others as much as you wish later."

He took Chana by the hand and supported her as he led her to a bench at the other end of the synagogue, and began to speak to her in a very low voice.

"Chana, your Hersh is dead like all the others, but he died differently. What I have to tell you is brutal, and if you would prefer not to know about it, then I will say no more."

"No, Moishe, please tell me. For my entire life, Hersh has been my greatest interest, every little thing he did, every movement he made. I want to know how he died."

"Very well, what I have to tell you is not pleasant, but I want you to know that when I first heard about it, it made me proud to think that he was *mishpoche* of mine."

"Where did you learn all this, Moishe?"

"Galdikas."

"Galdikas!" Chana spat out the name.

"Yes, Galdikiene, wife of Jonas Galdikas, considers herself to be a good friend of the people who are sheltering me. If she only knew how they are helping us, I don't think she would think of them as friends, and she wouldn't speak to them so freely.

"When the men were taken to the old mill, their first task was to dig the trench. Right from the beginning Hersh refused to have a hand in it, but because he was old, he was not forced to do it.

"When the trench was finished the men were made to approach the trench a few at a time, then shot so that their bodies fell into it.

"As long as I live, I will never understand why, but every single person obeyed the German orders, making it easy for them. That is every person except one...your Hersh.

"When his turn came, he refused to step forward, even when his own people shouted at him to hurry up. Two Lithuanians were ordered to move him, but he stood his ground, and couldn't be moved. Finally the German commander lost patience, and went to him and shot him four times, once in each shoulder and once in each leg. He was then taken to the trench and thrown in. Galdikas told his wife that he could hear your name and what sounded like a prayer coming from Hersh's lips as the next layer of people fell over him."

He looked into Chana's eyes, which were filled with tears.

"Forgive me, Chana, for I have only caused you further grief." He covered her shrunken hand with his own.

"No,.. thank you, Moishe. I am grateful that you have told me this. Please forgive these tears, for I did not think that any more tears remained in me. Thank you, for I loved him so much, and I was always so proud of him, and now I am even prouder...

"Do you know, Moishe?......That for me he would do anything,.. anything, to spare me from harm, and yet he was never afraid to suffer himself..

"....I did not believe that it was possible to love anyone more than I loved Hersh, and yet, now that he is gone, I feel that I love him more than ever....

"...Is is possible, Moishe, to love someone even more after he is gone..?"

"I suppose.....", answered Moshe Bloch, "But you are asking me a question that I cannot answer."

"Moshe, for the sake of Natan Beir, do you have any news about Elior and how he died?"

"No Chana, there has been no mention of him, and we can only assume that he went peacefully to his death like all the others.

"But there is something that might bring you some satisfaction, Chana. All that I have told you has been learned from Galdikas, through his wife, Galdikiene. She is now very concerned about the effect all this has had on her husband.

"From what I know of Galdikas, he would have enjoyed every moment of it," said Chana bitterly.

"From what has been told to me, this is not so. Like the other Lithuanians, he foolishly thought that the Germans were taking the Jews out of Dorbyan to be put to work somewhere, and to become someone else's problem. When he realized that they were to be shot, all three hundred of them, he was shocked. And because he was a part of it, he is now afraid that some people will consider him a murderer."

"And what else would you call him?", asked Chana.

344

Moshe Bloch did not attempt to answer the question. He shrugged his shoulders, and after a moment's pause, continued.

"Now she says that he wakes up every every night shouting that he can still see Hersh's face looking up at him before it was covered with earth. She is worried that he is losing his sanity, even though he insists that he did not lift a finger against any Jew personally."

"And what else would expect him to tell his wife? That he helped to murder three hundred people that day?"

"Exactly," answered Moshe Bloch, "But the story does not end there, and what happened afterwards has added to his torment.

"Whilst they were marching to the old mill, it seems that Hersh told him about your horse, Yoiphi. He said that the horse was behind the house, and that Jonas should go there and take her for his own. When Jonas returned later that night, he was shocked to find that the horse was dead, shot by the Germans."

"I'm not surprised," interrupted Chana. "If they will shoot people, then they will shoot any creature. Yoiphi would have been very hungry by then, and not at all friendly to any stranger unless he had food to offer."

"Jonas Galdikas loves horses, and could not understand how any human being could be so depraved as to shoot so fine an animal as Yoiphi. It left him a very confused and disillusioned man.

"Then on his way home he left the Polanger Gass to look at the spot where the men had been shot, thinking that perhaps it was only a bad dream. When he came to the trench where they had been buried, he said that the ground was still moving, as if there was still life underneath. There were hissing noises, and the sounds of vapour still escaping, and the soil was damp and spongy, and when he looked down, he could see that blood was oozing up through it around his boots.

"When he went to his father to tell what had happened the next day, his father had already found out, and refused to speak to him. Since that time his father has spoken no word to him, and will not eat at the same table or even sit in the same room with him.

"Galdikiene says that for her husband this was the final shock. He now has no ambition for anything, and has given up assisting the Germans. In fact he spends his days doing nothing at all, and has even lost interest in the farm and its animals. She is frightened, and does not know what will become of him."

Chana said, "It is better that Hersh did not live to learn all of this. He loved horses, and this would have broken his heart....It is strange,...but this is the one thing that Hersh and Jonas Galdikas had in common, - their love of horses. It is better that he went to his grave believing that Yoiphi would be well looked after."

She was silent, and Moshe Bloch took her hand.

"I think we should be getting back to the others. I have nothing more to tell. I will leave it to you if you wish to mention it to anyone else."

"Perhaps I shall tell Natan Beir, when the moment is right," said Chana.

They returned to the others, who were engaged in feverish low pitched conversation. Moshe sat Chana down and then turned to the other eager faces.

"I must go now, but I plan to return as often as I can, every night if possible. I have noticed that there are times when there is very little guard, and next time I would like to take one or two of the children with me, for there are good people who will look after them. You may discuss this after I am gone, and perhaps tomorrow night we can do something. Please see that the window in the same room is left the slightest bit open each night after dark, that I may enter. For obvious reasons the latrine room is best, for the Germans have weak stomachs."

"Who are the people sheltering you, Moishe?"

"I only wish I could tell you", answered Moshe Bloch, "But it would be the most foolish thing I could do. I worry myself that I may one day fall into the Germans' hands and be forced to tell what I know. If the Germans come to realize that there are some of us still free, then they will probably come to you for the answers........

"...And if they are somehow able to force it out of you, then it is the end not only for those who are hiding, but for the shelterers as well.

"I know just how much it would ease your minds to know who our friends are, but believe me when I say it is better that you do not know."

From the face of each woman came a nod of agreement.

"But there is one thing that you must know, and that is that we are not alone. The enemy is very powerful, and there are not many on our side, but there are some Lithuanians who are helping us. You may find this hard to believe, for you have only seen those Lithuanians who assist and encourage the Germans, and mock us in our misery..

"Yes, there are good Lithuanians, Lithuanians who are made ill at what is happening, and who are trying their best to do something about it. Some of them risk their lives for us, knowing that if they are found out, they will see their families tortured to death before their eyes. It does not seem to matter to them that we have lost all our possessions, and have no possible way of repaying them...

"So no matter what you may think about the Lithuanians, I beg you, do not try to blame *all the Lithuanians.* The ones who help us do it for righteous reasons. They are the true *tzadikim.* Their religion teaches them that it is the right thing to do, and their hearts tell them that they must do it,"

CHAPTER 13

The visit of Moshe Bloch lifted the spirits of those in the synagogue immeasurably. He had brought no good news, and their lot had in no way improved because of his visit, but the boost to their morale was undeniable. The one thought on each person's mind was revenge, and the thought that the Germans would one day suffer retribution. Until then the idea was unconceivable, for the Germans had proved invinceable at every turn, with no opportunity existing to do damage to them. Now, for the first time, the thought occurred that perhaps the Germans were not having things all their own way after all. The fact that Moshe Bloch was able to circulate undetected around the Dorbyan countryside was proof of this. The fact that Lithuanians, however few their numbers, were prepared to defy the cruelty of the German occupation was an even stronger sign. Perhaps it would be possible for Moshe to help some of the people leave the synagogue. For the first time since their imprisonment, a ray of hope existed.

For four nights the prisoners waited hopefully for another visit from Moshe Bloch. On the fifth night he appeared. The news he brought was not good.

"I have just come from the grave of Papa and Rabbi Weissbord beside the river. Before that I visited the grave of the men by the old water mill. I have been doing this every night that I am able.

"The area by the old water mill now smells of death, and the people who live nearby complain that it is unhealthy. There are rats and vermin burrowing and running about all the time. There is now talk that the Germans will have a fence built around the whole area."

His voice choked. "I would give my right hand to be able to say *Kaddish* over them, but I am not able. To say *Kaddish* there has to be a *minyan*......I don't think there would be enough men to form a *Minyan* in the whole Kretinger district..."

He swallowed, then continued.

"There is still no news of the last group. They may be still alive, as no special murder squads have been seen in the area, but nobody can say where they are. All I know is that nobody has heard any word of their deaths."

"How much longer will it be before they take away the rest of us, Moishe?"

"Who can say? The pattern they follow cannot be predicted, but I think that there is still a little time. They seem to have some sort of a plan. They send their murderers from one Jewish community to another and destroy it a little at a time, just as they are doing here. Exactly the same thing has been happening at Krettingen, Polangen, Shkud, Gorzd, Jakobovitch, and even Telz as has been happening here.

"They work out of Tilsit, and everytime they have completed a cycle they return to the first village to continue their butchering. It seems to take anything from two weeks to a month. They used to make no secret of their reasons to the Lithuanians. They say that by doing it this way they need fewer men and encounter less resistance. Theyhave learned that when people learn with certainty that they are going to die, then theyhave nothing to lose by resisting. When they think that there is some possibility that they may survive, then they do nothing."

"Moishe, even if they came to murder us all now, we could not resist. We are weak from hunger, and becoming ill from disease more and more of the time."

Moshe Bloch could only shake his head sadly.

"Is there noone, nowhere, Moishe, who can stop these butchers?'

"They are already being stopped," answered Moshe Bloch. "Already they are no longer winning the war against England. When all of England's empire becomes involved, the headstart that they have will be overtaken. Even though they are defeating the Russians at this moment, they must someday lose in the end."

"And what about the Americans, will they fight?"

"The Americans say that they are not part of this war, but their sympathies lay with England, and they are giving her help. Some Americans now go to Canada where they can fight for England. If America someday joins fully in the battle, then Hitler will be defeated that much sooner."

He added quickly, "But this will not happen soon enough to help us in Dorbyan. If we wish to survive, then we must help ourselves, and this is what I want to talk about."

He looked at his mother and sister.

"First of all, I want to get the two of you out of here. I can take the two of you with me when I leave tonight. Will you come with me?"

Rose Bloch shook her head.

"No, Moishe, I will not go with you, I am not strong enough. I cannot run, and would probably slow you down and bring about your death. There are younger people here who should be saved first, if possible. I am safer here.:

Moshe Bloch turned to his sister Chia, who was nodding her head negatively, and who had started to weep.

"No, I only want to stay here where I will be close to Mama."

Borh Moshe and Rose Bloch looked at Chia in surprise.

"Chia, you are only thirteen," said her mother. "You still have your whole life ahead of you. You must try to escape if you can."

Chia Bloch's tears trickled down her face, and she clung to her mother.

"No, Mama, I do not want to go! Not if I must leave you, Mama!"

Moshe Bloch put his arm around his sister's shoulder, and comforted her.

"Don't cry, Chia. It is alright. You do not have to go if you do not wish. I shall come back again before long, and you and Mama will have time to talk about it.'

He turned to the others, and looked into their faces searchingly.

"Is there anyone amongst you who would like to leave with me. I can take two of you. I believe that for the children it is the best thing, for there are good people outside who are prepared to shelter you."

He caught the eye of Natan Beir, who immediately read his mind, and said, "No, I am staying here. My whole family is gone, and I am the only one left. The only person I wish to be near is *Bobe*."

Chana glared angrily at Natan Beir, who withstood the stare.

"Very well," said Moshe Bloch. "There is still time. It is best if you think about it before my next visit, for you must be certain, for when anyone leaves it is forever. I can understand that you wish to remain together until the last, even though it may not be the best thing."

He stood up and made ready to leave.

"Before I go, if anyone wishes to come with me, I am able take two children. It would be better if two came with me now, that I can take two more with me next time."

There was no response. Moshe Bloch embraced his mother and sister, who followed him into the latrine room, and watched as he climbed through the window and into the night.

No sooner had Moshe Bloch disappeared when there was the sound of heavy tramping followed by the front doors of the synagogue being thrown open. A German soldier, pistol in one hand and flashlight in the other, stomped through the classroom area and into the synagogue. He was followed a short distance behind by a more senior officer who remained at the door, his pistol also drawn.

"All right! Where is he? I know that I have heard the voice of a man in here!

You are hiding him! Where is he?"

It was Chana who answered the German in a mocking tone.

"You may search until your eyes fall out child, but you will not find a man here,when there is no man here!"

The soldier glared at Chana.

"Quiet, woman! I know what I have heard! Where is he? I know that I have heard the voice of a man speaking!"

Chana stood her ground. She laughed aloud at the German, and then in a mocking voice turned to the others.

"He knows what he has heard! He knows what he has heard!"

Then she turned to the German again.

"You do not know what you have heard, child!"

She pointed to one of the women nearest hear.

"Shaine, would you please tell this youngster what he has heard!"

Shaine spoke a few words to the German, who stepped back in surprise, for Shaine's voice was abnormally low-pitched for a woman, to the point that it could easily be mistaken for a male voice.

"Now, child, perhaps you can tell me what you have heard!"

Chana gloated at the German triumphantly.

"Do you know, child, I think I know what your problem is! You are not yet old enough to know the difference between a man and a woman!"

The senior officer had followed the other into the synagogue, and now he tapped him on the shoulder and motioned him to leave. The two men turned and left, the younger one red faced. As he slammed the synagogue doors shut and locked them from the outside. he turned to his superior.

"Sir, do you see how that old woman taunts me? The old whore is like this everytime I enter. She is almost pleading with me to kill her. Why can you not give me permission to grant her her wish?"

The older man turned to him.

"Hans, I can understand your frustration with her, but I cannot simply allow you to shoot her. When we shoot people, it is according to a plan. We did not become a superior race by allowing our emotions to overcome reason. We have a plan to be followed, and it is my job to follow it."

"But sir, I cannot see how shooting the old whore upsets our plans. She is a disturnance, and when she is gone things will go more smoothly for us."

"She is a disturbance, true, but a harmless disturbance, Hans.

"I'm sorry, but I cannot grant you your wish. You have a lot to learn. If I allow you to shoot her simply because of your frustration with her, it would be a weakness on both our parts, and would not help our cause."

"I don't understand, sir, if she is a nuisance, then is it not better for all of us if she is eliminated?"

"No, Hans. She represents no threat to us. There is no way that she can cause us harm. It is the whole picture that matters. You see, we are fighting a war that many said we could not win. Yet we are winning now, and we will win in the end because of our brilliant *Fuehrer* and the other brilliant people in Germany who plan the campaigns, and because of people like you and me who are able to carry out the plans perfectly. As soon as someone disobeys his orders or takes matters into his own hands, the system breaks down, and the whole becomes less effective."

"But why, sir? I don't understand why we cannot kill all the Jews at once, just as we did with the men."

"I will tell you, Hans, and perhps you will understand. We are not the ones who perform the liquidations. Our job is to control the situation, to see that everything runs smoothly and that nobody escapes. We leave the liquidation to the specialists.

"The system we are using has been devised through a great deal of thought by the most intelligent brains in Germany. Adolph Eichmann, who is working on the final solution to the Jewish problem, has been studying Jewish customs for years, and has even visited Palestine.

"With his knowledge of the Jews and their habits, a system has been implemented where we are able to produce the greatest possible result using the least amount of resources. After all, we must not forget that we are fighting a war, and resources are not to be wasted.

"Wherever possible, we try to put the local people to use, for as long as it suits our purposes, and at the same time we try to achieve our goals with the fewest casualties possible to ourselves. Shooting everyone at once may be quicker, but it does not always achieve this, while the proceedures we have been following have been proven to work."

"Do you think, sir, that it is possible for anyone to have escaped us, without our knowledge."

"One would have to be very arrogant, Hans, to say for certain, but from what I have seen here in the Dorbyan area, I think not. This is one of the reasons that we first try to gain the favour of the local people, so that they will act as our eyes and ears for us. I believe that we have caught every Jew in Dorbyan in our net. If any had remained at large, then they would have been reported to us, and we would catch them, just as we did wth the Reizman brothers. There is quite simply, no place that is safe for them to hide."

"What about the forest, sir? I have often wondered if there might still be Jews hiding there."

"As I said, only a fool could be certain, but in my mind I am satisfied. Our Lithuanian allies know these forests well, from their struggle against the Russians before we came. If Jews are there, it would be known, and we would have been informed long ago. With our dogs we would find them in a very short time. You must remember, Hans, that the Jews are dispised in this country and have no friends anywhere.

353

"So you see, Hans, our system is working. We know from experience that if we separate Jews from their prayer and their Rabbis, then their spirit is weakened, and they are less likely to resist. They have a strong patriarchial tradition, and if we eliminate the men first, the women can be counted on to give us very little trouble. They can then be put to work and made of some use to us. If they are made to work for the local population, then we gain sympathy at the same time.

"You must realize, Hans, that the Tilsit administrative district is but a tiny part of the whole Jewish problem. In the towns of Garsden, Ktoettingen, Polangen, Skuodas and here in Dorbyan we had eliminated 1700 of them up to July 10. I haven't seen the figures since, but my guess is that we have now passed 3000, but this is nothing.

"The greater problem is that there are at least ten million of these vermin in the lands we occupy. They live like vermin, and they breed like vermin. They prey on the local populations and become rich at their expense. They are decadent, they carry disease, and they practise a bloodthirsty anti-Christian religion. Some of them marry into Aryan families, and the inferior blood that they introduce can take generations to disappear. Unless they are exterminated before it is too late, they pose a dangerous threat to the entire human race."

"Even the children, sir, even the very small ones?"

"It surprises me that I am asked this question so often, Hans, why it is necessary to eliminate the small children, who seem so harmless. But if you will think about it, you will realize that they are not so harmless as they seem. They already have their *scheiss* religion, which will remain with them for as long as they live. One day they will grow up and breed and continue to contaminate the human race.

"Let me put it to you in another way, Hans. Let us suppose that a plague of rats was threatening a town, would you eliminate only the larger rats, and spare the smaller ones which are not yet capable of biting? I don't think you need me to tell you the answer.

"We are doing our job well here, following the proceedures given to us, and the people in Berlin are pleased with the results. Other areas where the numbers are greater may require a different system, but that is not our problem. So far we are using less ammunition than expected, and although there have been casualties in other places, here in Dorbyan not one of us has suffered any injury. When our task here is finished, there is every chance that we will be sent somewhere where the problem to be solved is larger and the responsibilities are greater."

He slapped the younger officer heartily on the back.

"So you see, Hans. It has taken me awhile to say it, but you cannot shoot the old whore. But I can promise you this: things will not go on for much longer. I have advised Tilsit that all is *in Ordnung* here, and they have advised me that as soon as the next special liquidation unit is available, it will be sent here to finish the job. These *nutzlose esser* will not trouble us for much longer.

"Sturmbannfuehre Sandberger and Bohm are performing their jobs very efficiently, and I do not anticipate much of a wait.

"And the old whore, she shall be amongst the last to die. She shall see the others perish around her, That will be her punishment.

"And,......just in case you didn't know, Hans, Brigadenfuehrer Stahlecker has ordered that this district be *Judenrein* before Christmas. The way we are going, I am pleased to say that we will probably be able to give Dr. Stahlecker his Christmas present two or three months ahead of time."

CHAPTER 14

Two nights later Moshe Bloch entered the synagogue again, He was told about the episode with the German officers, and all agreed that it had been a narrow escape. Conversation would have to be kept to a lower voice, and under no circumstances near a window.

Perhaps he had also come close to misadventure when leaving, even though his observations had told him that the latrine side of the synagogue was generally unguarded. In future, before he was to leave, one of the women was to open a window and look out as casually as possible. If noticed by a guard, she would say that she was only allowing some ventilation into the latrine. Similarly, the window would remain open until after he had gone, that no sound be made in closing it until he was safely out of sight.

This time Moshe had news of a different sort. Relations had gradually been deteriorating between the Germans and the local population, as it became more and more apparent that the Germans had arrived not as liberators, but as conquerors. One episode in particular illustrated the contempt shown by the Germans towards the local inhabitants and their customs.

The last group of women to be killed had been working in the fields behind the Catholic church. Knowing what their fate was to be, some of them managed to speak to the parish priest, with the request that he ask the Germans that they be killed as painlessly as possible, preferably with a single bullet. The priest said that he would do as much as he could, but when he approached the Germans, he was shocked at their response.

The Germans told him flatly that it was none of his business how the women were killed unless he wanted to kill them himself.

When the villagers learned of this from the pulpit on the following Sunday, even those most devoted to the Germans experienced a change in attitude. Without exception, they were devout in their religion, and disrespect to their priests was unheard of, and unforgiveable. No longer did they smile towards the Germans in the streets; no longer did they offer assistance when needed; and no longer did the collaborators turn up for duty as before.

Not only in Dorbyan was this change taking place. Elsewhere the Germans had almost finished their task of ridding the countryside of "undesirable elements", and the usefulness of the locals had diminished. Partisans who had fought against the Russians were now no longer allowed to keep their arms. In the major centres, local councils were dismantled, and the parliament in Vilnius was ordered closed until further notice.

There were now more Lithuanians prepared to hide Jews. The problem now was that there remained very few Jews left to hide.

Moshe Bloch remained for as long as he dared, and when he left he took the only two children who were willing to go with him, Rachel Judel and Feige Simon. He had been disappointed that there were no others willing to leave, and he would have returned a second time that night had there been. He would take the children to where he himself was hiding, keep them there until the following night, and then move them to another safe house, more isolated, where they could remain safely for as long as necessary.

Perhaps the reason that these two children, of all present, had agreed to accompany Moshe Bloch was because they were alone in the world. The two girls of five and six years had lost their entire families during the past month. Unlike Natan Beir, they did not even have a grandparent remaining.

Moshe Bloch doubted that any other children could be persuaded to leave, no matter how much their mothers pleaded with them, and the thought left him depressed. With heavy heart he helped the two young girls out the window into the darkness, knowing that before much longer there would be no escape for anyone still in the synagogue.

CHAPTER 15

September 22, 1941, the 29th day of Elul by the Jewish calendar. was *Erev Rosh Hashanah*, or the day before the beginning of the new Jewish year. As the sun set, and the synagogue was once again shrouded in darkness, the new year, the year 5702 according to Jewish tradition, was ushered in. The words on everyone's lips had a special meaning.

"L'Shonoh habo b"Yerushalayim (next year in Jerusalem)". The year which had just passed had been as disastrous an any in the four thousand year history of the Jews,a history which had been characterized by catastrophe and disaster. The coming year showed no indication of being any better, but the prayer which had sustained Jews in exile over the millennia was not to be forgotten on this day.

Natan Beir, who said his morning and evening prayers every day, stood facing eastwards before the ark which still contained the hidden *Torah*, frustrated at not being able to remove it for a proper service. His head covered, as it had been during the entire ordeal except when he slept, he kissed his hand, reached inside beyond the false cloth front, and gently touched the sacred scroll, experiencing a spiritual uplifting as he did so. He withdrew his hand, and again gently kissed each of his fingers which had touched the *Torah*.

Later that night Moshe Bloch climbed through the latrine window. This time he was distraught and agitated, and he did not speak with his usual calm voice.

"The others will not be seeing in the new year," he said sadly. "Everyone of them has been butchered, including our Zelda."

He embraced his mother, and took his sister's hand

"I'm sorry, Mama. I have tried to think of everything......There was nothing I could do to save her."

Rose Bloch lay down again, still holding his hand. Although she had just lost a daughter, she and Chia were the only two in the synagogue still to possess an adult male in their family.

"I have also had news of Leiba Reizman. Although it happened sometime ago, I have just learned of it recently. He has been caught and murdered by the Germans...

"I was told that the two Reizman brothers tried to escape and were on their way to the Latvian border when they were recognized by Lithuanians on the road near Shkud. Someone betrayed them, for the Germans were waiting for them farther on and captured them. They were brought back to Dorbyan and tortured by the Germans in the fields behind the church. I don't know, but it is even possible that you would have heard the activity from here. It was more than a month ago.

"I am told that they were tortured very badly, and that in fact, it was so brutal that the priest heard it and came out and asked the Germans to stop. Before the priest's eyes the Germans then shot Leiba and his brother to death. Their bodies were taken away by Lithuanians in a cart, and it is believed that they were taken to be buried in the cemetery.

"The Reizman brothers were the most unfortunate of all, for they were not only Jews, but communists."

His voice choked.

"I knew Leiba, and I often argued with him, for I didn't agree with his views, but he was sincere, and didn't deserve this. He must have been a good man, for otherwise the Germans would not have hated him so."

"What about us in the synagogue, Moishe? Have you had any word?"

"No," said Moshe Bloch, his voice again choking, "But I can guess. From what I see I am certain that there is very little time left, and that is why some of you have to come with me tonight. What about you, Chia?"

His sister shook her head violently, and Rose Bloch spoke.

"Moshe, you must understand, after almost three months here, we have lost the will to do anything. Some of the children may be able to come with you, but most are ill. Even sitting up is now an effort, and when we attempt it, we feel faint. Our minds are as tired as our bodies."

Moshe Bloch allowed his eyes to survey the battered remnants of what had once been the Dorbyan Jewish community. He wrung his hands in frustration.

"Those who can must come! I will help you, I can carry one, maybe two children, and will help a third. There is little time. New Germans have arrived, and there was more activity around the synagogue tonight. I have a feeling that very soon, tomorrow morning perhaps, they will be taking the rest of you away."

His voice took on a pleading tone.

"Can you not see? Anyone who can escape, must escape! Do you not understand? Someday these murderers are going to lose this war, and they will be brought to account for their crimes. When the moment comes, there must be witnesses to what they have done. If there is noone to bear witness against them, they will escape punishment. It this what we want?"

There was almost no response, no panic, no tears. No longer was it possible to shock these people. The Germans had succeeded, in that they had carefully conditioned the Jews to accept their fate. Moshe Bloch shook his head in resignation.

It was at that moment that someone stated matter of factly, "I think I can smell gasoline."

The gasoline smell became stronger. Then came a crackling sound familiar to every Dorbyaner who had ever lived in the town since its founding. It was the sound of flames. The synagogue was on fire.

The crackling sound increased and the first puffs of smoke appeared. Moshe Bloch ran to the nearest window and flung it open, both to let in air and to look out into the yard. He drew back, as almost instantly a fusillade of rifle fire struck the brickwork only inches from the window.

The gunfire was followed by the sounds of laughter outside the synagogue.

"Leave quickly, my son! You know we cannot follow you! Go now before it is to late!"

Rose Bloch lifted herself and embraced her son for the last time as Chia clung closely to him. Moshe Bloch gave his sister a final kiss.

He looked imploringly at Natan Beir, who sat near to where his grandmother was lying. Natan Beir shook his head emphatically. He would remain.

"Take care of Lipman! He is so young! He is precious!"

"I shall, mother, I promise you."

He ran to the latrine room, which was on the oppposite side to where the fire had been started. He pushed the window open very slowly. There were no flames on this side as yet. The night was very black. Thus far all activity seemed to be on the other side of the synagogue. He climbed quickly through the window and dropped to the ground.

In a low crouch he scurried away from the synagogue to an adjoining wheatfield. Maintaining the crouch, he reached the edge of the wooded area nearby.

CHAPTER 16

Only when Moshe Bloch had reached the safety of the edge of the forest did he turn and look back at the burning synagogue. His heart sank, for any hopes he had held that someone else may have reconsidered and decided to escape the blaze were instantly dashed.

The flames were now halfway up the sides of the building and seemed to be being sucked inside the windows. Anyone managing to exit from the building would now present a perfect target for the German gunners. In the barely five minutes since he himself had fled, the flames had increased tenfold, lighting up the *Shul Platz* as if it were daylight.

He watched in fascination as the brick building did its best to withstand the onslaught, as though trying to protect its faithful followers inside. A canister of gasoline would be thrown at the flames, causing them to erupt into an inferno, then slowly subside as they failed to find any fuel to sustain them amongst the brickwork. Then another canister would be thrown and the process would be repeated.

Inside the synagogue Chana raised herself and sat motionless on the bench as the smoke began to fill the interior. There was heat, but this was not unbearable. It was the smoke which was becoming thicker and almost impossible to avoid. She seemed oblivious to it all, to the shouts, the screams and the incessant coughing, as the elderly women and young children dragged themselves from corner to corner in their attempts to find the smoke free areas. From time to time a gasoline filled bottle would crash through a window, starting an instant blaze where it landed, and causing a screaming, panicking rush in another direction. She watched it all, not attempting to move, as though in a trance, thinking back over what had happened during the past three months.

Yes, that was all it had been, three months, since the Germans had first entered Dorbyan, bringing their curse with them. They had wasted little time in beginning their persecution of the town's Jewry, which was shortly to change from persecution to extermination.

It was less than a week after their arrival when the first victims, Mordechai Bloch and Rabbi Iser Weissbord were taken, and only a day later when Hersh along with all the other adult males of the town were marched from the market square to their deaths. She could still remember Hersh managing one final wave to her before he was prodded along by the German soldiers and Lithuanian collaborators.

That day would remain in everyone's minds forever, the 4th day of Tammuz,for that was the day that the women and children of Dorbyan had set eyes on their menfolk for the last time. On that day Chana had not only lost her husband, but the husbands of her four daughters, and her grown up grandsons as well.

She thought of her four children who had chosen to migrate to North America. How long ago it had been, and yet it seemed so recent. First there had been their eldest, Chaia, then her next two eldest, Leah and Esther, and finally Joseph, their youngest born and only son. She remembered clearly the devastation she had felt asshe had farewelled each one, and although the letters from each had been frequent and regular, she had never fully adjusted to their loss, and the scars had never fully healed.

She remembered how the pain had been eased with the answering of her prayers as her remaining daughters Rocha, Ada, Mina and Breina had chosen to remain inDorbyan, and how her emptiness had been replaced with joy as each of her many grandchildren was born.

Now her four Dorbyan daughters were also dead, along with their own grown up daughters, taken from the synagogue to to slave in German labour camps until they dropped, and then beaten to death with farm implements. Now all that remained of her proud Dorbyan family was herself and Natan Beir, youngest child of Breina and Elior.

Natan Beir had been *Bar-Mitzvah* little more than a year earlier. He was good looking and clever and had promised a bright future. Chana could think of no reason why he should have to die. Yet as she watched him, her sadness was diminished by a sense of pride.

Natan Beir and three younger companions had stationed them-

363

selves in front of the ark which housed the sacred *Torah*, and were beating furiously at the flames which approached. Although the smoke was thicker there than elsewhere, they showed no sign of abandoning their project. One of the children had taken leave of the unequal battle, and was doubled over, but the other three continued their hopeless task, as much as their weakened limbs would allow. As long as a spark of life remained in any of them, the *Torah* would come to no harm.

Chana thought back to her own childhood, and the teachings she had received, of the heroes who had lived through Jewish history. She thought of Abrahan, Isaac and Jacob, the three patriarchs who had been the first Jews; of Moses and Joshua, who had carried out the task of leading the Jews from slavery in Egypt to the freedom of the promised land; of David the warrior king and his son Solomon, who had made the Jews into a powerful nation; of Shimon Bar-Kochba who, despite a hopeless cause, had defied the might of the Roman empire; and more recently, of Berek Joselovitch, the famed Jewish general from Krettingen. Any of these would have been proud of Natan Beir, and would have been honoured to have him as their son.

A plume of grey smoke drifted towards her. She coughed a few times, but made no effort to move. The other women had taken the children to the least affected areas of the synagogue, and were shielding them with their clothing and their own bodies, knowing that they had nothing more to offer them than a few extra minutes of life at their own expense. A thick wave of heavier black smoke billowed about her face. Again she refused to budge. Through the smoke she could still distinguish Natan Beir at his task. She suddenly began to cough violently, uncontrollably. A moment later her aged heart gave out and she slumped to the floor.

Moshe Bloch took one last look at the synagogue, which was no longer flaming, but filled with thick black smoke. Not only were his mother and sister there, but the hundred or so others also inside were almost to a person related to him in some way. The screams and the coughs coming from inside had become weaker, fading first into moans, and now only silence,

The Germans themselves had backed away from the building.

One of them sat apart from the others, his head in his hands, but amongst the others a bottle had been produced, and was now being passed around amidst laughter and joking.

He hissed the words at them.

"*Mamsers!* May God curse you and your *mamser* nation forever!"

Hs screamed the word several times, louder each time, "*Mamsers! Mamsers!*"

He turned sobbing into the forest.

"Goodbye, Mama......Goodbye, Chia......."

Dorbyan had ceased to exist.

DORBYAN
PART 8

CHAPTER 1

The following morning the Lithuanian townspeople passing through the market square saw a still smoldering synagogue which to all external appearances seemed largely intact. Thr brickwork was charred, the windows were broken, and a large portion of the roof had been burnt through, but from the outside the impression was that the building was largely undamaged.

The genocidal warriors of the *Einsatzgruppe* and their Lithuanian assistants were already busy at work, bringing bodies from inside the synagogue out and piling them into wagons. Few of the bodies exhibited burn marks, and it appeared that all had met their deaths through the inhalation of smoke or poisonous fumes. The villagers stood on the periphery of the *Shul Platz*, watching the proceedings in silence, and nodding to each other knowingly, recognizing many of the bodies. The few who plucked up the courage to ask what had happened were told gruffly that the building had suffered a direct hit during the night killing everyone inside.

The bodies, over one hundred in number, were heaped into the wagons and taken to the Wainaiker forest about a mile from the edge of town. Three large pits were dug. The bodies were thrown in, sprinkled with lime and covered with earth.

As the months and years passed, the synagogue gradually disappeared. The townspeople began helping themselves to the timber fittings of the interior, leaving an empty shell of a brick building. Then, towards the end of the war, some three years later, as the battered German armies were pushed backwards under the Russian onslaught, the town suffered further damage, with many homes destroyed and the synagogue sustaining direct hits from shells, leaving a roofless ruined building with partially standing walls.

This spelt the finish of the synagogue, for its strong red bricks were a scarce and valuable commodity to the impoverished people of the district, and particularly useful in the construction of ovens. By the time the war had ended, little more than a pile of rubble in the outline of the foundations was in evidence to indicate that the building had ever existed.

The official version of the synagogue's destruction came to be accepted, and was perpetuated by the Russians during their occupation of the country following Germany's defeat.

In time the story came to believed, and the only version of the event was that the synagogue "had suffered a direct hit during the war and burned to the ground." To this day this is the version that visitors to the town will be told, with no mention made of the fate of those inside.

Of the approximately eight hundred Jewish residents in Dorbyan on June 21, 1941, twelve are believed to have avoided the various German massacres. Ten of these were children, and two were adults, of these only the adults were male.

An exact discription of the events of Dorbyan's final days is difficult to ascertain. The problem is not one of lack of information, but rather of too many sources, none of .which seems to agree with any of the others.

The authoritative book *Yehuda Lita* contains a section compiled by survivers in 1967, It gives the most graphic description, but needless to say, does not agree with the official version. It makes no metion of the burning of the Dorbyan synagogue.

The version told by Moshe Bloch describing the destruction of the synagogue agrees with neither the official version nor with *Yehuda Lita*, and most versions of the burning of the synagogue originate from his testimony. Lithuanian villagers who are old enough to have been present at the time tell a different story, and believe that all Jews had been removed from the synagogue at the time of its destruction. They claim tohave no recollection of a fire in the building.

The above sources of information all come from personal accounts related many years after the event. Attempts have been made to go to the perpetrators themselves for their own version of events. Through the offices of Professor Konrad Kviet, an internationally recognized holocaust expert, documents captured from the Nazis and recently made available by the Russians have been provided. These describe the German operations in Gorzd, Polangen and Krettingen in the days leading up to the Dorbyan massacre. Unfortunately, to date no report on the Dorbyan operation has come to light.

One document does exist, however, which was written while the actual destruction was taking place, and although not complete in its description, it is accurate and graphic in the extreme.

A letter was written by Zelda Bloch, probably some three weeks before she was put to death in a German labour camp. Somehow she managed to smuggle the letter to Jadvyga Butkiene, in whose fields she was probably working. It was her hope that it would one day reach her brother Shevah, who was living in Palestine. The letter was never sent. Jadvyga Butkiene guarded the letter until the end of the war when she handed it over to Zelda's brother, Lipman Bloch.

The date on the letter, September 2, 1941, is suspect, as it was added by another hand, and gives an uncharacteristic Roman date rather than the Jewish calendar almost exclusively used in Dorbyan at the time. It is impossible to determine whether Zelda Bloch was still alive at this time or not, but in her letter there is no mention of the massacre of the women and children on August 18 and 19 as stated by *Yehudah Lita*. There is mention of her mother and sister, who would have been murdered by that time, if the version of *Yehudah Lita* is to be accepted. Her mention of her brother Moshe Bloch visiting the synagogue and trying to convince his mother to leave tends to substantiate the testimony given by Moshe Bloch himself.

One does not have to guess at the feelings of Lipman Bloch, a Dorbyan survivor, who passed the war both hidden by Lithuanian families and as a partisan fighter, when at the war's end four years later he visited his birthplace and was handed Zelda's letter and was able to read of his sister's final torment.

Dear Shevah, Rivkele and Dinele!

I am writing this letter in a difficult moment. Nobody knows our destiny, which is horrifying. You cannot imagine how gruesome our fate is. I will write to you a bit about our horrible lives. It is already almost three months since Papa is dead, shot by our beautiful enemy because his name was Jewish. The children Leiba and Gershon are gone from us since the 4th day of Tammuz. Papa died on 3 Tammuz. I stayed for a week's time with Chaike and Mama..............after the inhuman happening. How much pain *(Tsores)* we have suffered is difficult to put on paper. I have little paper and maybe little time because our moments are probably numbered.

We were alone and afterward Moshe came. He went to Polangen before the war. When the war started he returned to Dorbyan after the murder of the men. Now he is on the land by a Christian, Botkienen. I have learned to sew and Chaia is by Eknissen.

Mama is still in the *shul.* Our compound is there. They want to get her out, but she does not wish. Now we are not certain of life each time we are taken from the compound.....(Leah?) is worried for our lives and we about Lipman. We know nothing about him. Something from him is dear to me. If I could see you and tell you everything someday. But at present I think only of revenge and Palestine. My dear ones........this letter from Botkienen if I do not survive. I am writing because if you survive this ghastly war you should at least know the minimum. If this is my last letter before the end, we will be good pleaders for you from above. We are dying because we are Jews and we still pray for the coming of the Messiah. Keep healthy my loved ones. I send regards to you. If you have the possibility, repay

---

7   *Translation of the above letter initially proved a problem. Due to the hurried handwriting style the authour was able to decipher only about one-third of the content. A visit to the Yiddish speaking Rabbi of the Sydney Yeshiva allowed a further third to be translated, the Rabbi likewise baffled by the Litvak stetl handwriting. Then the authour copied the letter to the greatest possible enlargement and sent it to Sol Gilis of Yarmouth Canada, a native of Krettingen. Mr Gilis promptly returned a complete translation, saying that with the aid of a strong magnifier it was not difficult. He did mention however, that reading it and translating it "Took a lot out of me", and that when he showed it to Morris Attis, a native born Dorbyaner, Mr Attis could not bring himself to look at it.*

Botkienen together with Eknissen with gratitude because of the way they have acted toward us. Reply to them and from her you will know about us. Keep well. Remember us. Our only hope is to rise from the dead when the Messiah comes.

Zelda

CHAPTER 2

The Jews were gone from Dorbyan, almost without trace, as in hundreds of other east European villages, towns and cities. Less than four years later the Germans were gone also, beaten back to their own borders by the Russian army they had earlier so nearly defeated.

The Lithuanians, so unlucky in history, had simply traded one master for another,and were to endure a further generation and a half before they were to again become masters of their own country. Many of those who had collaborated with the Germans fled westward before the conquering Russian armies, and entered the western countries as refugees, eventually attaining respectable status. Those who stayed behind found themselves in a land under military occupation and forced to live under a communist system contrary to their religious and cultural traditions.

The name Dorbyan became forgotten to Lithuanians, who knew the place only by its Lithuanian name, Darbenai. Dorbyan survived only on the lips of Jews who were born there and had had the good sense or good fortune to leave before the German invasion. The name has been passed on to their descendants, to whom it is but a nondescript, far-away place where their ancestors were born.

Nor was there much reason for Dorbyan descendants to be interested in the birthplace of their forebears. Under the Russian occupation, entry was virtually impossible to any but those who could prove to have been born there. Even those permitted to visit would-have found little to interest them or bring back memories.

Many of the town's homes were severely damaged during the latter part of the war, and were replaced in the years afterward. In the town centre certain of the older houses still survive, long since taken over and occupied by Lithuanians, suspicious of any visit by a Jew, as it might mean the intention to lay claim to property lost during the German invasion.

Some houses are easier to identify and better remembered than others. Most older citizens can point to the property where Hersh and Chana Jacob lived. Although their house has been replaced with a newer, more comfortable home, some of the sheds and outbuildings in the rear would be recognizable to them. The homes of other Jews are known, but often subject to disagreement amongst the present day villagers as to which family lived in which building.

One of the Jewish homes to be easily identified is that of Leiba Reizmann, the former communist youth secretary. The house was turned into a small cultural centre by the Russians in commemoration of his contribution to their cause, and his extreme sacrifice.

The synagogue vanished slowly over the years as the bricks were pilfered by hard pressed villagers. A larger cultural centre was built in the *Shul Platz* area in front of where the building once stood. This building was in turn destroyed by fire in 1991, and the site has remained empty since then. A request has since been made that no future building be permitted on the site.

The *Mikve*, or ceremonial bath, still partially exists, although any Jew visiting the town could be forgiven for not recognizing it. The twin buildings have been stripped away, leaving a rectangular brick pond in front of a residence on the Kretinga Gatve, once known as the Krettinger Gass. The pond is decorative, and attractively covered in lilies, leaving no hint of its former use.

Outside of Darbenai is a large communal agricultural complex, one of the largest of its type in Lithuania. During the Russian occupation its director was Zigmantas Docsui, who fell from favour with the coming of Lithuanian independence in 1991. His place was taken by Albinas Simkus.

For many years the town suffered the isolation imposed by the Russians on most other parts of their empire, and visits from outside were few. When the righteous gentile Lekasius died, Moshe Bloch and his wife Esther visited the town to attend the funeral. Joseph Jacobson, of Pontiac Michigan, the son of Hersh and Chana Jacob, still fascinated with his origins and family connections, made plans to visit in the mid-1970's, but by then he was almost eighty years of age, and his family talked him out of it.

As more and more of the native Dorbyaners passed away, their descendants lost contact and interest in the town, but there were a few notable exceptions. One such was Raymond Whitzman of Montreal, Canada, who became obsessed with his family background, the study of which soon led him to Dorbyan.

Knowledge of the town was scant, as noone had had the foresight to document it when those with the knowledge still lived. Darbenai was known to be the site of the former Dorbyan, but how much of the Jewish era still remained? The Russians were unhelpful.

Rumours abounded: the cemetery had been destroyed by the Germans; it had been destroyed by the Russians[8]; it had been vandalized and desecrated by locals in the years since the war; it had been destroyed without trace. Only one glimmer of hope remained with the authour - a tiny entry in the Encyclopaedia Lithuanica under its description of Darbenai:

"...The cemetery is there, the sole remaining sign
of the Jews of the small town's tragic destiny...."

Then, in 1991, Lithuania gained independence from The Soviet Union, and the hopes of those who had dared to dream were realized. The district became open to visitors from outside. Morris Mendelson of Philidelphia, a Dorbyan descendant, was visiting the Lithuanian capital Vilnius on U.S. government business, and was able to arrange a day trip to Darbenai. He was taken to the cemetery by a local guide.

He immediately contacted Raymond Whitzman with the astounding news. The cemetery existed, was intact, and apparently not touched in almost fifty years! Many of the gravestones were legible, and some of these he photographed, including one of the best preserved, that of Mere Gite Kveril, the sister of Chana Jacob.

Immediately plans were made to clean up the cemetery, for fifty years of neglect had caused it to become overgrown with every type of vegetation from thorn bushes to mature trees with a valuable

---

8   *This brings to mind an anecdote which beautifully illustrates the Jewish custom of answering a question with another question, yet at the same time providing the perfect answer. Having heard that the Dorbyan cemetery might have been destroyed by the Russians, and unable to see the logic in it, I put to Mr Sol (Sliomas) Gilis of Yarmouth, Nova Scotia, the following question;* **"What possible reason could the Russians have for destroying the Dorbyan Jewish Cemetery?** *His reply:* **"Since when do the Russians need a reason ?"**

timber content. Many of the monuments could be partially seen in the earth, but were either overturned or inaccessible because of the dense overgrowth. Another Dorbyan descendant, Mervyn Jacobs of South Africa, visited the site and sent back a video tape to the author, showing the entanglement preventing access to most of the monuments. He made the observation at the time that the site was obviously a very old cemetery.

Through connections in the Lithuanian community of Sydney Australia, Albinas Simkus of Darbenai was engaged to oversee the restoration work.

Mr Simkus' first task was to engage a firm of architects to survey the cemetery, locating the surviving gravestones, then photographing and cataloguing them. Because of the foresight of Mr Simkus, the Dorbyan Jewish cemetery is now probably one of the most completely documented Jewish cemeteries in Eastern Europe.

His next task was to contact Joseph Bunka of Plunge, a holocaust survivor who is one of the few Jews living in northeast Lithuania. Mr Bunka made the trip to Darbenai and advised Mr Simkus on the most sympathetic ways of carrying out the restoration.

The restoration work lasted for about one year, after which funding ran out, but in that time a great deal was accomplished. Headstones were raised from the earth re-erected and cleaned, undergrowth was cut away, and the paths were redefined. It is now possible for a visitor to do what Morris Mendelsohn could not have done, namely to walk through the cemetery and examine almost every monument at leisure.

Since that time, the town has been visited by other Dorbyan descendants. One of these was Rabbi Aaron Koshitski, son of Liebe Katz and grandson of Leah, the daughter of Hersh and Chana. Fluent in Russian, he was, upon the directions of the authour, able to locate the former *Mikve* as well as identify the former occupants of many of the town's older houses. His visit to the Dorbyan cemetery confirmed that the work carried out had been worthwhile and represented value for money.

Unhappily the number of surviving native-born Dorbyaners is very small, and these are almost without exception too elderly or infirm to visit their birthplace. Interest in the town is growing, and it is the authour's hope that this book will further increase that interest, for Dorbyan, along with hundreds of other east European villages, represents a chapter in Jewish history which should not be allowed to be forgotten.

EPILOGUE

"Still stands the forest primaeval; but under the shade of its branches
Dwells another race, with other language and customs.."

from *"Evangeline"*

by Henry Wadsworth Longfellow

Dorbyan is gone forever, but if one is prepared to imagine, it is still possible to experience the town that once was, by taking a walk through present day Darbenai.

Start at the northern end of town, and approach through the Skuodas Gatve.Try to imagine that this now quiet street was once called the *Shkuder Gass*, and was the main thoroughfare running through the town. It formed the major part of the whole area then known as the *Jewish Platz*, and housed as many as one thousand Jews in its heyday.

Stop at the bridge over the river Darba just before entering the main square. Look down at the pleasant stream, close your eyes for a moment and try to picture earlier scenes of Jewish children, released from their *Cheder* classes, dashing toward this spot, to swim in the summer and to skate in the winter.

When the weather is hot, you may still see children at play here, but the squeals and the happy cries will not be in Yiddish, for that language is no longer known in Darbenai.

Continue along the main square towards the centre of the town. Picture the empty wide thoroughfare as it once was, a crowded market place lined by rough wooden houses tightly packed on both sides, where Jews and Christians traded every Wednesday. Picture the hitching posts along the sides of the street, and try to experience the noise and activity of the multitude of people, horses and wagons gathered there.

As you reach the large stone Catholic church, look across the

376

square to the overgrown area where the synagogue once stood, a building almost as large. Ask yourself how it came to be that two totally different races of people were able to co-exist in harmony for more than two hundred years, and try to imagine if you can, the depravity, the bestiality, which decreed that half the population should be exterminated, while the other half should be allowed to continue its existence.

Cross over to the overgrown area, and go back a distance from the street. Look down towards the ground. If you look carefully you should be able to make out the faint traces of the outline of a large building. The synagogue was sixty feet square, two stories, and had the capacity to seat five hundred worshippers. Try to think back to an earlier date, and try to picture an even larger synagogue. Then, think back even farther in history, and try to imagine the pride of a fledgeling Jewish community when it first managed to erect its original tiny synagogue on this very same site some two hundred and fifty years ago.

Look around on all sides. The area around and in front of the synagogue was known as the *Shul Platz*, and was the venue for celebration for the whole Jewish community. Try to imagine almost every Jew in the district, perhaps as many as two thousand, crammed into this area to celebrate a festival or a Jewish wedding held under the traditional canopy.

Continue past the synagogue outline and make your way to the nearby wooded area. Imagine, if you can, that you are Moshe Bloch, having just escaped the burning synagogue on the eve of *Rosh Hashana* of 1941. Imagine your feelings as, standing in the relative safety of the forest, you are looking back at a burning building where your beloved mother and sister are inside, not to mention the one hundred others who are all related to you in some way. Try to shut out of your mind the screams of those trapped inside, fading into moans, and finally silence. Picture yourself as the only person who has escaped the destruction, and ask yourself if you would be prepared to forget, or even forgive.

Finally, after you have walked through the town centre, make the effort to walk the mile or so along the Wainaiker Gatve past the edge of town. You will come to the long concrete wall along the left hand side of the road which encloses the Jewish cemetery. The area enclosed is vast, much larger than most cemeteries, and yet you will not see as many monuments as expected.

Shut your eyes once again and try to think of the reason for this. Think of the villagers who, over a period of seventy years, left their birthplace to be buried in distant lands, but at the same time to give us, their descendants, the chance for a better life, and, as it turned out, the chance simply to continue to exist. Think of those who chose to remain in Dorbyan to the end, those who were not given the dignity of a cemetery burial, and whose remains are to be found in an unidentifiable state in mass graves around the countryside.

Take a good, long look around you. This cemetery is the only remaining evidence that Darbenai was once known to most of its inhabitants as Dorbyan.

Perhaps Dorbyan does still exist, but if so, it is only in the imagination.

THE AUTHOR'S DREAM

Throughout my life, it has been a rare occasion when I can genuinely remember dreaming during my sleep. I am told that everyone who sleeps must dream, but if I have done so, as I am told I must, then I have almost never been able to recall what I have dreamt.

Of late a strange change has taken place. As the creation of this manuscript began to near its end, I have been subject to strange dreams, which for some reason I am always able to remember clearly.

The dreams have all been remarkably similar, and invariably begin with a cloud of swirling mist which after several minutes gradually clears to reveal the white bearded face of *Eliezzer ben Shmuel*, the Spanish born Jew who over a period of two generations led his flock across the breadth of a continent to eventually find refuge in the Lithuanian village of *Loigzim*. There is a gentle smile on the face of *Eliezzer*, which then fades away into the swirling mists.

A moment later the mist clears, to reveal the faces of *Arieh Leib* and *Breina Jacob*, the founders of the Jewish community of *Dorbyan*. *Arieh Leib*, the wine merchant, possessed the inspiration to leave the stagnation that was *Loigzim* for the greater promise that *Dorbyan*, thereby creating a community which was to flower in the generations that followed.. *Arieh Leib* and *Breina* are briefly joined by their son *Sender, Dorbyan's* first glazier, before the mist engulfs them.

The next to appear are *Chaim Nochum Jacob*, another wine merchant, and his wife *Anna*. Patriarch and matriarch of a large family, such was their legacy that most later *Dorbyaners* were able to claim ancestry from them.

The swirling mist forms, then clears again, this time to reveal the faces of *Joseph Jacob*, the carter, and his wife *Riva*, the parents of *Hersh*. They are joined by *Leiba (Zup) Jacob*, the fish pedlar, and his wife *Shora Hinde*, the parents of *Chana*. They manage a brief smile in my direction before being engulfed by the mist.

Then appear *Hersh Jacob*, the horse trader, and his wife *Chana*.

There is a strange feeling as these two appear, for these are the first Dorbyaners whom I have ever seen as likenesses in a photograph. The previous visions are all fantasies of mine as to their appearance, although there seems to be no doubt in my mind as to what they looked like.

As the smiling faces of *Hersh* and *Chana* recede, their place is taken by the faces of their Dorbyan children, *Rachel, Ada, Mina* and *Breina*, all of whom married and had children, and all of whom, like their parents, perished in the destruction of their community during the holocaust. Despite their tragic fate, all wear a gentle smile as they disappear from sight.

The final vision is that of the faces of *Hersh* and *Chana's* other children, *Chaia, Leah, Esther* and *Joseph*, the *Dorbyaners* who made the transition from the old world to the new. For these people there is no need to conjure up visions of how they might have appeared, for these are the *Dorbyaners* that I have met physically and come to know as living, actual persons.

There has been a span of over four hundred years between the lifetimes of *Eliezzer* and the Dorbyan children of *Hersh* and *Chana*, and yet *Eliezzer* would have found little in their lifestyles to surprise him. It is only after the migration from Dorbyan to the new world that the gap widened. The four who left for North America would have experienced the change to electricity, hot and cold running water, motorcars, telephones, plug-in radios and kitchen appliances, and finally, television and computers. Those left behind lived a lifestyle which for all practical purposes remained unchanged over a dozen generations.

Before the swirling mist closes in for the last time to end my dream, I see the entire *Mishpoche* gathered together, looking down on me, smiling gently. It is then that I realize the reason for their smiles. I realize that they are aware of my actions, and approve of them, and are pleased that their story is being told.

GLOSSARY

Aliyah — Hebrew, meaning 'to ascend'. Often used to mean migration to the Holy Land

Bar-Mitzvah — The attainment of adulthood by a Jewish boy at age thriteen

Beit (Ha)Midrash — Hebrew 'house of learning', often used in reference to a synagogue

Bima — The raised platform in the centre of a synagogue where the Torah is read

Bobe — Yiddish for 'grandmother'

Chalutz — Hebrew meaning 'pioneer'. Often refers to early settlers in Palestine

Chanukah — Jewish festival celebrating the rededicating of a temple in 165 BC

Cheder — Hebrew for 'room'. Yiddish for 'classroom'

Cyganas — Lithuanian for 'gypsy'

Daven — Yiddish word of unknown origin, meaning 'to pray'

Gan Eden — Yiddish via Hebrew, 'Garden of Eden", meaning 'paradise'

Gass — From the German word for 'lane'. Yiddish for 'street' In Yiddish the word for lane is gassel

Gatve	Lithuanian for 'street'
Gefilte Fish	Yiddish from German 'stuffed fish'. A fish cake or fish loaf made of ground fish, eggs, salt, pepper and onions.
Gehennah	From Hebrew, The Valley of Hinnom. Has come to mean 'hell'
Goy, Goyim	Hebrew, meaning 'nation' or 'people' Usually refers to gentiles
Hochum	Hebrew for 'wise person'
Juden	German for 'Jews"
Judenrein	German meaning 'purified of Jews'
Kaddish	Aramaic, meaning 'sanctification'. Commonly known as a mourner's recitation
Kol Nidre	The holiest of Jewish recitations, recited on Yom Kippur eve
Kosher	Food or Torahs which have been prepared according to proper Jewish law
Ma'ariv	Evening prayer said immediately after sundown
Mamser	Yiddish from Hebrew, meaning 'bastard'
Massada	Fortress near the Dead Sea where in 70 AD the entire Jewish population committed suicide rather than surrender to the Romans.
Mazel Tov	Yiddish "good luck', through Hebrew mazel meaning 'luck' and Tov meaning 'good'

Melamed	A Hebrew or sunday school teacher, often the Rabbi
Mensch	German meaning 'person' Yiddish meaning usually denotes a 'worthwhile person'
Meshugganeh	Yiddish corruption of Hebrew word meaning 'crazy'
Meshiach	Hebrew or Yiddish for 'Messiah', the saviour whom the Jews believe will someday arrive, bringing eternal peace and resurrecting the dead
Mincha	Afternoon prayer said prior to sundown
Minyan	A quorum of ten adult Jewish males necessary to hold a full service.
Minorah	The eight branched candlabrum used during the Chanukah service
Mishpoche	Yiddish from Hebrew, meaning 'family'. Often taken to mean extended family members and even extended family members of extended family members
Naches	Hebrew, meaning 'contentment'. Joy at any happy event
Pesach	Hebrew and Yiddish word for 'Passover'
Platz	Yiddish from German, meaning 'place'. Jewish Platz denotes Jewish quarter of a town, Shul Platz denotes area around a synagogue

Pogrom	Russian meaning 'devastation'. An organized massacre of helpless peoples, often Jews, usually with official sanction
Poirim	Plural of poireh, Yiddish, meaning 'peasants'
Rambam	Acronym formed of the initials of Moses ben Maimon, renowned twelfth century Jewish phiposopher of Spain and Egypt
Rosh Hashanah	Hebrew 'head of the year'. Jewish New Year falling on 1 Tishrei
Seder	Passover feast and service held in the home celebrating the deliverance of the Jews from Egypt as described in the Book of Exodus in the Old Testament
Sepharad	Hebrew for 'Spain'. Has come to refer to oriental Jews
Shabbes, Sabbes	Yiddish from Hebrew 'Shabbat', meaning 'Sabbath' The word is derived from the Hebrew word for "seven".
Shabbas Goy	A gentile hired to perform tasks forbidden to Jews on the Sabbath, such as the feeding of animals
Shaharis	Morning prayer said after sunrise
Shichsa	A gentile girl
Shochet	A person authorized to carry out the ritual slaughter of animals, often a Rabbi
Shul	Yiddish from German, meaning 'school', but which has come to refer to a synagogue

Simcha	Hebrew 'rejoicing'. Any happy occasion
Tishe b'Av	Hebrew 'Ninth Day of Av', a day commemmorating tragedy in Jewish history, and observed through fasting and mourning
Torah	Hebrew, meaning 'teaching'. Consists of the Five Books of Moses, the first five books of the Old Testament. Always produced in scroll form
Trafe	Food which is not Kosher
Tsores	Yiddish from Hebrew, meaning 'trouble', has come to mean 'pain and suffering'
Untermenschen	German term to describe Jews and other so-called inferior races Literal meaning 'subhuman'
Yeshivah	Hebrew, meaning 'Sitting'. Refers to a seat of learning
Yom Kippur	The Day of Atonement, holiest day of the Jewish year
Yuntif	Yiddish from Hebrew Yom Tov, meaning 'good day'. A holiday or festival

APPENDICES

APPENDIX 'A'

LOIGZIM (Laukzemis)
(The Genesis of Dorbyan)

In Loigzim, a small Russian hamlet near the Baltic Sea, in the early nineteenth century,lived a man named Rachmael. He was an honest man, small in stature, with a flowing beard and eyes burning with zealous righteousness .He was very learned in the Talmud and very pious. But to eke out a mere living, Rachmael was obliged to ply the trade of a tailor, at which he worked day and night, save on the Sabbath.

"Rachmael", called his wife Sarah, one morning, "The baron's son has come for his father's uniform!"

"Tell the young drunkard that I am working on itnow. It will be ready tonight."

But the young man did not wait outside for Sarah to bring the answer. He staggered to the tailor shop, howling, "Why don't you come out, you damned Jew? Don't you hear your lord and master calling? Aren't you making your living from us?"

Rachmael tried to placate him. "Yes, Yes my lord."

"Then when are you going to pay the fifty rubles for your rent, which is long past due?"

"When I deliver your father's uniform tonight, my lord," answered Rachmael quietly. "I will settle all up." He begged the unreasonable youth to be patient and go home peacefully. And the young sot finally took his leave, first delivering himself of an avalanche of oaths

The old Baron of Loigzim was a hard man to get along with. He lived beyond his means and exacted heavy taxes from all who came under his rule. The young baron, in his early thirties, was worse than his father. He was always trouble, but as the law was in his father's hands,he did not care what capers he cut. Under their caprices the hundreds of peasants who worked at the baron's villa did not have an easy time of it.

When Rachmael promised to deliver the baron's uniform that night, he had reckoned without thought of the Sabbath, which, it being Friday, would begin at 4:30 in the afternoon. And Rachmael would not break the holy Sabbath even if it cost him his life. At dawn on Sunday he stood at the baron's gate, begging the gatekeeper to permit him to enter at once, with the finished uniform.

Thus it was that, having incurred the baron's displeasure, Rachmael, Sarah and Mailki (their daughter aged 12) were exiled from Loigzim and moved to Darbyon. Darbyon had a population of some 8,000, of which 95 per cent were Jews. In the outlying rural district lived many farmers, who were Litvanians and all Roman Catholics. The Jews were on very good terms with their neighbours as the priest at that time was their friend because his mother had been a converted Jewess.

But in Darbyon, Rachmael was unable to make a living. The grief of it made him sick, and losing heart, he died in the prime of his years. He was taken back to Loigzim for burial at the side of his father in the old Jewish cemetery, which dates back to the Spanish Inquisition, when a company of Jews emigrated to Loigzim as refugees. Part of that company went on to Prussia and became German Jews.

Poor Rachmael, the pious tailor, was the last to rest in that old cemetery, for the Jews of Darbyon now had a new burial ground. And every year on the ninth day of Ab (August), Mailki his daughter would visit his grave and shed tears in his memory.

(From "Three Oceans, from the Baltic, Across the Atlantic, to the Pacific", the autobiography of Harry A Jacobs, born in Dorbyan in 1875 and migrated to the USA in 1889)

Note: The old Jewish cemetery in Loigzim still exists, for it has been mentioned in recent correspondence to the authour.

APPENDIX 'B' -
THE DEVELOPMENT OF DORBYAN

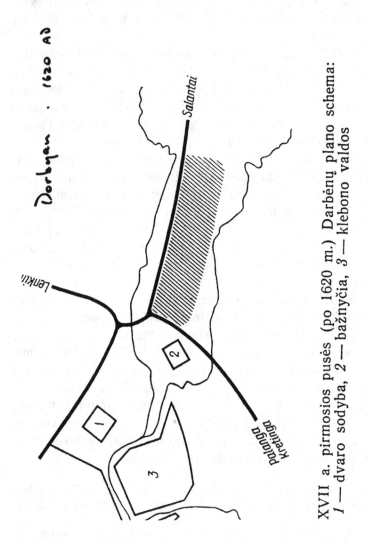

In 1620 Dorbyan was little more than the agricultural estate of the nobleTytschcovitch family located ar the junction where the highway crosses the River Darba.

1779 - 1781 Plan of Darbenai. Original. (Drawing of same below)

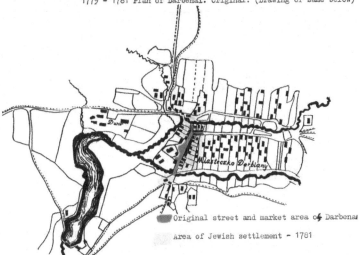

Original street and market area of Darbenai

Area of Jewish settlement - 1781

37 pav. 1779—1781 m. Darbėnų plano kopija su paryškintais pagrindiniais vietovės elementais

In 1781 Dorbyan had 12 Jewish homes and 18 Jewish fmiles.

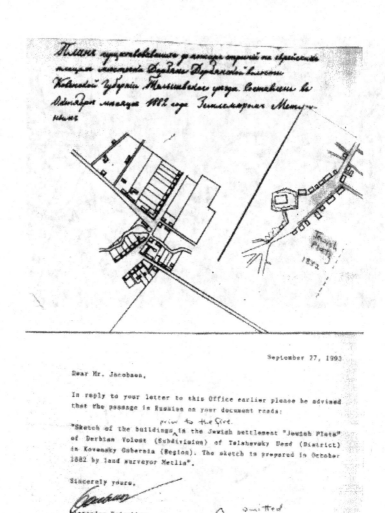

September 27, 1993

Dear Mr. Jacobsen,

In reply to your letter to this Office earlier please be advised that the passage in Russian on your document reads:

"Sketch of the buildings, in the Jewish settlement "Jewish Plate" of Derbian Volost (Subdivision) of Talshevsky Uesd (District) in Kovensky Gubernia (Region). The sketch is prepared in October 1882 by land surveyor Metlis".

Sincerely yours,

Alexander Kolsobbes

In 1882 Dorbyan had reached the peak of its development, which it was to maintain for a further 15 years, until the migrations started to have an effect.

The population at the time appears to be slightly less than 2000, of whom the vast majority were Jews, particularly in the town centre.

APPENDIX 'C' -
THE DORBYAN CEMETERY

(The Dorbyan cemetery is the sole remaining feature of Dorbyan which indicates the former Jewish occupation of the town.)

(The Dorbyan Cemetery, Photographs)

1. The entrance to the cemetery.

2. Building for ritual preparation of bodies for burial. (Outside the cemetery walls)

3. Gravestone of Mere Gite Kveril, sister of Chana, died 1934.

APPENDIX 'D' -
THE DORBYAN SYNAGOGUE

(Above – Photo and description of the last Dorbyan synagogue, which was completed in 1909 and destroyed in 1941)

(Below - A sketch of the layout of the synagogue according to the memory of Morris Attis, who left Dorbyan in 1923, aged between 9 and 10 years)

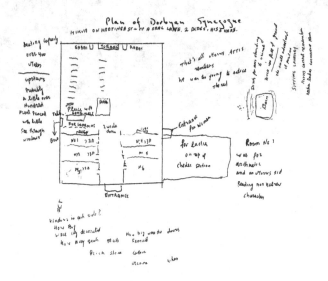

APPENDIX 'E' -
THE DORBYAN MARKET

In 1701 AD Darbenai was granted commercial priviledges, which included the right to hold its own market. Shortly afterward the first Jewish traders arrived to settle in the village. Jews sold textiles and threads to the gentile population. These in turn sold farm produce to the Jews. The market was held almost every Wednesday until 1941 AD, when the extermination of the Jewish community decimated the town's population and destroyed the market's reason for existence.

42 pav. Darbėnų aikštės pietryčių kraštinės fragmentas. Fotografuota apie 1930 m. (ČDM LS, Nr. 2044)

APPENDIX 'F' -
BIRTH CERTIFICATE OF MORRIS ATTIS

(English translation produced after his arrival in Canada. The Rabbi was Benjamin Perski, chief Rabbi of Krettingen (Kretinga) in Lithuania. Krettingen was the district capital, some 8 miles from Dorbyan and all Dorbyan births had to be registered there. Rabbi Perski was married with one daughter. He perished in the holocaust in 1941 and would have been in his mid-fifties at the time.)

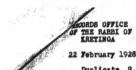

RECORDS OFFICE
OF THE RABBI OF
KRETINGA

Given in
matters not
requiring
excise tax.

22 February 1928

Duplicate   9 January 1928   No. 4

BIRTH CERTIFICATE

Son or Daughter	Son
Name of person born	Mordche
Name and surname of father	Rachmielis ETIS
Name of mother	Chanè
Maiden surname of mother	- - - -
Occupation of father	- - - -
Place of residence of parents	Darbènai
Nationality	- - - -
Citizenship	- - - -
Date of birth, in words (Christian era)	The fourteenth day of June in the year one thousand nine hundred and fourteen.
Place of birth	Darbènai
Date of circumcision, in words	The twenty first day of June in the year one thousand nine hundred and fourteen.
Name and surname of person performing circumcision	Assistant Rabbi

This certificate is copied word for word from the Registration Book of Births, Records Office of the Rabbi of Kretinga (Darbènai Branch Office), for 14 June 1914, which is recorded there as No. 30, and this certificate has the same validity as the record in the books.

(Signed)   B. Perskis

Rabbi of the Records Office

Annex "A"

Geo. Marchetti
Consul General

(SEAL)
OF THE RECORDS
OFFICE OF THE
RABBI OF KRETINGA

APPENDIX 'G' - FAMILY PHOTOS

(Top) – The family photo taken in 1920 prior to Joseph's migration to North America. The elderly lady in the centre of the front row was Shora Hinda Jacob, mother of Chana. (Bottom) – A photo of Natan Beir Jacob, youngest child of Breina and Elior.

The photo was taken in 1927 at one year of age.

APPENDIX 'H' -
LETTER OF ZELDA BLOCH

This letter was written shortly before Zelda Bloch was put to death by the Nazis in September 1941. The letter was given to a Lithuanian who guarded it until the end of the war. A more complete description and a translation from the Yiddish can be found inside the text of this book.

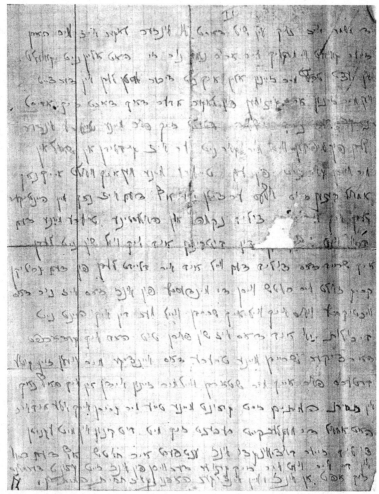

Letter Of Lipman Bloch (1992) Translation from Yiddish

To Mr Daniel, Shalom!

I am sending you the map of Dorbyan according to my memory. I am away from Dorbyan for fifty years. In Dorbyan lived 250 Jewish families, 1500 Jews. Sadly, all were exterminated by the murdering bloody enemy. Ten Jewish children were rescued. If you will learn more, you may contact the Lithuanian Jewish Society. I enclose the address. Be healthy. Shalom Rav to you.

Bloch

יקירי נכדי שלום!

כתבך עם הברכות די נעימות מן
לוודא... הגיעו. אני שמח על מכתבך. אני
הייתי פה בעולם לון שלי 50 ישר.

אני נוכחתי... הברכות בסך 250
בעולם... 15 לירות, ...
... ... לכם די...
... 10 ...

אני שולח לך ברכות ומיטב
... לך לכל הטוב
... ...

שלך הדואג לך תמיד
סבא

APPENDIX 'I'
THE BURNING OF THE DORBYAN SYNAGOGUE – FACT OR MYTH?

"Talking on her siblings; Yosef and his family, Villi (Welve) and his family, Chia and her family and Rifka and her family were burned alive in the synagogue according to Moshe Bloch who escaped from a synagogue window in the month of Av, (1941). It was his good luck that he escaped from the gun fire of the German soldiers. He fled through a wheat field and was in hiding in a Gentile village until the end of World War ll. However all other members of Moshe's family were killed.

(As related by Esther (nee Jacob) Cohen born in Dorbyan, migrated to Palestine before World War ll, presently living in the communal settlement of Kfar Warburg in Israel.)

Rachel – Oldest
Aida
Minnie
Bryna – youngest

\} live in Russia.

Joe Jackson – son U.S.
Chia   Canada
Esther   Canada.
Leah   Canada.

Family that remained in Russia lost
their lives in the holocaust. They were
placed in a tiny Shul and told –
there would be work for them – but
Germans burned the Shul and they
all died except 2 little girls about
6 yrs old that are distant relatives of
the family, they escaped and are
supposed to be alive in Israel
Got this info from Uncle Joe Jackson
Mar 8/81 – He wasn't well at the
time + had difficulty speaking +
subsequently died of Ca of larynx.

402

Authour's Comment: This note was written on the back of a family photograph provided by Bernie Bloom, son of Chaia and Leizer Bloom, and grandson of Hersh and Chana. The information was gained from his uncle Joseph, son of Hersh and Chana and good friend of Moshe Bloch from whom he would have heard the story.
However the account raises questions, as the Dorbyan synagogue was anything but tiny, seating 500 persons. The authour does not know of any other synagogues in and around Dorbyan.

Interview of Antanas Kramilius with Dargis? Vlacovas.

Dear Daniel

This is the interview with Vaclovas in Darbenai recorded on video A.K.
I am speaking with a local resident of Darbenai who was 7 year old boy in 1941 when the Germans occupied Lithuania. If you do not mind,could you tell me your name ?

Valcovas. Dargis ? Vaclovas,born and bread in Darbenai.I remember those days very clearly. The Jewish women and children were kept in the Synagog.They were there for approx. 3 - 4 weeks.Progressively they were taken to the forest of Darbenai and never seen again...

A.K. They were women and children ?

Vac. Yes women and children.The men were killed on St Peters day, 29th of June 1941,near the mill on the road to Palanga.

AK.The information received by Daniel Jacobson in Australia from Mrs Ruzgailiene told the official version of the fate of the Synagog.The Synagog received a direct hit by a shell and burned to the ground.What can you tel me about that ?

Vac. I can tell you that there was only a small damage visible in the roof,possibly hit by a fragment of a shell. The rest of the Synagog remain standing.After the women and the children were killed the synagog was pulled down brick by brick by the local people.

AK. Just a moment. The other story is that the Synagog was burnt down with the women and children inside by the Germans ?

Vac. That is an absolute lie.

AK. That is what I wanted you to confirm.I take it that after the women were killed,only then the Synagog was pulled down and bricks were used for various purposes.?

Vac. That is correct. The bricks were solid red bricks and possibly was used to build ovens etc.

AK. Can you tell me what has happened to the place where the Synagog stood.?

Vac. The spot now remains empty.The soviet (communist) administration have built a Cultural Centre which burned down some two years ago.

AK. The most important thing I wanted to know about the fate,that it was burned down ?

Vac. That story is absolute rubish and untrue.

AK. The next question is: what has happen to the books in the Synagog ? Did they burn with the Synagog ?

403

Vac. No, that is not true. The books were carried out by the Germans and the Jews outside the Synagog and burned outside the Synagog. I saw that myself.After the fire was extinguished,there were scraps of leather etc., and we kids scavanged them from the ashes. Yes it is sad,but these are the facts. The books were burnt on purpose.

AK. That is nothing new. Hitler burned all other books which did not agree with him. Are there any Jews living now in Darbenai ?

Vac. No I dont know here,but there is a family in Klaipeda.

AK. I had some correspondence with a Jewish man from Plunge ?

Vac. No. I am not aware of this man.About the buildings in town,yes they were mostly owned by the Jews. I remember the Kindergarten,Hospital,the Rabi residence and others.

AK. You were a small boy at that time.Do you remember if any Jews were hurt during the Independent Lithuania times ?

Vac. No, the Jews were best of neighbours and friends.We kids mixed freely with each other.

AK. We were told that certain Moshe Block got inside the Synagog to the women and escaped from the burning Synagog.Do you know this man Block ? Are there any truth to his story ?

Vac. I do not know if he was connected with the museum,but that the Synagog was burned down is a complete fabrication.

AK. Did you knew Moshe Block.?

Vac. Yes,I knew him very well .He had a shop and as kids we used to receive some sweets from him. He had two sons and two daughters.

AK. Do you know where is Moshe Block now ?

Vac. No. I got no idea what has happen to him,whether he escaped or was shot with the others...

This is the interview with Vaclovas,the surname I could not identify from the video.The rest of the video is in English at the Cemetery.

Antanas Kramilius

The following question was asked
of Lipman Bloch by the authour:

When was the Dorbyan synagogue burnt? I have heard two versions, Tisha b'Av and Erev Rosh Hashanah, which is correct?
Lipman Bloch's reply: "I have no answer."

APPENDIX 'J'
DORBYAN 1941

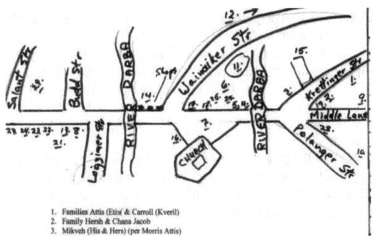

1. Families Attis (Etis(& Carroll (Kveril)
2. Family Hersh & Chana Jacob
3. Mikveh (His & Hers) (per Morris Attis)
4. Drug store
5. Medical Doctor
6. Synagogue
7. Market Place
8. Yiddische Folkschool
9. Rail Platform
10. Mass grave of men murdered by the Nazis
11. Graves of women and children murdered
    in the synagogue by the Nazis
12. Jewish cemetery – 2 km
13. Rabbi's home
14. Hardware store at bridge
15. Thoroughfare through forest with a few
    Jewish homes.
16. Home of Govsa Yankel Kveril, photographer
17. Home of Simon (Zymon) family (Hardware?)
18. Home of Reizmann Family (Barber Shop)
19. Home of Elberg the chemist
20. Home of Yitzhak Jakobi
21. Library
22. Home of Itse Cohen
23. Home of Mordechai & Rose Bloch & 7 children
24. Home of............
25. Home of Gershon & Shora Hinda Jacob, parents
    of Esther Jacob Cohen
26. Home of Leiba Koshutski
27. Home of Abraham Bloch
28. Mikveh on Pirtes Street (per Lipman Block)

APPENDIX 'K'
LIPMAN'S LISTS

At the request of the author, Lipman Bloch, a Dorbyan holocaust survivor, created two lists.

The first was a list of Dorbyan residents who actively assisted Jews in avoiding the barbarities of the Nazi Germans during their occupation of the town. In all cases these were gentiles who sheltered and hid Jews from the Germans despite the fact that it was made known that anyone assisting a Jew would be treated as if he were a Jew himself.

Despite the threats and obvious peril to their families a small number of gentiles sheltered Jews and managed to keep them safely hidden until the end of the war and the defeat of the Germans. These people can truly be said to deserve the title of *Righteous Gentiles*.

List No. 1	List No 2
Barbara Zaluta	Vladas Yashinskas
Lekasius	Galdikas
Bagdanavitz	Zavueras
Skripkaviscius	
Galdikas	
Girasaikis	
Butkus	

The first list names people who helped and sheltered Jews without asking payment during the Nazi occupation of Dorbyan.

At the top of Lipman Bloch's second list (as he is at the top of everyone else's list) is Vladas Yashinskas. His dastardly deed is mentioned in the pages of this work.

Readers will notice that the name *Galdikas* appears on both lists. Family split-ups were not unknown, and the authour took it upon himself to assume that it happened in this case in Dorbyan.

APPENDIX 'L'
PAMDENAC, NEW BRUNSWICK

Pamdenac is a small locality roughly 12 miles from Saint John on the Frederickton road, which became unique in Jewish life in North America. In the 1920's Jews from Saint John (mostly of Dorbyan origin) began visiting the location, and finding it to their liking, began building holiday homes there, which they would visit and live in during the summer months. The process continued into the 1950's by which time most Saint John Jewish families were spending their summer months in Pamdenac.

As the Dorbyan Jews spread out through North America, relatives converged on Pamdenac from as far away as Montreal, Boston, New York, Pontiac, Michigan and points farther. Summertime Pandenac had become a focal point for Jews from many distant places, and became unique in North America.

The writer well remembers the earlier days when Yiddish was the preferred language and English was used only in the presence of children. A Dorbyaner or any other eastern European Jew for that matter would have felt immediately at home in Pamdenac. Also remembered were the squeals of joy and the passionate embraces which greeted the passengers of every car as it pulled up to a family cottage.

Towards the end of the 1950's and during the 1960's Pamdenac went into decline. There are several reasons for this, of which the main ones are as follows:

The popularity of Camp Kadimah:
Camp Kadimah, a Jewish summer camp in Nova Scotia, had increased in popularity and grown to the point where it proved a more attractive proposition to Jewish children than a summer cottage. With their children no longer with them many families no longer felt the need to maintain a cottage in Pamdenac.

The passing of a generation:
The migrants from Dorbyan and elsewhere were an extremely tightly knit group, having all shared the same background. As this generation passed from the scene their children did not feel the same sentiment and did not find Pamdenac as attractive.

The decline of the Saint John Jewish community: From 1920 to 1950 Saint John boasted the largest Jewish community east of Montreal, with some 1400 members. In 1950 it went into decline as members sought out the greater economic benefits offered by other centres. By the year 2000 the community had dwindled to 140 members, many of these elderly, and its synagogue had been sold to avoid its maintenance costs. There was simply no longer a population base which could support a society such as Pamdenac.

Today, as in Dorbyan, there is no Jewish presence in Pamdenac, and it is simply a picturesque locality, much like many other similarly sized dots on the map. Future Jews are unlikely to be aware of its existence, but those old enough to remember it in its heyday will look back on it with fond memories.

SUMMARY

Was the Dorbyan synagogue burnt down, killing those inside? The matter is certainly open to question. The authoritive Yehuda Lita makes no mention of this in its description of the final days of Dorbyan. Lipman Bloch, a survivor, does not confirm the story, although his reluctance may be simply a desire to avoid a controversial subject.

In 1941 the Germans had not yet adopted the tactic of herding Jews into synagogues and setting them alight. The first case of this known to the authour occurred in 1943 in Vilna (Vilnius).

In 1941 the main synagogue in Krettingen was burnt down, but under completely different circumstances. The fire was set by a disgruntled gentile who was later praised by the Germans for his services. There was no loss of life in this fire.

Here is the problem: Esther Jacob, Bernie Bloom and Joseph Jacobson, who tell of the event are all reputable people whom the authour trusts implicitly, and who would never knowingly falsify evidence. In addition, the authour does not feel himself qualified to contradict the testimony of Moshe Bloch, who is no longer living and able to present his case. It is perhaps possible that sometime in the future further evidence will come to light which will resolve the question. Until then readers will have to draw their own conclusions.

Printed in the United States
By Bookmasters